The Facemaker

The Facemaker

by Richard Gordon

McGraw-Hill Book Company
New York   St. Louis   San Francisco

THE FACEMAKER

Library of Congress Catalog Card Number: 69-12264

Second Edition 23796

Book I

The Facemaker

1

HE HAD BEEN in the sanatorium three months and was glad to find everyone apologetically giving up the idea that he really ought to die. He knew perfectly well he had the fatal *habitus phthisicus* described by Hippocrates. His skin was soft, pale and veined. The whites of his eyes were tinged blue. His shoulder-blades stood out like wings, and they could almost count the ribs of his flat chest across the room. It was not at all the sort of chest the sanatorium liked to see. It was a chest which gave in to tuberculosis without the flicker of a fight. A cowardly chest. He ought to be ashamed of it.

They put him to bed in the cold January air, with a mackin-tosh sheet as a counterpane to catch the rain dripping monoto-nously under the verandah. They gave him a spittoon with a cap like a German beer-mug, fed him like a fighting-cock, submitted him to the indignity of bedpans and bottles, measured his weight once a week, his spit once a day, and his temperature four-hourly. His doctors and nurses were solicitous to the point of tenderness, which depressed him, as he soon found this attitude reserved for the most desperate cases. They forbade him to wash and shave himself, to sit up or even to read. He had nothing to do but chase his thoughts round his head, and no news of the world except sometimes carried by the rumble of the guns across the Channel.

The sanatorium's medical superintendent was a sad-faced Scot, whose scrawny frame and club-like finger-nails told know-ing eyes that he was seeking revenge on his own disease, by spending what it had left of his life in treating it. He had the habit of declaring at the bedside, 'Only *Mother Nature* can cure tuberculosis, not the physician. We provide fresh air, rest, a suitable diet, a carefully balanced regimen—we are but Mother Nature's handmaidens, standing at her elbow while she performs her healing work.'

His patient thought this had at least the advantage of justifying the sanatorium's shortcomings in advance.

It was impatience to get out of the place rather than desperation to get better which made him ask the superintendent for remedies more specific than Mother Nature, dragging from his own half-forgotten lectures such nostrums as gold by injection, creosote by inhalation, or iodine mysteriously liberated internally to disinfect the body by the drinking of chlorine (which struck him as likely to taste very nasty). But the superintendent looked sadder than ever and said, 'Placebos, placebos! I should prefer to insult neither your body nor your intelligence, Dr Trevose. More important than any drug in the world is your will-power, your determination to recover, your *strength of character*.'

Young Graham Trevose found this Presbyterian bleakness more depressing, having suspected for years that the strength of his character was even more fragile than that of his chest.

Graham's misfortunes had started at two in the morning, an hour when our resistance is supposed to reach some mysterious lower ebb, a favourite one in the mythology of hospital sisters for birth or death to shake the human frame. He had woken coughing a salty taste from his mouth, and hastily lighting the bedside candle found an alarming red stain staring at him from the sheet. When John Keats, another young doctor, underwent the same unsettling experience he cried with poetic quick-wittedness that he saw the seal on his death-warrant. There occurred to Graham only a less spectacular idea—now he'd get out of military service.

It was over three years since most of his fellow-students at Blackfriars Hospital had gone off to join Kitchener's army, in the same spirit as they went off to play football matches. But

2

Graham's puny frame clearly being no use to a drill-sergeant he had stuck to his books, braving such inconveniences as Zeppelins and white feathers, until graduating before Christmas in 1917. Then he found King and country wanted his new qualifications however insecurely they were embodied, and conscription threatened to scoop him up with the other scrapings of the barrel.

The First World War being a more informal one than the Second, his Aunt Doris could persuade her brother, a captain in the Royal Navy whom Graham had disliked since birth, to pull a few strings for the lad. It was settled that he should be commissioned as a surgeon-lieutenant and posted to his uncle's own command, the *Inviolable*, a brand-new battleship bristling with guns, her sides the thickness of a medieval castle, advertised by the Admiralty to friend and foe as unsinkable. Aunt Doris thought the sea air would do him good.

But a haemoptysis in the middle of a cold January night of 1918 seemed likely to change this and many less immediate plans. The household was roused, the gas-mantles lit, hot-water bottles filled, a fire kindled in his bedroom despite the dissuasive level of coal in the cellar. A chest physician was summoned later from his breakfast—Dr James Wedderburn, F.R.C.P., of Blackfriars Hospital, plump, side-whiskered and prosperous, with an air of such smug good health as deeply distressed his more self-pitying patients. He arrived, radiating confidence like a lighthouse, in a magnificent Rolls-Royce Silver Ghost chauffeured by a man so pointedly past military age as in seeming danger of dropping dead over the wheel. Graham's father, Professor Trevose, waiting to receive him in the hall of his tall and gloomy Hampstead house, knew the physician well. The professor was in charge of the anatomy department at Blackfriars, and frequently pressed his company on Dr Wedderburn, who found it tedious to the extent of sometimes forgoing his lunch to avoid it.

The consultant's examination was more impressive than conclusive. He fancied the right upper chest might move a little less freely than the left, the note on percussion with his pudgy

3

fingers could be a little impaired, the breath sounds rustling up his expensive stethoscope a shade diminished. There might be an area of tubercular consolidation at the apex of the right lung —though on the other hand there might not. But fever conspiring with blood-spitting in such a fragile body was a deadly alliance. Experience alone told him the disease would gallop through the poor young man and bear him off to Heaven in the year. This view he put privately to Graham's father downstairs, suggesting the course of events should more fittingly occur in a sanatorium.

'This damnable Koch's bacillus,' cried Professor Trevose. He tugged his heavy moustache irritably, wondering why God was so unkind to him. If the calamity had put him in a doubly bad temper, it was his normal reaction to any emotional stress. 'Hasn't it done us enough damage already? It's the curse of our family.'

'Ah, it was so sad about your poor wife.' Remembering she had expired from tuberculosis in his care, the physician added even more devoutly, 'I did all that was humanly possible, of course.'

'Of that I have no doubt, Wedderburn.' They stood in the dark-panelled hall, with its elaborate hatstand and pair of prints from Leonardo da Vinci's anatomical sketches. 'But of course, the boy's been foolish. He was overworking badly for his finals, that must surely have made him run down generally? It was his own fault. Entirely his own. He lived in bone idleness till a month before the examination, however severely I chivvied him.'

'We can hardly expect our students to spend their lives with such unpleasant experiences as examinations hanging perpetually over them, can we?' Dr Wedderburn took a cosy view of everything, even illness and death. The young flat-chested maid with acne handed his top hat and grey gloves. 'Have you noticed Graham off-colour for long?'

'No. Not at all. It's a bolt from the blue.'

'No night sweats?'

'None that I have been informed of.'

4

'The weight has been pretty constant, I take it?'

'Certainly in my observation. Of course, it may not be as serious as we fear,' Graham's father hazarded. 'A burst vein in the throat, something like that?'

'Possibly, possibly,' said Dr Wedderburn. Both knew well enough this was the first of many straws grasped by the tubercular sufferer. 'We shall need a specimen of the sputum to stain for acid-fast bacilli. Perhaps you would have the kindness to leave the bottle at the bacteriology lab in Blackfriars? Naturally, we would revise our ideas of the diagnosis should it prove negative.'

The professor suggested an X-ray. Dr Wedderburn was shocked. Such dodges were not for the responsible physician. He spread out his gloved hands. The good Lord has blessed the doctor with his five senses. The hallowed tetrad of the bedside—inspection, palpation, percussion, and auscultation—was powerful enough to evoke the most evasive diagnosis, and ever would be. Those gentlemen with their crackling and dangerous machines produced only time-wasting photographic plates of November fogs. The professor apologized. The physician then left, scattering a few more grains of comfort to be pecked at leisure.

The professor went into his study and sat at his roll-topped desk, struggling with the new situation. Graham ill in bed upstairs would be an enormous complication to the single-handed running of a wartime household. Life was worrying enough already, with one son in France, a medical officer at the front. It would be better, as Wedderburn suggested, to tidy Graham away in a sanatorium where they specialized in such tragedies. He could visit the poor boy regularly, though wartime train journeys were becoming unbearable and the fares deserved thinking about. He wished crossly that Graham's mother were alive to halve the burden. It was a grave distraction for the professorial mind, which should have been freed from domestic responsibilities both trivial and weighty to soar like an academic eagle over the bleak and mountainous problems of human anatomy. He pulled the bell-handle for the young maid with

5

the acne spots. It was only ten in the morning, but he asked her to bring him a glass of port.

The sanatorium recommended by Dr Wedderburn was on the Kent coast near Pegwell Bay, surrounded by scummy-looking sea, mud, scrubby sand-dunes and fields full of cabbages, which gave off a smell setting Graham's heart against the vegetable for the rest of his life. Three months passed before its authorities even let him see a newspaper, from which he learned that the *Inviolable* on her first foray to sea had sunk, guns, armour-plate, crew, uncle, and all. From that moment he got steadily better.

'*Spes phthisica*,' muttered the medical superintendent, using a mildly contemptuous technical term for the hope which was keeping so many of his patients alive when clearly nothing else was. But the angry spikes on Graham's temperature chart subsided to gentle ripples as the disease blew itself out. Perhaps the substitution of the chance of dying for the certainty had stimulated the will-power prescribed by the superintendent. Perhaps Graham was tougher than he looked. Perhaps—an almost unthinkable possibility—Dr Wedderburn had made a mistake in diagnosis. By the spring of 1918 even the superintendent had to agree the young doctor might live, and allowed him the luxury of sitting up.

With nothing to fill the time between having his temperature taken, Graham started to draw. He drew everything in his world, the cherry tree flowering charmingly a yard from the foot of his red-blanketed bed, the neighbouring patients, Harry the boot-faced orderly, even Sister Constable. She was square-faced, red-cloaked, and medal-ribboned, disliked in the sanatorium far more than the Kaiser who, Graham decided with a few strokes of the pencil, she would closely resemble if she let her moustaches grow. He was surprised at his skill. He supposed he had inherited it from his mother, along with his chest.

6

2

DR OLAF SARASEN—he disclaimed the English surgeon's self-assumed title of 'Mister'—had plunged impatiently into the war long before it submerged his own country. In the summer of 1915 he arrived at Liverpool from New York unannounced, unknown, and unowned by any authority, with several crates of operating equipment, a pair of gorgeously-fitted ambulances, and apparently unlimited money. He wore a uniform of double-breasted leather-buttoned khaki jacket, twill breeches, cavalry boots, and spurs, each shoulder decorated with the Stars and Stripes and an announcement in gold thread, 'U.S. Medical Volunteers'. This body, like the costume, he had invented entirely himself.

Once in London, Dr Sarasen trumpeted a single-minded doctrine of plastic surgery across the tranquil though arid plains of medical thought, by exploiting indiscriminately lectures both professional and public, influential dinner-tables, the pages of any publication prepared to print his views, and the ears of any doctor trapped into hearing them. His motives were taken by English surgeons as either charming native enthusiasm or some sort of complicated swindle, his manners regarded somewhat as the old aristocracy regarded those of the new war profiteers. Such advertising was thought of as all very well among those Yankee fellows, but not for the discreet doctors of Harley Street, who anyway had more soft-footed ways of advancing themselves. The plastic surgeon was laughingly dismissed as 'The Wild Saracen', a bounder, probably a quack, and worse still terribly vulgar.

7

But with men of power rather than men of physic 'The Saracen' got on splendidly. He talked their language, especially about money. The quicksilver tongue which raised funds in New York persuaded a junior minister of Asquith's to suggest that the War Office should loose him on the troops, and surprisingly the War Office agreed. Though the idea of reconstructing battle-damaged features was pretty footling—the duty of medical people in wartime was returning casualties to the front as quickly as possible to be shot at all over again—the generals felt it good for morale. A man would know that should his face get blown off, someone was employed to put it back on again. And with the Saracen providing his own pay and equipment the scheme was attractively cheap. They commandeered half a sanatorium on the Kent coast and packed him off.

The skill which the Saracen applied to New York noses was almost defeated by the ravages of battle. He raised pedicles of skin from chests and shoulders to plug holes in cheeks, so at least a man's tongue no longer worked in full view of his comrades. He took grafts from hip-bones and ribs to remake shattered jaws in patients fed on fluids by an enema syringe stuck down their throats four-hourly. He covered raw areas of flesh with paper-thin grafts of skin cut by a Thiersch knife like an oversized barber's razor. Everywhere he tidied up busily, undercut tissue, and tried to join it up again without tension or scarring. About half his repairs survived and half sloughed away through sepsis. Some of his patients left hospital unblemished, most looked peculiar, one or two died. 'Maybe we're not making Greek gods,' he would claim proudly, 'but at least we're turning out something their mothers won't scream at.' Every afternoon, under King's Regulations, the convalescents were put on parade, ordered to form fours, and were marched round the countryside by a sergeant-major.

To the nearby villagers the 'Face Hospital' was a place to be mentioned in whispers, the haunt of freakish monsters beyond the imagination even of H. G. Wells. Old ladies shuddered and sometimes screamed at the patients' approach, mothers locked up their children, and pregnant women feared (or welcomed, as

8

may be) the possibility of sudden abortion. A deputation hurried to the sanatorium, puffing righteous indignation like an overtaxed railway engine. They demanded the village be put out of bounds. The Army obliged. With nowhere else to go, the men started wandering along the beach.

Graham first noticed the Saracen's patients from an isolated summerhouse where—a doctor mysteriously remaining a doctor even when a patient—he alone was privileged to sit that summer and inhale, though without undue exertion, the reputedly therapeutic Channel breezes. At a distance he imagined they were curious congenital monstrosities, like the London Hospital 'Elephant Man' befriended by Edward the Seventh's appendicectomist, Sir Frederick Treves. But with their approach, hospital blues proclaimed the deformities man-made rather than born. There were three of them, holding back as they caught sight of his deck-chair, but he struck up an acquaintance easily enough through the reassurance of his medical title and the cigarettes bought in the village by Harry the orderly (on a commission basis). He was smoking them with a two-inch bandage bound with professional neatness round his fingers, to baffle Sister Constable's witch's eye for tobacco stains.

'Sit down and let's swap grouses,' he invited. 'Life's a bore down here, isn't it? Do you get anything but Tickler's plum and apple jam on your side? We tubercules are fed to the teeth with it.'

They were soon getting on splendidly. The patients were glad of anyone taking an interest in them—and they weren't even officers, either—with the village barred any diversion was welcome, and a man could always do with a few extra fags. Besides, the poor young bastard had T.B. Nothing cheers the afflicted like discovering someone to be sorry for.

They were relieved that Graham showed neither horror nor pity towards them. He felt neither. No doctor seems so heartless as a newly-qualified one, his brain bristling aggressively with cures for cut-and-dried clinical conditions, his experience rich in demonstration cases if not yet in human beings. He was simply interested in them as specimens. Particularly the

9

corporal with no nose, but a bump instead, like the beak of a hen, in the middle of his forehead.

'Next month it'll be my new nose, Doctor.' The man fondled the lump with a mixture of amusement and pride. 'Last month it was a bit of my rib, down here. Oh, he's very clever, Dr Sarasen.' He spoke with the reverence of any man for another who has cut him about sufficiently often and extensively. 'Mind, we looks a bunch of bogymen, I suppose. Can hardly blame them in the village, can you? But it's not very handy if you're wanting to buy a pint or some smokes.'

'Where did you get wounded?'

'Wipers. That there big push last summer.'

'Would you object if I drew you?' Graham asked suddenly.

The man looked alarmed. 'Draw me? I ain't no oil-painting, am I?'

'You're more interesting to me than anything in the National Gallery, I assure you. Do you know what you are? You're a medical pioneer. Yes, I'm not joking. The whole elaborate paraphernalia depends on a few guinea-pigs and brave fellows like you. You're like Jupille, the shepherd lad Pasteur tried his anti-rabies serum on. Or Eben Frost, who risked his life sniffing an unknown anaesthetic to lose a tooth. Or little Jimmy Phipps, the boy Jenner first vaccinated.' Graham was well up in medical history, which he found by and large more interesting than medicine itself. 'They put up a statue to Jupille in Paris. Maybe they ought to raise one in the village to you. Think of yourself as a benefactor to humanity.'

The corporal's grin disclaimed such hollow honours. 'What worries me, Doctor, is which bit I blow if I gets a nasty cold in the nose.'

In a world which shutters its windows and hides its children at your approach, you have to develop a highly specialized sense of humour.

The more Graham drew, the more the patchwork faces fascinated him. He had heard nothing of reconstructive operations in the tuition condescendingly bestowed on him at Blackfriars Hospital. Their great surgeon Sir Horace Barrow, though acclaimed in amputating a limb to have no equal in speed, dexterity, or relish, ran his practice strictly on the principle that if thine eye offend thee, pluck it out. Graham drew half a dozen of the wounded men from a score of angles, sometimes pencilling slight improvements of his own. He thought the sketches rather good, almost worthy of a textbook. Then one morning his interest in the subject was brought abruptly to a halt.

It was after breakfast, when the sanatorium verandah was busy with nurses and orderlies tidying away the bedpans, bowls, trays and other domestic trappings of illness, presenting the patients in a neat clean row for stately inspection by their medical attendants. A stranger came down the line of beds, a pink-cheeked, red-eared tall young man rather older than Graham, in a well-valeted khaki uniform with lieutenant's pips on the cuffs, a Sam Browne, breeches, and shining boots, his intensely military appearance hardly softened by the twined-serpent R.A.M.C. badges on his lapels.

He saluted. 'Dr Trevose, isn't it?'

Graham nodded.

'My name's Haileybury. I'm attached to the plastic unit in the other block.'

It was clearly no social call. The visitor looked as unfriendly as a barbed-wire entanglement. 'It's my duty to speak to you on an important matter.'

It suddenly struck Graham how much in an argument a man flat on his back is at a disadvantage to one standing on his feet. 'In that case it's my duty to listen.'

The officer seemed to seek words. Then the colt frisked through the trappings of a war-horse. 'Look here, you're jolly well infecting my patients,' Haileybury burst out boyishly. 'We take tremendous trouble keeping our chaps separated from you T.B. people. Surely you appreciate that? And there you are, hobnobbing with them every afternoon. It's not playing the game at all, you know.'

Graham's reply was a laugh. Haileybury looked quickly up and down the verandah. He had started out aware that a row between two medical practitioners must always be a delicate affair, and he hoped there was no possibility of being made to look at all foolish. 'It doesn't strike *me* as the slightest amusing,' he said bleakly.

'But I'm not infective. Honestly. There're no Koch's bacilli in my sputum. None at all. They only found them twice, and I think they were cheating because I didn't fit the classical pattern of the disease. If you don't believe me you can always look at my notes.'

'Oh, I wouldn't doubt your word.' Haileybury's tone underlined the hideousness of one medical man's lying to another. 'Then perhaps you'll oblige me by giving up drawing the poor fellows? You must know how they feel about their appearance. It's bad enough with the village shying away as though they were in the last stages of leprosy. If those pictures got into the wrong hands—or into a newspaper . . .' His almost colourless blue eyes expressed horror. 'Why, it would be terrible. Our work here might become wellnigh impossible.'

As a civilian, even a sick one, Graham was faintly alarmed at any clash with the military. But the man was clearly a bore. He must not be misled that the drawings, the patients, nor especially himself, had in Graham's eyes the slightest importance.

'They won't get into anybody's hands. I only did them for my own amusement.' Graham handed a sheaf of papers from his bedside locker. 'You can take them if you want to—tear them up, do what you like with them. I'll go back to drawing the seagulls, if it makes everyone happier.'

The young medical officer hesitated but took the sketches. He had not allowed for this. He was piqued. He was as touchy as the fuse on a shell over his position as the only Army officer on the Saracen's staff, or over association with such an inglorious unit at all, and felt the mysterious doctor in the summerhouse was somehow straying on to the parade-ground of his authority. But as he ruffled through the drawings he had to admit the interloper's knack for art, and that sort of thing. It occurred to him they might possibly tickle the fancy of the Saracen. And any such stimulation would make life easier in the other half of the sanatorium.

12

'Well . . . if you really don't want them, I'll take them.'

'Do.'

'We've got an artist chappie on the unit, of course, but he's not much good.' Haileybury's tone set such occupations in their place. 'Thank you,' he added.

'Please don't mention it.'

'By the way, I've put that summerhouse out of bounds.' He saluted. 'Good day, Dr Trevose.'

An amusing idea struck Graham. 'Dr Haileybury—'

He turned. 'Yes?'

'Fetch me a bedpan, old man, will you? They're in the cupboard by the door. I'm absolutely bursting.'

Haileybury went pinker. 'I'll send a nurse,' he snapped.

He disappeared down the verandah, with the dignity of the Guards in retreat.

'*What* a bore!' thought Graham. 'Thank God I won't see him again. What a frightful, crashing, A-one bore.'

It was a term he used freely at the time, to embrace any unpleasantness from the lack of a cigarette to the loss of an uncle.

3

GRAHAM DIDN'T NOTICE the girl until she was almost on top of his deck-chair. He was concentrating on sketching the rotting black timbers of a breakwater, stretching forlornly after its departed tide. His reaction to any rebuff being immediate loss of interest in the subject, the man (or more often the woman) who offered it, the faces which had fascinated him one day dropped from their slot in his mind the next. He had turned his talents to the seagulls, as promised.

Three weeks had gone since the row, and he was becoming as bored and dispirited as a prisoner of war. He tried reading, but the sanatorium's stock of books was as tattered as they were old and uninteresting, new ones were beyond his pocket, and no circulating library could possibly allow their volumes into such an infective midden. He had only the newspaper, the *Strand Magazine*, copies of *Tit-Bits* fingered by the whole ward, and his elder brother Robin's letters from 'Somewhere in France', as the address went. These were inclined to be ponderous, filled with sound advice, and impregnated with vinegary morality, like Robin himself. Even the excitement of his father's monthly visit was denied him, the professor writing that weighty matters of academic anatomy unhappily tethered him to London, though Graham suspected his own returning health made the sooty carriages of the South Eastern and Chatham railway less endurable. He had even stopped smuggling cigarettes. His only aim was to exchange the sanatorium beach for the wider shores of life as soon as possible.

14

But now a girl. He caught her in the corner of his eye. Quite a flapper.

'I hope you're keeping your distance only because you're afraid I'll infect you,' he asked, without looking up.

'Oh, no!'

She was pretty, unmarried, and very young—about eighteen, he calculated. She wore a blue-and-white striped civilian dress, her long fair hair loosely drawn into a bun below her wide-brimmed hat. A refreshing change from the drab-uniformed, middle-aged, war-cropped V.A.D.s in the sanatorium.

'I was just watching you drawing.' Overcoming scruples about tuberculous or moral contamination she advanced a pace or two. 'I hope you don't mind the liberty?'

Her voice is a disappointment, he told himself.

'I don't mind a bit. Any artist is flattered by an audience, even a man painting a pillar-box.' He was anyway a natural exhibitionist, a trait which furrowed so many lofty professional brows later on. 'May I introduce myself? Dr Trevose. Though at present locked up here serving a sentence.'

'I work on the other side,' she volunteered. 'Helping with the letters and records for Dr Sarasen.'

'*That's* very brave.' He was being honest. 'Putting your head in a nightmare factory.'

'Oh, it's not that bad.' Now her smile's quite nice, Graham decided. 'You soon get used to the boys. And it's awfully good work, isn't it?'

'Oh, very praiseworthy,' he said off-handedly. Anything connected with Lieutenant Haileybury deserved scant respect. 'How about letting me draw *you*?'

She blushed, such a suggestion striking her as much too intimate for a few moments' acquaintance.

'Yes, come on! If you don't like it I'll set fire to it. I promise. Perch yourself on that flat stone. It won't take a minute.'

'No, *honest*,' she protested. 'I'm not worth a picture.'

'Nonsense! You'll make a very pretty one.' She blushed more deeply, but sat as directed. 'May I ask your name?'

'Miss Pollock.'

15

'I mean the name people call you.'

No reply. Under the rules of courtship in a more leisurely age the exchange of christian names was a milestone far down the primrose path.

'Forgive me,' apologized Graham gallantly.

'It's Edith,' she decided to impart.

'Isn't that a nice name?'

He sketched until she started to fidget, then abruptly tore the paper up. 'It was far too unflattering,' he told her, as she gave a charming little cry of disappointment. 'You'll have to come back tomorrow.'

Wooing Edith without the usual accompaniments of theatres, chocolates, flowers, and even nightfall struck Graham as an uphill task. But after six months of feverish chastity woo her he must. He felt it unfortunate that the raised bodily metabolism in tuberculosis should increase the desire, while the treatment precluded the performance. Rumours regularly ran round the sanatorium of unexpected bursts of co-operation by the nurses, of irregular shapes in the female beds at night, even of attempts on Sister Constable herself. They were good for the patients' morale, and if they came to the ears of the medical superintendent he dismissed them. He had long ago stopped believing that people in the care of himself and Mother Nature dared indulge themselves in the feelings of ordinary men and women.

A few afternoons later, sitting with their backs against the summerhouse in the sun, the pretence of sketching wordlessly abandoned, Graham judged the moment had arrived to kiss her.

'No, no!' she protested, automatically.

'But I'm not in the slightest infective,' he assured her considerately.

In her attempts to explain this was not the point, the first step to Edith's downfall was mounted.

'Do you actually live somewhere in the san?' asked Graham, resuming the conversation.

She collected herself. 'Oh, no. I cycle over every day from Ramsgate. My father's in business there.'

'Really? What sort of business?'

Edith picked a blade from a tuft of grass, and fixing it between her thumbs blew into her cupped hands, producing what struck him as a very unpleasant noise.

'He's a butcher.' She blew at the grass again, but this time it didn't work. 'I used to help in the shop, behind the cash-desk. Then I learned the typewriter. I wanted to better myself, you see.' He was struck by the power of this motive force, as expressed by the solemnity of her tone. She extruded a piece of grass with the tip of her tongue and added more cheerfully, 'Anyway, we've all got to do *some* sort of war work, haven't we?'

'My father's a butcher, too. Well, a professor of anatomy.' Seeing this meant as little as announcing his father was a troglodyte, he added, 'He cuts people up. Dead ones.'

'*Dead* ones!'

'Yes, he finds it very interesting.'

'Where's he get them from?' she asked, aghast.

'Oh, they don't have to dig them up any more. From poorhouses, infirmaries, jails. People with no relatives, no friends, nothing at all but the flesh and bones they stand up in.'

It thrilled him to feel her shiver against him. He had won over a few girls with this Bob Sawyer approach, easy familiarity with the unmentionable, and even the unspeakable, giving any young man an undeserved fascination.

'I shouldn't like it to happen to me.'

'That's not very likely. You know, my father always smells of formaldehyde, even on holiday. That's what they pickle the corpses in. They hang them up in racks by their ears till wanted, like suits of clothes—'

Edith decided to change the subject. 'He must be dreadfully clever, your father. Being a professor, and that.' She had a natural reverence for intelligence. 'Tell me about your mother.'

'She died when I was a child. T.B., same as me.' Graham switched to a tone of tragedy, adding with enthusiastic pessimism, 'I suppose it'll carry me off too, in the end.'

This on top of the clothes-racks of corpses melted Edith. She started to cry. 'Don't say that, Graham! Oh, don't say that!'

She was torn from the misty contemplation of his distant

17

death to grappling with his immediate vitality by feeling his hand groping up her skirt.

A week later Graham faced a complication spared other young men with similar plans in cornfields or punts. He knew he had the choice between copulation and convalescence. His regimen was such a finely balanced one of rest and carefully graduated activity, he had taken pencil and paper and tried to express his much-desired expenditure of energy with Edith in terms of his daily exercise allowance. How far would the pulse rate rise? And the respiration? What about the muscular movement? He finally equated it with a mile, walked on the level at an even pace.

He prepared himself by cutting a mile from the prescribed three of his morning walk, and getting Harry to buy the necessary apparatus in Ramsgate (also on a commission basis). But Edith seemed horrified by his suggestion of a 'bit of fun'. The eager young fellow was rushing her down the primrose path with the speed of launching the Ramsgate lifeboat. But she agreed to go inside the summerhouse. After all, it had just started to rain.

The admittedly misleadingly simple occurrence had so many terrors for the girl Graham almost despaired. He explained pressingly his medical knowledge put the better-publicized sequelae out of the question. After all, he reflected a shade impatiently, not every young woman had the privilege of being deflowered by a dissector of the entire female pelvis. But there were sighs and tears, regrets and recriminations. He grazed his knee badly, and in the confined space there was a great deal of dust. He felt he had won a hollow victory. And he worried dreadfully that night it would put his temperature up.

Graham's experience of the female pelvis being unfortunately greater than his experience of the female as a whole, he was unprepared for the adoration Edith now beamed on him. In the hot pursuit of love she became the hare and he the tortoise. It made him worry about his temperature more than ever. She brought him gifts—chocolate, strawberry jam, calf's foot jelly, which everyone knew was good for tuberculosis. She also brought him a tenderness which he had never experienced from girls picked up in the hospital or shops, in his motherless home, nor anywhere else, except in the sanatorium during the strictly limited period when everyone imagined they would be transferring him any day to the mortuary. They enjoyed the intimate exploration of each other's personalities almost as much as of each other's bodies. For the first time in his life Graham felt someone cared that he was living. When the summerhouse started becoming too cold in the afternoons he found himself taking a solemn step. He asked Edith to become his wife.

She burst into tears, but agreed, quite quickly. They decided nothing could be announced until his discharge from the sanatorium with a clean bill of health, or the medical superintendent would find too many awkward questions. If he were faintly surprised at himself, he supposed it a feeling shared by all young men proposing marriage. Every night in his red-blanketed bed he felt obliged to find a hundred reasons for asking her. All of them were really irrelevant. With nobody else nubile in sight they were joined together as compulsively as Adam and Eve in that tubercular Garden of Eden.

4

FOUR GENERATIONS OF the Trevose family had been doctors of one sort or another. Like many other Cornishmen they had once reaped a living from the sea, by fishing, the service of their sovereign, or smuggling. Then about the time of Queen Victoria's accession, the same bacilli lodging briefly in Graham's chest settled permanently in the spine of young Enoch Trevose and he suffered Pott's disease, in sad ignorance of the splendid eighteenth-century London surgeon who had dignified it with his name. The tuberculous process turned Enoch's vertebral bone into a cheesy mass, which in time solidified as a wedge of misshapen chalk and plainly closed the family livelihood to him. Like many sufferers from chronic illness he developed a lively interest in medical matters generally, and decided to set up as a quack. He felt his sinister hunchback would be a valuable asset.

Enoch started by peddling among Cornish villagers cures for over-indulgence in the pleasures of board and bed. Then he flirted with phrenology, assessing underlying mental aptitudes from bumps on the scalp, but found it too sophisticated for his patients. He tried instead mesmerism, which scared them from their wits. He finally prospered by reviving the medieval craft of uroscopy. From inspection of the urine in a crystal flask Enoch could advise not only on his patient's disease but on his problems in affairs of commerce, agriculture, or the heart as well. A shrewd judge of human nature, he died with a practice extending from Truro to Bath and a gold-headed cane as grand as any sported by a fashionable London surgeon, his only failures occurring once or twice a year when some joker substituted for the vital fluid the offering of his mare or cow.

Money blurring even the worst deformity, Enoch married the pretty daughter of a Camborne innkeeper, and produced a son who was put to looking after the ledgers and leeches of a local apothecary. The young man found in himself a skill at setting the bones of men injured down the tin mines, or of their masters dropping drunk from their horses above, and grew to bask in the respect of learning rather than of witchcraft. Then the Medical Act of 1858 blew a blast through the profession which stripped like beggars' rags the gorgeous privileges in which he had clothed himself. In official eyes he was unexamined, unregistered, probably unlettered, unfit to practise and unallowed to use the title of 'Doctor'. Bitterness almost killed him. He prized the title more than the shameful fortune of his father. He determined his own children should learn proper medicine at a proper hospital, much of it in Latin. A daughter travelled to Edinburgh behind the bustling skirts of Miss Jex-Blake. His sons went to Blackfriars Hospital in London. One of these rewarded him—admittedly less through brilliance than availability, being handy when the former occupant of the chair cut his finger dissecting a carelessly-pickled corpse and died of blood-poisoning in a week—by flowering into the professor of anatomy who stood in his study one grey morning in January 1919 contemplating the psychological ruins of his household.

It was a disturbing time not only for the professor but for everyone. As Boccaccio described an earlier visitation, many valiant men and many fair ladies breakfasted with their kinsfolk and that same night supped with their ancestors in the other world. A fearsome influenza virus had leapt on a populace congratulating itself on escaping death in the hands of one another, to make short work showing how Nature could outdo her creatures in the matter of mass-destruction.

The week of the Armistice had left Britain two thousand citizens the less from 'Spanish flu'. Families crawled helplessly round their houses or died together behind locked doors, as in the Great Plague. Jails and nunneries suffered impartially. The

Army which had conquered a too apparent enemy dropped in thousands to an invisible one. Telegrams warned next-of-kin of men dangerously ill, who were already blue-faced and dead in the mortuary. Lloyd George caught it. Pneumonia, the 'old man's friend', instead of releasing him from the pains of senility marched in the epidemic's footsteps and asphyxiated his grandson. Undertakers were reduced to papiermâché coffins. The doctors' only treatment was a poultice to deaden the pain in the chest, and straw to deaden the traffic in the street.

Professor Trevose had sneezed that morning, five times—he had counted them. A nervous, edgy man, he worried if the ultramicroscopic thunderbolt was now descending on himself. His bodily resistance was surely lowered by overwork, channelling the flood of post-war students into his anatomy department at Blackfriars. (The corpse situation was extremely tight.) His precious professorial thought had still to be dissipated on a home sadly short of coal, food, and the woman's touch. His younger son Graham, sent to a sanatorium to die, had not died at all, but returned engaged to a girl ridiculously below his social station. His elder son Robin, in the professor's opinion mistaking a natural smugness for piety, had announced that on release from the Army he was disappearing as a medical missionary to the remote Straits Settlements—he certainly wouldn't get very fat on *that*. The cistern was leaking into the professor's bedroom and the butcher's boy had been rude. All were unbearable distractions, he reflected bad-temperedly, from the essential tranquillity of academic life.

There was a noise from the breakfast-room next door. His two sons were quarrelling as usual.

Graham and Robin had quarrelled about many things since their fights over rocking-horses and bicycles, but now Graham refused to take his brother's new vocation seriously their disputes took on a loftier air.

'Mind you, I bear God no ill-will,' Graham told him amiably over the remains of his breakfast. 'No more than any other distinguished gentleman I've heard a lot about but don't see much prospect of meeting.'

22

Robin glared. He was still in his R.A.M.C. uniform, with broad shoulders, sleek black hair, and glowing complexion—the family genes, shaken in the professor's reproductive process, had landed heavily in his favour. He found much to disapprove of in Graham—his unstarched collars, his atheism, his laziness, this girl in the sanatorium (even before submitting to the pain of meeting her), above all his general underestimation of the earnestness of life. 'I'm sorry you should deny the existence of the human soul. Genuinely sorry. It grieves rather than angers me you should deny yourself the comfort of a life hereafter. Perhaps if you'd served in France you'd have come back with different ideas.'

'Oh, come, Robin, that's below the belt,' Graham told him cheerfully. 'I ended up C-three, totally rejected. I'm not a conchie. No-one was more eager to do his bit. I couldn't help getting T.B., could I?'

'There you go, deliberately misunderstanding me as usual. Of course I didn't say you were a shirker.'

'I'd like to believe it all. I really would. It would be great fun existing for ever, playing the harp and sitting on a cloud. Though that would be rather dampish, and likely to give you piles. But why flatter only we top dogs in the evolutionary scale with souls? It strikes me a bit hard on the runners-up, like the apes.'

Robin banged on the tablecloth with his coffee spoon. He was a flamboyant breakfast-eater, always getting down first and surrounding himself with a nest of letters, torn envelopes, and pages of newspaper, attracting all the jugs and bowls to his own end of the table as if by magnetism. He was a man who saw each new day as a challenge, and liked to fortify himself to meet it. It all irritated Graham very much. 'I agree that man is, zoologically speaking, an animal. But you must concede that we are the only animals God created with an awareness of our own inevitable death. Surely that suggests some difference?'

'Then I only hope there's some mechanism for opting out of immortality. There're plenty of people I want to avoid in London, let alone in Heaven. But what on earth are we discussing

23

things like this for at breakfast time? It's far too early for serious thought.' He was becoming bored with teasing his brother. He had long ago decided his own intelligence bettered Robin's, and was coming amiably to suspect it exceeded that of his father the professor. He took out a cigarette. 'Let's change the subject.'

'Yes, you're smoking too much.'

'Nicotine hasn't been shown to do people any harm. Only cats.'

'That statement applies only to *normal* people.'

'I do wish you'd stop treating me as one of the chronic sick.' It was Graham's turn to be annoyed. 'I've no sputum, no cough, no temperature, nothing. I'm cured. My lesion's calcified. If it wasn't by now I'd be dead.'

'I don't believe you're even taking your temperature, are you?'

'Of course I am. Well, when I remember. Anyway, I'm not going to be bewitched by a damn thermometer. It ruled the sanatorium like a rod of iron.'

Graham got up and started wandering round the shabby breakfast-room looking for a match. Like everywhere else in the Hampstead house it had a medical air as inescapable as the stench of iodoform in hospital. On one side was a mahogany case with rows of old anatomy books imprisoned behind lattice-work for life. On the other stood a sideboard with copies of the *Lancet* scattered round an old brass microscope under a glass dome like wax fruit. One wall exhibited a black-and-white reproduction of Rembrandt's *Anatomy Lesson*, the other an equally harrowing photograph of the newly-qualified professor, in academic robes brandishing his rolled diploma at the world like a truncheon. Over the fireplace hung a water-colour of a highly eventful storm at sea. It had been executed by the professor's wife when sent to Cornwall to convalesce and paint, during their weird triangular courtship with the tubercle bacillus always in the third corner.

Graham struck a vesta. 'I'm feeling fit enough to start work, you know.'

Robin looked up from the *Morning Post*. 'What as? Demonstrator in the anatomy rooms, I suppose, as Father suggested. That's a fairly light occupation for an invalid.'

'No, I'm taking a surgical job, I fancy.'

'But I didn't think you were much interested in surgery.'

'Well, yes and no. At best, I've thought it mutilation as a fine art. At worst, a generally losing battle against sepsis and haemorrhage—all chloroform, pus, and slipping tourniquets. Most depressing. But this is reconstructive surgery.'

Robin laid down his paper in horror. 'Not *plastic* surgery?'

'Plastic surgery, reconstructive surgery, cosmetic surgery, facio-maxillary surgery, call it what you like. In the san I did some drawings of Olaf Sarasen's patients. He must have been impressed, because now he's moved to Town he's written offering me the job of clinical assistant. I'm seeing him this afternoon.'

' "The Saracen"! You can't work for that mountebank.' Robin sounded more shocked at his brother's attitude to his profession than his attitude to God.

'I don't believe he is a mountebank. No one at Blackfriars could take more care over his patients.'

'Of course he's a mountebank! Everyone in London says so,' Robin corrected him flatly. 'Take up throats, eyes, orthopaedics, anything you like. But not this trivial face-lifting business.'

'Listen.' Graham leant on the table. 'Do you know what the Saracen can do? He can take a cartilage from a man's rib, transplant it to the middle of his forehead, wait till it's developed a new blood-supply, then draw it down to remake a shot-away nose. Isn't that fascinating? Just think—soon we'll be able to replace precious fingers with toes, make rosy cheeks from the broad unseen acres of the abdomen, even transplant whole organs from one patient to another—if they're prepared to put up with the inconvenience of being Siamese twins, which will anyway be comparatively trifling and strictly temporary. Once the new blood-supply's taken, we'll just snip them apart, like a pair of paper dolls.'

Graham Trevose had imagination. It was a quality in medical men uncommon, and probably downright dangerous.

'We shan't have people dying from Bright's disease with shrivelled kidneys any more,' he went on enthusiastically. 'We'll simply graft in a new kidney from a condemned criminal, or some other co-operative donor. Plastic surgery's going to take the whole subject by the ears, shake it up, and revolutionize it. You mark my words. It's like Morton's ether, or Lister's carbolic spray.'

'Poppycock,' said Robin.

Graham shrugged his shoulders. 'Well, if I don't like it, in six months' time I can always get a job doing something else.'

'Not after working for an adventurer like Olaf Sarasen you won't.'

'Oh, rats!' said Graham, losing his temper, throwing his cigarette into the fire, and abruptly leaving the room.

The professor heard the door slam and pulled his moustache irritably. There was no peace in the house since the boys had come home. Academic contemplation had been so much easier with one in the trenches and the other on his death-bed. And another thunderous disturbance was rising above the horizon. He had better weather it as soon as possible. He pulled the study bell-handle again for the little maid with the acne.

5

GRAHAM MADE HIS way to the Saracen by his favourite form
of transport, well wrapped up in the frontmost seat on top of an
open General omnibus. The capital was settling down from the
flag-waving of the Armistice, but there were plenty of khaki
vehicles on the roads and khaki uniforms on the pavements.
Apart from Tommies there were Canadians, Australians, and
Americans kicking their heels and occasionally authority while
waiting for ships home, and women were still to be seen in
khaki caps and baggy service jackets. But the flu virus had
replaced the excitement in the air. People hurried about with
scarves drawn protectively over mouth and nostrils, and anyone
sneezing was regarded with the outraged suspicion recently
reserved for possible spies and traitors.

Graham found the Saracen himself bald and amazingly fat,
smoking a cigar which he flicked into a large ashtray shaped
like an American eagle. The surgeon had so enmeshed himself
in the British military machine he proved impossible to detach
when the sanatorium pleaded for its wards back with peace.
Having nowhere else to put him, the Army transferred him to
Princess Alexandra's Hospital for Officers in Kensington, one of
several peculiar London institutions never certain if they were
really hospitals or nursing-homes, where the Saracen was un-
daunted to find himself restricted to six beds and use of the
operating theatre only on Saturdays. He had a talent for
expansion in the teeth of competition which would have brought
admiration from his many friends on Wall Street. He had

already achieved eviction of the hospital secretary from a down-stairs office, where he received Graham behind a large desk with a signed photograph of Mr Woodrow Wilson and the American flag on one side, and a signed photograph of Mr Lloyd George and the Union Jack on the other.

'Tell me, Doctor,' he asked at once. 'Why did you choose our profession?'

Graham always found this embarrassing. His family had expected him to 'go in for' medicine, and he had been too young to resist such unoriginality. As he searched for a fittingly solemn reply the Saracen saved a lie by adding genially, 'It's the family business, isn't it? Well, medicine owes a lot to its dynasties.' He picked up the sketches Graham had given Hailey-bury. 'You've got quite a talent for drawing, Dr Trevose. Maybe it isn't great, but you don't find it much among medical people at all. I guess the Renaissance has to answer for divorcing science from art.' He waved the cigar in his other hand. 'I don't need to tell you what we do here—or what we try to do, which is more to the point. Do you think you could become interested in this branch of surgery?'

'In my present state of inexperience I'm in the happy position to become interested in anything, sir.'

The Saracen grunted. 'No "Sir", if you please. We're civilians.' He spread out his well-polished cavalry boots under the desk. ' "Doc" is my title on the unit. Now we're reorganizing I'm looking for another pair of hands in the operating-room. I could take a young fellow out of the Army or some place, but I'm after a man with feeling for the job.' He assessed Graham through the cigar-smoke. 'Are you ambitious?'

Graham had never asked himself. 'Averagely, I suppose.'

The Saracen chuckled. 'Are you interested in money?'

This struck Graham as frankly indelicate. The consultants who trained him at Blackfriars would no sooner have discussed in public their financial dreams than their sexual ones. Besides, he was still in the charming stage of any professional career when the rewards seem as irrelevant as they are insubstantial.

'I won't believe any man who tells me otherwise,' the

Saracen continued cheerfully. 'Not outside a madhouse or a monastery.' He leaned back in his chair, cigar aimed at the ceiling. 'Do you know what I'm going to do with this hospital? I'm going to make it the greatest centre for plastic surgery in Europe. In the world! People from the four corners of the earth will come to see our work, as pilgrims.' He leant abruptly forward, chins wobbling earnestly. 'Oh, I know the war's over and the wounds are healing and there's some Jeremiah telling me every week we plastic surgeons have nothing left to do. Out of a job, they say. We'll have only warts, club feet, girls scalping themselves in machines. By God, they're wrong! "For the children of men, they are but vanity."' Graham thought he had a good voice for Biblical quotation. 'Vanity, Doctor! That's going to bring us more casualties than the Germans did. I'm a man of vision. I see the day when we'll provide mankind with new noses, new ears, new chins, as easy as drawing a tooth. We'll change the contours of its breasts and its buttocks. We'll wipe away the ravages of age. The features you're born with won't signify any more. We'll usurp the functions of the Almighty! And if you dedicate yourself,' he explained, coming down easily from lofty generalities to commercial particulars, 'I can guarantee you an income in five years' time— Come in!'

This itinerary of the road to Eldorado was interrupted by a knock on the office door and the appearance of Lieutenant Haileybury. The two young men stared at each other. Haileybury silently inclined his head. With the population of the world shifting like sand at the end of the war, both thought a second encounter terribly bad luck.

'Think it over, Dr Trevose.' The Saracen started busying himself with some paperwork. 'I'll give you two days. Don't write. Use the telephone. Time is money. Eric, show the doctor out, will you?'

Haileybury nodded again, without speaking. The pair crossed the over-polished parquet of the small hall, which like everything else at Princess Alexandra's had an air of decorous homeliness, broken only by an elderly V.A.D. arguing crossly with someone down a brass voice-pipe in the corner.

'Do I gather the Saracen's invited you to join the circus?' he asked at last. 'I'm just back from leave.'

Graham nodded.

'Of course, the man's no end of a card.' Haileybury's tone indicated that offers of any sort from this source were suspicious, if not sinister.

'Then how come you're working with him yourself?'

'Oh, the Army posted me. To keep an eye on him, I imagine. He's an impossible spendthrift, and no idea of discipline among the men.' They reached the glass-panelled street door. 'I wouldn't accept, if I were in your shoes.'

'Why?'

'There's no future in it.'

'I don't know if I agree.'

A wintry smile relieved Haileybury's features, which had frosted over at the sight of Graham. 'But you've just been subjected to the sales patter.'

'Well, he certainly did most of the talking,' Graham agreed.

'Oh, that's typical. He'd be wanting to see your reactions. He's got a full enough dossier on you somewhere, don't you worry. Anyway, the Saracen's completely impossible to get on with.'

'I don't know if I agree with that, either.'

Haileybury smiled again. 'I see you're an enthusiast, Trevose. Take my tip. Don't make up your mind till you're clear of his magnetic field. You wouldn't be the first it's lured in the wrong direction.'

Graham was puzzled. Was Haileybury's cocky attitude merely showing off, or a genuine attempt to scare him away? And why? Because he had asked the man to fetch a bedpan? Some people take life immensely seriously.

'Thank you, Haileybury. I'm much obliged for your advice.'

'I'm only trying to be helpful. Plastics is a very new specialty —if it's a specialty at all. Nobody knows where they are yet. Have you got transport?'

'I'll walk, thanks. It's a fine afternoon.'

As the glass door swung shut behind him Graham made the

second biggest decision of his life. As impulsively as he had decided to marry Edith he decided on the Saracen. Throughout his life, inside the operating theatre or out, no path beckoned him so invitingly as one the angels feared to tread. It was his natural luck that so often the angels were standing about afterwards looking foolish. It struck him that for the first time in his life he had entered upon gainful employment. He started to whistle like an errand-boy.

Inside the hospital, Haileybury made straight back to the office. The Saracen looked up impatiently. He was calculating how to buy some speculative shares with money he didn't have, an exercise giving him as much pleasure as reconstructing a nose.

'Eric, it'll wait, won't it?' he asked shortly.

'I think I should have a word with you, Doc.' The young medical officer looked awkward. The subtleties of the game of life were beyond him, he felt demeaned even by having to play it at all. 'About Trevose.'

The Saracen flicked ash from his cigar. 'What's the matter with him? I checked at Blackfriars. He's got a good brain, when he's pushed to use it. A bit lackadaisical and over-concerned with number one, but we can straighten that out. He looks a fragile specimen, but his lesion's healed. Do you know anything else?'

Haileybury went pinker. 'He isn't exactly out of the top drawer.'

The Saracen grunted. He disliked the British idea of society as some sort of tallboy. 'His father's a distinguished professor.'

'You know he's engaged to marry Miss Pollock?'

The surgeon raised his eyebrows. 'No?' He grinned. 'Pretty girl.'

'He was carrying on with her in a most distasteful way,' Haileybury went on. He disliked discussing such things, but he disliked Graham more. The man was encroaching on his little kingdom. He wished ardently he'd torn up the drawings. 'Yes, in that beach hut. I wondered where she was going in the afternoons. I made it my business to find out.'

The Saracen laughed. 'Well, well! So you were Miss Pollock's chaperon? Or was he putting your nose out of joint?'

'There was no question of that,' said Haileybury hotly.

'As long as it doesn't interfere with his surgery, I don't care what the hell the boy does with his spare time,' the Saracen told him amiably. 'Now let's have a little peace, eh, Eric?'

Haileybury retired, baffled. The game of life, played against the Saracen, always seemed to be a losing battle.

Graham reached home to find the psychological dilapidation of the household completed by Sally, the flat-chested seventeen-year-old maid with the spots, having been found pregnant. The professor's diagnostic suspicions had been aroused that morning over his breakfast by noticing her acne had vanished, pregnancy being an infallible if drastic cure for this skin condition. She was summoned to his study, an intimidating room with curtains of Nottingham lace excluding the light from the window, and another of red velvet over the door excluding the world in general from his rarefied anatomical thoughts. Tall, stooping, heavily moustached, the distinguished academic towered before the marble fireplace as the embodiment of Divine wrath on her miserable failings. She burst into tears, confessed, and so forgot herself as to sit in his presence.

But the veins in the hand which grasped her little rough one seemed that morning to run not with blood but the milk of human kindness. The man of science perched on her chair, encircled her with his arms, and let her sob into his austerely-trousered lap. He removed her little starched cap, the more soothingly to stroke her dark hair. The culprit, it emerged, was an assistant at the greengrocer's. For a moment he had even suspected Graham, with his new penchant for the lower classes. The professor promised to shoulder the massive diplomacy not only of interviewing the youth, but of Sally's return home to Edmonton and her eventual admission to the maternity wards at Blackfriars. Afterwards he dried her tears on his handkerchief and kissed her tenderly, not once but several times.

When Aunt Doris, up from Brixton for the afternoon, nosed out the news she had to lie down and be brought tea with chocolate biscuits. She blamed the professor roundly for employing such wretches, as she had blamed him for bullying Graham over his books and ruining his health, indulging Robin's religious mania and catapulting him from the family bosom across the face of the earth, even for marrying her poor delicate sister in the first place and killing her by exposure to housework, childbirth, and the London fogs.

This emotional explosion made the professor rude to Miss Timworth, who came two days a week to do his typing. Though he was often rude to Miss Timworth, that afternoon she was feeling unwell and pinning on her hat left for ever, embarrassingly eloquently. She was typing his monograph on the synovial membranes lining the joints of the body, a topic of deeply-argued interest to his brother anatomists, if its fascination escaped a wider public. Like the flower on the cactus the book represented fifteen years of quiet unseen effort, and there it was in useless bundles of illegible longhand all over the floor. This was the bitterest dose to swallow of all.

With everyone in such straits it was remarkable that among the rare jollifications of the professor's home the supper-party that evening should count an outstanding success.

6

'WE ARE SUCH a masculine household you mustn't expect anything elaborate,' the professor apologized to Edith, inspecting her for the first time as though she were some interesting anatomical specimen in a bottle.

'I'm sure it'll be ever so comfy,' she said. 'Oh! what a lot of books!'

It suited the professor's ideas of economy to hold the feast in the shabby breakfast-room, pleading the continued scarcity of coal as an excuse for not broaching the big front dining-parlour. And with the country's convalescence from the war insufficiently advanced for meat to be freed from its coupon, he felt the fare could be blamelessly—indeed, patriotically—unsumptuous.

'What a lovely house!' Edith exclaimed. 'It must have looked a treat decorated for Christmas.'

'We celebrate such occasions very quietly,' said the professor.

'Perhaps you would like the chair nearest the fire, Miss Pollock?' invited Robin.

'Oh, thanks,' said Edith. She fluttered a smile. 'Ever so much.'

They made a peculiar quartet in the gaslight, sitting on well-repaired plush-seated chairs round a table decked with a shining linen cloth and the family silver, eating cold ham and pickles. The professor himself, dark-suited and heavily watch-chained, smelt of his corpse-preservative as usual. Robin was anatomizing Edith with his eyes as closely as his father, though the pain he feared on meeting his prospective sister-in-law seemed somewhat anaesthetized by her transparent desire to please. Besides, he was fidgeting to talk interestingly about kala-azar, yaws, trypanosomiasis, latah, chappa, chiufa, kubisagari, and other complaints unknown in the world of sanitation, street lighting, and taxi-cabs. Edith herself wore the blue-and-white dress Graham had first seen her in, though she had taken it up a daring six inches above the ankle, and her fair hair had been submitted to a fashionable crop. She was perfectly at ease. Professional gentlemen were becoming to her very ordinary creatures indeed. As for Graham, he sat in unusual silence, feeling like the author of some passionate, secret correspondence seeing it produced as a red-taped bundle in open court.

Graham's first uncomfortable adjustment on coming home from the sanatorium was to the distance Edith lay beyond the outermost ripples of his social circle. His father made plain that the dissectors of humanity and the dividers of Sunday joints simply did not mix, though seeming less concerned over the alliance than with scotching any hopes it might have of financial assistance. Aunt Doris burst into tears, finding consolation in Graham's mother no longer being alive to witness the disgrace. The young man began to wonder if he had perhaps been a trifle over-enthusiastic.

He tried blowing cold on Edith's passions by post, but this only made them blaze the brighter. At the first Christmas of peace his escape-hatch closed with a crash. Now the Face Hospital was shut and air-raids were over for ever, she was coming to London to live.

In the new year they made a rendezvous at Charing Cross station, where he watched her appear through the steam of the suburban platform wondering nervously if she would cling to him outside W. H. Smith's bookstall as passionately as outside the sanatorium summerhouse. That would never do, under the eyes of the railway employees. But she kissed him politely, asked after his health and his father, and said she wanted a cup of tea.

Across the marble-topped table at a Lyons' teashop Graham discovered with some disappointment that the attraction of London lay less in himself than in the previously declared and

35

still pressing idea of self-betterment. Edith was living in a suburb with the refreshingly pastoral name of Hither Green, with a sister who had already undergone the betterment process by marrying a barrister's clerk in the Temple. The clerk had found Edith a typist's job in the chambers of a neighbouring silk, Mr Wellingford—*K.C.*, she emphasized, this tenuous connection with Buckingham Palace apparently being gratifying. Her affection for her new job seemed so much warmer than for Graham, and in the less bracing air their relationship seemed no more wonderful than any joining the other office-girls and boys around them. He suddenly panicked at losing her, particularly as he had forgotten how pretty she looked. He told her hastily that his intended wife must come home to meet the family. So there she was, with the professor holding her hand.

'The anatomist's snuff-box.' The professor filled the hollow below Edith's thumb with salt. 'You see that little triangle? It is formed by the tendons of the muscles *extensor pollicis longus* and *extensor pollicis brevis*.' The edge of his false teeth appeared under his moustache as he smiled. His idea of small-talk was a string of anatomical jokes, unintelligible outside a dissecting-room. 'Should you wish to indulge in snuff, you would find it a convenient repository for each dose.'

'Why, fancy that!' Edith sounded quite breathless.

'*I*'m going to need all the anatomical knowledge I can muster,' Robin interrupted. 'I'm off overseas shortly to a missionary settlement. I shall be completely single-handed. For medicine, surgery, obstetrics—everything. It's quite a challenge.'

Edith's eyes widened. 'Won't you be eaten by cannibals?'

They all laughed. Only Graham knew she really meant it.

'I shall be much more likely eaten by mosquitoes.' Robin's tone nevertheless implied that any cannibals straying on the scene would get short shrift from *him*. He was about to give a lecture on yaws, but the professor forestalled him by tickling Edith behind the ear.

'There!' he exclaimed. She looked startled. 'I have stimulated your *alderman's nerve*. Through its connection with the vagus nerve, which descends from the brain into the abdomen, you know, it stimulates that much-abused organ the stomach to empty. Very useful after a Lord Mayor's banquet.' He laughed heartily. 'That's the legend, at all events.'

'Well!' Edith was amazed at the scientific wonders unfolded for her. 'Who'd have guessed it?'

'It seems rather optimistic invoking the reflex tonight,' remarked Graham morosely.

'This rationing,' sighed the professor. 'Will it ever end?'

He took a sip of the wine, which had as its main virtue value for money. He was enjoying himself. With no female patients, and the nurses at Blackfriars as far beyond his department as its lady students were in the future, he had no opportunity of talking to young women at all. But a chance word from a girl on a bus could set him aglow, he warmed to the touch of young ladies serving in shops, a waitress leaning across with his teacake inflamed him with thoughts far from academically anatomical. Well, it was lucky to be attracted more by girls as the years advanced rather than less, he told himself. There was no fun withering into a dry old stick. And, of course, no one could possibly notice.

Frustrated over yaws, Robin started a dissertation on faith in healing. Graham looked up. 'Oh, you mean like Monsieur Coué? "Every day in every way I am getting better and better"? If you run your practice on those principles, Robin, you'd better make jolly good friends with the coroner. That's if they run to such inconveniences out where you're going.'

Robin looked angry. 'You're misunderstanding me again. Quite deliberately.' In respect for Edith, he decided not to pursue the argument. He started talking about the flu epidemic instead, holding it as an illustration of Divine wrath on the wrongs of warring mankind.

'My dear fellow!' Graham didn't like the way his brother was taking the stage in front of his girl. 'Now you're confusing theology with bacteriology.'

'I do wish you wouldn't make sweeping remarks,' said Robin. 'But be reasonable. If faith in God can save us from our

37

ills, what's He want to send the epidemic for in the first place?'

'It's all due to the low state of nutrition,' the professor declared, dabbing his mouth with his napkin. To strangle the row he suggested playing his violin.

The breakfast-room was cramped for Mozart, with airs from *Chu Chin Chow* and *H.M.S. Pinafore* as light relief, but all three listened attentively. Particularly Edith. She thought his music less of a strain than his conversation. As he finally packed his instrument away the professor brought up the topic of type-writing.

Edith blushed. She suspected such modest achievements unworthy of the company. 'I only learned so as to do my war work,' she explained hastily. 'I'm helping Mr Wellingford as a personal favour, you know. Strictly temp.'

'I am writing a book,' the professor revealed. 'It is a labour of love, but nonetheless a labour. My last typist left, some-what unexpectedly, and I am hard put to find a suitable replacement. I don't know if I could poach a little of your time—'

'I'd be very glad to help, I'm sure.' Edith smiled round. 'I mean, it's all in the family now, isn't it?'

'But Father will pay for your trouble, of course,' said Graham.

The professor looked irritably at his son. 'The fee must per-force be small. Academic life, I'm sure you understand, is totally unmotivated by financial considerations.'

'Oh, yes,' said Edith.

The professor mellowed into a smile. 'Which may or may not be a disadvantage.'

'I expect I could come on Saturdays.'

'That would be a great help.'

'When I can manage, of course.'

'I think you will find the material very interesting. It is on the subject of the synovial membranes.'

'Is it really?' said Edith eagerly. 'Yes, I expect I shall.'

The professor bowed low over her hand. Then, exhausted with sociability, he made straight for bed.

Returning from leaving Edith at the Tube station, Graham found Robin standing thoughtfully before the dying fire.

'Well? What do you think of her?'

'She's certainly very gay and very agreeable. *And* very pretty.' Robin paused, and added, 'I congratulate you, Graham.'

'Thank you.' Graham sprawled in a chair.

'You wouldn't know she was common at all.'

'Thank you,' Graham repeated.

To be 'common' was such a hideous social disfigurement during the meal they had tactfully not mentioned Edith's parents. It was like avoiding the topic of noses if entertaining the Saracen's patients. She certainly hadn't brought the subject up herself. To sup with a professor and a doctor son you were about to marry was such a shining milestone up the hard road of self-betterment father and mother could be temporarily ditched.

'You mean her table manners weren't too bad?' Graham lit a cigarette. 'Or too good, which would have been worse?'

'When are you getting married?'

'Oh, some time this summer.' Graham flicked the match into the grate. 'It depends what we can screw out of the old man. She made quite a hit with him, didn't she? And I'll make a bit on the side assisting the Saracen in private. It all helps. I expect he's pretty generous.'

'So you've really made up your mind over the job? You realize plastic surgery is not thought even respectable in the right circles?'

Graham blew a chain of smoke-rings. 'Neither was chloroform.'

'You know that isn't the answer, Graham.' Robin shook his head sadly. 'You seem to forget our family has a certain position to uphold in the profession.'

'Yes, our grandfather was a quack bone-setter and our great-grandfather was a piss-prophet,' said Graham, getting up and going to bed.

39

7

SHE WAS THE most beautiful, or anyway the smartest, woman to come within range of Graham's handshake. Her hair was as fashionably short as her jade-green dress. Her hands rested on a matching silk parasol. A fox fur hung over her shoulder. She got more effect than displaying a load of jewellery by wearing one enormous pearl on a golden chain. He fancied she was older than himself, but such elegance baffled his calculations. As she turned to smile he saw on her right cheek a hairy mole an inch across, as ugly as a stain on a bridal gown.

'I'd like have you meet Dr Trevose, one of my staff,' the Saracen introduced Graham grandly from behind his desk. 'Dr Trevose will be assisting me with your operation.'

This was news to Graham, who had been planning to leave early that hot Saturday afternoon.

'Miss Cazalay is giving us the privilege of creating perfection where there is yet only beauty.' The Saracen flourished his cigar. He had abandoned his uniform, but not his smoking habits. 'As I shall be performing the procedure under local, I should like you to administer a sedative.'

'Oh, no!' objected Miss Cazalay at once. 'I utterly refuse to be doped.'

The surgeon looked doubtful. 'We've got some pretty frightening-looking toys up there.'

'Now you're trying to make my flesh creep.'

That's the voice of a woman who knows what she wants, thought Graham.

'You're just as bad as all the other doctors,' Miss Cazalay smiled. 'They say you're harbouring the most *awful* things, just to make you more grateful when they find they've made a mistake and you aren't. I want to keep my mind *perfectly* clear. I'm not going to miss the chance of telling absolutely everybody about my operation. Particularly in the hands of the famous Dr Sarasen.'

Possibly mollified by the praise, the surgeon surrendered.

The events of the hot, arid and consequential summer of 1919 included the peace treaty signed at Versailles and the German fleet scuttled at Scapa Flow, but not so far the marriage of Edith to Graham, who was beginning to feel the snowflakes would be descending on his shoulders before the confetti. For the Saracen's dreams had been roughly ended, and Graham's prospects had faded with the rest of the highly insubstantial pageant.

At first Graham had revelled in assisting at operations performed in flesh and blood rather than confined to his pencil and paper. He even struck a workable relationship with Haileybury for the good of the patients, though careful to disagree with him about everything from the quality of the postwar surgical catgut to the wave of postwar strikes, Ireland, the gold standard, and the collapse of morals generally. It all induced in him mildly socialistic views, which Edith's father on their single meeting over Sunday lunch in Ramsgate found so distressing.

Professionally, the two young surgeons' ideas drew further apart daily. Haileybury was the son of an engineer officer in the Indian Army, who on retirement had dabbled in jute and found to his alarm this unexciting commodity caused his swift impoverishment. Afterwards he sang praises of the simple, trustworthy Service virtues in the ears of his son, who struggled on short commons to finish his education and was rewarded almost at once with a chance to cut the figure he envied—a uniformed surgeon. When the casualties of war were regrettably supplanted by the more trivial ones of peace, Haileybury still brought to his work the mind of the military doctor. Graham thought he brought also the mind of the sempstress and municipal architect—though admitting this a valuable corrective to

41

the Michelangelo approach of the Saracen, to which he inclined himself. To Graham, plastic surgery was artistry in flesh,
creation in the most exciting of all media. To Haileybury, it was
the prosaic repair of injury and deformity. The acorn of discon-
tent sown between them in the sanatorium ward so flourished
in this disputed ground, its sturdy branches overshadowed the
pair of them all their lives.

Though for now, Haileybury simply dismissed Graham as too
clever by half.

'Why don't you sew the two free edges of the pedicle
together?' Graham asked him one afternoon in the operating
theatre.

The pedicle was a thick two-inch-wide six-inch-long strip of
skin raised from the patient's shoulder, to which one end was
still anchored. The free end plugged a crater in the man's
cheek, a Canadian officer whose misfortunes had begun two
years before at Vimy and, bedevilled by sepsis, were at last
coming to an end.

'Join these?' Haileybury ran his needle-holder up and down
the raw edges. 'Why?'

'Because it would help preserve the blood-supply of the
pedicle, cut down the risk of sepsis, and what's as important be
less painful for the patient.'

Haileybury considered this for some moments. 'No,' he
decided. 'You'd end up with a sort of septic sausage. The whole
pedicle would slough away in a week.'

'But can't you see how the two edges are curling together, like
a scroll of parchment?' Graham insisted. 'Why, they're simply
asking to be joined up.'

'Put the dressings on please, Trevose,' said Haileybury,
closing both the operation and the discussion.

'Won't you let me put three or four stitches in?' Graham
pleaded. 'We can take them out if there's any sign of infection.
Just as a favour.'

'I remember the last time you asked me a favour.' Haileybury
stripped off his gloves. 'You wanted a bedpan.'

By June 1919 Graham could sew up the pedicles as much as

42

he liked. Some movement in the mystic machinery of the War Office demobilized Haileybury, as much to his own surprise as the Saracen's. With Haileybury out of the way the Saracen let Graham work alone at operations which, though comparatively minor, were intensely flattering to his junior status. He realized excitedly that he had a flair for the handicraft of surgery, the cutting, stitching, snipping, and remodelling. This gave him a satisfaction which for long periods of the day put all else from his mind, including Edith. Now he stood on his own feet any doubts about his marching to the head of the specialty were dispelled. He had self-confidence, as essential in a young surgeon as in a young politician or young pugilist. But Graham's thanks for relief from his vinegary overseer were brief. A month later the Saracen announced with extravagant regret that he must go himself.

The Saracen had underestimated the toughness of the charming London consultants, lurking to slip their own cases into his profitable beds at Princess Alexandra's. Like many other gay upstarts tolerated during the war, he found himself shunned in the more formal society of peacetime. Though nobody could send him home because nobody had dispatched him, and he showed no inclination to repatriate himself (it was said through the imminence of prohibition), his cases simply trickled away until the once lusty unit became too enfeebled to support even a single assistant. His right to practise at all on New York qualifications was publicly doubted, facing Graham with perilous questions of assisting an unlicensed practitioner, which the young man recognized as a professional crime as grave as committing adultery with your patients, if less enjoyable. The Saracen was sad. He had expected a gift of ready-made British qualifications in gratitude for his work during the war, but the serious-minded surgeons who decided such things read rather too much in their newspapers about his fondness for large motor-cars, race-horses, champagne parties, and any attractive woman he could lay hands on.

Graham's next discomfiture was an admission that his brother was right. His impulsive foray into plastic surgery had not only

43

ended in defeat, but a testimonial from the Saracen was an invalid passport to the most respected hospitals. He felt he should have some sort of employment before marriage, even though he had arranged to live with Edith on the top floor at Hampstead, over the professor's bedroom. The ceremony must perforce be delayed. Meanwhile, his bride-to-be came every Saturday afternoon and typed about synovial membranes.

8

'I FORGOT TO ask how your try at that throat job in Islington went,' the Saracen said to Graham as they creaked and wobbled towards the top floor in the lift, having left Miss Cazalay to prepare for her unsedated ordeal in charge of the Princess Alexandra's matron.

'It didn't go at all.'

'That's tough. A throat job would be useful. It's next-of-kin to plastics, and maybe you could have tried your hand reshaping a few noses on the quiet. But don't lose faith in yourself, son.' The Saracen opened the lift gate. 'You've got the mind and the hand for this sort of surgery. Your idea of stitching up the pedicles—it's a great advance.' Chuckling at his own wiliness, he went on, 'You've got quite an attraction for the ladies, too. It all helps in our line. I've noticed it with the nurses, the stenographers, the other girls around.'

Graham looked surprised. 'I've never flattered myself at cutting a particularly romantic figure,' he objected modestly.

'Looks don't count all that much.' The Saracen was sensitive over his own waistline. 'Maybe it's because you keep them amused. There's not much amusing in a woman's life. It's all menstruation, constipation and backache.'

'But Doc!' Graham grinned. 'You seem to forget I'm shortly to be a married man.'

'Maybe I did. Your little girl must be getting mighty impatient.' The surgeon threw his cigar into a fire-bucket outside the anaesthetic room, in respect less for professional convention than the explodability of ether vapour. As they brushed past the new Boyle's anaesthetic apparatus like a display of water-filled jampots, he added over his shoulder, 'I guess our patient won't faint. Miss Cazalay's a tough baby.'

'She's an actress?' If Graham had never heard of her, actresses the Saracen associated with had never been heard of by anybody.

'Christ, no! You know Lord Cazalay?'

Graham raised his eyebrows. Everyone had heard of Lord Cazalay during the war. He was always cajoling or coercing the population from posters, newspapers, or flag-hung platforms, honoured by the Germans with the threat of postwar hanging. Graham felt the quantity of the Saracen's practice might be dropping, but the quality seemed to be keeping up.

'She wanted the operation back in her place, but I wouldn't have it. Risk of sepsis, any number of things. It'll be a simple job. I took the same sort of thing off the tit of a girl last week. It seemed her boy-friend kept confusing it with her nipple.' The Saracen laughed. His patient had put him in a splendid temper. 'Don't use the brush on your skin, son,' he warned as they started scrubbing up. 'It'll give you a dermatitis and maybe in thirty years a cancer.'

The operating theatre was a small, plain room with a long window down one side admitting the afternoon sunshine. It was sketchily furnished with a spindly-legged operating table under a wide-shaded electric lamp, a couple of enamelled slop-buckets on the lino floor, and a tier of hand-bowls opening like a teatime cakestand. Along one wall a white-painted Welsh dresser bore flat dishes of suturing materials submerged in carbolic, shiny metal drums of sterilized dressings, flasks of brightly-coloured antiseptics, and bundles of swabs in jars like those in sweetshops. Graham looked round as the patient appeared, lying on a trolley. Without her hat she looked older—thirty at least, he thought. Her dress was stripped to her waist, and she was wearing what they called a brassière.

'This *is* very elaborate,' complained Miss Cazalay. 'For a minor operation.'

46

'My dear, no operations are minor.' The Saracen deftly covered her shoulders, neck, and eyes with white sterile towels. Taking a syringe of local anaesthetic from Graham and announcing cheerfully, 'Just a little flea-bite!' he ran the needle through her skin.

'Ouch!' she complained through the towels. 'That hurt.'

'Sorry, my dear.'

'Now remember—you're to tell me absolutely *everything* that's going on.'

'Sure, my dear, sure.'

Miss Cazalay found doctors trying. She had been brought up to assume as much without vanity as without question that no-one could occupy a better position on the stage of life than herself. Her acquaintances were no bother because they recognized it too, but parsons and doctors demanded a tiresome readjustment of the personality. Even parsons weren't too wearisome, any she met being accustomed to treat such personages as herself and the Almighty with equally well-bred respect, but she felt you *surrendered* so to doctors. Your frame might be your housemaid's, if rather cleaner. In their power you became a nobody. And Miss Cazalay could never allow herself to be a nobody. She therefore made up her mind to impress her personality on her operation.

But operations like battles unhappily do not always run as smoothly as in the minds of their planners. For a start, there was too much bleeding. The Saracen decided crossly that the adrenalin mixed with his local anaesthetic to constrict the cut blood-vessels had deteriorated in the sunlight. Trickles began to evade Graham's swab and run across Miss Cazalay's shapely but unanaesthetized chin. Her demands for a running commentary became steadily less enthusiastic. The Saracen impatiently pulled the half-detached mole with his forceps, and she cried out.

'Not long now, my dear,' he muttered. 'Not long.'

No reply.

At last the mole was detached. The Saracen picked it with forceps from its bloody bed and dropped it into a waiting

47

kidney-dish on the operating table. Unfortunately he had over-looked the towels being pulled awry in the struggle, and the scrap of pigmented oozing flesh lay squarely in its owner's view. Miss Cazalay screamed.

'Get some water!' he commanded, slapping a swab on the open wound.

Graham hastily found a feeding-cup like a small teapot. He dashed in some water and held it between Miss Cazalay's lips. She remembered somehow to say, 'Thanks most awfully.' She had been extremely well brought up.

The Saracen then ordered Graham to hold her hand for the rest of the operation.

It occurred to the surgeon after such a performance he really should escort the patient home in her car, particularly as the sight of his bill would be as severe a shock as the sight of her mole. But in half an hour he had an appointment with a man he was hoping would lend him money. For a moment he struggled between duty and solvency. Then he told Graham to accompany her instead.

With a rug round her knees in the back of the Daimler Miss Cazalay apologized torrentially for her stupid behaviour. Graham made most sympathetic remarks. The woman was clearly as sensitive to the terrors of surgery as to the blemish it had removed.

'I don't know why I bothered to have it done,' she told him distractedly. 'Except that Dr Sarasen kept persuading me. And he *is* terribly persuasive, isn't he? I was really awfully fond of that little mole thing. I shall feel quite lost without it. Anyway, it was awfully sweet of you to hold my hand, Dr Trevose. I do hope it wasn't a bore, when you'd so much rather be cutting me up. And now I shan't be fit to be seen for a month. Thank heavens it's the end of the season! I shall be able to vegetate in total solitude. For weeks I've been working like an absolute slave.'

The idea of Miss Cazalay slaving so startled Graham he exclaimed, 'What sort of work?'

'Oh, all sorts. The Red Cross, the Cazalay Mission in Canning

Town, the Belgian Children's Charity, the Sunshine Fund, the Free Medicine Club . . . I never have a moment.'

'Oh, I see. Well, I suppose it's best not letting yourself be bored.'

'Bored?' She looked irritated. 'I could never possibly get bored.' He might have suggested it were some disgraceful illness. 'Here we are,' she said abruptly.

They had arrived at a house in Half Moon Street, off Piccadilly. It was not a part of London Graham frequented, or even knew. As the chauffeur opened the door and he helped Miss Cazalay from the car he noticed with alarm that she was pale and starting to tremble.

'Are you sure you're all right?' he asked anxiously. 'It might be a delayed reaction from the local.'

'Of course I'm all right!'

The front door was opened by a tall figure in dress clothes. The hall was high and dark and seemed full of marble and paintings. As Graham helped Miss Cazalay inside she said, 'Now I'm being silly again,' and he caught her as her knees gave way.

The figure in dress clothes, whom Graham took to be a butler or footman, stared at them in horror. Lord Cazalay's only daughter was a person of such assertive importance in the household, round whom his own life distantly spun its humble daily revolutions, to see her suddenly insensible was as though the sun had gone out.

'Shall I get a doctor, sir?' he gasped.

'I am a doctor,' Graham told him briefly. 'Fetch some brandy.' The butler still stared. 'Hurry up! Can't you see it's urgent?'

Graham sat Miss Cazalay on a chair and pushed her head between her knees. Her hat fell off. He wondered whether to lay her on the floor and rip open her dress to free her breathing, but perhaps the intense decorum of the surroundings inhibited him. He looked round hopefully for some relative or other female help. Two girls in maids' uniforms were leaning over the banisters, more alarmed than the butler. It was unbelievable to find Miss Cazalay in such an undignified posture. Fainting in front of the servants was really not done at all. As his patient showed no signs of recovery, Graham panicked for a second that she were dead. He felt her pulse, beating away threadily. The butler reappeared with a decanter and glass on a silver tray, his hands shaking. He had been so paralysed by the irregularity he automatically served the stimulant as if ordered from the dining-room after luncheon.

With the brandy Miss Cazalay gave a gasp.

'Where's the lady's bedroom?' Graham demanded.

The butler hesitated. Even in such a crisis he doubted the propriety of directing a strange and rather unkempt young man to the shrine. Graham picked her up. 'Come on! She's got to lie down somewhere.'

The butler led the way upstairs. Graham was not strong and Miss Cazalay was rather heavy. He smiled as he suddenly pictured the pair of them tumbling down the dignified staircase and ending as not one but a couple of insensible patients in the hall. Miss Cazalay's room seemed all mirrors and orange silk hangings. He laid her on the bed and covered her with the eiderdown. One of the maids, who had recovered from the shock sufficiently to think action expected of her, appeared helpfully at his elbow with a large bottle.

'What's that?' Graham demanded.

'Jeyes' fluid, sir.'

'Good God!' he muttered. 'It's a disinfectant for drains.'

Miss Cazalay opened her eyes. 'I've got an awful headache.'

'Haven't you any aspirin?' he asked the maid irritably.

'There's some in my dressing-table,' murmured Miss Cazalay, colour hesitatingly taking repossession of her cheeks. 'What a performance! I *am* stupid,' she apologized again as the maid returned with tablets and water. Miss Cazalay had been brought up to see all illness as a form of weakness. 'How did I get up from the hall?'

'I carried you.'

She managed to smile. 'How romantic.'

The door burst open, and a woman in street clothes threw

herself upon Miss Cazalay in a torrent of Italian. Lady Cazalay came from a noble family in Venice, and when overcome by her emotions found only her own language adequate to express them. Her only recognition of Graham's presence was repeating loudly to him that Dr Whitehead be summoned at once.

'But, madam! Miss Cazalay will be right as rain if she lies down for a while.'

'No, no! We must have Dr Whitehead. He always attends my daughter. Since she was a little girl.'

Graham thought this doubtful, Dr Whitehead not being a practitioner of advanced years. But he dutifully sought the butler to summon the royal physician. After all, they could call who they liked, as long as they could afford to pay. He watched the butler reluctantly make for the telephone room off the hall, to pick the instrument from the Louis XIV table on which it was displayed with the pride of all the Cazalays' privileged possessions. The poor fellow felt after the upheaval of the afternoon this was the final blow. He was never comfortable with the telephone, someone having told him it could attract dangerous atmospheric electricity from miles around.

It seemed Graham had no more to do. The patient was recovering, and Dr Whitehead might be displeased to find him on the scene in his shabby suit. He opened the door and quietly let himself out. He walked along Piccadilly in the sunshine, to the corner of Bond Street opposite the Ritz Hotel, and sat reliving his experiences on the foremost seat on the top deck of an open Hampstead bus.

9

GRAHAM REACHED HOME to be greeted in the hall by a pair of black metal trunks, securely roped, sealed in lead, and stencilled neatly in white, DR ROBIN TREVOSE NOT WANTED ON VOYAGE. Having a natural fussiness which he mistook for conscientiousness, Robin had started packing weeks ago. His books were carefully crated, his tent, mosquito-net, hip-bath and hot-water bottle (it was liable to become quite chilly at night, he told Graham severely) all boxed and garlanded with pretty steamship labels. A passage being difficult to extract from the tangle of postwar shipping, he had spent the entire summer amassing a mountain of kit and presumably an equally large knowledge of tropical medicine. But at last he was due to sail, by White Funnel to Singapore in a fortnight. He seemed to his family to have been on the point of leaving home all his life.

Graham heard the rattle of a typewriter from his father's study.

He had found London a cruel place for lovers. He had taken Edith hopefully into the country now and then, but her terror of discovery by passers-by proved so totally inhibiting he even sighed for the quarantined seclusion of the sanatorium summer-house. Now he recalled that his father was delivering some ceremonial lecture at Blackfriars, Robin was buying a compass from a particular shop in Greenwich, the maid was absent through family illness, and the cook as usual was visiting her mother and leaving a cold supper.

It was worth a try.

Edith looked up from rolling a clean sheet of paper into the ungainly machine. 'Oh! It's you, dear.' He seldom got home on a Saturday afternoon. 'I didn't hear the front door. Anything exciting happen at the hospital?'

'Yes, I had to take some woman home after we excised a mole from her face, and she fainted in her own front hall.' He did not elaborate on these facts, Edith sometimes asking unending questions once her interest was aroused. He slipped his hands over her shoulders and felt her breasts under her white blouse. 'How about a bit of fun?' he suggested.

'Fun?' Suddenly understanding he meant the serious sort of fun she looked startled and asked, 'What? Here at home?'

'Why not?' he grinned. He noticed the erectile reflex of her nipples.

Edith's mouth opened. 'Where?'

'In my room.'

She looked even more doubtful. 'Something might happen.'

'But we're absolutely alone.'

'I mean babies and that.'

'What of it?' He laughed. 'We're getting married anyway, so it wouldn't matter.'

'Oh, it would be awful! Everyone would notice. Just think.'

'Nothing happened before, did it? Science is truly wonderful.'

She laid her hands on his. 'When are we going to get married, dearest?'

He had been afraid of this question. 'As soon as I get a job. The very next day if you like.'

'You're sure you *want* to, Graham?'

'Of course I am!' He sounded deeply offended. 'Why on earth should you ask?'

'Oh, I don't know. You've been a bit down in the mouth recently.'

'Things haven't been particularly cheerful at Princess Alexandra's. The physician St Luke himself would have been a bit down in the mouth. How about coming dancing tonight?'

As he expected, she brightened up at once. Edith loved

dancing. She was particularly good at the bunny-hug. 'Then come and have a bit of fun first,' he persisted.

She giggled. 'Oh, all right, then.'

He took her by the hand upstairs. His own bed looked rather cramping for fun. An idea struck him which could bring a lifetime of amusing memories. 'In here,' he directed.

The professor's room had mauve patterned wallpaper, brown paintwork, and heavy crimson curtains. In the middle his big brass bedstead stood under its purple coverlet as impressively as a catafalque. Underneath, brilliantly tinted and embossed, was a chamber-pot of the highest quality.

'Not on the professor's bed!' Edith gasped. She had a strong sense of propriety.

'Why not? It'll be so much more comfortable.'

'Supposing he comes in?'

'He's addressing a lot more anatomists. About synovial membranes. Though we'd better look sharp.'

She started to giggle again, and began taking off her silk stockings.

The broad soft bed played genial host, though the springs creaked like arthritic ligaments with the unaccustomed exercise and in the middle one of the big brass knobs fell off, bounced like a cricket ball, and rolled noisily across the lino. Edith lay afterwards with a reverent expression she felt fitting to the moment. Graham couldn't help himself thinking it gave her a half-stunned look. He inspected her nose, an inch or two away. It really did turn up too much at the end. If you made an incision through the mucous membrane inside, thus avoiding a scar, then with a pair of curved scissors snipped away the tips of the little alar cartilages—

She leapt up. 'Listen! There's someone downstairs.'

'Probably the boy with the joint for tomorrow.'

'No, no! It's in the house. Honest.'

She looked so frightened Graham said, 'I'll go and see.' They both hastily began pulling on their clothes. In the hall Graham found his brother, looking disagreeable.

'Where have you been?' Robin asked shortly.

54

'Getting some cigarettes.'

'Where's Edith?'

Graham raised his eyebrows. 'I wouldn't know. In the old man's room, I think. Fetching some notes.'

'From his *room*?' Robin frowned. 'Everything's kept in the study.'

'Oh, he probably took them to read in bed.'

'I've never heard of him doing such a thing.'

'What are you so worried about?' Graham demanded crossly. 'Do you suppose my future wife is going through his pockets, or something?'

Robin looked flustered and replied more civilly, 'I just wondered why she wasn't at her work, that's all.'

The brothers stood staring at each other. Graham wondered anxiously if Edith had remembered to screw the knob back.

'Did you get your compass?' he asked.

'Compass?' Robin seemed puzzled. 'Oh, the compass. Not in the end. I decided to try somewhere nearer on Monday.'

Graham glanced at his wristwatch. Somehow he had to shift Robin from the hall. Edith might appear in the most suspicious physical and mental disarray. 'How about a cup of tea?' he suggested. 'As everyone's off we'll have to brew up ourselves.'

'Yes, go ahead.' Robin nodded. 'I'll be in the drawing-room. I've got another bundle of those Customs forms to fill in.'

Graham watched him close the drawing-room door before making through a green-baize one leading to the kitchen. He suddenly noticed how hot and stuffy it was inside the house. No wonder they had been sweating so much, their bodies slapping together like a pair of fresh Dover soles. He hoped it hadn't shown. Robin's eye was trained for physical abnormalities like his own. Feeling for a match, he put the black iron kettle on the gas and started to whistle 'Alexander's Ragtime Band'.

Robin waited. He was close against the drawing-room door, peering through the crack. Edith appeared on the stairs. No notes, no other documents. And what of Graham's cigarettes? He certainly wasn't smoking, and a man doesn't traipse up to his bedroom for a packet unless in pressing need of a gasper.

55

But before he could say anything Edith smiled and remarked blandly, 'Hello, Robin! Well, *I*'ve got work to do, if no one else has,' and made serenely for the study.

'What were you doing upstairs with Graham?' he asked angrily, following her.

She placed her hands on the typewriter keyboard. 'Nothing.'

'You swear it?'

'Go on with you! Don't be daft.'

Robin fell on his knees, grasping both her legs, and in his enthusiasm those of the chair. 'My darling, my darling! You won't go back on me?'

'Of *course* I won't.'

He looked up anxiously. 'You haven't said anything to him?' She shook her head. 'My angel, I could stoop and kiss your little feet,' he continued, though contenting himself by lifting her skirt and caressing her knees with his nose.

'You'd better go, my sweet.' She smiled. Robin was such a hot-headed, vigorous man. Like a bull. Very exciting, really. She softly stroked his head and he groaned loudly. 'He might come in, mightn't he?'

'He's got to know some time.'

'But not just now, dear. Not just now.'

Robin got to his feet. 'It's not easy for me—having to face him morning to night.'

'Yes, we're ever so naughty, really,' said Edith. 'Aren't we?'

As the door shut, she turned back to her work. Graham had interrupted her while transcribing, 'In the knee-joint the *meniscus medialis* and the *meniscus lateralis* are devoid of synovial membrane: now it becomes necessary to turn our attention to the interesting fact that the surfaces of these cartilages are fully and normally clothed with synovial membrane—' She looked for her place and added, 'in the foetus'.

She often wondered what that funny-looking word meant.

10

A LETTER, DELIVERED by hand, was waiting for Graham at Princess Alexandra's the following Monday morning. It depicted a Miss Cazalay as apologetic over her failure to have him shown out properly as over her unforgivable lapse of fainting at all. Then she explained that a branch of the Red Cross (Graham never discovered what it was or did) met at her house once a month for a talk by some medical man. Unfortunately, the Dutch doctor with the completely impossible name, invited the next Saturday to unravel the mysteries of psychology, had been obliged to excuse himself through illness (she fancied the poor man had been forced to enter some sort of mental home, she added with a gay little exclamation mark). Could Dr Trevose step into the breach? The audience would be small but appreciative. Tea would be served. She so hoped he found the date convenient.

Graham did.

To demur that he was hardly an authority on plastic surgery after a few months' practice, most of them under Haileybury's irritatingly close supervision, never occurred to him. If he were given the stage he was confident of providing the show. It was again his natural exhibitionism. Later he lectured in countries still unborn, to peoples then dismissable as savages, about surgery at the time undreamable, but none had the importance of his little talk before tea in Miss Cazalay's upstairs drawing-room.

As armour against the treacherous shafts of stage-fright he

simply reduced his hearers to a collection of hats—the lampshade, all fringes, shimmering in front of his nose, the shoe-bag drooping to his right, an affair like the frill on a mutton-chop very upright to the left, something right out of *Alice in Wonderland* nodding at the back, probably asleep. The group were all women, middle-aged to elderly, he supposed rich, mostly titled, and dreadfully arrogant. The flattery of the crush in the drawing-room was unmarred by his ignorance that Miss Cazalay had drummed up the audience by telephone, through feelings of obligation, even of guilt, towards her involuntary physician.

Graham spoke without notes, rustling the ladies with a little laughter, shaking them with a mild shudder, explaining with great gentility the principle of moving skin and bone from one part of the body to another. His feeling for an audience was as natural as Gerald du Maurier's. They found themselves quite taking to this pale, slight, soft-spoken young doctor with such magical powers at his finger-tips. Particularly as Graham had gone to the trouble of sprucing himself up, even stealing some of the fragrant lotion which Robin bought (as he carefully explained) to nourish the roots of his hair. He ended by passing round a few of the most undisturbing photographs he could find in the Saracen's office, which were eyed by about half the audience, shivering dutifully. He invited questions.

Could you move skin from one person to another? asked a hat. He regretted not, though it might be possible with identical twins. Another enquired in more theoretical tones if the shape of one's nose could *really* be changed by an operation. Certainly! You had the choice of Greek, Roman, retroussé ... More theoretically still, what exactly was this 'face-lifting' one heard so much about? Quite simple! An incision was made at the temple, buried behind the hairline, the skin was drawn upwards and the excess snipped off. It was 'putting a tuck in' the face, if they cared to see it that way. He fancied they stole looks at one another. Quite a few quids' worth of work for the Saracen in the room, he told himself cheerfully. The lecture was ended only by the butler whom Graham had psychologically dismembered in the hall appearing to serve tea. There were cucumber sandwiches, for which he shared the passion of Wilde's Algernon Moncrieff.

'You were awfully good,' smiled Miss Cazalay, a square of plaster on her cheek. She was relieved that the risk of inviting him instead of the Saracen had been justified. He thanked her, reaching for a second sandwich. 'Have you always been a face doctor?'

'I haven't been a doctor of any sort very long. For most of my first year I was in a sanatorium—as a patient.'

'*Were* you? How awful!' Contracting tuberculosis was perhaps the most shameful weakness of all. 'Then what made you *become* a face doctor?'

He took another sandwich. 'More or less accident. I suppose it's the same with everything of fundamental importance in life.'

She pouted. 'What a pity. I thought you might be some Pygmalion hankering to create your Galatea.' This was lost on Graham, who had a strictly scientific upbringing, but it sounded pleasant. 'Well, there's time yet, Dr Trevose. Perhaps half London will be at your door one day.'

'That depends on whether I get another job or not, I'm afraid.'

She looked amazed. 'Do doctors have *jobs*? How peculiar! Fancy thinking of Dr Whitehead having a job.'

This reflection was inspired by Dr Whitehead himself, who had promised to look in. He was a skilful looker-in at fashionable gatherings, finding it a convenient way of impressing himself on prospective patients without overstraining the liver or stomach. A tall, spare, pink-and-white man, he wore the frock-coat many of his colleagues in the Harley Street area had abandoned during the war (as many of them had abandoned their practices as well for the Forces, he had started doing handsomely). He was a specialist who specialized in nothing, much sought after by people making money enough to afford distrusting the homely ministrations of their family practitioners. He had a delicacy of manner in not only the drawing-room but in the most unpromising clinical circumstances, which had endeared him to

59

greater personages even than Miss Cazalay. His name always appeared on bulletins hung from the Palace railings, varying its company according to the occasion.

'This is Dr Trevose, and he wants a job,' Miss Cazalay said at once.

Dr Whitehead regarded Graham loftily. 'You're with the Saracen, aren't you?'

In his confusion at finding himself facing the royal physician, Graham had taken another sandwich. He told himself sharply such gross functions as appetite must never be displayed in the salons of Half Moon Street. Reference to the Saracen disarrayed the young man even more, but Dr Whitehead smiled and said, 'We should be grateful for his livening the London scene for us. Is it true he has one Rolls-Royce for himself and another for his instruments?' He could appreciate the noble qualities of the successful as sensitively as his colleagues in the East End appreciated the noble qualities of the poor. 'So you're after a job, eh? I heard the Saracen was having to cut down.' He took a cup from a footman. 'What sort of a job? In plastic surgery I should say they were non-existent.'

'I was hoping for something in E.N.T., sir. At least it would keep me going while working for the Fellowship.'

'There's a throat job coming up at the Sloane, I believe.' He implied a kingly disinterest in minor promotions. 'I'm on there, of course. Grafton wants a junior—you've heard of him doubtless?'

Graham nodded eagerly. The Sloane was a small hospital tucked behind Oxford Street, its consultant appointments bitterly fought over through its liberality with private beds. To land a junior job there would be a most valuable by-product of the afternoon.

'I fancy a word from me would settle the matter.' Dr Whitehead broke a biscuit. 'Though you'd have your visiting to do. At the Sloane we're rather a club, you know. We like applicants to call on the consultants beforehand. With their wives. It's a practice which used to be common in London hospitals before the war. I'm sorry to see it dropping out.'

60

'I haven't a wife,' said Graham hastily.

'Ah, you are at the fortunate age when the chase is more satisfying than the choice.' He smiled. 'Well, take your time. I've seen more promising careers wrecked by the wrong wife than by the wrong diagnosis. I'll mention it to Grafton, if you like.' Abruptly turning his back, he started talking to someone else.

Graham noticed through the window it was going to rain, and he had brought no overcoat.

'*Must* you go?' asked Miss Cazalay, as they descended the marble staircase. 'But perhaps you're right. You'd only be badgered with a lot more silly questions. Did you know I drove an ambulance during the war? Though I probably endangered far more lives than I saved. I'm a terrible driver.' She laughed. 'But it was the only way to go on living in my own home. Biddenden was turned into a convalescent hospital, you know.'

Graham remembered pictures of this Kentish mansion in the *Bystander*. Very grand. Officers only, he supposed. They reached the hall. A door opened and a short, fat, black-jowled man in morning clothes hurried across, followed by a younger one carrying a red dispatch-box. 'Daddy! This is Dr Trevose. You remember—he was talking to my Red Cross people. He's a *plastic* surgeon.'

Lord Cazalay registered a look of intense interest. He extended his hand and shook Graham's earnestly, holding his elbow. 'Very pleased to meet you, Dr Trevose. You people did tremendous work during the war. The country owes you a debt of gratitude.'

'Thank you,' said Graham, remembering to add, 'My lord', just like he'd read in novels.

Lord Cazalay switched off the look, withdrew the hand, and disappeared through the front door. It was his principle that a politician must butter up his public like a shopkeeper his customers, however neatly he manages to short-change them. He was so adept at this little scene, performed without interruption to his buzzing inner thoughts, he could have played it in his

61

sleep—indeed he often did, awaking muttering earnest platitudes to all manner of well-deserving citizens flying away in his dreams.

'But we must see you in Biddenden one week-end this summer,' Miss Cazalay invited vaguely. 'Perhaps when the Whiteheads are there, then my mother can talk about all her complaints at once.' A footman opened the door. 'Are you interested in plants? We're supposed to have one of the most splendid collections of exotic vegetation in the country. In the greenhouses are Chinese rhododendrons, Himalayan bamboos, Singapore forest orchids . . .' She ticked them on her fingers. 'No, I expect you'd be bored with them. I am, terribly. The footman will get you a taxi.'

'It's all right, I'll walk.' Graham had been brought up to number taxicabs among dissipations.

'But it's teeming!'

'I've got to visit a shop—just round the corner.'

'Oh, well, good-bye, Dr Trevose. Thank you *so* much for all your trouble.'

She smiled and held out her hand. By then Graham had touched a good deal of Miss Cazalay. But innocently taking her invitation as a suggestion she thirsted after his company, it gave him an excitement almost impossible to keep unnoticed. The door shut. He walked down Half Moon Street in the rain.

As he reached the corner of Bond Street the downpour started to take itself seriously. The buses were full, the top-deck passengers huddling miserably with their laps under the tarpaulins. He started making for Dover Street Tube station, but impulsively decided to walk home. Walking, a man was self-contained and alone, and he had something to think about.

11

EDITH.

My God, Edith! He didn't want to marry her at all.

It had been worrying him all summer.

He had just enjoyed a day excursion into a delightful world which contained marble staircases, plentiful servants, glass-houses full of idiotic plants, 'work' that disguised bone idleness, ornamental hats, beautifully cut cucumber sandwiches, and Dr Whitehead. Why shouldn't he, Dr Trevose, take up permanent residence in it? Miss Cazalay's drawing-room fired him with more ambition than the Saracen's operating theatre. He had brains. As good as Dr Whitehead's, at any rate. He had energy—he'd work twenty hours a day. But of course pure intelligence wasn't enough, no more than pure gallantry in war.

For success in modern medicine you needed social position, money, connection, airs and graces. Dr Whitehead, Graham seemed to remember, married the daughter of a duchess. He wondered gloomily what she would make of Edith. Or for that matter, what would the wife of any ill-qualified g.p. struggling with a large panel and a larger mortgage? She'd turn up her nose and probably make it twice as plain. His family were right. Graham Trevose, the great plastic surgeon, couldn't start married to a girl from a butcher's shop. He had not only magical skill but charm with the ladies—the Saracen had told him as much, and he was a sound judge of both. His depression was fleetingly lightened by recalling his taming the roomful of overbearing rich harridans. But charm, like artillery, was useless, wasteful, and downright dangerous if directed on the wrong target.

Besides, he didn't love Edith.

Or did he? He wished the condition had clearly recognizable signs and symptoms, like typhoid fever. His life with Edith was happy enough, but surely the great passion was different, running like a fever in your blood? It looked like it in the moving pictures, anyway. Would he *ever* really know if he loved her? Would he ever really know if he loved anyone? It was a wretched disability. Or perhaps he was incapable of love? He began to feel even more sorry for himself.

But he was engaged. It was a solemn bond, he had given his word, only a scoundrel would break it. He must go ahead like a gentleman. Besides, he totally lacked the cruelty to make the final break with her. Well, the courage, anyway. He supposed everything came down to that lack of character so lamented by the Scots medical superintendent. He reached Oxford Street, and it started to thunder. He turned up his jacket collar, aware of becoming remarkably wet.

The storm had stopped when he reached Hampstead, but the afternoon was still dark and the gas in the house ablaze. It was a Saturday, and Edith would be still there, tapping out wisdom on the synovial membranes. He couldn't face her. He would plead a chill, go to his room, and smoke cigarettes. He opened the front door, and found Robin standing in the hall amid his luggage.

'Graham—'

'Oh, hello.' He stripped off his jacket. 'I'm damned soaked. Couldn't get a bus.'

'Graham, I've got to talk to you.'

'What, here and now? Can't you see I'm drenched to the bone? Do you want me to get pneumonia?'

Robin jerked his head. 'There's a fire lit in the study.'

His expression was so funereally grave Graham followed him. He wondered with alarm what was up. Their father? Perhaps he had met the same anatomical accident as his predecessor. He was surprised to find Edith away from the typewriter, sitting beside the grate with her hands crossed in her lap. As he ripped off his wet tie, Robin announced, 'Edith and I are going to be married.'

Graham paused in the motion of undoing his front stud. 'You're *what*?'

'Going to be married. Edith and I. Next Friday.'

Graham's first thought was that Robin would no longer need to take his hot-water bottle.

'Yes, I should have told you everything before.' Robin stuck his hands into the pockets of his clerical-grey suit and started pacing the carpet with much agitation. 'I admit freely I've been deceiving you the past few weeks. Deceiving you—my own brother! It's a terrible thing. But I did it only for your peace of mind. Honestly, Graham. For the peace of mind of all of us. It would have been impossible, wouldn't it, for you and I to have shared the same roof?'

Graham said nothing. He's quite frightened of me, he thought. A refreshing change.

'I suppose I could have gone somewhere else,' Robin admitted with a shrug. 'But it would have been terribly awkward with all my preparations for the journey. Now that I'm off next week—we're off next week,' he corrected himself, 'it can wait no longer.'

Graham decided to play his part in the scene. 'You bloody hypocrite,' he said impressively.

'Yes, revile me. Revile me as much as you like. I deserve it.' Robin stood looking his brother nervously in the face, his ruddy cheeks starting to tremble. 'But you'll understand, Graham— you *must* understand—out East a man needs a companion. Particularly for the sort of task I've undertaken. It's absolutely essential. I need a companion to look after the women and children. A companion to look after *me*. I'd go mad, otherwise. There're no other women out there, you know. Only natives. Yes, I'd go mad. Quite mad. And Edith's so suitable. She knows a lot about medicine. Working in that plastic surgery place prepared her for the horrors—'

65

'You and your claptrap about faith and the beautiful life hereafter! Setting yourself up as the personal friend of God—'

'I'm still a sincere Christian, Graham,' Robin protested lamely. 'This has made no difference.'

'I don't know how you've the face to appear as a medical missionary. You've just driven a coach and pair through the Ten Commandments.' Graham was uncertain which ones applied, but felt it a telling phrase. 'You're disgustingly selfish. You're dragging Edith away just to suit your own damn convenience.'

'No, no, that's wrong! I love her.' Robin was too self-centred to allow Graham's possibly sharing this attitude. 'Unless I loved Edith with all my heart and soul how do you imagine I could endure this present agony—'

To Graham's alarm, his brother fell on his knees at his feet. 'We must pray, pray,' he started muttering. 'O God forgive thy humble and weak servant, O God forgive me! I am wretched, weak, I cannot support the turbulent passions in a man—'

'This is really getting us nowhere,' said Graham.

'Graham, you must forgive me. Please forgive me, Graham. I beg you! Scourge me, flay me, but in the end forgive me.'

Robin broke into sobs.

It occurred to Graham this was exactly the situation he had longed for all his life. Here was Robin the paragon, Robin the handsome, Robin the righteous, Robin with the chest impenetrable to tubercle bacilli, Robin who always got down first to breakfast, grovelling round the dripping ends of his trousers. He was wondering how to make the most of it when the door opened. The professor was bad-temperedly complaining about the commotion.

'What's this? What's going on? Robin, what's the matter? Has there been an accident?'

Graham slung his wet jacket over his shoulder. 'Robin's going to marry Edith instead of me.' He looked at his wife-to-be of that morning. She was sitting by the fire with exactly the same placid expression. He thought he should say something to her, but no remark particularly fitting or self-flattering coming

66

to mind he decided to leave the room in dignified silence instead.

The professor twitched his moustache nervously. The scene was so beyond the experience of an academic gentleman he simply withdrew, in great haste. He sat in the cold and dark breakfast-room rocking backwards and forwards on the edge of an overstuffed chair muttering, 'My God, what has come upon us now?' It was an emotional tangle far too complex for a mind attuned to the solid mysteries of anatomical thought. Even an attempt to unravel the mess would be an impossible distraction from professorial life. Had his ears heard aright? Surely not! Was *Robin* to marry Edith? To carry her off to the Straits Settlements? He leapt up with an angry cry. The synovial membranes! Now they would *never* be finished.

In the study, Robin groped his way to Edith, laying his head on her lap and muttering, 'O God, what have I done? What have I done? Edith, my darling, you must punish me. You must *punish* me, severely, severely . . .'

His voice soaked away, into the shifting dark sands of his psychology. Edith thought he became rather fanciful sometimes. She put her hand gently on his. She had been afraid of rather a scene, but everything had really gone quite well. 'Don't worry, my love. We'll soon be far away over the sea.' A thought struck her. 'Oh!' she exclaimed. 'Did you remember to tell the shipping line about the double cabin?'

Her severely practical mind would be a great help to them out East.

Upstairs, Graham threw himself on his bed and laughed. He laughed so much he began to choke. He had to jump up and vomit into the slop-bucket under his washstand, where he had rinsed the streaks of blood from his mouth after his haemoptysis eighteen months before. Floating round in the brownish froth he could see dozens of little pieces of cucumber.

12

FOR THE NEWLY-ENGAGED couple's last week in Hampstead Graham maintained an attitude of dignified sulkiness. As Robin took care never to leave him alone with Edith, their only exchange was by chance on the stairs.

'I hope you will be very happy with my brother,' he said.

'That's ever so nice of you, Graham.' She sounded as though they had just been formally introduced rather than ripped asunder. Going down a step she turned and added, 'You didn't want to marry me, not really, did you?'

Graham affected a look of such pained surprise she remounted the stair, bringing herself close to him. 'No, you didn't. You're going up in the world, aren't you?'

'What's that got to do with it?'

'You've got the power to make something of yourself.' She tapped her forehead. 'Up there. You'd resent me. I'd be just a milestone round your neck,' she told him charmingly. 'You're going to be famous some day. Like Dr Sarasen. You're not afraid to strike out, you see.' She glanced round the dark, ill-decorated, untidily masculine hall. 'You want something better in life than this. Don't you?'

Graham smiled. 'That all sounds very clever, Edith.'

'I'm not clever. Not a bit. Only about the way I get people to think of me. And then not all the time. Anyway, Graham—good luck.'

Her smile flooded him with regret that his mind had been made up for him. 'Come on!' he exclaimed. 'Let's just run off together, the pair of us. To Gretna Green. We don't need any luggage, only a wedding-ring.'

She laughed and waved her finger. 'Don't be daft,' she said.

She ran downstairs, still laughing, her dress flying up and showing her calves.

Robin quickly lost his remorse in a cloud of fussiness over steamship tickets, special marriage licences, medical supplies, flowers, letters of introduction, Keating's anti-bug powder, hymn books, and contraceptives. He even expressed surprise at Graham's refusal to attend the wedding, which was performed quietly in the missionaries' chapel at Woolwich by one of his brethren. There was a reception afterwards with a large cake and a little champagne. Robin made a speech which would not have disgraced a groom taking a more straightforward path to the altar. The barrister's clerk from Hither Green made a speech which would not have disgraced Marshall Hall. The butcher and his wife looked stunned, but they supposed if their daughter found one doctor as good as another they were hardly in a position to challenge her experience. Aunt Doris provided the tears, and the Professor provided a smallish cheque. The couple spent the night at the Euston Station Hotel, early the next morning leaving for Liverpool and a high-minded if impecunious future.

Edith felt the greatest adventure of her life had begun. It was even more exciting than working in the Face Hospital. There was no-one on the dockside to bid them good-bye, but they stood and waved wildly from the rails just the same, Robin observing heartily, 'That's the last we'll see of the old country for a bit, my darling,' to which she replied breathlessly, 'Isn't it such *fun!*'

Everything fascinated her—the docks with their gawky cranes, warehouses the size of cathedrals filled with strange-smelling sacks, her new husband flashing their new blue-and-gold passport, the ship's ventilators drooping like unwatered plants, the fascinating gusts from the hatchways of burning oil or roasting pork, Englishmen in gold braid and Chinamen in starched jackets. She even giggled excitedly over the printed instructions

69

for donning lifejackets, with their hint of the stirring perils of the sea, which Robin made her read carefully before leaving harbour. The prospect of sleeping in a bunk tickled her more than of watching some eight thousand miles of blue water pass under their porthole.

They were quickly picked out as newly-weds, though Robin being such a poor sailor was obliged to let several nights pass before putting this circumstance into action. He approached his duties with great enthusiasm, having in the back of his mind notions of embellishing the plain fare of human intercourse with such piquancies as embracing Edith's feet and submitting himself to some indignity, or even violence, in her hands. But she only said, 'Robin, don't be daft,' and he realized such plans had to be left, however regrettably, theoretical. He had suspected that women took a different view of such ideas. He would have liked to discuss the topic with Graham, with his wider experience of the sex, but recognized that might have been somewhat difficult.

The other passengers were civil servants, officers, planters, and businessmen making for the East to restore or start their fortunes after the war. Once the ship passed Suez the sun shone hotter than Edith believed possible, awnings were rigged on the decks, and metal scoops fitted to direct the clammy atmosphere of the Red Sea into the portholes. A change overtook the commonplace middle-class people who had filed aboard in Liverpool. In their white ducks the men strode the decks like lords, talked more loudly, laughed more heartily, and clapped their hands for drinks not only more resoundingly but more often. Their wives showed even better the strange aggrandizement kindled in the British by strong sunlight. Edith was too happy to appreciate at first the little condescensions by which they made plain their relief at being spared the embarrassment of her company after Singapore, and too eager to chatter to notice that the few seeds of conversation she carried in her head were increasingly nipped by social frost.

'That woman at our table—she's a real cat,' she complained to Robin when the ship turned east round the foot of Ceylon.

'When I said I'd never learnt to play bridge, she just sniffed and said, "Mrs Trevose" '—she imitated the astringent voice—' "I'm sure you were much better advised putting your hands to *work*." '

Robin frowned. Though he generally described Edith as a nurse, he knew it was stupid to delude himself that without the eye of love she struck the world as most definitely and distressingly 'common'. 'I don't see anything particularly offensive in that, dear.'

'You should have *heard* her,' Edith told him spiritedly. 'Oh! I'd like to scratch her eyes out.'

Robin sat on the bunk and reached for his Bible. He read a passage every day, and found it a handy way, in the tiny cabin, of quashing conversation. 'We must draw strength from God to overcome such maliciousness, and ask Him to forgive them.'

Edith pouted. She had accepted God as something that came along with Robin, and genuinely did her best to please both. But she didn't want the woman at their table forgiven by anyone.

'I'm afraid there is an awful lot of petty snobbery out East,' Robin went on sorrowfully. 'Or so I hear.'

'Snobbery?' She had been gazing from the porthole and turned with such fury she startled him. 'Then what have we got to worry about? We're the snobs now. Aren't we?' The road to self-betterment, stretching behind her all the way to Ramsgate, had been triumphantly marched. To find the destination much the same as the start was heartbreaking. 'Aren't we?' she repeated.

But Robin was deep in the Scriptures.

Edith quickly forgot her rebuffs in renewed excitement over Singapore. She revelled in such strange sights as girls in cheong-sams split to the thigh (which she thought would be fun to wear), the vertical writing outside the cupboard-like shops, women squatting with babies slung from their backs eating rice with chopsticks in the street, toddy shops, and even death houses, where ailing relatives might be conveniently stacked away in rows of bunks until extracted for a joyous and extremely noisy

Chinese funeral. They stayed a week or so with an old Scottish doctor and his wife, who had lived out East so long as to have Chinese complexions but talked with the undiluted accents of Inverness. Their final journey was to Province Wellesley, the northernmost of the Straits Settlements opposite the island of Penang, a three-day voyage by steamer up the coast broken at Port Swettenham. A motor-lorry brought them and their possessions at last to the mission settlement at Kapala Batas, which consisted of three buildings the size of a village hall, the one with the bell the church, another housing the school, and the most dilapidated the hospital with its dispensary. There were three bungalows, one for the doctor, one for the schoolmaster, and one for the reverend missionary, who they found had taken the chance of moving into his medical brother's larger and more comfortable and temporarily vacated premises.

Even when the novelty of four servants to order about became simply a matter of domestic routine, Edith never felt bored. Her placid nature was as incapable of boredom as of malice. She found something of interest every day, a new plant or a new bird, or the surge of battle in their war against the ants. Besides, isolation saved her from the daggers of social ambushes. Their only companions were the schoolmaster and his wife, a dried-up couple who had come to Province Wellesley before the war, and the missionary, who was old and talkative and inclined to dribble down his beard. These three thought the newcomers agreeable enough, though from experience were reserving judgment for a reasonable spell, say a year or two.

Robin quickly became very bored indeed. He arrived seeing himself as a crusader, simultaneously bringing health and enlightenment to people well advertised as lacking both. He found neither offering particularly welcome. He was regarded with suspicion and fear, not as the adversary of illness and death but their closest associate, into whose view it was unwise to stray. He was so clumsy over the finer adjustments of human relationships he regarded his ungrateful and reluctant patients with short-tempered puzzlement. He stubbornly avoided advice from his missionary colleague, partly through pride and partly through the danger of finding himself deluged with saliva and conversation. Most frustrating of all, instead of presenting him with interesting tropical diseases to be cured by white man's magic, his patients mostly had ordinary European complaints and a shocking number suffered from syphilis. He began to worry if he really wanted to practise such strenuous medicine, though as he had committed Edith and himself for five years, not only morally but on paper, this was a theoretical doubt. They would just have to put up with it.

Meanwhile, the professor in Hampstead was still wondering bad-temperedly why one of the knobs on his bed kept falling off.

13

THE TIDE OF life, once it had borne Robin and Edith away to Asia, turned in Graham's favour.

Dr Whitehead was as good as his word, though more out of respect for Miss Cazalay's guineas than Graham's talents. Graham anxiously called on Mr Grafton at the Sloane Hospital, finding him a large prosperous surgeon so goodhearted he welcomed a nominee to spare him the pain of disappointing unsuccessful applicants.

'You'll find life here quite a holiday after all that pioneering stuff,' he told Graham amiably. Unlike most throat surgeons he was an admirer of plastic work.

'I'd better tell you, sir, I've had no experience of E.N.T. work at all.'

'You'll soon pick it up,' said Mr Grafton. 'Mostly I do tonsils.'

Tonsillectomy was as much a feature of conventional English education as confirmation, both procedures doing the candidates as little observable good. Graham certainly got the hang of Mr Grafton's technique quickly enough. The little patient was dumped on the operating table by a nurse, then John Bickley, the sharp-featured young anaesthetist, muzzled him with a wire-and-lint mask and hurtled him into unconsciousness with a jet of sweet-smelling ethyl chloride from a miniature soda-syphon. At some precise point between wakefulness and death John whipped away his machinery and retired to watch the proceedings, wearing the cheerful Sam Weller expression of a perceptive servant common to all anaesthetists. A twist and snip of Mr Grafton's long tonsil guillotine produced the offending organs, a deft scrape with a curette removed the adenoids as an encore, then Graham held the victim upside down by his heels, to prevent drowning in his own blood while coughing and retching his way back to the world.

After the operating list, when the hot little theatre resembled the Place de Grève at the end of a busy day during the Terror, Graham had to collect the tonsils and adenoids to present in a jar to his chief. He imagined this was for some deep otorhinolaryngological research until he discovered the surgeon put them on his strawberry beds, for which they apparently had no rival as fertilizer in the seedsmen's catalogues. As all the patients were private ones—not losing your tonsils being one of the few contemporary blessings of poverty—as Graham got a guinea or two a case, and as Mr Grafton achieved the turnover of a skilled Chicago slaughterman, he began doing quite well.

During the winter of 1919, when the world abolished war for ever by creating the League of Nations, Mr Grafton promoted Graham his registrar. Then the Saracen suddenly became eager to stuff guineas into his pockets. Leaving Princess Alexandra's after a complicated row (with the Saracen's fading glamour the secretary had demanded his office back for a start) the American had rented with borrowed money a suite of rooms in Wimpole Street, which he fitted out magnificently as an operating unit. Graham hesitated to accept the invitation to assist him. In the eyes of the General Medical Council the Saracen did not exist. But John Bickley, who gave the Saracen's anaesthetics, reassured Graham that legal proceedings were afoot against the G.M.C., in which the Saracen had put his own money and was therefore plainly expecting to win. And reshaping a nose, Graham found, could be worth several jarfuls of tonsils.

Even the professor added to Graham's affluence. Possibly feeling his younger son had suffered a little roughly in the hands of his brother, his fiancée, and the tubercle bacillus, he unexpectedly offered a small allowance. As he had no longer Robin to house he calculated the overall outlay would not be large.

75

Besides, he was in a good mood because the synovial membranes had started up again. They were typed by a girl of eighteen called Sibyl, who wore the closest crop in London and smelt like a hothouse of violets.

Of more value than money was Graham's Fellowship of the Royal College of Surgeons. He was allowed to sit the examination on turning twenty-five in the winter of 1919, having already kicked aside the stumbling-block of the Primary examination in anatomy and physiology at his father's insistence while still a student. Passing at the first try, he could revert from the still novel title of Doctor to the grander one of plain Mister, a complicated exercise in surgical snobbery he was never able to fathom. With a Fellowship he had a future. He began to dress more smartly. He bought a small Jowett car. He was in the position to think again of taking a wife.

This time, he had already decided, I know what I'm after.

His uncoupling from Edith had left him free to forgo the simple pleasures of marriage for love in favour of a woman with money and position, but the difficulty lay in finding one. Now, Miss Cazalay, he calculated, must have friends, and a man had to start somewhere. He wrote to Half Moon Street on the pretext of thanks for his new job, suggesting pointedly he hadn't forgotten the invitation to Biddenden. Miss Cazalay was irritated. If everyone insisted on taking her at her word, she could have filled Windsor Castle every week-end. But she asked him for the following Saturday. Graham bought a new set of plus-fours and was so on his best behaviour he bored everyone.

But Maria Cazalay's mother took to him. He listened patiently to all her ailments, many of which were unknown to medical science. During the autumn of 1919 she asked him regularly to Half Moon Street for tea. She thought him more *simpatico* than Dr Whitehead, who was inclined to be vain, and anyway treated tea as a consultation and sent in a bill for a guinea. Maria was often there, between dashing to meetings of the Cazalay Mission, the Belgian Children's Charity, the Sunshine Fund, and the Free Medicine Club. Graham began to see a good deal of her. She began to think he wasn't so boring after all.

76

One afternoon the pair of them were talking about free medicine, when Maria burst out impatiently, 'The poor really have no sense of responsibility. Some of these lower-class families produce enormous broods of children—eight, nine, ten or more sometimes. And they haven't a penny to bless themselves with. No wonder they all get rickets and scurvy and nits and such things.'

'The world suffers an unhappy division—into couples who want to have children and can't, and couples who have too many and don't know how to stop.'

Graham was sitting in an easy chair, swinging his leg over the arm. He was now perfectly at home in the drawing-room. Maria's mother had gone to lie down with a headache, induced by a surfeit of clinical recollections.

'Yes, of course.' Maria looked awkward. 'I've heard there are ways in which one can stop . . . well, breeding.'

'Oh, birth control,' said Graham lightly.

Maria blushed. It was not at all the sort of subject one mentioned to young gentlemen. Only a year or two previously, she seemed to remember, people were sent to prison for advocating the use of such apparatus, whatever it happened to be.

'You must have heard of Marie Stopes?' Graham suggested.

'The name, certainly.'

'She's planning to open a clinic next year. That'll let off a splendid fuss. Questions in Parliament, thunderings from the pulpit, that sort of thing. It'll be just as bad as Mr Willett's Daylight Saving Time.'

'I can't say I altogether agree that *clinics* are necessary,' said Maria primly. 'It's such a very private matter between husbands and wives.'

'There'll have to be some sort of clinics for these new diaphragms. They don't go in by instinct, I'm afraid. It's amazing the average woman's lack of knowledge of her own anatomy.'

He saw Maria bite her lip. But they were talking about 'women', a detached and philosophic subject, she told herself, like the poor. 'I don't think even I know how these things operate.'

77

'The diaphragm sits snugly under the neck of the uterus—the womb.'

'The womb . . . that's different from the other . . . the other passage, is it?'

'I'll draw you a diagram,' Graham offered.

She brought him a sheet of writing paper, which had a coronet on it.

It amused him to see the flushed discomfiture of the leading light in the Sunshine League and Free Medicine Club. It was his Bob Sawyer approach again. He never shook off the grinning ghost of this Dickensian roustabout all his life. With Edith he used racks of corpses, but a lady of Maria's intelligence and sensibility he confronted with the womb.

At their next meeting the subject of contraception somehow brought itself up again.

'But the *poor*, what method do they use?' Maria asked. She had beaten down her embarrassment. After all, it was perfectly permissible to discuss such intimate generalities with a young man if he happened also to be a young doctor. And it was also rather exciting. 'These implements cost money.'

'*Coitus interruptus.* As free as the air we breathe.'

'I don't think I understand.'

'It's a ceremonial salute to the goddess of love rather than firing in deadly earnest.'

'I still don't understand.'

'I'll draw you another diagram.'

He began to wonder if she were really quite innocent. He could tell from the *Tatler* she floated through life on a cloud of 'admirers', well-born and well-tailored young men who could buy half Bond Street for her presents, but perhaps she was not the generous bestower of gay favours he imagined. Perhaps, it struck him suddenly, there was even a chance for a serious-minded professional young gentleman like himself. An exciting thought. At least she seemed to find him more interesting than the committee of the Sunshine League.

And Maria began to wonder how much of his knowledge he had got from books.

During that winter Graham occupied her thoughts quite as much as her committees. She was touched by his simple attentions. After all, he was kindly, he was amusing, he was sensitive, he had perfectly passable manners, and he knew all about the female pelvis. She fancied he was falling in love with her. Graham fancied he was, too—if she encouraged his advances, he was ready enough to supply the passion. At Christmas she let him take her to the Sloane Hospital Ball, a sumptuous annual affair in Park Lane when the rich dutifully fed and frolicked to raise funds for the undernourished poor. She decided afterwards she was really becoming quite fond of him, and he danced wonderfully. He had enjoyed plenty of practice with Edith.

Maria finally made up her mind to marry the little doctor as clear-headedly as she decided anything on an agenda. Many men had confessed themselves tortured with love for her, but none in the end seemed inclined to make his agonies exclusive— she knew the reason well enough, though at the moment preferred not mentioning it. And she had to marry *someone*. At Easter 1920 she asked him with three other admirers down to Biddenden, but one developed mumps, another was suddenly dispatched by the Foreign Office to make peace with the Turks at Sèvres, the third, a gay fellow in journalism, wired last-minute excuses in expensive profusion. She suddenly saw herself an old maid, banished from the stage of life altogether to the wings, a cheerless prospect. She was already thirty-four. She told Graham twenty-nine, but she knew he didn't believe it. He was an admirably shrewd young man as well.

After tea on the Easter Monday she invited him into the hot-houses. She knew she would leave them a betrothed woman. Once she had firmly made up her mind on a subject, she couldn't envisage anything whatever standing in her way.

That evening found Graham opposite Maria's father at the dinner-table, waiting a chance to ask his formal blessing. He felt not only overwhelmed by the events of the afternoon but most uncomfortable. The points of his dress collar were sticking into his neck. The coming interview had blunted his appetite for the food while sharpening it for the drink, leaving him flushed and muzzy. Not that he needed Dutch courage, he told himself. After all, he had been through the experience once already. But the Ramsgate butcher had been a simple hurdle to mount. Lord Cazalay was more in the nature of a portcullis.

Graham watched the man across the table. He was talking animatedly, banging the cloth, his face scarlet, his starched shirt-front crackling as if unable to contain the passion surging in his bosom. Graham had given up following the trail of the argument, an elaborate diatribe balanced on some delicate point of party politics. People who knew, or who said they did, awarded Lord Cazalay a mastership of intrigue bettering Lloyd George's, who, they hinted, became Prime Minister only through some refined shaft of Cazalay's treachery towards Asquith. They whispered that Cazalay had not only ruthlessly engineered the sinking of the Dardanelles expedition through hostility to Churchill, but equally ruthlessly engineered the sinking of the *Hampshire* through hostility to Kitchener. Graham found it simple to imagine such ferocity behind his exterior, which at the moment resembled an ape sitting unexpectedly on a wasps' nest. On the intelligence which had carried him to command the country's affairs in the Cabinet he was unable to form an opinion, any remarks by Lord Cazalay to himself on their few meetings being polite, formal, brief, and wholly automatic.

Lord Cazalay disposed of his port and his point, extinguished both his cigar and his outraged expression and rose from the table. The dinner-party was as informal as anything could be in his company, and to Graham's alarm his host would not for once be rightly joining the ladies. Instead, he made for a panelled door leading to his study, with a call of, 'Here, Arthur!' indicating a desire for words with a fellow Cabinet minister. Graham stood gripping his chair. He had only that evening to settle his business, and hadn't counted on forcing precedence over the Home Secretary. His resolve stiffened by wine, he pushed forward and asked, 'May I have a word with you, sir?'

Lord Cazalay looked startled, but gave a quick smile. 'Let's leave it till the morning, young man. You're staying overnight, I hope?'

'It's about Maria.'

Lord Cazalay resumed his ape-like expression. 'What about Maria?' As Graham found himself incapable of reply the politician's brain busily swept up a pile of suspicions. 'Would you mind biding a moment, Arthur?' he muttered.

'Our young friend seems possessed of information of some importance,' smiled the other politician. 'If we leave him to boil, it may well vaporize away.'

'Charles! Henry!' Lord Cazalay snapped his fingers to summon his two sons, neither of whom Graham knew very well through their having addressed him hardly a remark between them. 'And you, George,' he added to the secretary Graham had seen with the red dispatch-box. They all went into the study. Lord Cazalay took up battle-positions in front of the grate. 'Now—what's all this about Maria?' he repeated, scowling.

This was not the scene Graham had pictured. For a start, he hardly expected to find himself so heavily outnumbered. Unfortunately he had overlooked the total lack of communication in the Cazalay family. Lord Cazalay was far too deep in politics to pay attention to the others, Maria had for years stepped her own way, and if Lady Cazalay had been terrified of her husband before her marriage the event had done nothing to relieve it. When Lord Cazalay snapped at Graham, 'I know of nothing you need discuss with me about Maria,' it was one of the few times in his life that he meant what he said.

'We want to become married,' Graham told him, simply.

'Did you hear that, Charles?'

'Yes, I did,' agreed one of Maria's brothers, grinning.

Graham suddenly felt angry. After all, he was a registered medical practitioner, a surgeon, a healer. He was a man entitled to respect in the world. 'I have a very good position in the Sloane Hospital,' he said defiantly. 'In the throat department,' he added. 'And now I have my Fellowship.'

'What Fellowship?'

'The Fellowship of the Royal College of Surgeons.'

'Never heard of it,' said Lord Cazalay.

Graham was stunned. Ignorance of such precious honours was unbelievable. Then it struck him sickeningly that the lives of Lord Cazalay and himself were calibrated on widely different scales.

'I agree there's a gap socially between Maria and myself,' he retreated. 'But she and I have discussed it—'

'Maria and *you* have discussed it? What's it got to do with Maria and *you*? It's Maria and *me* who'll discuss such matters, if they are to be discussed at all. Who are you? I don't know anything about you. Does anyone know anything about you?' Lord Cazalay implored in general. 'What are you doing in my house anyway?'

This seemed a crashingly discouraging turn in the conversation. Graham was about to defend both himself and the Royal College of Surgeons, but suddenly losing heart made abruptly for the door.

'Don't run away, you fellow. I haven't finished with you yet. I know the type of people about these days—'

Graham slammed the door behind him, catching Maria's brother exclaiming, 'Throat hospital!' and roaring with laughter.

He ran from the house, ripping off his collar. The alcohol had evaporated from his blood. He fancied he was going to vomit. He knew perfectly well he would for years have cut a petty figure at Maria's side, but having his nose rubbed so vigorously in the malodorous fact took away his breath. He wanted to get away, to escape to the academic security of Hampstead. He didn't want to see anyone in the place again. He started wandering round the grounds, getting lost, somewhere or other dropping his collar.

Lord Cazalay had no need to summon Maria. Hearing the door bang she sensed something amiss and hurriedly excused herself from the drawing-room. She found her father haranguing the other three about the dangers of fortune-hunters, quite as fiercely as he had harangued gatherings in Trafalgar Square about the dangers of the Germans.

'Don't be stupid,' she said angrily. 'Do you imagine I'm fool enough to give myself to a gigolo?'

This subdued Lord Cazalay. He had respect for his daughter's mind, which he felt shared something of his own. 'But surely, Maria! You can't be fond of him?'

'Of course I am! It is unworthy and wounding to suggest otherwise.'

She also shared something of his ear for a phrase.

'But what of all the other men you've been mixed up with?' Lord Cazalay continued briskly. 'I've lost count of them. There isn't a woman in London who's had your opportunities. Why do you want to pick on this throat doctor, or whatever he is?'

'Do you wish me to die before I marry?' She clapped her hand to her cheek. 'Why do you think I had this thing cut out? Every affair in the past has come to nothing. I'm going through with this one, whatever anybody says. There're things about me you don't understand—couldn't understand. I know what I want, and I'm going to get it.' She sat down abruptly in an armchair.

Everyone fell silent. They saw Lord Cazalay was thinking. The lightning mind which flashed clarity on so many obscure political situations was trying to decide the inevitable first question, 'Where is the advantage to me?' An unmarried daughter was somehow a reflection on himself, particularly when the misfortune was so clearly not through want of trying. He had never understood Maria's failure in that department. He supposed she was clear-headed enough not to be duped by an out-and-out rogue. Perhaps it would be best to give in. Anyway, she generally got her own way in the end. The door opened, and Lady Cazalay appeared, erupting Italian.

'Oh, shut up, for God's sake!' said Lord Cazalay. 'Charles— fetch that doctor fellow back.'

They found Graham sitting beside the lake, smoking cigarettes. It occurred to Maria he might have been contemplating throwing himself in, which though the water was only three feet deep would have made a pleasant gesture. In the study Lord Cazalay shook him warmly by the hand, explaining his petulance as the result of shock—which Graham, as a medical man, would easily understand. The house burst into uproar. Everyone congratulated him heartily, even Maria's brothers, who followed their father's opinion in everything, and the Home Secretary, who followed the novels of Elinor Glyn. The servants were summoned with champagne. The emotional see-saw left Graham stunned, until at last he escaped to bed, when he discovered he still had no collar on.

They were to be married in September, as fashionably, socially and spiritually, as possible. Graham was stopped in the street by reporters, his photograph appeared in the *Illustrated London News*, *Punch* made a heavy-handed joke. The professor was delighted, particularly as financially the flow of current had been repolarized. Aunt Doris was rapturous. Dr Whitehead promised to look in at the wedding reception. They were to honeymoon on the Riviera, spending the first night at Dover. It had never crossed Graham's mind to suggest any fun with Maria beforehand. When she undressed in the Dover hotel he found she was covered with really rather a lot of moles, from one end of her thin trunk to the other.

14

THE MOST THRILLING event of Graham's honeymoon was his discovery that the tides of the Mediterranean really did not come in and go out at all. He had never believed this distinction from less sophisticated waters. But there were the waves, beating as regularly as a pulse all day long on the same filthy strip of shingle. He felt a Galileo, making some original observation in astronomy.

It was a wonderful holiday, the best of his life, his first abroad. It fascinated him to hear people chattering in French, to handle the fragile-looking coins with holes in the middle, to post letters with gay, complicated stamps rather than the solemn monochrome features of the British king. He took an appropriate scientific interest in the aquarium tucked below Prince Albert's castle, and in the plants of the *Jardin Exotique* up the hillside. He was struck by the spotless artificiality of the Casino square, crammed with flowers as thickly as a London coster's barrow, where even the excreta dropping from the cab-horses seemed made of some synthetic and totally inoffensive material. He easily adapted himself to the food and attention lavished on them by the Hôtel de Paris, and there was no other 'high life' to test him. After the excitement of the wedding, his wife declared she wanted a quiet time of it. And anyway, gambling bored her. Graham sketched her on the Casino terrace every morning and organized picnics in the mountains every afternoon. She was always gay, smart, and a creditable companion. The sea stayed blue and the weather was charming.

It was soon clear why Maria had ripened so long on the topmost branches of the nuptial tree. Her promiscuity in London had been virginal. She was frigid.

Every night the fortress lay defenceless and eager for surrender, but the gates defied the battering-ram. It was most exhausting for both of them. When she demanded why she was cursed with such a disability Graham explained patiently it was a sort of spasm, like the cramp when swimming. A form of hysteria, he added—most unwisely, because she told him quite severely through the darkness she was not hysterical in the slightest.

'I didn't mean it in that sense, my darling,' he apologized. 'But you mustn't *worry*. That only makes it worse. You worry that you can't do it, then you worry that you worry that you can't. You understand?'

She understood very well. It had worried her for years, more than her moles. So many men had started making love to her but retired hurt and baffled, she had begun automatically expelling them from her life once she sensed their taking range for an attempt. But Graham she expected would be different, with his knowledge of the female pelvis. Though she had rather feared a fuss, remembering a novel where a similar honeymoon terminated with the husband short-temperedly strangling the wife.

Graham was not over-upset. An exchange of intimate confidences was hardly to be expected *before* a marriage. After all, he hadn't told her anything about Edith.

'But what can we *do*?' she demanded.

'We can but persist.'

He persisted there and then, but it still didn't work. He persisted the following night, several times. He persisted when the waiter took away the bedside trays after their *petit déjeuner*. He persisted suddenly in the middle of the afternoon, remembering from some gynaecological textbook that success might occur when there wasn't time enough to worry about achieving it. But they stayed out of luck. He began to wonder if persisting in a relaxing warm bath might do the trick.

86

Then suddenly it happened. It may have been the reward of Graham's considerate handling of the situation, or simply of his physical endurance. It may have been two bottles of champagne at dinner dissolving Maria's inhibitions, or it may simply have been the rest and fresh air doing her good. But everything clicked as precisely and excitingly as the little ivory ball on the roulette table dropping into its slot. She was terribly grateful. And terribly proud. She had been perfectly right in her choice. He really was a clever little doctor after all.

They went home. Mentally, she rolled up her sleeves. The honeymoon was over, and Graham had to be fitted into place with the rest of the household.

The ambition of her womanhood achieved, Maria slipped almost immediately into middle-age. She dressed more drably and drew back her long black hair into an intimidating bun. She abandoned with relief the gay calendar of flirtatious parties for the more substantial and less tiring joys of domesticity. She had rented a house in Great Ormond Street, not far from the children's hospital, where she intended they should live in fairly modest style with only half a dozen servants. The district would be convenient for her work with the Red Cross, the Cazalay Mission in Canning Town, the Belgian Children's Charity, the Sunshine Fund, and the Free Medicine Club, to which had been added the Garden City Housing Trust, the Libraries for the Poor Scheme, the Keep Fit Society, and the general feeding and care of Graham. She entertained only at home, conscientiously rather than lavishly, and Dr Whitehead looked in repeatedly, remaining under the dictates of professional ethics Maria's personal doctor (he charged a guinea for tea, but appeared for dinner gratis).

Graham never saw Lord Cazalay, who seemed to be fully occupied persuading the miners to take lower wages. He occasionally met Maria's brothers, who still had nothing to say to him. He first came across the man who would in time mean more to him than any of them—Valentine Arlott, a young Australian who had founded the London *Daily Press* on Lord Cazalay's money before the war, and during it had praised both

Australia and Lord Cazalay so handsomely his readers might be forgiven for imagining the pair could have beaten the Kaiser without outside assistance. He was starting a newspaper insurance scheme, and questioned Graham closely about the cash value of various items of anatomy. Short, pudgy, ginger-haired, and bouncy, he asked across the dinner-table if an arm was worth more than a leg. How much more? What about an eye? What were the chances of losing both in an accident? Not very high, Graham assured him. Splendid! He'd make a big feature about eyes. It would set the public shivering. It amused Graham to see his casual remarks inspiring the next morning's headline. Even his father the professor couldn't have managed that.

A month after the honeymoon the black vulture of gloom settled on his shoulder. It was not an unknown visitant. He knew he had a manic-depressive personality, his mood swinging from bright sunlight to black night, never lingering in the comfortable greyness of more stolid minds. Even as a child, a casual rebuke from the professor, or refusal of cake for tea, could throw him into the sulks for a day. Now he was more miserable than he could remember in his days of impecunious irresponsibility. He hadn't entered a new world with Maria—the struggle of putting himself on terms with her friends told him that. He had simply excluded himself from his old one. At the Sloane he was no longer the up-and-coming young Mr Trevose. He was Maria Cazalay's husband. The clash between his social and lowly professional status seemed resented by everyone, even the good-natured Mr Grafton, perhaps because Graham arrived to work in a better car than he did. He felt he was becoming a social waif and began feeling terribly sorry for himself. Particularly when Maria started discussing his career, a project in which she took even keener interest than in the Garden City Housing Trust.

There was no plastic surgery post at Blackfriars, nor any of the grand London hospitals—Harold Gillies himself had got back to Bart's only as an assistant in the throat department. Graham wanted some small hospital as a springboard, somewhere he could, like Gillies, start doing throat work and later teach himself plastics without the world seeing too much of his failures. But where? The Sloane was no use. When Maria insisted he leave it to her he raised no objection. After all, she was far better versed in the ways of the world than he was. Also, she was about nine years older.

The day after they buried the Unknown Warrior in Westminster Abbey the Saracen invited Graham to assist with a case. He drove to Wimpole Street with John Bickley in the anaesthetist's Wolseley (the chauffeur-driven Lanchester Forty went back from the Sloane for Maria's use), the dickey crammed with cylinders of nitrous oxide gas and oxygen, lengths of rubber piping, and pieces of anaesthetic apparatus. They found the Saracen in a good mood, for four reasons.

First, his patient was female, young, and wealthy, the daughter of a City man who had sought his assistance without even a breath of canvassing.

Secondly, his lawsuit was snowballing to a climax. If the General Medical Council refused to recognize the Saracen's qualifications there was nothing he could do, the Council being as much above the bother of appeals against its wisdom as the Star Chamber. But he had cunningly started a libel action against a member of the body, a worthy general practitioner elected by his medical peers, who had unwisely strayed outside the stockade of privileged speech to comment severely on the Saracen at some otherwise unexciting medical meeting.

The lawyers found his case interesting, which should have been warning enough. When doctors find a case interesting the patient is generally doomed. A judge and jury of the King's Bench also found his case interesting, but rejected it. Then three judges in the Court of Appeal, equally interested, threw it out as well. But agreeing the case of interest to the country in general they allowed a final plea to the House of Lords, which the Saracen was convinced would award him damages, restore his costs, and gloriously settle his professional status. He could simply have gone home to New York instead, but like many Americans of nobly expensive tastes he enjoyed the life of decadent old Europe. And he was so shouldered with debt even his appearance in the Cunard offices would have produced writs like a snowstorm.

The third reason for the Saracen's good mood was meeting Graham for the first time since his marriage. He felt the young man could now start being useful to him, particularly as he had brought the happy pair together. The fourth was having a proposition to discuss. A proposition always made the Saracen happy.

The patient was so pretty her hare-lip was doubly disfiguring, making Graham think of some vandal daubing the smile of the Mona Lisa. The Saracen set to work excising its edges and undercutting the skin, taking care not to shorten the lip and leave it worse than before, gathering up the superfluous red tissue in a fetching Cupid's bow. He operated as usual in silence, only when inserting his final stitches asking Graham abruptly, 'Are you a Catholic?'

Graham wondered if they were in for some ethical discussion about tampering with girls' features, but the Saracen went on, 'You know St Sebastian's, out Uxbridge way? It's a small Catholic hospital. I've been working on Sir John Blazey, their chairman of governors. They're starting a plastic unit out there. Nothing colossal, mind, just a few beds, less than we had at Princess Alexandra's. I'm to be made surgeon-in-charge.' The Saracen took another needle-holder trailing fine catgut from his theatre nurse. 'How'd you like to be first assistant?'

'But I'm *not* a Catholic,' Graham objected.

The Saracen chuckled. 'What's wrong with a sudden conversion? I guess the good Lord would have to look mighty sharp to find I was still one of the Faith. It doesn't signify much with the hospital, though it helps, maybe. Think it over.' He dropped his voice as though passing confidential information of monetary value. 'It's the chance of a lifetime. You'd be crazy not taking it.'

'But first assistant—' The offer was so unexpected Graham felt confused. 'I'm too young, surely?'

'This is a young man's specialty!' The Saracen cut out a stitch which displeased him and inserted another. 'Ours is a stern discipline,' he reflected as an aside. 'Other surgeons' scars

90

are but lights under a bushel. Ours shine on the world for life. I guess you wouldn't mind making a small investment in these rooms—to join me in partnership,' he added as casually. 'They cost a mint to run.'

'When's your case reach the House of Lords?' asked John Bickley sharply from the head of the table.

'Oh, pretty soon,' the Saracen replied vaguely. 'Pretty soon.'

This had a dampening effect on the conversation. The Saracen was always having to tell himself his anaesthetist was smarter than he looked.

Graham decided to discuss the idea with Maria, because he discussed everything with Maria. She was working at her desk alone in the drawing-room when he came in.

'St Sebastian's—yes,' she decided. 'Partnership with the Saracen definitely *no*. You mustn't give the man a penny piece. I don't trust him.'

Graham shrugged his shoulders. 'You trusted him to remove your mole.'

'Really, Graham! That's hardly the same thing. Anyway, I was prepared to put up with him to get rid of it. No, you must go and see Sir John Blazey yourself, my dear. I can easily arrange an introduction.'

'I couldn't possibly see Blazey without asking the Saracen's permission.'

'Why?'

'That would be going behind his back.' She made a contemptuous pout. 'It's the Saracen who's offering me the chance of first assistant, not the hospital. Don't you see? The partnership in Wimpole Street is part of the bargain.'

'Now you're talking rubbish.'

Graham's resentment awoke. 'I don't need any advice about the Saracen's morals or character. I've seen him working among patients long enough to form my own opinions, thank you very much.'

'Well! I'm only trying to help with your career.'

'Are you? Or is it an excuse for running my life for me? I can't call my soul my own these days. The house is filled with

91

people I don't know or I don't care for. I can't even eat what I like or dress as I like. You don't seem to want a husband at all. You want a puppet.'

'Now you're being stupid.' She sat with her lips tight, wondering if she were angry or simply afraid she might cry—an unthinkable weakness. 'You ought to be grateful for meeting so many useful people.'

'Do you imagine I enjoy everyone pointing a finger at me?' It was the first row he'd had with her. In fact, it was the first row he'd had with any woman. He and Edith had parted with never a cross word. Like many outraged spouses, he seized the chance for amateur dramatics. 'People everywhere say I only married you for your money. What do you think *that* does for my self-respect?'

'Who says that? Who? I haven't heard of anyone.'

'Everyone at the Sloane. I can't endure working in the place much longer.'

'Oh, the Sloane! They're envious, that's all. Surely you've sense enough to see that? *Why* should they think such things?'

'You're nine years older than I am, for a start.'

It was the first time this weapon had been drawn from its sheath of tact. 'Why do you accuse me of that?' Maria demanded furiously.

'It isn't an accusation. It's a statement of fact.'

'God! You're being horrible to me.' Graham folded his arms and stared at her nobly, an effect badly upset by her adding in a low voice, 'I'm pregnant.'

His mouth fell open. 'What?'

'Yes, I'm certain of it. I haven't seen anything for two months. My breasts are getting bigger.' She clasped them. 'That's a sign, isn't it?'

He recalled she had recently been emitting a new radiance, remarked upon by her friends and taken as a compliment by himself. Now he realized this was enjoyed by all newly-pregnant women, and due to an upsurge of hormones rather than cohabitation with himself. He told himself crossly he should have spotted the diagnosis weeks ago.

92

'Aren't you pleased?' she asked, looking at him timidly.

'But, my darling . . . of course I am!' He sat on the edge of her chair and put his arm round her. He supposed all men were pleased when their wives became pregnant. 'Of course I'm pleased! As pleased as anyone in the world.'

He smothered her in a blanket of solicitude, and arranged for her to see Mr Harold Berkeley from Blackfriars. Mr Berkeley smilingly confirmed her suspicions. The baby would be born the following June. He put it tactfully that a primiparous lady of thirty-four should take her state seriously, reduce her activities, avoid riding horses or the possibility of falling downstairs, and leave all theatres and cinematographs the instant the plot threatened to become too exciting. Maria wrote jubilantly seeking leave of absence from the Red Cross, the Cazalay Mission in Canning Town, the Belgian Children's Charity, the Sunshine Fund, the Free Medicine Club, the Garden City Housing Trust, the Libraries for the Poor, and the Keep Fit Society. All the freed energy was concentrated on her pregnancy. With every mouthful she ate, every breath she drew, every movement of her swelling body, she thought of the foetus inside her. No mother could have lavished on her child greater intrauterine devotion.

Lady Cazalay came into residence at Great Ormond Street at once. Lord Cazalay, after briefly and earnestly congratulating Graham, put the matter from his mind in favour of more important affairs. The dinner-parties stopped. As a doctor-father, Graham found himself pulled into the limelight of their marriage. He arranged the consultations, collected the specimens, and explained in detail to both wife and mother-in-law the anatomical, physiological, obstetrical, embryological, and psychological facts. He became almost as favoured a figure in his own home as he had been in Half Moon Street before the wedding. Even Maria's brothers took him aside and asked in confidence if the going was likely to be heavy. He felt the pregnancy was doing him a deal of good.

Every afternoon at four, Dr Whitehead looked in for tea, and charged a guinea.

15

PERHAPS DECIDING THAT Maria's delicate condition called for all consideration possible, Graham fell in with her views and visited Sir John Blazey at St Sebastian's. He found the little hospital charming, with its atmosphere of graciously bestowed charity, its nursing nuns in billowing coifs (which he feared were terribly unsterile), and its crucifixes on the walls of the operating theatres. He saw he would have to overcome a puritanical disapproval of religious trappings in medical surroundings. He failed to see the connection between medicine, which was a science, a business of cutting and curing, and religion, which was a highly unscientific matter altogether. Though he supposed it was a comfort, believing you passed from the care of your physician not simply to that of your pathologist but to the more enlightened solicitude of St Peter. As he had once told Robin, he wished he could believe it himself. But doubtless the priests who made so free with the wards kept the patients' peckers up wonderfully, and at very moderate cost, for he understood the poor fellows' stipends were pitiful.

Sir John Blazey was a thin, colourless man, fussing to explain the new unit was certainly not for such questionable practices as face-lifting and nose-making, but for the crop of accidents from the factories sprouting all round the hospital. He showed Graham the wards with such fussy diffidence the young man left for home in the Lanchester feeling more depressed than ever —Sir John would have awarded some unknown registrar from a throat department a more dusty reception. And he still had to explain the visit away to the Saracen.

94

He was spared this awkwardness. From that evening's paper Graham learned the world the poor man was struggling to balance on his shoulders had finally flattened him.

Five judges of the House of Lords, unmatched for experience, wisdom, and senility, had considered his case. Two thought he was right, three thought he was wrong, though all five found it most interesting.

The decision came at a bad time. In the winter of 1920 the goods which were to flood from Britain into a threadbare post-war world were somehow left silting up the factories, and unemployment grew as credit diminished. The *Daily Press*'s front page announced the Saracen's bankruptcy, hinting the more exciting whiff of a criminal charge was in the air—even the surgeon himself recognized his creditors had been treated to more enthusiasm than frankness. The rooms in Wimpole Street were locked, his instruments and his racehorses were impartially impounded.

'Always knew he'd come to a bad end,' Dr Whitehead told Graham, taking his hat after looking in for tea. 'Commercial motives have no place in our profession.' He paused at the front door. 'I was most interested in the news of your father.'

Graham looked blank. Had the longed-for Fellowship been awarded by the Royal Society temporarily out of its collective mind?

'You don't know?' Dr Whitehead gave a smile. 'Then perhaps you'd best hear it from the professor himself. It's anyway hardly more than a rumour.'

'Nothing discreditable, I hope?' asked Graham quickly. He had in his time overheard plenty of students' gossip in the dissecting-room, where his father was known as 'The Rubber', not through any erasive qualities.

'Far from it! Highly creditable.'

'Then tell me. Surely you can tell me what it is?'

But whatever the pearl of information, Graham failed to prise it from the oyster. In Dr Whitehead's practice he learned to take professional discretion to extremes.

With St Sebastian's and Maria's pregnancy Graham had too

much on his mind to seek his father out. He was also expecting the Saracen to appear any day at Great Ormond Street, but the American delayed his visit till the week before Christmas. He was perhaps hopeful of the seasonal atmosphere, having his eye on a loan.

'Things haven't been going too well,' he admitted, sitting by the drawing-room fire with a cigar. It was the first understatement Graham had heard from him. 'Though I still know I'm right. What man before God could say otherwise? It needed only one of those law lords to think just a little differently. Judges are like horses, I guess,' he sighed. 'You can never tell which way they're going to jump all the time.'

Graham expressed sympathy.

The Saracen explained that matters were not so black as printed in the newspapers. His powerful friends in New York would straddle the Atlantic with a financial lifebuoy before seeing him go under. But rescue operations took time. He hated asking—because he regarded Graham as a personal friend rather than a professional colleague—but he would much appreciate two or three thousand pounds for a while. When Graham shook his head he generously reduced his demand to a single thousand. Graham shook his head again. The Saracen began to lose his temper.

'Don't you feel you owe me anything? Aren't you going to make your life's work in plastic surgery?'

'Yes, that's what I hope, certainly.'

'And who gave you your chance?' Graham made no reply. He would gladly have handed the man the money, but Maria was against it for more than economic reasons. If he were seen siding with the Saracen his own professional status might be called to question. Besides, the purse-strings were in her hands as firmly as if they had remained in Lord Cazalay's own. Suspecting the true frustrator of his hopes, the Saracen added sourly, 'Would you have the courtesy to tell Mrs Trevose I called to ask after the health of my grateful patient?' He then left with dignity, wondering if he'd the chance of a less ambitious sum from John Bickley.

Sir John Blazey came fussing into the house on Christmas Eve. He apologized for calling on business at such a time, but the situation at St Sebastian's had to be resolved as a matter of urgency. Now that Dr Sarasen was so painfully out of the question—Sir John made agitated little bounces on his heels—the committee had met and decided more care must be expended on his replacement. They had carefully considered Graham's application for the post of first assistant—thank you, he must decline a glass of sherry, he was sorely pressed for time —and notwithstanding Graham's age felt his experience and obvious talents, in the strictly circumscribed specialty of plastic surgery, merited their appointing him as deputy to the surgeon-in-chief. He could start the good work of the new unit until a suitable senior could be found. Would he accept such heavy responsibility?

Graham would.

He found himself in full charge of his own plastic surgery beds around his twenty-sixth birthday. Whether his work was so brilliant or the committee shirked the risk of appointing another trickster like the Saracen he never discovered, because the appearance of the threatened overlord was never mentioned from the day he joined the hospital staff to the day he retired from it at the age of sixty-five.

16

IN THE NEW YEAR Graham's father called at Great Ormond Street to congratulate his son on his new appointment. Their meetings were becoming fewer and increasingly embarrassing, the professor being so overwhelmed by his son's marrying riches he treated the young man with a grotesque respect. He wore his usual dark suit and emitted his usual smell of corpse antiseptic, but something struck Graham as different—his eye had a sparkle, and even his drooping moustache seemed to wear a sheen. First they discussed Maria's pregnancy. Everyone coming to the house first discussed Maria's pregnancy. Then the professor brushed his moustache and announced coyly, 'Well, Graham, my boy, I have some news which will surprise you. Though I fancy your autonomic nervous system will survive the shock.' He paused. 'I am to be married again.'

Graham looked aghast.

'Well, Graham? Aren't you pleased? Eh?'

He sounded painfully impatient for a reply, but Graham could only stare and ask, 'Marry? Marry who, Father?'

'Mrs Fanshaw,' said the professor.

It had been a sad little episode for the academic gentleman.

At first, during that summer, he had come into his study only to help Sibyl with the difficult words about synovial membranes, which she'd misspelt for months.

' "Epiphysis",' he explained smilingly over her shoulder. 'With the "i" first, then the "y". If I may explain, that is the portion of bone separated in early life from the main shaft by a ring of cartilage. But as we grow the cartilage disappears, the bone becomes one entity. Now—' He ran his long fingers up the sleeve of her cotton dress to grasp her elbow. 'Here we have the lower *epiphyses* of your humerus—"es" in the plural, you understand. How old are you, Sibyl?'

'Nineteen, sir,' she told him in a crushed voice.

'At such a delightful age the lower *epiphyses* are as yet un-united with the shaft. That occurs only with the onset of senility, at twenty.' He laughed. 'The humerus at its *upper* end ossifies in the same way, from centres at the head and at the greater and lesser tubercles. They are eight in number.'

He felt her shoulder through her dress. He considered making the demonstration more accurate by slipping his hand in her neckline, but decided against it.

'Just here,' he said.

'Thank you, sir.'

Sibyl found such difficulty with anatomical nomenclature that the professor often felt obliged to sit with her, patting her wrist, and sometimes her thigh, to emphasize the quaint classical words. But the girl's attempts were hopeless. He had to correct whole pages beside her, so close he could feel the hard line of her femur through her skirt. Reaching for a book or a pencil his hand might accidentally brush her breasts or sometimes lie in her lap, quite forgotten, often for minutes on end. Recognizing young Sibyl was doing her best, even his severest reprimands were delivered with his arm round her. He knew that she would interpret such attentions as kindly and fatherly.

But Sibyl was more experienced than he imagined. In her last post at a tea merchant's in Mincing Lane the merchant had done exactly the same.

Arriving home one summer afternoon from Blackfriars the professor advanced with jaunty step into the study to find with his typist an overweight high-coloured woman in a flowered hat, knitting.

'Oh! Good afternoon.' He pulled his moustache irritably.

'This is my mum,' said Sibyl, looking guilty.

'Very pleased to meet you, Mrs Fanshaw,' said the professor, leaving little doubt that he wasn't.

'I hope my Sibyl is giving satisfaction, Professor Trevose?'

'Perfectly. She is having a little trouble grasping the nomenclature, but that will doubtless be overcome in time.'

'My Sibyl's an intelligent girl and a good worker, I've always said.'

'Most intelligent. For her age. It is of course not given to all of us to comprehend the embryology of the synovial membranes at first blush.'

'That's why I was glad of her working for a professor. "You take the post, my girl," I said. "It will improve your mind."'

'I expect she has found me merely dull,' said the professor, a shade hopefully.

'Though it's a sacrifice for me, and that's a fact. I'm a widow, you know. Without Sibyl it's lonely in the afternoons at Cricklewood. If it's all right with you, I'll come over to sit with her.'

The professor said he would be delighted, backed out hurriedly, and sat in the breakfast-room next door in a bad temper.

Sibyl remaining in strict quarantine all summer, the professor could hardly avoid paying attention to Mrs Fanshaw, whom he discovered to be the widow of some official on the Great Western Railway. By September he started inviting her to join him for tea in the breakfast-room, leaving Sibyl floundering among synovial membranes alone.

'It must be wonderful your son marrying the daughter of Lord Cazalay,' she told him. 'I read all about it in the papers.'

'A satisfactory match,' the professor admitted modestly. He handed her the wedding photograph of Robin and Edith, next to the silver-framed one of his late wife on the mantelpiece. 'I have another son, you know. He is, alas, far away in the Straits Settlements, engaged in missionary work. He has a most praiseworthy sense of vocation.'

Mrs Fanshaw took a bite of madeira cake. 'Pretty girl.'

'Edith will be a great help to him out East, I fancy.' The professor added with unthinking accuracy, 'She is very adaptable.'

'So you're quite alone, then?'

'I suppose it comes to us all.' The professor replaced the photograph. 'It is a bitter discovery—realizing how much we rely on our children's companionship. We only make it when they are grown up and gone.'

'It's a shame,' agreed Mrs Fanshaw. As he fell silent she added, 'It's a wonder to me how you manage. A man by himself. Things aren't back to normal even yet, not after the war.'

The professor sighed. 'Sometimes it *is* a struggle. Responsibility for the household is such a distraction, when really I should be concentrating on my work. Academic life is extremely trying, you know. There is no holiday, no escape. One's brain can never be unfettered from its problems. I have servants, of course, but sometimes I feel them more trouble than they're worth.'

'They don't know their places these days, none of them.'

He nodded. 'Now all the girls are working in factories you have to pay them the earth.'

'It's a scandal,' said Mrs Fanshaw, taking another mouthful of cake. 'Money's changing hands.'

The professor agreed with all these sentiments. The shared pains of the postwar middle-class so distracted him he finished his tea without mentioning anatomy once.

By November the book was finished. The last word on synovial membranes stood in two three-inch piles of typescript, presenting no problem but the pleasant one of transferring it to the medical publishers. If the professor's great task was over, so was Sibyl's. He asked Mrs Fanshaw to marry him.

After all, the house *was* a terrible burden. He was becoming dreadfully lonely, and would be more so as the years galloped by. Besides, she hinted at a little money of her own. She agreed readily, her sharp mind having outwitted the organ of academic contemplation by assessing his income and total assets with far keener accuracy than he imagined.

'Yes, the ceremony is to be in February,' the professor told Graham in Great Ormond Street. 'Very quietly, of course. I think a registry office would be more suitable.' As Graham tried to stumble out appropriate congratulations, his father gave a weak smile and added, 'How strange that in such little time Robin, you, and myself should all find brides? We're quite gay dogs, aren't we?'

But he suspected any such frolicsomeness was for him at an end. Mrs Fanshaw was beyond the desirable age in his eyes by some forty years, but the man who wants the moon must philosophically content himself with a candle.

17

THE PROFESSOR FELT crossly that becoming a grandfather twice within three months was unfair on a comparatively newly-married man.

It had seemed to Graham the whole of London stood still and waited breathlessly for Maria's confinement. She had given up the exertion of everything except reading the untaxing works of Mr Wodehouse and Mr Maugham. He had bought her a crystal set as a diverting toy—Northcliffe and the *Daily Mail* had produced Melba singing through the earphones, while Val Arlott and the *Daily Press* were hoping to produce Chaliapin—but she was spared the danger of such excitements because however much Graham fiddled with the catswhisker the receiver never seemed to work. A room upstairs was stripped for obstetrical action, a nurse was engaged, Dr Whitehead looked in twice daily. But the mother-to-be continued to pass her days on a sofa in the drawing-room, every twinge of backache sending a ripple of agitated expectancy through the whole household.

It happened on Midsummer Day. Maria was scrupulously punctual, as usual.

'The first stage has definitely begun,' Mr Berkeley smiled to Graham while coming downstairs with Dr Whitehead. 'As you know, with a primiparous subject, it may be anything up to eighteen hours before we have full dilatation. Whitehead will telephone when I am needed.'

It was at two in the morning when they judged it time to resummon Mr Berkeley. He announced the child to be born in a couple of hours. Graham sat downstairs with Dr Whitehead, who had apparently looked in for the night, at unthinkable expense. The royal physician entertained him with stories of royal personages, but Graham wasn't listening. Despite his knowledge of the female pelvis he was worried. Everything to do with Maria's reproductive system seemed so inefficient. When Mr Berkeley reappeared, still smiling but regretting matters not as smooth as he had hoped, Graham leapt from his chair with a cry.

The obstetrician explained calmly the lie was a breech with extended legs, even drawing a little diagram of the balloon-like uterus with the baby trying to kick its way out instead of butting head-first. In the case of an elderly primigravida—he hastily excused himself, he used the word 'elderly' in the purely relative and technical sense—extraction under anaesthesia was indicated.

Graham was shattered. His wife, whom he felt he had come to love deeply amid the tenderness bestowed on her in general, was running into unthinkable dangers.

A nursing-home overlooking Regent's Park was hastily telephoned, an ambulance ordered. Lord Cazalay was called from Half Moon Street, and arrived with his secretary as though his daughter were already on her death-bed, scowling thunderously at Graham as the author of her misfortune. Lady Cazalay had gone into Italian at the onset of labour, required sal volatile with the return of Mr Berkeley, and now had to be laid down and attended by the nurse. Then Graham suddenly felt irrelevant again. When one of the Cazalay line was to be born, and in dangerous circumstances, he was merely someone else to get in the way.

He drew Mr Berkeley aside and asked the risk.

'I'll tell you,' the obstetrician said frankly, still smiling. 'For a manual extraction after version under anaesthesia, the accepted figure of maternal mortality is thirty per cent.' Graham flinched. 'In my hands, I would say fifteen.'

'Couldn't you perform Caesarean section?'

'I'm afraid the chances would be no better, Graham.' He

paused. '*Even* in my hands. It's a desperate operation once labour's started, even in these days.'

Graham's lips trembled as he went on, 'How about puerperal sepsis? After all these complications?'

He remembered too many cases in the maternity wards at Blackfriars, seeing the first horrifying swing of the new mother's temperature chart, watching it mount until the fever burnt her life out under the helpless eyes of her doctors.

'I shouldn't worry overmuch. Admittedly there's a chance of puerperal infection, but it's very much a danger of the public wards, you know. Private patients in single rooms largely escape such things. And we've the new antistreptococcal serum up our sleeves, which is a comfort.'

'If it works,' said Graham.

'Well, yes,' said Mr Berkeley.

As Mr Berkeley left for the nursing-home Graham realized he hadn't even asked the chances of the baby. The unborn child had become so much a possession of Maria's no-one seemed able to imagine its independent existence at all.

The obstetrician was as good as his word. Before daybreak Desmond George Arthur Graham Trevose was scrambled out of his mother's exhausted uterus, battered, blue, but ready to breathe. Lord Cazalay ordered champagne, and congratulated Graham handsomely. If his daughter were going to live, he took it as a compliment to the Cazalay constitution. She certainly made splendid progress, after a week becoming physically almost herself again. After a month, even Lady Cazalay had started to recover.

On the other side of the earth, Edith's pregnancy was a welcome diversion for the entire mission settlement.

Her married life had been placid. The couple grew fonder of one another, much because it was her nature to scuttle away from quarrels like a rabbit from a gun, and Robin fussed more over the pregnancy than she did herself. Edith declared the child would be born in October, and their year's local leave being due Robin arranged for them to travel a month beforehand to Singapore, where his wife could enjoy the best obstetrical attention in south-east Asia. Edith was so excited about the trip that she had the trunks brought out to start packing a good fortnight before sailing. It was trying work in the heat and her back began to ache, but she was never given to complaining and told herself cheerfully a pregnant woman must tolerate a discomfort or two in the good cause. She suddenly felt exhausted, sent the cook-boy to make her a cup of tea, and collapsed in a wicker chair in the bare living-room. She felt something warm between her legs. Only when the flood of amniotic fluid drenched her dress did she realize things were seriously amiss. As badly befitted a girl once behind the cash-desk of a butcher's shop, Edith had made a mistake in her dates.

Robin was brought hurriedly from the dispensary. He had a sketchy experience of midwifery—his patients neither tolerated nor needed the interference of a stranger—but everyone else for hundreds of miles had even less. He gathered Edith up and moved her to the bedroom, issuing orders for boiling water, clean towels, and bottles of antiseptic. He left her on the bed with hasty expressions of reassurance, and hurried back to look up *Practical Obstetrics*. The schoolmaster couple were away on some expedition. The missionary's assistance he quickly ruled out. He wondered if he should pray for Divine guidance, but he decided there wasn't time, and anyway he hoped supernatural intervention wouldn't be necessary.

The labour was as uncomplicated as Edith herself. A few hours later, the professor was turning in his fingers at Hampstead a cable bringing the name of Alec Quentin Trevose into the family. Well, it was splendid enough, he thought sadly, but the grandsons underlined that his active life was nearing its end. He feared less his years pressing on him than his days, once he retired from Blackfriars and had nothing to call him daily from the house. His marriage had brought some wearisome complications. His wife, though companionable, was not intellectually stimulating. His new stepdaughter had refused to move in, found another job, and sought the roof of an aunt in Southsea. Aunt Doris simply refused to speak to him. And the second Mrs Trevose was alarmingly extravagant. She had already redecorated the house and herself out of recognition. She also insisted on doubling the servants, on one of whom she discovered the professor demonstrating the bony origin and insertion of the *gastrocnemius* muscle in the calf.

'But, my dear,' he complained pathetically, 'the girl had hurt her ankle. I was only trying to calm her by explaining exactly what went wrong.'

'You keep your hands off young women,' snapped Mrs Trevose.

The professor looked shocked. 'You must please remember that I am a medical man. The human body is my rightful province.'

'Don't give me that! You're always pawing and fondling girls, rubbing yourself up against them when you get half a chance. Why, the way you interfered with my Sibyl! Disgusting, it was.'

'How can you say such a thing?' cried the professor, though with more pathos than conviction.

'It's as plain as a barn door. You should see some of the looks behind your back when we're out, in shops and that. You'll get run in one day if you don't mend your ways, you just mark my words.'

The professor was saddened. He really didn't think anyone ever noticed at all.

18

GRAHAM FOUND THE burden of fatherhood lay lightly on him. Maria took control of his son as she took control of everything else. His longest contact with the lad lasted for half an hour each evening, when Desmond was presented in a state of abnormal cleanliness by the crisp-aproned nurse. But the dramatic birth of the child had a dramatic effect on the mother. Desmond left Maria feeling the fragility of her own life. For the first time she realized that death must be allowed into the scheme of things. She pondered over it deeply and morosely, confiding in no-one, not even Graham, any more than she had over her sexual shortcomings. She turned for comfort to works of philosophy (religion she dismissed as too frivolous). She entertained little, and withdrew from half her committees. Some days she became totally introverted, sitting for hours on the drawing-room sofa as she did when pregnant, staring before her. Graham asked himself if some subtle change had occurred in her endocrine system, possibly some minute thrombosis in her pituitary gland. Whatever it was, a shade had been drawn over her personality and life in Great Ormond Street became chillier. He began to wonder how Edith was these days.

The London season Maria now preferred to spend by the sea in isolation—apart from four maids, the cook from London with a couple of girls in the kitchen, nurse and nursery-maid, and a few gardeners. Seeing no reason why her own child shouldn't enjoy the same fresh air provided for the beneficiaries of the Sunshine Fund (who were dispatched once a year in relays to take a day's ration of it at Southend), she bought a house in Cornwall overlooking Falmouth Bay where she took Desmond from June to September. Graham joined them for a week or two, killing the long days painting the view and tracing his ancestors, delighting to find in the nearby churchyard sloping so prettily towards the setting sun that many of the headstones where the fat gulls dozed belonged to his kin. It amused him to discover that other adventurous Cornishmen were recorded as meeting their end through drowning, gunfire, or fever in distant lands, while his family always seemed to die in their beds. He supposed they were naturally lucky, the one quality essential for the successful doctor if never for the good one. The rest of the year he busied himself at St Sebastian's, writing papers for the medical journals, lecturing whenever he had a chance, and generally making a name for himself. Maria read every word before it was printed or uttered.

In 1924 Maria took Desmond to Cornwall early, declaring that the crowds jostling for the British Empire Exhibition at Wembley made London doubly impossible. Graham doubted if he could travel down before August. His father was doing as well as expected after prostatectomy in the hands of Sir Horace Barrow, but the cells in the histologist's section had shown large dark nucleae, the malignant eyes of cancer. If a crisis occurred, diplomacy might be needed as much as surgery—he doubted if Aunt Doris and his stepmother would speak even if adrift in the same lifeboat. Anyway, his presence in London during July was essential. He seemed likely to achieve so youthfully the ambition of his life, a consultancy in plastic surgery at Blackfriars.

He admitted freely it was Maria's doing. If Graham wanted a department of plastic surgery at Blackfriars, she would create one. She sought the aid of Val Arlott, whose *Daily Press* then struck its readers as less of a newspaper than a Santa Claus insisting on Christmas every day of the year. Any of them wishing to insure against their deaths or against the loss of bits of themselves meanwhile, to refurnish their houses with six-piece suites of fumed oak, to own the new Austin Seven, to read

Dickens and Shakespeare from beginning to end, or to holiday in the millionaires' playground of Biarritz, had simply to register as a regular subscriber and try one of the paper's amusing and untaxing competitions. If the prizes were less often fumed oak and the company of millionaires than the works of Dickens, Val Arlott bought literature in bulk and showed a profit on the transaction.

Maria's idea tickled him. Therefore, it would tickle his public. He would start a campaign for this wonderful new science to be established in a great hospital in London—it was a public disgrace no such unit existed—he would raise funds, get important people interested. And what better institution to house the centre of healing than Blackfriars, hardly a newsboy's shout from the *Press*'s own offices?

But Blackfriars was not a stable for everyone's gift horses. Though younger than St Bartholomew's at Smithfield, whose walls were already ancient when darkened by the fires of Bloody Mary's martyrs, it was a City institution like the Old Bailey. It was backed by the shrines of the nation's liberties in Fleet Street, flanked by the repository of its legal wisdom in the Temple, fronted by the soft-running if no longer sweet Thames, and had the Church of England embodied in the bold redoubtable dome of St Paul's looking over its shoulder. It was controlled jealously by its board of governors, the State not presuming to meddle with the health of its citizens, beyond seeing their water was clean and they didn't catch smallpox too often. As the governors were City worthies knowing nothing of medical technicalities, their power had as usual in great and lazy institutions fallen into the hands of the four most pushful professionals. These were Dr Wedderburn, who had consigned Graham to his grave, Sir Horace Barrow, who resembled a retired prize-fighter with a good tailor, Maria's obstetrician Mr Harold Berkeley, who resembled an actor with an even better tailor, and Mr Cramphorn, a clipped-moustached, pipe-smoking, short-statured surgeon, given to pepper-and-salt suits, half-moon glasses, elastic-sided brown boots, and enigmatic grunts.

The *Daily Press* was not the sort of newspaper these four enjoyed reading, or at least enjoyed being seen reading. They feared a 'stunt'—a horrible ravishment of the hospital's dignity.

'I suppose we could preclude any distasteful advertising at our expense,' Sir Horace decided. 'The lawyers might draw up something to that effect. I don't think we should reject the offer out of hand. After all, money's money.'

The other three agreed. But they feared even more a plastic unit would upset the delicate balance of surgical power in the hospital. Sir Horace, backed by Dr Wedderburn, felt strongly that the cause of many chronic diseases which irritated the human frame—things like headache and rheumatism—though admittedly totally unknown, lay somewhere among the churning coils of the patient's gut. It was perfectly logical. Such problems were traditionally ascribed to intractable constipation, and Sir Horace had cut the Gordian knot by slicing out the colon. But relief unfortunately evading both him and the sufferer, he now chased higher and higher up the alimentary canal in pursuit of this elusive mischief, removing more and more of the intestines until he seemed in danger of being the first surgeon to perform tonsillectomy from below.

Mr Cramphorn was a 'pexy' man. He believed these baffling complaints, in which he included dysmenorrhea and migraine for Mr Berkeley's benefit, sprang from undisciplined organs straying from the sites ordained by God and anatomy and careering round the belly like sailors on a Saturday night. Every morning he performed splenopexy by tacking the errant spleen sternly into place with strong catgut, or nephropexy by suspending floating kidneys from the last rib like monkeys on a stick. The hospital was finely divided over the merits of these two panaceas, and the new plastic surgeon would swell one camp or another.

But Mr Berkeley depicted the problem as more complicated still.

'If we *don't* accept a plastic unit,' he said, lighting another of his Turkish cigarettes, 'we shall be under irresistible pressure to start one in neurosurgery, or thoracic surgery, or some such.

These specialized departments are springing up everywhere nowadays like asparagus.'

It was a telling point. A nerve surgeon or a chest surgeon would steal everyone's glory by inventing his own operations for rheumatism and headaches. But the interference of a plastic surgeon could never be more than skin deep.

'If we do have a plastic unit, then who will be our plastic surgeon?' asked Sir Horace.

'Trevose's boy, of course,' grunted Mr Cramphorn. 'He's going great guns at St Sebastian's.'

'He's very well off,' murmured Mr Berkeley.

This was another consideration. Graham wouldn't take more than his fair share of the precious beds in the private block. The doctors had to live as well as the patients.

'The post must be properly advertised, naturally,' declared Sir Horace sternly. 'It would be most irregular otherwise. There must be no suspicion of favouritism.'

'No, none at all,' the others agreed.

As the surgeon was to be installed before the building, the post was advertised by early summer in the medical journals and *The Times*. All aspirants had to provide each of the hundred or so established consultants with a *curriculum vitae*, printed at their own expense. It was Blackfriars' practice, impressing candidates with the solemnity of trying to join such a majestic institution at all and, like an election deposit, scaring off the more faint-hearted or eccentric ones. The short-list interviews were fixed for the last week in July, and Graham was requested to attend.

Three days beforehand Maria sent a telegram announcing she was coming home. Graham was alarmed. He met her at Paddington to find her pale and agitated, trembling beside him in the car. He thought she was ill, his mind automatically searching for a diagnosis.

'No, I'm perfectly well,' she said firmly. 'And so is Desmond.' The child had been left in Cornwall. 'It's my father. He wishes to see me. He's coming to the house in half an hour.'

It was beyond Graham why the rendezvous should be so shattering—he never presumed to pry into the Cazalay family affairs. Lord Cazalay arrived punctually, hurrying into the house alone. It was the first time Graham had seen him unaccompanied, his habit being to plough through life like a battleship, screened by escorts. He was scowling as usual, and hardly noticed his son-in-law. He took Maria into the study and locked the door.

'Something's gone wrong,' Maria told Graham when her father left an hour later.

He frowned. 'Is he ill?'

'No, no!' she cried impatiently. 'All the disasters of life aren't bodily ones.' She paused, biting her lip. 'We're ruined. Penniless.' Graham looked at her blankly. 'Oh, it's a long story. I don't understand half of it. It goes back to the war. Everything seems to have crashed all of a sudden.'

'When will this get out?' he asked impulsively. 'In the newspapers? It would never do, not before I go up for the interview at Blackfriars.'

'My God!' she shouted angrily. 'Is *that* all you worry about?'

She left the room, slamming the door. Graham couldn't believe her. For Lord Cazalay to come down in the world was like Lord Nelson crashing into Trafalgar Square. She had been running through bouts of depression recently, and brooding alone in Cornwall had done her no good. He should have made the effort of travelling down for a week. But he fancied she had left the room crying, for the first time since he had known her.

The next three days were crammed with confusion. Men Graham had never seen before kept appearing at the house with heavily-sealed envelopes for Maria. Whatever they contained she kept to herself, hardly sparing a word for him at all, refusing all soothing by drugs or words. The afternoon of his interview at Blackfriars she hardly noticed he had quit the house.

The candidates had to wait on hard chairs outside the hospital committee-room, in an anteroom where the staff left their hats and coats. It was a bare apartment, decorated only with a board showing the day's operations and post-mortems, penned in elaborately handwritten lists like the menus outside French restaurants. Graham hated the room. He had waited there often enough as a student, and it always meant something unpleasant was going to happen, even if it was only meeting his father, who always left committees in a bad temper. He found one candidate waiting already.

'Hello,' Graham greeted Eric Haileybury. 'I heard you were putting in for the job.'

Haileybury was wearing a severe blue serge suit and holding a grey trilby hat on his knees with bony red hands. His fair hair was thinning, and Graham thought he showed the five years since their last meeting. But he remembered the man always affected a seniority beyond his age. He wondered absently why he always imagined the fellow shaved with cold water, a blunt razor, and carbolic soap.

Haileybury inclined his head. 'I think I owe you belated congratulations, Trevose. On your marriage.'

'Oh, thank you.' Graham gave a nervous laugh. He felt it hardly the best time to receive them. 'I hope they are congratulations I can reciprocate?'

But it appeared that wedded bliss had evaded his fellow-surgeon.

Graham sat down. There was a silence. 'You're at the Radcliffe Infirmary, aren't you?'

'Yes. Officially I'm doing orthopaedics. There're no plastic beds, of course. It's very much a little country town hospital. The ancient university, I fear, turns up its distinguished nose at anything more vulgarly useful than Latin and Greek. But I'm managing to apply a good deal I learnt during the war. Thiersch grafts to heal up old osteomyelitis, bone grafts in general, pedicles for burns, or for any sort of tissue-loss after injury. It's really remarkable the number of casualties being caused by motor-cars.'

The warmth they felt for their common subject began to melt the ice. 'I'm doing work on wrist pedicles.' Graham demonstrated, moving his wrist from his stomach to his forehead. 'You raise a pedicle of skin from the abdominal wall, like we did in the old days. You attach it to the wrist till it takes. Then up

114

goes the wrist and you fix the free end to the face, or wherever you want it.'

'What happened to the Saracen?'

'He escaped to France. Beyond that I've heard nothing.'

Haileybury gave his thin smile. 'He's probably making a fortune lifting the faces of these fast-living Frenchwomen.' He fiddled with the brim of his hat, and went on, 'This is all a formality, isn't it, Trevose? The job's booked for you.'

'Of course it isn't.' Graham sounded indignant. 'The committee will pick who they fancy.'

'Oh, come, Trevose! Everyone knows your wife got that newspaper to drum up the money. If you *don't* get it, I can only say it will be a gross miscarriage of justice.'

Graham's irritated denial was scotched by the arrival of the other candidates—two assistants of Gillies and Pomfret Kilner and a sallow, moustached, middle-aged surgeon from Manchester no-one had heard of. Graham folded his arms and stared straight ahead in silence. Life was too short, he told himself, to bother with its Haileyburys. Of course the job was his. He deserved it. Quite simply, because he was the better surgeon. Nobody spoke. The man from Manchester produced a penknife and nervously cleaned his nails. Haileybury blew his nose. The clock on the wall ticked away like a trip-hammer, irritating everyone.

Unhappily for Graham the selection committee's deliberations were more open-minded than they deserved. His life's ambition was in danger of frustration by the caecum. This inoffensive bulge of bowel near the appendix was the venue of a furious new battle between Sir Horace and Mr Cramphorn. Sir Horace fell upon the caecum with his scalpel like a tramp handed a hot dinner. Mr Cramphorn tacked it the firmer into place. The two men were hardly on speaking terms.

'The caecum,' Sir Horace had thundered over his lunch that very morning, 'lying at the extreme blind end of the colon, is a sump, a sewer for every intoxicant in the patient's faeces.'

'Nonsense,' disagreed Mr Cramphorn shortly. 'The caecum

115

is to the colon as a breech-block to a gun. Without a breech-block both won't fire properly.'

'Balderdash,' said Sir Horace.

Meanwhile, patients with such disabilities as headaches and rheumatism had their caecums either totally extracted or embedded like foundation-stones, depending on which morning they happened to present themselves at Blackfriars for a consultation.

Haileybury was surprised after the usual questions to be invited to express views on the caecum. Should it be excised? asked Sir Horace. Or immobilized? demanded Mr Cramphorn. Haileybury said guardedly it depended on the experience of the surgeon. But Graham declared flatly the caecum should be left utterly alone, even delivering something of a lecture on interference with Nature by her surgical handmaidens. His departure was followed by a hostile silence. The half-dozen other doctors round the table were against him already, purely because he had money and influence. It is always sweet on committees to adopt high principles at someone else's expense.

After an hour's wrangling the only choice seemed the man from Manchester, a throat surgeon who had done no plastic surgery at all. Dr Wedderburn, the chairman, wisely adjourned for tea. Graham found himself alone in a teashop round the corner, his cup and sandwich untouched. This was serious. Supposing he was rejected? The job suddenly meant more than ever. He could hardly set up in Harley Street and keep a newly-impoverished Maria from his foothold at St Sebastian's. If they *were* impoverished. But the unthinkable to both himself and Lord Cazalay was with every moment becoming the feasible.

Luckily Dr Wedderburn unveiled after tea his monolithic argument—Trevose was a Blackfriars man. This sobered the committee up. Moreover, his ailing father was a Blackfriars professor, his brother and two uncles had walked their cherished wards. The hospital staff must stick together. Even Mr Cramphorn and Sir Horace agreed. Both had sons and nephews with ambitions along the same lines as Graham. They sent the secretary to summon him from the anteroom, where the clock had become deafening.

Graham reached home elated. In the hall he found a detective and two policemen, looking for Lord Cazalay. Maria was unashamedly in tears. When he tried to comfort her, he might have been a stranger. She never asked about Blackfriars. He suddenly felt disgusted with the whole Cazalay apparatus. What of them anyway? He had made use of them, he had got what he wanted. Now he was his own master, a consultant at Blackfriars, irremovable, irrefutable, irreproachable except in his own eyes. The detective left after furious writing in his notebook and Maria locked herself in the bedroom. Graham took his hat and quit the house.

He hailed a taxi in Southampton Row and gave an address in Pimlico. Brenda was at home, in her short skirts, her shocking nude-looking beige artificial silk stockings, her cigarettes of black tobacco and yellow paper, her holder eighteen inches long. Since Desmond's birth Maria had shut up sexual shop, and Graham had no urge to play the monk. He supposed Brenda was a 'bright young thing', while Maria was increasingly plainly neither. In many ways the girl reminded him of Edith. And Maria? She reminded him of his mother's photograph on the professor's mantelpiece. One day he really must settle down to a serious study of this fellow Freud.

19

THE PROFESSOR HAD come to smell worse than ever.

He had spent his second honeymoon in Brighton, at a hotel away from the sea-front chosen through the modesty in its accommodation, menus, and bills. It was the middle of February and bitterly cold, the sea leaping angrily to drench unseasonable intruders on the promenade. He thought the change would do him good. His wife felt even the provision of two separate piers poor compensation for the midwinter bleakness, which was liable to trigger off her rheumatism. And she was sleeping badly, through her new husband's habit of rising once or twice a night to make noises in the bedside chamber-pot. Mr Fanshaw certainly hadn't submitted her to such interruptions, but she supposed such things were normal in men, of whom he had exclusively provided her virtuous experience.

The professor's disability grew gradually worse. After a year or so he had trouble on cold mornings getting through his lectures, despite a hurried though often ineffective dash to the basement beforehand. Usually a wordy expounder of anatomical mysteries he began boiling down his wisdom, to the relief of both himself and his students. He hesitated submitting himself to professional advice. After all, the process was entirely natural. The book he opened on the subject gave him the philosophical balm of Sir Benjamin Brodie, the nineteenth-century surgeon at St George's—

'When hair becomes grey and thin, when atheromatous deposits invade the arterial walls, when there has formed a white zone about the cornea, at the same time, ordinarily—I dare say invariably—the prostate increases in volume.'

It was inescapable, the professor accepted. Though it was sad. Life was becoming gloomier, and his marriage instead of brightening it with forgotten joys made it even blacker with unremembered pains. It was poor comfort to learn that the affliction worried elderly retrievers just as badly.

His clinical crisis occurred almost six years to the day after Graham's in the bedroom next door. The flow had abruptly stopped and no effort, mental or physical, could restart it. The professor lay with a hot-water bottle clutched hopefully to his bursting abdomen, and Sir Horace Barrow was summoned from a City banquet. He was not surprised. His views on prostatic hypertrophy were summarized less elegantly than Sir Benjamin Brodie's with the dictum, 'By their boots ye shall know them', and for months he had noticed evidence of uriniferous dribbles on the professor's. He even felt relief the enlargement might account for the man's conduct, the unuttered scandal of the hospital. Only a week before the professor had come into Sir Horace's own wards on some anatomical pretext, and the nurse he had called behind a screen to assist his examination complained red-cheeked to the ward sister. The ward sister told her briskly she was imagining things. Such conduct was by definition impossible in a Blackfriars' man.

After the operation the professor fell as totally into the power of his wife as a baby. Catheterization had often to be performed, and he instructed her in the art. She was not a cheerful nurse, having certainly not bargained for this sort of complication to her marital duties. The professor began to remember bitterly the old London surgeon's nightly prayer, 'Lord, when Thou takest me do not take me through my bladder', and became more bad-tempered than ever.

'There's one or two matters we've got to go into,' his wife told him firmly one afternoon. 'The will, and that. After all, you never know, do you?'

The professor thought this in most questionable taste. He knew well enough from Sir Horace's guarded reassurance the cancer might recur, but prying into his private financial affairs on any pretext struck him as indelicate.

'Everything's in order,' he told her crossly. 'In apple-pie order. The relevant documents are safe with my solicitors.'

'That may well be. But I want to know how I stand, don't I? It's only right.'

'You stand very well indeed. Surely you can take my word for it?'

'Well! I don't know, really I don't. What are you keeping everything so secret for? Anyone would think I wasn't your wife but your woman.'

'The details are extremely complicated,' he told her hopefully. 'Only solicitors and such people can understand them.'

'I'm no fool, you know.' She patted the curls ringing the base of her neck. 'Fanshaw told me everything, every single thing. Like a gentleman.'

She dropped the subject, until the next occasion when the professor had to be catheterized. The following morning they went to his solicitor.

'I think it's scandalous!' she declared, once told the details. The estate was to be split three ways between Graham, Robin, and herself. 'What's Graham want the money for? He's rolling in riches. I come first, don't I? I'm your lawful wedded wife.'

The professor's brain was not the sharp organ of anatomical thought it once was. With the failing of his excretory apparatus the level of urea in his blood began to rise, leaving him fuddled, listless, and prone to headaches. He finally changed his bequests, mainly to get peace from her nagging, particularly during the catheterizations. His new will stood unaltered a week after Lord Cazalay's flight filled the newspapers, when the professor died in his brass bedstead, and in a bad temper. A lifetime of economy and shrewd investment had left no less than thirty thousand pounds. Graham and Robin were awarded a thousand apiece, the residue passing to his widow.

She set about the Hampstead house, where she was determined to live in a style compensatory to the victim of a double widowhood. The place was decorated over again, and all the medical books and medical furnishings thrown out for what they could fetch at an auction. She summoned Sibyl back from Southsea. Both mother and daughter agreed that the house during the professor's lifetime, with all those gruesome reminders of mortality scattered about, was enough to give any healthy woman the creeps.

20

IN 1930 GRAHAM'S new unit at Blackfriars was producing the goods with enough confidence to put some in the shop-window. A conference was arranged of plastic and throat surgeons from all over the country, with demonstrations of patients and operations. It was to be the finest moment of Graham's career.

It had taken him six years to find his feet at Blackfriars, which he decided was no better nor worse than any other big hospital. Its specialists gave the London poor the same care as the London rich—often better, any hospital at all outdoing the fashionable West End nursing homes with their small resources and large bills. The patients came mostly from Islington and Shoreditch in their shawls and their corduroys, burdened with their symptoms, their specimens, their strings of children, and often their unseen companions, against which the doctors ostentatiously buttoned themselves up in long white coats. The specialists treated the patients kindly, as Tolstoy's enlightened Dmitrich Levin treated his serfs. But their worlds could only possibly touch at the point of disease, and even this was thought more the doctor's possession than the patient's, few being considered intelligent or refined enough to be let into the secret of their maladies. Neither could the beneficiaries of free care expect the comforts of private patients, Blackfriars adding to the enfeeblement of illness the austerity of a workhouse and the discipline of a barracks. Apart from several hours' sitting on long hard benches in the reek of strong disinfectant before anything happened at all, the patients' inferiority was underlined by bullying porters and brusque sisters, insensitive after years of handling bemused humanity. They accepted it all with the stoicism of everything else in life. When half your street was on the dole, you had to.

The consultants ruled their little empires, rubbing shoulders as uneasily as the states of the prewar Balkans. As Sir Horace had foreseen, a plastic surgeon would be the odd man out, even something of a freak. Graham's self-centredness anyway made him a neutral in hospital politics. Even physically he was isolated in the new Arlott Wing, which had displaced the old hospital bakehouse, obliging its cockroaches and mice to seek alternative accommodation. He was unbothered by students, who saw no reason to waste time on plastic surgery, which was never asked in examinations. He shared a houseman with orthopaedics, but had a full-time registrar, Tom Raleigh, a short, dark, plump young man with tiny hands and feet, his mole-like appearance matched by the blind earnestness with which he followed Graham in everything. There was a sister in charge of the dozen beds, another in the theatre, and a mechanic with a lathe for turning out facial splints and prostheses. Graham did most of the sketching himself, but had called in a commercial photographer.

Graham's private practice was disappointing, most of the cases finding their way to established men like Gillies. This was awkward, because bank-managers shied away as though he were contaminated with the same financial leprosy as his father-in-law, who had disappeared with Lady Cazalay to Venezuela, a well-chosen destination from which it proved impossible to get them back. Graham had first mooted a loan to Dr Whitehead, but that experienced skater on thin ice skilfully cut a few delicate figures before dropping him into very cold water indeed. Then he found that impoverishment, like everything else in human experience apart from virginity, pregnancy, and death, was strictly comparative. True, they exchanged the Great Ormond Street house for a flat in Ladbroke Grove, the one in Cornwall was sold, the Crossley was replaced by a Morris Cowley, and the army of servants was demobilized, but his first impression that they would have to call on the Salvation Army for coal and hot soup proved exaggerated. There was an enormous 'scandal', of course, the tongues of London wagging like ears of wheat in a storm. But under darkening skies the shadow of the Cazalay family no longer fell on him, and he found it on the whole rather stimulating.

Maria herself was badly hurt in the crash. She rarely left the flat at all, except for taking Desmond every afternoon round the streets—Kensington Gardens, where she might cross paths with the nannies of former friends, was forbidden territory. She developed insomnia, and vague aches in the joints and abdomen, disastrous had they come to the attention of Sir Horace or Mr Cramphorn. Graham wisely treated her with small doses of aspirin and larger ones of sympathy. After all, she was now nearing forty-five and such symptoms might be expected.

The plastic surgery conference over which Graham had worked so hard and worried so much was to start on a Monday morning early in September. It was to be different from anything seen before. No-one was to be bored, no-one would miss a point. Graham would stage-manage the show with the panache of C. B. Cochran at the Palace Theatre. It was to be held in the eighteenth-century hall of Blackfriars, a stately apartment brought to life by the sweetest breath of English architecture, pillared, vaulted, and lined with the delicate tones of tight-packed leather-bound books. He arranged photographs and sketches with typed case-histories connected to their relevant points by coloured ribbons, everything as clear and as enjoyable to follow as the cutaway battleships and motor-cars in the *Illustrated London News*. At one end slides of interesting cases were displayed in stereoscopic viewing boxes, like those inviting seaside holidaymakers to share the butler's voyeurism. At the other was a screen for lantern slides and a lectern on the dais, which Graham mounted with some excitement to open the proceedings.

'My first case,' he explained, as the curtains were drawn and the lights lowered, 'is an unfortunate girl whose mammary appendages I can only describe as resembling in size and shape a pair of vegetable marrows.' He indicated with his pointer the lantern slide. 'If her physical discomfort was considerable, her mental discomfort was immeasurable. She was denied the sports for which the "modern girl" we hear so much about in the newspapers regularly half-undresses herself—swimming, tennis, sunbathing, and so on. And, far more sadly, courtship too. Can you imagine even Romeo bringing himself to fondle a Juliet equipped with monstrosities like these? Though admittedly, gentlemen, we must beware of accepting *any* plea for a reduction mammoplasty. A girl's fashions change. So do her young men. She may come back wishing to restore the *status quo*.'

There was a murmur of embarrassed laughter. From the start, Graham's exhibitionism struck a false note. The audience felt it hardly right referring to such things as breasts light-heartedly. After all, theirs was a stripling specialty, badly needing clothing in an outfit of dignity. General surgeons never spoke of the stomach except with the greatest solemnity.

Graham described an operation he had invented himself, the cutting out a wedge of fatty breast tissue like slicing an overripe orange. It was simple, surgically crude, and sometimes a failure, but it was the forerunner of more elaborate manipulations some fifteen years later when the female breast threatened to turn from a decoration to an obsession.

'May I end by impressing upon you, gentlemen,' declared Graham, 'the most important step of the operation occurs in the ward beforehand. It is then the site of the new nipple is measured and marked out with Bonney's blue. It must stand at the apex of a triangle, formed by a perpendicular running through the centre of the clavicle'—he demonstrated on his jacket—'and another line seven-and-a-half inches long, drawn from the suprasternal notch. Symmetry is everything, gentlemen. A lop-sided Venus de Milo would be more amusing than admirable.'

The lights went up. A door concealed in the bookcase opened behind him. His ward sister appeared with a brown-haired girl in a dressing-gown, which she silently slipped from her shoulders

125

with the air of a prospective purchase in an ancient Oriental slave market.

'You see the transformation?' Graham exchanged a smile with his patient. 'I hope you will agree that these neater organs are as today favoured by dress-designers, emperors of the cinema, and other less drastic creators of the female shape than ourselves.'

The patient withdrew. Haileybury rose from his seat at the front.

Graham tightened his jaw. It was their first encounter since his rival had been appointed plastic surgeon to King Alfred's Hospital, an institution equally splendid as Blackfriars across the river. Doubtless he was anxious to make an impression.

'I think we would all congratulate you on an admirable result, Mr Trevose.' Learned heads nodded. 'But might I enquire precisely your indications for performing this type of operation at all?'

'Certainly, Mr Haileybury. You ask my indications. For the physiological enlargement of puberty—never. For a patient under twenty or over fifty—never. For chronic mastitis—I would advise total amputation. For any other healthy woman sufficiently deformed to demand it—always.'

Haileybury folded his large hands in front of him. He was still wearing his blue serge suit. Graham found himself wondering if it were the only one he owned, or if he bought them in job lots. 'Then it is always in your opinion a purely cosmetic procedure?'

Graham was ready for this. 'I think I would be unfair if I suggested you equated "cosmetic" with "trivial". You yourself must agree the mental and social benefits of the operation are tremendous.'

'The knife seems rather a drastic innovation in psychological treatment,' returned Haileybury dryly. 'Freud, Jung, Adler and such gentlemen are hardly renowned for their surgical skill.'

This caused a laugh. Mention of psychologists in gatherings of more practical doctors always had the effect of Mr Leslie

Henson's appearance on the stage. Graham began to feel annoyed. The man seemed set on ruining his effects.

'As for social reasons,' Haileybury persisted, 'might I question the correctness of surgery straying into the province of the beauty-parlour?'

'The benefit of this operation is quite as great as that of gastroenterostomy to kill the pain of duodenal ulcer,' Graham told him shortly.

That was unwise. Gastroenterostomy, the by-passing of a troublesome duodenum, was less of a surgical procedure than a sacred rite. The operation was starting to busy the abdominal surgeons of the thirties, as much as the abdominal surgeons of the forties were busied dismantling it. Dissent broke from the audience. Graham bit his lip, but controlling himself announced, 'Gentlemen, we have hardly begun the day's proceedings. I think we can discuss such general questions more pleasantly over lunch. May I pass to the next case?'

The body of his lecture was less sensational. As he showed them his surgery of burns—a new branch, in which he had become intrigued—of fractures of the jaws, of injuries to the fingers, of Dupuytren's contracture closing up the palm, even Haileybury was denied ammunition for criticism. Finally Graham came to Miss Constantine.

She appeared through the bookcase door, tall, heavily boned, in a short frock, artificial silk stockings, cropped hair, and a hat with an enormous feather.

'Please inspect the patient, gentlemen.'

She posed a minute in silence, then disappeared.

'Perhaps you were struck by Miss Constantine's gait?' Graham suggested. 'She strode into my consulting-room like some huntswoman of the shires, though she had never mounted a horse in her life. I discovered she worked at a famous emporium in Oxford Street, behind the sports goods counter, where her athletic appearance was doubtless thought an asset. Now, gentlemen, I must reveal to you there is a disgraceful amount of flirting behind the scenes in such places. But Miss Constantine was not at all amused. She complained that even the most polished advances of the gentlemen floorwalkers simply embarrassed her. As for accepting their invitations to cinemas or dance-halls, the very idea was repulsive. She became worried, understandably enough. But worse was to follow. She found herself developing a strong romantic attachment to a girl in the millinery department.'

Graham called for a lantern slide.

'Observe, gentlemen, these genitalia. They are at a careless glance feminine, and the nameless practitioner who brought Miss Constantine into the world must have been very careless indeed. Look more carefully. This clitoris is in fact a penis, these *labia majora* an ill-developed scrotum. There are no *labia minora*, no hymen, no vagina.' He rapped for another slide. 'I operated on this deceptive state of affairs. You will see the organs are now undeniably male. I was glad to rectify an error of a somewhat fundamental nature.'

The lights went up. Through the door appeared a smiling, dark-haired youth in a double-breasted grey suit. 'Miss Constantine,' Graham added smugly, 'has become Mr Constantine. A fine figure of a man.'

As the patient left Haileybury was on his feet.

'I fear I cannot share your equanimity at changing a fellow human being's gender.'

'I did *not* change the sex,' Graham told him irritably. The man was a fool, thick-headed and thick-skinned. 'The patient has been male since conception.'

'But she had been brought up as a girl. You talked about the mental aspects of your surgery. I should imagine the psychological effects of the abrupt change highly detrimental.'

Mr McMannus rose beside him. He was short and fat with a squeaky voice, a throat surgeon who hated Graham with an intensity in the profession restricted to close colleagues at the same hospital. He was outraged at Graham's filching the broken noses, cleft palates, and hare-lips he thought his personal property. Worse still, Graham refused to recognize the new doctrine of 'septic foci'. The cause of the headaches and rheumatics had been transferred from lazy guts and errant kidneys to malevolent pockets of pus lurking all round the body, for which Mr Cramphorn rummaged the abdomen like an earnest Customs official and Mr McMannus cracked open sinuses with his hammer and chisel, or extracted teeth like shelling peas, particularly if the patient that morning came in with smelly breath.

'I feel it my duty,' the throat surgeon squeaked, 'to express my distaste at the manner the case was presented.'

'I found nothing in the slightest distasteful,' Graham told him shortly. 'The patient gave her willing consent. *His* willing consent,' he stumbled.

To relieve tension over the exchanges the audience laughed. It made Graham lose his temper.

'I may be somewhat old-fashioned,' continued Mr McMannus, drunk with the heady wine of righteous indignation, 'but I find such theatricality sadly out of place at Blackfriars.'

'If you cannot distinguish knowledge from dullness, then I'm sorry for your students.'

Mr McMannus glared. 'If we are here for an exchange of insults rather than an exchange of views, I withdraw.'

He sat down, to some applause. Graham saw he'd been a fool. 'I apologize,' he said hastily. 'I'm sure, with your great experience in the pathology of the tongue, you will agree that running away with itself is one of that organ's more desperate conditions.'

There was a sympathetic murmur, but the damage was done. Graham's authority was broken. Most of the assembly agreed with McMannus. The lecture was 'flashy', an insult to the austere intelligence of a medical audience. Besides, this young fellow Trevose was already getting himself a bad name for pushfulness. They nodded their heads. At what age was he appointed to Blackfriars? Less than thirty. Disgraceful! They all seemed to remember at once he had been linked with the infamous Saracen.

Graham decided to end the lecture. He left the hall without a word. He went straight to his room in the Arlott Wing, sitting alone in a mood of unbearable gloom. He had worked hard for originality, and the dunderheaded audience were blind to it. He compared himself tragically to Manet presenting the world with *Le Déjeuner sur l'Herbe*. It was all Haileybury's fault. He'd started them off. Graham felt the hospital was unbearable. Tom Raleigh could handle the afternoon demonstrations. He hurried out to his Alvis and drove to Queen Anne Street, where he had taken consulting rooms.

He wondered afterwards how he managed to drive through the London traffic without hitting anyone. He was preoccupied with the sickening realization that a fundamental belief in his life was wrong—the charm, humour, and fairly cynical flattery which had carried him so handsomely right from Maria's drawing-room lecture through countless awkward committees at Blackfriars was not enough. His skill as a surgeon was as genuine as his flair as a lecturer, and both had been sneered upon by a bunch of pompous, self-satisfied, haughty men encased in their own sense of importance like a limb immobilized in plaster of Paris. At least, Graham told himself bitterly, I'm not a hypocrite. I'm pushful, I suppose I'm selfish, I like the limelight, but I make no bones about it. Right! If they're going to look down on me as a flash Harry, an upstart, a moneymaker, I'll live up to their little expectations. I'll make a fortune out of face-lifting, let my burns and repair work go hang, and the lot will die painfully of ingrowing jealousy.

He arrived at his consulting rooms. His desperation for originality had led him to decorate them in Japanese style, so he greeted his patients alarmingly before a painted screen like some medical mikado.

'I didn't expect you,' exclaimed Kitty Rivers. She was a slight, fair girl in a white overall, his secretary. She studied his face and asked, 'What's wrong?'

'Oh, everything's wrong!' He fell into the chair behind his consulting desk. 'The meeting's a flop, a fiasco, even before it's started.'

'But how? You were so confident about everything.'

'I overestimated the intelligence of my audience.'

She put her arm round his shoulder. 'Oh, darling! I'm sorry.'

He took her hand eagerly. This was why he had hurried from the hospital, he supposed, to attract some sympathy. He sat in silence for a moment, then seeing no point in doing things by halves asked, 'Can't we go round to the flat?'

She shrugged her sharp shoulders. 'But, darling . . . I mean, it's broad daylight, with patients buzzing about everywhere. Someone you know might easily see us. Someone from Blackfriars.'

'I don't give a damn who sees us. Not today, anyway.'

As he fell silent again, she added in her meek voice, 'I loathe this hole-and-corner business as much as you do.'

'Now please! Don't start that all over again.'

Kitty bit her lip. She never dared argue with him about anything, from a slip in the appointments book to the relationship which had grown in the little garden of her life to overshadow everything else. 'I wasn't really starting anything *again*.'

'Weren't you? Well, there's no point anyway. You know the situation perfectly well. I'll leave Maria as soon as I can. I've told you dozens of times, haven't I? I'd leave her today if I could. I can't, and that's all there is to it. Surely you don't imagine I *want* to go on living with her?'

'But *can't* you get a divorce?' She looked down at him imploringly. 'It wouldn't hurt your practice. I'm sure it wouldn't, darling. Everyone's getting divorces these days.'

'Oh, it's more complicated than that. Maria's a sick woman. And there's the boy.'

'Of course, I appreciate the difficulties.'

It irritated him when she made herself pathetic—it was the only effective weapon in the pasteboard armoury of her personality. 'We've got to be patient. You can't switch one marriage off and another on, you know, like the electric light.'

She brought herself to put something terrible into words. 'I suppose there isn't anyone else, Graham? I mean apart from Maria?'

'Don't be stupid.'

'You really went to Paris alone?'

Graham lost his temper for the second time. 'Why do you keep on about it? I went to Paris alone to sell some pictures. I didn't. I came back again. Still alone.'

'I just wondered, that's all.'

Her capacity to sound totally crushed enraged him more. 'Well, don't wonder. I don't like people wondering about my activities. Now leave me in peace, for God's sake. I want to think.'

It really was being a most trying morning.

21

GRAHAM HAD TAKEN Jean Dixon to Paris, and it had been a dreadful failure.

Jean was a red-headed, green-eyed cockney, who had been proudly started at art school one year and sadly withdrawn the next, when her father, in the building trade, was crushed into bankruptcy by the depression. She thought herself lucky to find a job with a West End photographer, a young man Graham had once treated for some minor blemish, which led to her appearing at Blackfriars to take pictures of the patients. Graham soon asked her to dinner at the Savoy, and noticed she ate like a horse.

After a few weeks he supposed she was a tart, more or less. She seemed to have plenty of men friends and plenty of presents. He felt a trip to Paris a reasonable *quid pro quo*, for it seemed not only risky but indelicate inviting her to the little flat near his consulting rooms in the engineered absence of the mistress-in-residence. Besides, Paris was romantic, as everyone knew. And he had been overseas only once since his honeymoon, the Cazalay family not being keen on 'abroad'. He had accompanied Maria and her mother to Venice, a dreadful crawl by railway across the roasting face of Europe, with Lady Cazalay devastated by everything from palpitations to the incomprehensibility of ticket-collectors, both of which she expected Graham instantly to rectify. Venice itself had been hot and smelly, his painting things had been lost on the way, and Lady Cazalay's family were exquisitely impolite to him.

133

First he'd had to break the news about Paris to Maria.

'It's a bore going all alone,' he complained, 'but I don't suppose you feel up to the trip.'

'Paris? I must have been hardly a girl when I was last there.' Maria sighed. She was spending another day in bed. Her headaches and pains now conspired with fits of depression to poison her with feelings of inadequacy for life, so she simply retired from it between the sheets. Graham's modestly rising affluence ran to a cook and a maid, who between them looked after Desmond and shuttled him to day-school round the corner. They had moved from Ladbroke Grove to a terrace house in Primrose Hill, a tall, poky place with steep stairs, a narrow hall floored with cracked tiles, and a front-door which borrowed gay patterns from the sun through a panel of gaudy stained glass. He recalled this afterwards as his 'suburban phase', and had even equipped himself with suburban trappings—a dog, a cabinet radiogram, and a lawn mower, which he pushed on one or two occasions.

'I remember the underground railway stations in Paris,' Maria reminisced. 'All curly green ironwork, like some strange sort of plants growing out of the pavements. There was a ball at the British Embassy, and several of the girls fainted. It was a terribly hot night. I suppose we all dressed so unsuitably in those days. I met Clemenceau, a kind-looking old man, nothing tigerish about him at all.'

'Clemenceau—another qualified doctor,' Graham told her. He was wondering if Jean had a passport.

'Was he? Didn't he die last year? These days I can't remember who's alive and who's dead. Where shall you be staying?'

He mentioned a small hotel out at the Porte Maillot—'After all, I'm on my own.' She was shocked he had overlooked the Crillon. He had noticed for some time how the focus of her mind was falling more and more sharply on the past.

Jean Dixon was at first girlishly excited by French sounds and smells, the racing taxis, the musical-comedy policemen, the tables on the pavements, the stuttering advertisements for Dubo ... Dubon ... Dubonnet, the posters of the lugubrious Nicolas man with his fists sprouting dozens of bottles—the sudden, breathtaking, dirty Paris of the Gare du Nord, memorable for ever. The trouble really began with the cockroach in the bidet. The whole hotel frightened her. It was tall, gloomy and airless, with ill-painted shutters, smelling like a museum, its windows apparently incapable of opening without a set of joinery tools. Graham telephoned down about the cockroach, but nobody understood the French he had been painfully learning from the Berlitz booklets. Then he developed gastroenteritis.

It must have been something he had eaten on the boat—he suspected the ham had definitely turned. It necessitated an urgent and colicky search for a *pharmacie* stocking the only trustworthy remedy known to British travellers, the intestinal equivalent of Keating's Powder, the famous Dr Collis Browne's Chlorodyne. The shop produced only the mockery of a bottle of Eno's Fruit Salts, until Graham finally found it stocked by a smart chemist's in the Rue du Faubourg St Honoré, rather as the smart bars in the neighbourhood stocked Scotch whisky. He swallowed the opiate mixture with glasses of neat brandy, feeling the alcohol might sterilize the interior of his gut, or at least make him appear more cheerful. But it was a sadly unromantic disability.

Still, Jean tackled the Louvre with the same youthful enthusiasm as she tackled the *marrons glacés*, and they both agreed the Mona Lisa was ridiculously overrated. His excuse for being in Paris at all was selling a few of his paintings, but art-dealers on the banks of the Seine seemed as insensitive to his talents as their counterparts beside the Thames. One blunt fellow, an Englishman Graham met long ago in the sanatorium, even described his work as 'distinctly amateurish'. He was hurt. He was as proud of his canvases as of his operations, which could hardly be shown off to impress his friends.

The essential part of the excursion was even more devastating. On the first occasion he threw himself at young Jean so eagerly he suffered *ejaculatio praecox*, which was quite a social embarrassment, as he really knew her only very slightly. On the next he had taken either too much cognac or too much chlorodyne, for the opposite occurred. He had never suffered before the dreaded students' condition of 'whisky prick'. He lay wondering if he were already too old for such adventures. He pictured his endocrine glands, the cherry-like pituitary below the brain, the bilobed thyroid embracing the windpipe, the neat adrenals capping his kidneys, the twin plums of the testes themselves— was the whole constellation cooling down from blazing suns to sterile planets? But he was only thirty-five, dammit! he consoled himself. And it always seemed to work with Kitty Rivers.

Most depressing of all, he met the Saracen. Graham never discovered how the surgeon knew he was in Paris. He simply appeared at the hotel, his fat cheeks sagging, his clothes untidy, his cigar replaced by pungent Gitanes. The three of them went to a café and drank Pernod, the American seeming to accept the redhead as too natural to require comment. It appeared the French were no more eager than the British to recognize his qualifications and he had given up surgery for finance, for which he felt an equal flair, until the Wall Street crash had put an end to that career as well.

'I guess you'd call me a retired man.' He opened and closed his pudgy fist. 'Though I still feel the itch to use the knife, almost every day. Maybe they'll let me give them a hand at the American Hospital at Neuilly, if I ask nicely enough. I've something left to offer humanity, even now.' He stared at the milky liquid in his glass. 'But I've been misunderstood too often to care much any more.'

He cheered up as they explored with rose-tinted lamps the caverns of the past, remarking in a low voice only as they broke up, 'And Maria?'

'She's in rather poor health these days, I'm afraid.'

'I'm sorry. Please convey my regards. It was too bad about her father.' He paused. 'The lady must think herself very fortunate, having married a gentleman with a profession.'

'That man!' said Graham bitterly, undressing for bed. 'He has brains, skill, imagination—the same imagination that brought Morton to use ether or Harvey to discover the circulation of the blood. And what happened to him? He was beaten.

136

By snobbishness, small-mindedness, envy, greed, and arrogance. Instead of enriching the stream of human happiness, his talents were deliberately thrown out like dirty water. My God! They might as well have chopped Rembrandt's arms off.'

Jean was lying naked on the bed, eating Swiss liqueur chocolates and reading the *Continental Daily Mail*. She made no reply. She never understood half that Graham said to her. Of course, as she told her friends, he was terribly brainy, by which they understood she meant he was terribly dull. She often wondered if he behaved as oddly with his wife.

22

'I'M IN A mess,' Graham told John Bickley.

The anaesthetist looked up from the menu. 'Oh, there you are. I was just going to order. I thought you'd been trapped by that jamboree of yours at Blackfriars.'

Graham smoothed the black tie against the points of his dress-collar. 'The governors are giving a reception, but I got away on some excuse or other.' It was the evening of the first disastrous day of the plastic surgery conference, but after his rebuff of the morning Graham was already losing interest in the cherished project. 'It's good of you to come along at a couple of minutes' notice, old man. I simply had to talk to someone.'

John put another Abdulla in his cigarette-holder. 'What about?'

'Women.'

'Oh, dear.'

'It's serious.'

'In that case, you need a drink first. The sidecars they make here are excellent.'

They were in a small, underground, smoke-filled restaurant in Soho, as yet 'undiscovered', but where, John explained, on a clear day you could often see as far as Tallulah Bankhead. He was doing pretty well. Since the war anaesthetists had transformed themselves from seedy practitioners creeping in their surgeons' shadows, a bottle of chloroform in one tail pocket of their coat and a scrap of lint in the other, frequenters of coroners' courts and merchants of death rather than passing oblivion. With the growing complexity of both surgery and their own apparatus they were becoming respectable specialists entitled to ten per cent of the operation fee, which allowed John Bickley to lead a life of bachelor ease with a Green Label Bentley, chambers rather than rooms, and even a manservant. As he administered most of Graham's anaesthetics they had become close friends. They saw too much of each other's mistakes to be otherwise.

After the cocktails they ordered the six-shilling dinner. They had decided to be extravagant.

'Do you know about Kitty Rivers?' asked Graham, coming to the point. 'I never confessed I'd installed her in a flat near my rooms, round the corner in Marylebone High Street.'

'I'd be the only qualified man in London who didn't know about it.'

Graham shrugged his shoulders. He always hoped his misdeeds would be somehow overlooked by the world, like his father.

'Well, it was better than her own place, over a sweet-shop in Shepherd's Bush. You could only get upstairs through the shop, which was always full of the most horrible-looking and extremely inquisitive children, buying humbugs.'

John summoned the wine waiter.

'Do you know, Kitty was my secretary for an entire year before anything in the slightest shaming happened,' Graham went on. 'I remember selecting her for that fair, well-scrubbed look. I thought it would lend an appropriately hygienic air to the waiting-room.' He tipped a glass of sherry into his turtle soup. 'She also struck me as having an amenable, undominating personality. That's her strongest weapon. She keeps imploring me pathetically to kick out Maria and marry herself.'

John Bickley smiled. 'There's a tendency for this complication to set in, Doctor.'

'But how can I?' exclaimed Graham. 'Apart from anything else, it would play hell with my practice. Far too many people know Maria's more or less bedridden. You can't keep these things quiet. Though I try. I'm rather ashamed of Maria, I

139

think. What do you imagine our nose-in-the-air brethren would say if I abandoned her? And I can't afford to drop a guinea. I'm living beyond my income as it is. I got used to having money, before the Cazalay business. It's always been damn difficult doing without it.'

John nodded. Anaesthetists, who serve many masters, are the profession's gossipmongers like Shakespeare's servants. He had a fine sense of the monetary value of scandal.

'Besides, there's Desmond,' Graham added, as an afterthought. He swallowed his glassful of burgundy in three gulps. 'I've a clear conscience over Kitty, mind you. I deserve some fun. You can't live without love, can you? No more than you can cook without salt. God knows, I don't get much of a ration of it at home.' As the waiter refilled his glass he promptly emptied it. John's idea about a drink was a good one. 'That's how it all started, you know—Kitty being beautifully sympathetic to me about Maria's disabilities. Peculiar.'

'How long's Kitty been going on about marriage?'

'Oh, months. Why do people keep talking so airily about divorce these days? It's the cinema, I suppose. They aren't easy, not at all. I went to a solicitor once, just to keep her quiet. Maria would have to divorce *me*. And she doesn't even know of Kitty's existence. Just imagine how I'd introduce *that* topic into the conversation.'

'And are you in love with Kitty?'

Graham shrugged his shoulders. 'I don't know. I don't know if I'm in love with Maria, either. I've never known if I've been in love with anyone. Perhaps I've an inborn immunity to the condition, as some people have for tuberculosis. I can't give love, and, what's worse, I can't receive it. That's what makes me so cold and callous in the eyes of a lot of people. Perhaps I'm a bit schizophrenic—emotional blunting, you know the thing. Anyway, it's all come to a head. I took a girl I met in a photographer's studio over to Paris. I suppose Kitty's found out. It's terribly worrying. Yes, I suppose I must love Kitty. I wouldn't care otherwise, surely?'

John laughed. 'Really, Graham! Look yourself in the face.

One woman's much the same as another to you, isn't she? As long as she's got a vagina in working order, you're happy.'

'Perhaps so. We're a terribly randy family.' He sounded self-pitying, as if describing some sad congenital affliction. At least, he told himself, he had insight into his faults. He couldn't help what Nature had made of him. If only people would *understand*. 'But what's the odds? I've got to stay and look after Maria. Though she doesn't want a solicitous husband. Rather a solicitous doctor. Do you know why I picked Maria in the first place? It wasn't the money, or the kudos, or all that. I wanted a mother-substitute.'

'Oh, steady! Let's keep Freud out of it. You've enough on your hands as it is.'

'But it's true,' Graham told him seriously. 'Now she's my poor sick mother, I'm giving her all due devotion and running after girls my own age. How can I sort the mess out? I've my brother and his wife coming home on leave this month, too. That's another story I won't go into,' he ended despondently.

'We must do a lot more drinking. Then the answer will come to us,' John decided cheerfully. 'Brandy's a wonderful cerebral stimulant.'

After the meal and the brandy he suggested to Graham, 'Would you like to go on to a bottle party?'

'What's that?'

'They're all the thing just now. People can't afford to give parties because of the depression. You bring your own bottle and in you go.'

'All right. I'm game.'

The bottle party was in a top-floor room in Pont Street, with sloping ceilings and cuboid furniture. As most of the men and girls were wearing pyjamas it was apparently a pyjama party as well, which Graham supposed too was all the thing. He also supposed he was rather drunk. He had no idea who the hostess was, nor any of the guests either. He found himself on a divan covered with a leopard-skin rug, talking to a pyjamaed girl wearing not only the newly fashionable long, pink-painted finger-nails but—he observed with intense fascination—painted toenails as well. She asked him what he did for a living, and he said he was a bank manager.

There was a gramophone on the divan, which he wound up to play Bobbie Howes and Binnie Hale singing 'Spread a Little Happiness'. Everyone was making too much noise to notice. He took the record off, and somehow broke it in two. The girl with the toenails giggled and handed him another. He joined in the vocal himself, shouting very loudly and tunelessly, 'I lift up my finger and I say, "Tweet tweet, shush shush, now now, come come!" ' As he tried to change the needle he was surprised to find the manœuvre beyond him, spilling the little tin of bright metal spicules all over the floor. He began to feel terribly ill. He never drank much, but they had bought a bottle of whisky and another of Gimlet, and they felt they might as well enjoy their entrance-fee.

He lay back on the leopard-skin with his eyes shut. When the girl with the toenails asked if he was all right he felt disinclined to reply. Somebody got John Bickley, who like all anaesthetists —possibly through daily contact with gusts of powerful narcotics—had an inhuman resistance to alcohol. John got him down the stairs. Graham insisted he wanted to go to a night club. John found a taxi and took him instead to his own front door, where Graham remembered to ask, 'What about Kitty? What do we do about Kitty?'

'Give her a nice diamond bracelet and tell her to go to hell.'

'And what about Jean?' Graham asked soulfully. 'I can't leave little Jean.'

'Little girls who work in photographers' studios aren't lonely for long.'

Graham burst into tears.

The next he knew it was the morning. He woke aware of three unfortunate facts.

He was lying on the bed in his own room wearing his dress-clothes and patent-leather shoes. He remembered being sick on the stairs. And the maid was declaiming a Mr Haileybury wished to see him in the hall. He groaned.

'I'm sorry I'm not shaved,' Graham greeted Haileybury

bad-temperedly, appearing in a dressing-gown after hastily splashing his face with cold water from the washing-jug. 'I don't usually expect visitors at this hour.'

Haileybury was standing holding his grey trilby, in a trench-coat wet about the shoulders. From somewhere inside he silently drew a copy of the *Daily Press*.

'I get this newspaper myself, you know,' said Graham shortly. He took the copy, noticing on the front page,

WOMAN INTO MAN
LONDON DOCTOR'S FEAT

'Then possibly you have already enjoyed reading the middle pages?'

Graham ripped open the paper. There were two photographs, one of Miss Constantine holding a bouquet of flowers, another of Mr Constantine holding a golf club. The columns of type in between seemed to cover her confusing past, her eventful present, and her hopeful future as a husband and father.

'You must forgive me for thinking such self-advertisement quite disgraceful, Trevose. Though I don't think I shall be the only one.'

'My God, man! Surely you don't suppose I had any inkling the rubbish was to appear? The newspapers are always getting their hands on these titillating little stories. They paid Constantine handsomely, I have no doubt.'

'Your name is mentioned.'

'What of it? *I* can't help it. The *Press* must have thought it of public interest.'

'I should be more inclined to believe you were you not a close friend of the paper's proprietor.'

This was too much, especially on such a morning. Graham's head hurt terribly. 'If you want to call me a liar, please do it in as many words, then leave me in peace, for God's sake.'

'A liar is not something I would lightly call any man. It just strikes me as an unhappy coincidence that you should owe your position at Blackfriars to Arlott.'

'You've got the wrong end of the stick. Quite the wrong end. Barrow and the others insisted from the start that Arlott renounced any right to interfere with the unit or the appointment of its staff. *Or* to use it for any sort of advertising. There's a document to that effect. If you still think I'm lying, I'll have the governors' clerk bring it to you by lunchtime.'

Haileybury said nothing. Then his humourless smile appeared. 'That won't be necessary. I only wish I had known of this document's existence when we faced the appointment committee together. It would have given me more heart.' He turned towards the front door. 'I shall not be attending the conference any further, Trevose. I did not wish my absence to go unexplained. I will bid you good morning.'

What a fool the man is! Graham told himself, hurrying upstairs to shave. What a priggish, sanctimonious ass! But a dangerous fool, always lurking to do a mischief. He must himself that very morning write to the medical journals, plainly disclaiming foreknowledge of the article in the *Daily Press* and seeking protection for the profession from such abhorred publicity. Val Arlott had strongly advised such a course when they had discussed the case of Miss Constantine together the week before.

23

ON THE THIRD Sunday morning of September Robin's family
arrived at Primrose Hill via Tilbury and Fenchurch Street
Station, with the same white-stencilled tin trunks strapped to
the roof of the cab. Robin had assumed as a matter of course
Graham would be putting them up.

Robin hadn't taken home leave until 1930 because he
couldn't afford it. Their spell on the mission station had been
five years of ill-paid boredom, broken only by the schoolmaster's bungalow burning down one night and the talkative
missionary's spectacularly falling silent for ever in the middle
of one of his sermons. They decided to settle in Singapore but
somehow it hadn't worked, then Robin took a job in Kuala
Lumpur as medical officer to a Scottish engineering company
with a thrifty view of salaries. These adventures he had painstakingly spelt out in many-paged monthly letters to his brother,
some of which Graham had read all the way through. But now
the time had come to install his son Alec in an English boarding-
school, the child having already defied the principles of contemporary paediatrics by showing a young white skin in the
tropics at all—particularly as the poor little boy had turned
out so depressingly delicate.

Edith left the cab first. She wore a plain blue cotton dress,
her skin was as brown as boot polish, the hair under her
tight-fitting hat was bleached by the sun as savagely as any
London girl's by hydrogen peroxide. Like many English-
women in the tropics she had grown thin to the point of

scrawniness, but Robin lumbered out behind her as fat as the Saracen, pale-faced and puffing, his hair grey, his gait shuffling, his suit as though he had slept in it all the voyage, his voice so husky Graham wondered with alarm that his brother might have succumbed to the tropical hazard of drink. Though few words passed between them, all three were overcome by the meeting more than they liked to show. As for the circumstances of their parting, Robin and Edith seemed to have buried them in forgetfulness with the equanimity of a pair of municipal gravediggers.

'Here's Alec,' announced Edith proudly. 'Alec, darling, this really *is* your uncle Graham.'

Graham became aware of a pasty, large-headed, spindly-legged boy of nine, looking at him in terror. He felt the lad hardly looked strong enough to survive an outing to the Zoo, let alone the rigours of English residential education.

'I expect you've noticed a lot of difference in London,' said Graham, leading them into the house.

'Haven't had much chance to look,' mumbled Robin.

'Yes, the buses have got tops on,' Edith declared brightly.

Robin stopped to appraise the hall. Graham seemed to be doing quite well.

'It was a pity about father.'

Graham needed to remind himself the professor had died after Robin's departure. He had reached the age when memory starts to shuffle the years. 'Yes, it was sad.'

'The sordid details—the will, and that? They stood, I suppose? One can't do anything now?'

Graham shook his head.

'What's she like?' Robin asked. 'The woman?'

'Well . . . perhaps you'd better go up to Hampstead and see. After all, I suppose we've a perfect right to call on our stepmother.'

'And how's your wife?' smiled Edith. 'We're dying to meet her.'

'Maria will be down by and by,' said Graham.

Maria didn't appear until immediately before lunch.

146

'I must apologize for not greeting you,' she began stiffly, coming downstairs in a black dress. 'But I have been rather poorly. I hope you will be comfortable with us.'

The newcomers were shocked. They had suspected Graham sold his manhood for a mess of pottage—which was anyway soon dashed from his lips—but they imagined him married to the smart, active woman who, they remembered from the papers, strode through postwar society. Certainly not to the thin, bent, greying invalid shaking hands so unsmilingly. It had taken all Maria's old courage to force herself down that Sunday morning. She had become terrified of strangers. But she felt she owed it to Graham—his brother must not fancy anything amiss. After all her husband deserved it. He was very good to her.

'I'm sure we'll be comfy,' Edith said quickly. 'Ever so.'

'I have so long admired you from my husband's description,' Maria told Robin. 'One seldom meets an Empire-builder these days. Well! We are to have a family lunch. That will be very pleasant. Two generations at the same table. Graham—it's cooler than I expected.'

Graham fetched a shawl and draped her shoulders. Maria led them into the small green-papered dining-room, almost filled with an oval table, the relic of more spacious days. 'I'm afraid you have come back to a sad country,' she went on, taking her seat. 'We have two million unemployed, we shall be abandoning the gold standard at any moment, and we have a government of red revolutionaries.' She rang a little hand-bell and added to Edith, 'You must be hungry after your long journey,' as though they had accomplished it by open boat.

Robin noticed Graham busy at the sideboard, half-filling one graduated medicine glass with red liquid and another with green, placing two white pills on a spoon laid neatly across a tumbler of water. Maria swallowed the medicaments, apparently unaware of Alec's fascinated gaze. He thought she might be some sort of witch.

'I take it you're doing pretty handsomely?' Robin eyed his

brother's establishment more critically. 'Well, we should have plenty to talk about.'

'Oh, I stored up thousands and thousands of grains of gossip,' smiled Graham, starting to carve the joint with the calm authority of any less distracted suburban paterfamilias. He had thoughtfully ordered roast beef and Yorkshire pudding, the edible counterpart of the white cliffs of Dover. 'But it's a peculiar thing, now you're actually here I seem to have mislaid the cache. Tell us about Malaya instead.'

'Didn't you keep my letters?'

'Should I?'

Robin looked annoyed. 'They might have made an interesting book.'

'Not too much meat for Alec,' Edith interrupted hastily. 'He has such a small appetite.'

'*I* haven't got a small appetite,' growled Desmond. He had been sizing up his little cousin across the table with the intense suspicion of one small boy for another.

'I myself eat nothing, nothing,' muttered Maria, who like all chronic invalids could not imagine her symptoms less interesting to her hearers than to herself. 'It is all something to do with my low blood-pressure, so Graham says.'

Graham thought she was conducting herself rather well.

'I've one piece of news,' he added casually. 'I'm going overseas myself next week. To Egypt.'

Robin looked up. 'Oh?' He felt he had a proprietorial interest in the world beyond the Mediterranean.

'I'm flying,' Graham went on more sensationally. 'In the new airship. Do you know Val Arlott—the man who owns the *Daily Press*? He fixed it for me at short notice. It seems he persuaded the powers-that-be a doctor aboard would be a good thing. For the first leg of the flight, anyway. The rest are going on to India. Cairo takes only thirty-six hours, you know. *Thirty-six hours.* Imagine that!'

Edith gasped. 'Graham! Do you suppose it's quite safe?'

He grinned. 'You can hardly expect me to funk a comfortable ride in a sky-borne hotel when Amy Johnson went all the

148

way to Australia in a tiny little aeroplane by herself. Besides, the Air Minister's coming with us. I can't imagine a better guarantee of safety.'

'It can do over sixty miles an hour, and there're five power-cars,' Desmond interrupted eagerly. Since the news of his father's adventure he had become an expert on airships. 'If it crashes, they press a button and cut open all the fuel tanks with special knives. I saw it at the air pageant over Hendon,' he continued proudly in Alec's direction. 'It's as long as the *Mauretania*.'

'I sailed in the *Mauretania* once,' observed Maria, more to herself. 'When my father took me to America before the war. It was all very gay, but of course everyone made a fuss of us in those days.' She shivered. 'Graham, the window's open.'

The conversation was then stopped by Alec's going white in the face and fighting for breath.

'Oh dear! It's one of his attacks,' said Edith apologetically.

'Bronchial asthma,' explained Robin.

Graham looked alarmed. Like all surgeons his knowledge of pure medicine had atrophied like a disused limb, but he recalled the disease came from spasm of the tiniest tubes in the lung under the influence of something baneful, in either the air or the psychology, which had so far evaded the wisdom of the doctors. Only the week before a young girl had died at Blackfriars in *status asthmaticus*, despite oxygen, camphor injections, and two professors.

'Do you want some adrenalin?' he asked anxiously, though from the calmness of Alec's parents to the attack the poor child seemed to come under fire pretty frequently. 'I've some in my bag, for mixing with locals.'

'A tablet of ephedrine will have him right.' Robin took from his breast pocket a grubby envelope, handing the wheezing boy a small white tablet with the air of distributing sweets. Without a word or even a sip of water, Alec dutifully swallowed it. Desmond looked fascinated. He hadn't witnessed such excitement since the maid fell in the kitchen underneath a scalding kettle.

'An asthmatic attack is always more frightening for the onlookers,' Robin pointed out.

'How unfortunate to be ill at his age,' said Graham sympathetically. It suddenly struck him how sturdy young Desmond resembled Robin, and puny little Alec himself. His head buzzed with figures in a fundamental calculation. No, it was quite impossible, he and Edith couldn't have managed it even had they been a pair of elephants. Oh well, he told himself, heredity is as full of surprises as any other game performed in the dark, and if the human race is so earnest about its reproduction Nature must get a laugh from the antics now and then. Maria, who had taken no notice of the disturbance, rang her handbell for the maid and said, 'Illness is unfortunate at any age.' Robin then started on tropical medicine, though sticking to the clinical side. It seemed to Graham that since the days in Hampstead his brother and God had somehow fallen out.

After lunch, Maria retired immediately to bed and Desmond insisted that Alec and Robin admire his model railway, displayed in full complexity in a back room recently upgraded from his nursery to his 'den'. Graham took Edith into his small study beside the front door. It was almost the first time they had been alone together since the afternoon the professor's bed-knob fell off.

'All those books!' exclaimed Edith. 'Just like the old house at Hampstead.'

'In which I should, by rights, now be living.' Graham smiled. 'In which *you* should, by rights, now be living. With me.'

'Yes, I might have.' She seemed not put out by this reminder. 'It was a rum do, wasn't it? I mean about your father marrying that woman. I'd never have thought it, not of the professor. He was always so learned.'

'In my job you come to expect anything of anybody. Even your own father.'

'Whatever happened to the professor's book?' Her face lit up. 'All about . . . oh, what was it? Something funny to do with bones.'

'It came out! Didn't he send you a copy? Perhaps he thought it would be rather extravagant, with the overseas postage. Do you know, in the eyes of a lot of people I'm only the son of the greatest authority in the world on synovial membranes?' He paused. 'It's very touching.'

'Go on, Graham—you're standing well enough on your own feet. I said you'd be a success, didn't I?'

'But I'm not a success. Not yet. It's still a struggle. There's an awful lot of prejudice against plastic surgery. There's an awful lot of prejudice against *me*. I'm ambitious, I suppose, which is thought most ungentlemanly in our bigoted and back-scratching profession. Not that it worries me. Only my dear colleagues. Are you happy with Robin?' he asked abruptly.

'Oh, yes,' she told him cheerfully. 'We're happy together, all three of us. It's lovely really. I never thought I'd deserve it, back in the old days.'

'But is he all right?' Graham added with concern. His brother's leaden complexion had been as much of a warning in his eyes as a leaden sky in a sailor's. 'Physically, I mean. He's changed terribly.'

'Yes, he's been rather poorly,' Edith admitted. 'Headaches, and that. He tries to keep it from me.'

'Any vomiting?'

She looked surprised at the question. 'Now and then. In the mornings, when he gets up. How did you guess?'

Graham frowned. 'What's his blood-pressure doing?'

'I don't know.' She suddenly sounded helpless. 'He's fainted once or twice, and we had the other doctor in. But he's an Irishman who drinks a lot. I don't think he's much good.'

'He really ought to see someone in London. Wedderburn's gone, of course, but there're plenty of bright new sparks about. And you ought to think pretty carefully before going back out East.'

'He wants to go back all right.' She smiled again. 'He's already fussing about the journey—you know Robin. His life's there.' She turned to stare out of the window at the small, dusty London garden. 'He's always trying to . . . well, debase

151

himself. It's funny. When we left the mission station he wanted to work in a leper colony. I told him he was daft. That partnership he had with the doctors in Singapore—it didn't come to anything, because he said he didn't like making money out of ill people. Mind, there was a row as well, over the terms of the agreement. I don't know what, but they were all very angry. It's a pity. We could have had a nice house in Singapore, near Farrer Park up on the hill with the nobs. After twenty years we could have come back to England for ever, living like lords. In 1944—it isn't all that far away. But he's happier in Kuala Lumpur, though it's rough. Perhaps it's because he feels more important.'

'He always put the practice of his profession before its rewards,' Graham told her charitably. 'Unlike me, I suppose.'

'Then there's other things.'

'Oh?'

Edith still stared through the window. 'Funny things he does sometimes. With the natives. I've found him kissing their feet, and that. He always seems to like treating their sores, the nastier the better. Once something happened when . . .' She swallowed. 'Well, he was all naked and tied up. I shut my eyes to it.' She turned towards Graham and smiled once more. 'It's peculiar, isn't it? I've never breathed a word of this to a soul before.'

Graham wondered how to comment on this arresting spectacle. 'I think we're realizing these days that the sexual urge, like other blessings, comes in some strange disguises.'

'I expect it does. Well, Graham—if I *hadn't* married him you'd have left me on the shelf, wouldn't you?'

'Nonsense!' he said stoutly. Emboldened by her confidences, he tried to kiss her. He was startled at her force pushing him away.

'Don't be daft,' she said.

The phrase was her fire-extinguisher on the blazing insanities of the world.

24

ROBIN BRUSHED ASIDE questions on his health, seeming more concerned in fussing over Graham's preparations for his adventure in the air. Graham had already been vaccinated at Blackfriars against smallpox (which went septic) and inoculated against typhoid fever (which he felt as unpleasant as having the disease), but Robin insisted he also buy a spirit stove to boil every mouthful of water as protection against the deadly *vibrio* of cholera. Robin spent his most enjoyable afternoon for months in the Army and Navy Stores fitting his brother with tropical kit, while delivering a running lecture on the perils of the direct sun falling upon the head, of mosquitoes, of bedbugs, and the rapid sapping of even an Englishman's moral fibre in tropical climes. He counselled a *sola topi*, ample supplies of quinine, a small Bible, and that powerful agent of British colonialism, Keating's Powder.

The airship herself was seven hundred and seventy feet long, at once the queen of the air and the nursling of British engineering. She had rows of double-bunked passenger cabins, reassuringly lit through artificial nautical portholes. Her saloon provided not only hot meals for sixty, but hot music through the wireless loudspeaker. She had a promenade deck with a ship's rail and deck-chairs for enjoying the view. The lounge was the size of a tennis-court, decorated as tastefully as any transatlantic liner's with little pots of ferns and palms. The furniture was lightweight wicker, to be rearranged in the evenings for dancing.

The airship was to flash past Paris, Tours, Toulouse, and Narbonne, skirting the Pyrenees (the Alps were considered inadvisable), to Ismailia on the Suez Canal, where a mooring mast had been built for her like a desert-bound Eiffel Tower. There was to be a ceremonial dinner while attached to it, with the High Commissioner of Egypt taken aboard—though no fuel, the stench of diesel oil being thought too nauseating for high official nostrils. Then she was off to Karachi in India, awaited by another Eiffel Tower and the R.A.F. with gas cylinders, the whole journey finished in an incredible seventy-two hours. The passengers for this maiden flight were restricted to a distinguished six, whom Graham would treat presumably for sickness, nervousness, or other unknown hazards of the air.

Graham was to disembark at Ismailia, a convenient P. and O. was leaving Port Said for Genoa, then he would take train and Channel steamer home. He would be away from Blackfriars a bare month. He was looking forward to the trip excitedly, having discovered in himself a taste for travel. Besides, it would give him a breathing-space with Kitty Rivers. And it was always rather pleasant for a while to get away from Maria.

Graham's coming absence had brought a flurry of work at Blackfriars and St Sebastian's, but he found time to give Robin and Edith a treat or two. He took them to *Bitter Sweet* at His Majesty's, and even Robin, whose puritanical views of the stage saved him the expense and effort of theatre-going, admitted this man Noël Coward had a deal of charm with a scene or a tune. Graham even made an impulsive offer, immediately regretted, to drive them to Alec's school at the seaside resort of Birchington-on-Sea, on the tip of Kent not far from the sanatorium where he was sent to end his days. He supposed he'd made the suggestion through pride in both his new Alvis and his skill as a motorist, though it was an enormous distance—almost eighty miles. Robin and Edith would be returning later by train for the thrill of seeing him leave for Egypt, staying meanwhile with Edith's mother in Ramsgate. The butcher himself had some time before gone the way of all flesh, edible or otherwise.

154

Little Alec's school had been chosen through its connection with Robin's old missionary society and its modest scale of fees, but above all for its air. The air circulating round the Isle of Thanet, Robin declared, had no equal in the whole therapeutic armamentarium for a chesty child. Graham hoped so. Alec had thrown an attack of asthma regularly twice a night, which was extremely noisy in the house and becoming a shade boring. Graham wondered if they were caused by the dust or by the emotional effect of Desmond, who awarded his cousin sly punches and kicks whenever he had half a chance without detection.

They were to leave for Birchington early on September the twenty-fifth, which was a Thursday. The weather had turned so bad Graham telephoned the Air Ministry to see if the airship's flight the following week might be postponed. An official tetchily assured him only the most tempestuous skies could delay such a monster, and anyway the Air Minister must be home in London to make a gloriously prompt entrance at the Imperial Conference in mid-October. Besides, it was a matter of British prestige getting her off on time, and British prestige, with Gandhi and the depression, was having a thin time of it. They set off for Kent, Alec as pale as his new wooden iron-bound tuck-box. Graham feared the child might be sick continually on the way, and he was.

That afternoon Graham's housemaid, still in her brown morning uniform, was asleep in the kitchen, when the front-door bell jangled in the rack above her. Desmond was at school, her mistress as usual upstairs in bed, and they expected no visitors. Rubbing her eyes and smoothing her apron, she clicked across the tiles of the hall and found outside a slight, fair-haired young woman in a plain brown coat and small round black hat, which had, in fact, been bought specially for the occasion.

'Could I see Mrs Trevose, please?'

'Which Mrs Trevose?' asked the maid, half-asleep. 'There's two living here, madam.'

'Mrs Maria Trevose.'

'Is she expecting you?'

'No. I don't suppose she's even heard of me. But I must see her at once. It's vitally important.'

The maid looked alarmed. Such announcements, though commonplace on the talkies, were rarely uttered by human tongue. 'Not an accident?' she gasped, alive to the untrustworthiness of such contraptions as motor-cars.

'No, it's nothing like that. But I *must* see her. Please.'

Maria faced her visitor sitting up in bed, a shawl round her shoulders, a book from Boot's library on her bed-rest, her medicine bottles and pills neatly at her elbow. She carefully inserted a leather bookmark, closed the page, indicated a chintz-covered upright chair, and apologized. 'You must forgive me for receiving you in my bedroom. My poor health I hope is excuse enough. Do please sit down. I'm afraid I didn't catch your name properly. That silly girl was almost incoherent. Reliable servants are unfortunately things of the past.'

'It's Miss Kitty Rivers. I'm your husband's secretary.'

'Strange,' mused Maria. 'He has often spoken about his secretary, but I can't recall his once mentioning your name. Well?' She lay back on her pillows, as though already weary of the interview. 'What have you to tell me?'

For a girl of such meekness as Kitty Rivers the confrontation had been almost unthinkable. But when desperation failed her revenge urged her on. Now she wondered what to say. Words came only because there lies in every woman an actress, waiting in the wings for the cue which comes too rarely in the humdrum performance of life. 'I am your husband's mistress,' she declared startlingly.

Maria said nothing. She stared at her visitor with dark eyes, as though some remark had been made about the weather.

'I've been living with him. He got me a flat near his consulting room, in Marylebone High Street. He used to come round, often. It's been going on almost two years now.' As Maria still looked blank she said more nervously, 'Don't you understand? We were lovers. We were *intimate*,' she added, falling back on the more comfortable sexless language of the newspapers.

Maria continued to stare.

'It's true!' Kitty insisted. 'I swear it. I thought I loved him, you see.'

'I don't believe you,' said Maria.

'But why should I make it up? Why on earth? I could prove it, if you like. I could tell you all sorts of things about Graham. Yes, I could. Some things I don't expect you know yourself. You've *got* to believe me.'

Maria still stared. 'I don't believe you.'

'I'm sorry.' Kitty began to sound miserable. 'I didn't really want to hurt you. But it is true—every word.'

'You're a liar, Miss Rivers.'

'I'm not!' she exclaimed. 'For two whole years—'

'I have been expecting your visit, Miss Rivers.' Maria slowly smoothed the sheet with her thin hand. 'It would be you, or somebody else. I know my husband is an attractive man. There must be any number of young girls at his work or among his patients likely to lose their heads over him. Since my health started to fail I have prepared myself for one to come out of spite and jealousy to poison my mind against him. You don't know my husband, Miss Rivers. You don't know him at all. You could never have spoken about him in such a manner if you did. He is devoted to me. Devoted! And I to him. How do you imagine he could bring himself to give me such tenderness, such sympathy, and such love, if he were diverting his affections to another woman?'

'But, Mrs Trevose!' Kitty jumped up. 'I ask God as my witness, *it's true!*'

'I don't see any necessity for calling the Almighty to your rescue,' said Maria shortly. 'I must ask you to leave me. I tire very easily these days. You will find the maid to show you out.'

'You *horrible* woman!' Kitty started to cry. The staircase, the stairs, the hall, the maid—who had dutifully changed into her afternoon black frock—were a blur. Graham was an utterly damnable man. For two years he had used her body, regularly, twice a week, on Tuesday and Thursday afternoon, after private consultations. Now he had not only humiliated her over some girl in Paris. He had denied her the gratification of infuriating his wife.

As Maria heard the front door slam downstairs she reached calmly for her novel. She removed the bookmark and stared at the page. She was still staring at it four hours later when the maid, worried at no summons from her bell, came to draw the curtains and switch on the light against the gathering dusk.

It was eleven that night before Graham reached home. It had been a trying drive, particularly in the dark. He noticed a light under Maria's door at the back of the house—unusual, because she always took her hypnotic mixture of chloral at ten. He found her sitting up in her shawl, with her book.

'Oh, Graham, dear! I'm so glad. It was getting terribly late and I was worrying. You had a safe journey?'

He smiled. 'Haven't you taken your medicine?'

'I stayed awake because I have some news for you. About Miss Rivers.'

Graham felt as though his stomach had turned to ice.

'I'm afraid you will have to find yourself another secretary, my dear. Miss Rivers has tendered her resignation. Or so I take it. She came here specifically this afternoon to blacken your character.'

'Oh?' Graham's trembling hand reached for the bottle of colourless sedative medicine. It seemed a good idea getting Maria off to sleep as soon as possible. 'What did she say, for God's sake?'

'She was accusing you of making advances to her. It was a very silly attempt. I wouldn't bother repeating all she said, even if I could remember it. I was alone in the house with Bridget, and half-asleep anyway. It was too ridiculous even to be embarrassing. I know you too well, my darling.' She smiled at him. 'And she is, after all, only a working woman.'

'But it's unbelievable!' Graham hastily covered his moral nakedness with a fiery cloak of indignation. 'I just can't understand it. I suppose it's because I've been meaning to sack her—she's got terribly inefficient lately. Always making mistakes of one sort or another. A stupid girl, really.'

158

Maria swallowed her dose. She turned up her mouth to be kissed. He could taste the sickly chloral hydrate on her lips. 'Graham, you really know very little about women.'

He escaped. He paced up and down his own room. He wanted to dash to Marylebone High Street at once, but even with Maria drugged leaving the house was too risky. Early the next morning he made straight for Queen Anne Street, to find the trivial belongings Kitty kept on her desk in the hall—a flower vase, a travelling clock, a photograph—were ominously absent. In his Japanese consulting room one of the desk-drawers was half-open and the contents of all of them awry. She had been having a good rummage round before leaving. He went to Marylebone High Street to find the flat deserted, her clothes gone. He stood in the tiny bedroom, cursing. Where did her family come from? Norfolk or somewhere. She'd probably bolted back there. But there wasn't time to start chasing her now. He had an operating list at Blackfriars in half an hour. He drove to the hospital, thanking God Maria hadn't taken the little bitch seriously. The dulling of her senses with the years had a few advantages.

Graham's last week in London was too full of worries at Blackfriars and complications over his journey for him to suffer as Kitty intended. She didn't even send him a letter. He thought of trying to trace her, even of employing a detective agency, but decided against it. It might leak out among his colleagues at the hospital. Then he began to tell himself it was perhaps all for the best. Now he could hold his head up, behave decently in future, act as a good husband, father, and Blackfriars consultant. As for the girl in the photographer's, John Bickley was right—she didn't merit a second thought. He was well rid of both. His life henceforward was to be virtuously uncomplicated. The long-standing anxiety of deception had evaporated overnight. The feeling was quite exhilarating. Though he had to admit he rather missed Kitty, particularly on Tuesday and Thursday afternoon.

Saturday arrived. The airship was at last to leave. Graham was going to Bedford by train with Robin, Edith, and Desmond, where an official car would be waiting. He was to rise from the airfield at six in the evening, and the weather that morning was horrible. It had turned bitterly cold and the wind ripped the trees half-naked in the sedate avenues of Primrose Hill. At breakfast-time Graham rang the *Daily Press* to be told everything proceeded smoothly, with Mr Arlott already in Bedfordshire to observe the departure on behalf of his readers and the nation. Graham had hardly hooked up the earpiece when the bell rang again. It was Tom Raleigh from Blackfriars. One of his cases was badly infected, and perhaps he should look in before leaving.

Graham hastily arranged to meet the others at St Pancras Station, and hurried upstairs to say farewell to Maria. It suddenly struck him how old she looked. How old *was* she? he asked himself. Mid-forties. Good God! That morning she seemed at least sixty. Perhaps it was the greyness of the light.

'I'm off now,' he told her cheerfully. 'I've got to call into Blackfriars.' She looked alarmed at the unexpectedly sudden parting. 'Don't worry, darling, such are the miracles of the modern world I'll be back in a month. Robin will look after your medicines and things, he promised that. He's a very good doctor, you know.'

As Graham kissed her, she said, 'Perhaps your absence will be relieved by another visit from some hysterical woman?'

Graham gave a laugh. Even to him it sounded as hollow as Mr MacDonald's promises of prosperity just round the corner.

At the door he heard a cry. He found her staring after him, her hand at her throat. 'Desmond—you're not taking Desmond? Not on the airship?'

'No, of course I'm not.' He was desperately impatient to get to Blackfriars. 'Why on earth do you ask?'

'Oh, I don't know. I get so confused sometimes. I didn't think it was this morning you went at all.'

He came back and stroked her cheek. 'You mustn't worry about yourself,' he said as tenderly as he did a dozen times a day to his patients, and as automatically. He sometimes worried that his feelings for his fellow-humans, like his work on them,

160

went no deeper than the skin. 'Desmond will be right here, with Robin and Edith. You won't be alone.'

She clasped his hand. 'Without you I am always alone.'

Holding his bag with his *sola topi* tied to the handle, Graham hurried into the blustery cold, wearing the lightweight suit Robin advised for the autumn sun of Egypt. The airship, Graham had been repeatedly assured, enjoyed even central heating.

The patient at Blackfriars was a twenty-year-old girl who had neatly amputated her thumb with a guillotine machine in a cardboard-box factory. Graham had made her a new one, on the same principle as the Saracen made his corporal another nose. He had first chipped away a strip from the crest of her hip, leaving it still attached to the main bone and sticking out like a little pyramid under the skin of her groin. A few weeks later, he brought down her injured hand and stitched it to the lump. Later still, once the chip of bone was newly nourished by the arteries of the girl's arm, he freed it from her hip completely. 'It may not look very elegant,' he told Tom Raleigh at the time, 'but at least she's got a grasp—it's something to pick up a knife and fork or a bar of soap, to feed and wash herself in a civilized manner. You can use the rest of your fingers for wearing rings, but your thumb's essential. It's what keeps us ahead of the animals, isn't it?'

Tom Raleigh had objected mildly, 'Some of the new artificial limbs are very good, sir.'

'I will not have my patients going about with hooks like pantomime sailors,' Graham told him curtly.

But something had gone wrong. As Tom Raleigh gently removed the dressings from the girl's hand that morning Graham saw too clearly the classical tetrad of Celsus, *calor, rubor, tumor, dolor*—heat, redness, swelling, and pain, the danger signals of inflammation. The girl was shivering. A new four-hourly temperature chart had been started, an ominous sign in itself, recording a hundred and three. Graham carefully raised her arm. Two long red fingers of infection were reaching past her elbow for the lymph-glands in her armpit.

161

'When did this all begin?' he asked Tom Raleigh quietly.

'Sister noticed the temperature was up last night, sir.'

'When was it normal? Where's the ordinary ward chart?' Graham saw from this a sudden and violent infection had taken hold. 'You'd better get a swab across to the lab.'

'I did last night, sir.'

Tom Raleigh handed over a pink slip of paper, the bacteriologist's report. The girl's attacker was, as Graham suspected, a virulent streptococcus. Such cases were common enough among pathologists, slaughtermen, and others whose occupations drew their fingers into unhealthy nooks and crannies. Too often a gruesome leap-frog ensued, the surgeon amputating the hand with infection already on its way to the elbow, then a second amputation at the shoulder was performed too late to prevent generalized blood-poisoning which snuffed out the flames of fever for good. If only, Graham thought bitterly, we had some chemical, something like Ehrlich's arsenicals against the spirochaete of syphilis, some other 'magic bullet' to kill the everyday bacteria marauding as dangerously as tigers all round us. He returned his attention to the patient. 'My dear, you are very ill.' He stroked her burning cheek. 'You have an infection in your hand which can spread up your arm and reach your heart. You understand? We are going to make you better—and quickly, too. Though I am afraid you are going to lose your arm.'

The girl stared at him. Graham knew nobody could grasp the significance of his sentence at once. He moved away from the bedside. 'I'll send Sister to speak to you.'

'Wouldn't incision and drainage be adequate, sir?' asked Tom, as they walked down the ward.

'Either I amputate today with the chance of saving her life, or someone amputates tomorrow and she's dead on Monday. Tell the theatre to prepare for a forequarter. You'd better call Cramphorn if you're worried about her afterwards. I've got to leave London on the afternoon train whatever happens.'

'Yes, sir.'

'And I want her isolated, or we'll have the whole ward

infected. How did she get it in the first place?' he demanded brusquely. 'I'm careful enough about asepsis in the theatre. Are you?'

Tom said nothing. His chief's temper seemed to be worsening these days. He sometimes threw instruments in the theatre, blamed the nurses for blunt knives and broken stitches, and himself for everything else from the unit's mortality-rate to the patients' food arriving cold. He was becoming a shade tired of it. 'We'll have to get her parents' permission, sir,' he remembered, 'she's under twenty-one.'

'Damn her parents,' said Graham.

He wished Tom didn't sound so bloody meek. He reminded him of Kitty. Perhaps that was why he had chosen both of them.

25

THE OPERATION WAS barely completed when the telephone rang in the tiny surgeons' room behind the theatre. Graham impatiently laid aside the board on which he was finishing his notes. It was Robin.

'Graham? You've got to come home. At once.'

'That's out of the question. I've just done an emergency forequarter, and the patient isn't even back in the ward.'

'It's Maria.'

His tone was enough. An idea which for years had been dissolved almost invisibly in the fluid of Graham's mind abruptly precipitated in spiky crystals.

'What is it?' he asked nervously.

'I can't tell you on the phone. It's a matter of life and death.'

'Do what you can. Don't call in anyone else,' Graham ordered hastily. 'I'll be there straight away.'

He left the patient in the care of Tom Raleigh, grabbed his bag with his *sola topi*, and took another taxi back to Primrose Hill. The house was in confusion. Edith was trying to quieten Desmond, who was insisting loudly on seeing his mummy. The maid in the brown dress was crying hysterically. The dog was barking. The cook was sitting in the hall staring straight ahead of her, and from the kitchen came an alarmingly strong smell of burning. Only Robin seemed as stolid as usual.

'Is she dead?' asked Graham at once.

'No, she's still got a fair pulse.' The two brothers started upstairs. 'Her breathing's shallow, but there's no cyanosis.'

164

Maria was lying on her back, snoring loudly. Graham saw Robin was wrong, she was tinged with blue. On the bedside table, beside a glass in which her teeth had been left with customary precision, were two empty medicine bottles. Graham had prescribed a double supply to cover his absence, and as he was giving a small nightly dose of fifteen grains of chloral hydrate in solution he calculated that she must now have some fifteen doses inside her—two hundred and twenty-five grains, enough to be fatal.

'How on earth did she swallow it?' he asked distractedly. 'They usually vomit on half as much.'

He tugged up her chin, easing her noisy breathing by drawing her flaccid tongue from the back of her throat. He felt her pulse and raised her eyelid. The pupil was not widely dilated, which was hopeful. He touched the eyeball with his finger-tip, but the lid failed to flicker in response.

'When did she do it?'

Robin shrugged his shoulders. 'I don't know. She gave orders not to be disturbed and we thought she was just upset at your going. Then Edith came in about something or other.'

Graham grabbed his wife. He tipped her head and shoulders over the edge of the bed and rammed his fingers into her throat. Nothing happened.

'I thought of an emetic—mustard, or something.' Robin sounded plaintive. 'But she was already unconscious—'

'Damn it! If only I had some apomorphine to inject! That would bring it up.'

'Hadn't we better get her to Blackfriars?'

'No, no, not Blackfriars! I don't want her seen there. We'll take her to the Sloane.' He replaced Maria on the bed, tugging away the pillows so she lay flat. 'Saturday's John Bickley's day at the Sloane—he'll know how to handle this. If it isn't too late for anyone to handle it.'

'I'll ring up for an ambulance.'

'No ambulance,' Graham insisted. 'I don't want ambulances outside the house. People talk. We'll take her in the car. Tell Edith to get Desmond out of the way.'

165

They carried Maria downstairs wrapped in a blanket, her mouth sagging open, her head lolling on her shoulder, one naked foot sticking out of the bundle. Graham dumped her in the back of the Alvis with Robin. John Bickley had been warned by telephone and was waiting in the downstairs casualty room. He laid Maria on the leather-covered couch and tipped one end until her head touched the floor. He pumped oxygen into her from his anaesthetic machine, squeezing a bag like a red rubber football bladder. Then he ran a thick tube down her gullet and into her stomach, washing it through with salt solution. Graham had lost Robin, who decided to stay in the corridor either through delicacy or because he found with a pair of nurses the little room was most uncomfortably crowded.

'I'll give an injection of strychnine.' John Bickley drew up the dose in a syringe. 'With luck it'll get her breathing going. I only wish I'd one of those new German analeptics. They'd wake the dead.'

Graham muttered, 'What are her chances?'

'Oh, we'll pull your wife through.' John had an anaesthetist's professional optimism. 'But it's a pretty awful penalty for such a simple mistake.'

'Mistake?'

'Yes. The mistake of dosing herself from the wrong bottle.'

Graham looked at him silently. Both saw how the lie could be established if they lied to each other. 'Yes, a most unfortunate mistake,' he said.

Maria groaned and moved her head.

'You really must read her a lecture on studying the labels, you know,' said John. 'Like we give the nurses.'

Graham sat on a short wooden bench, suddenly exhausted. His heart glowed towards the anaesthetist. Maria's essay in self-destruction must somehow be kept quiet. It was disgraceful, a reflection on himself. No-one must suspect at Blackfriars. As she moved an arm John Bickley shifted her to a less drastic slope, reached for a sphygmomanometer, bound on the cuff, and listened with a stethoscope at her elbow.

'The diastolic pressure's not too bad,' he announced, 'which

166

shows we're getting on. Though she's having a few extrasystoles.'

Graham looked round as the door of the casualty room opened. To his consternation Mr Cramphorn appeared, with pepper-and-salt suit, half-moon glasses, brown boots, and puffing pipe. Damn! Graham thought. He had overlooked Saturday was Cramphorn's day at the Sloane as well.

'Halloa! Trevose, what's this? Your wife, isn't it? Not serious, I hope?'

'Yes, it's Maria. She took an overdose of chloral hydrate. By mistake.'

'I say, I'm sorry. That's bad luck. I hope she makes a speedy recovery. Anything I can do? I fancy she's in good hands. Please accept my sympathy.'

Graham cursed. The man could see perfectly well what was up. On Monday all Blackfriars would know of the suicide attempt—if they got away with merely an attempt. The valley of the shadow of death from which John had rescued Maria led only to further shades, of heart-failure, bronchopneumonia, or delayed collapse. If there was the publicity of an inquest . . .

'I think we can put her to bed,' said John Bickley.

The two nurses laid Maria on a trolley, moving her upstairs to a private ward. Outside the casualty room Robin was still waiting. 'You know, it's very late,' he told Graham. 'The train for Bedford's left already.'

'I'm not going.'

'But surely you don't want to miss the trip? Not after all the preparations?' Robin sounded cross. His valuable advice about Graham's kit and health might all be wasted. 'She'll be all right now, won't she? Edith and I can stay here to keep an eye on things. We can get a car to take you to the airship. You'll still be in good time.'

'It's out of the question. Completely out of the question. I've got to stay with her. Get on to Val Arlott—he's at Cardington, waiting for me. Tell him my wife's seriously ill. He'll have to make my excuses to Sir Sefton Brancker and the rest.'

'Oh, very well, I suppose it's up to you,' Robin agreed

morosely. 'Though it's going to be no end of a job getting through to this Cardington place. Where on earth can I find the telephone number?'

They put Maria to bed with her feet still tipped up, to prevent her own secretions filling her lungs and drowning her. They laid a row of rubber hot-water bottles down each flank like sucking pigs and left Graham alone with her. The day grew prematurely dark and rain started dashing against the window. Nurses came and went, but he hardly noticed them. He smoked cigarettes until his packet ran out. He sat staring across the small room at his wife, white-faced and with her mouth open, illuminated by the dim light of a bedside lamp.

The moment seemed to have arrived when he really ought to decide if he loved her or not. She was admittedly hardly a decorative consort at the best of times. He often thanked God her withdrawal from the world saved him the trouble of hiding her from his friends. But his work was leaving him progressively disillusioned over the value of beauty. How many wives had come to him with wrinkles, baggy eyelids, or misshapen noses for the magical transformation of their marriages with a wave of his scalpel? And how often did surgery on the wife have the slightest effect on the husband? Not once that he knew. Well, only once, he reflected. The operation was such a success the woman went off with another man, leaving the husband furious and threatening litigation.

He took a sheet of blank paper from Maria's folder of notes. He wrote at the top, 'History of Present Condition'. Underneath he put, 'Ten years ago, I married Maria through a combination of impulsiveness, ambition, self-flattery, disappointment, and lack of maternal influence during formative years. Plus need for regular sexual outlet, of course.' He suddenly wondered what had happened to Brenda of the foot-long cigarette-holder. He seemed to have lost her somehow during the General Strike. 'A few hours ago, I was overwhelmed at the tragic possibility of my wife's death. Compare: her labour, in 1921.' He paused, and added, 'Or at my own responsibility for both?' He screwed up the paper and stuffed it in his pocket. It

168

really was a difficult diagnosis. 'Why aren't I a nicer person?' he asked himself. 'My God, why aren't I a nicer person?'

It was a frequent plea, and the inner voice always sounded most pathetic.

Some time during the night Maria regained consciousness.

'Graham . . . !' She held out her hand.

He went over to her. 'My darling . . . you're all right.'

Without moving her head from the pillowless bed she looked round the white cubicle. 'What happened? Where am I?'

'You're in hospital. You've been ill. You're getting better.'

'Oh, I remember . . .' She gave a faint smile. 'I was silly, wasn't I?' It reminded him of the afternoon she fainted in Half Moon Street. 'You hurt my pride, Graham.'

He nodded guiltily. Somewhere in the doped blood circulating in her prematurely wizened body lingered the spirit of the old Maria Cazalay.

'How did they find me? I thought you were already gone on the airship? I've been confused lately.'

'Edith discovered you. I was still at Blackfriars.' He held her hand tighter. 'I promise there'll be no more of this—no other women. I was foolish, selfish, heartless. It'll never happen again. Never!'

'Graham, don't leave me—don't leave me alone. Not in the hands of strangers. Everyone's a stranger to me now. Except you.'

'I won't leave you. I'll never leave you.'

The flicker of a smile lit her white face again. 'You were always so considerate to me. Even on our honeymoon.'

She relapsed shortly afterwards into normal sleep. Graham sat beside her, taking her pulse every half-hour. At six in the morning it occurred to him he had eaten nothing since breakfast the previous day. Maria was out of danger. He could go home. It was still dark, a terrible morning, cold and wet. There were no taxis, and he'd told Robin to take the Alvis. He turned up his jacket collar and walked north from Oxford Street in the rain, as he had walked years before from Maria's house in Half Moon Street. He felt equally gloomy, and what was worse, shameful. From now on, he decided solemnly, he was to be Maria's alone. He would turn for satisfaction to his work, give more time to patients like the factory girl he had been obliged to mutilate less than a day ago. He would be Maria's lawful wedded husband, in sickness and in health. Well, she always got her way in the end, somehow or other.

The house in Primrose Hill was dark, the newspapers sprawled on the front step next to the milk. Graham absently gathered them, feeling for his key. On top was the *Sunday Times*, with its unexciting front page of advertisements. Underneath, as their usual *Daily Press* ran no Sunday edition, lay the *Sunday Express*. The headline caught his eye.

R 101 DISASTER: 45 DEAD

His hand started to shake. He read down the column.

AIRSHIP CRASHES IN FLAMES
FAMOUS AIR ACES PERISH
Lord Thomson and Sir S. Brancker Dead
ONLY EIGHT SAVED: 45 TRAPPED IN AN INFERNO

He found Edith in the kitchen, in her dressing-gown boiling a kettle. Seeing his expression she gasped, 'Maria!' but he told her quickly, 'Maria's all right,' and laid the newspaper silently on the table. Edith read it, her eyes growing wider. 'Oh, Graham!' She threw her arms round him, hugging and kissing him. 'Oh, Graham! You're alive, you're alive!'

'I'm very much alive! Thank God I didn't go.'

'Oh, Graham, darling Graham!' Edith started to cry. 'I don't know what I'd do, in a world without you in it somewhere. Honest, I don't. I always think of you, wherever I am, however far away.'

He took her head gently in his hands. The shock of his reprieve was starting to wear off. 'Why, you're still in love with me,' he accused her smilingly.

'Oh! Don't be daft,' Edith told him faintly. She blew her nose. The news was too much for her vocabulary. They just stared at each other in silence. 'I expect you could do with a cup of tea?' she said.

She was as practical as ever.

During the day, as the telephone woke him with enquiries and even condolences, a strange feeling came over Graham of living through it all before. Suddenly he remembered. It was the *Inviolable*, all over again. He wondered wryly if his luck could turn as handsomely twice.

On the Monday the *Daily Press*, piqued by young Arthur Christiansen's scoop in the *Express*, ran a front-page story of Graham's escape. He later learned with amusement that even Haileybury had seemed quite sorry to learn of his supposed incineration in a wood outside Beauvais. The *Daily Press* continued its discreet puffs in the sails of his career, speeding him on his course. He was amazed at the effect of Miss Constantine's story in its pages. Patients who had never heard of him, or even of plastic surgery, besieged his door in Queen Anne Street with all manner of structural complaints. His notion of revenging himself on his sneerers with the terrible weapon of their own jealousy became a reality. Miss Constantine was the hinge to the lid which opened suddenly on the riches of his career.

Maria left the Sloane after a week. The girl Graham had operated on in Blackfriars died the same day from streptococcal septicaemia. She suffered one of the bitterest human misfortunes, contracting a fatal disease while its fangs were already being drawn by a man in a white coat busy among his testtubes, unknown in a foreign land. It was five years before the bacteria-killing properties of a red dye called prontosil were described in a German medical journal, inaugurating as some compensation for the age of Hitler the age of antibiotics.

After all the fuss Graham intended to give up the Marylebone High Street flat, but decided at the last moment against it. The rent was modest, and you never knew.

26

ALEC TREVOSE REFLECTED afterwards that his school on the Kent coast was arranged architecturally like the ocean liners of the time, steaming thrustfully across the Atlantic after the profitable Blue Riband. It was divided strictly into three classes. The headmaster with his scrawny wife and pair of small daughters went First, in the manor house of Kentish ragstone which looked so well on the cover of the prospectus and emitted sadistic whiffs of savoury cooking. The masters were Tourist, in a brick lodge converted from servants' quarters and stables, which smelt of cheap tobacco and linseed oil or dubbin according to the cricketing or football season. The hundred and fifty-odd boys went steerage. Behind the manor house spread a wake of remarkable buildings, all different, their only common factor being economy in construction. The predominant materials were asbestos boarding, corrugated-iron roofing, concrete flooring, reluctant and pungent plumbing, broken windows, and dim electric bulbs. Throughout the year they always smelt the same, of freshly-sharpened pencils, spilt ink, sweaty shirts, and urine.

Still, the famous air was there. It was provided liberally, whistling across the North Sea unhindered from Scandinavia all winter, through the ill-fitting doors, window-panes and floorboards, chilling the boys' raw and scarred bare knees, piercing their bedclothes, and freezing over the washing-jugs in the dormitories. It all took Alec's mind off his asthma, if it didn't improve it.

The headmaster, known for some forgotten but undoubtedly entertaining accident with his trousers as 'Old Flybuttons', was a pinched, gloomy fellow with dark clothes and a wing collar, a frustrated—or, Alec wondered afterwards, unfrocked?—clergyman, wearing a mixed expression of piety and dyspepsia. He appeared in the school mainly to supervise prayers and to teach divinity, though regrettably not holiness. But he seemed a jovial enough man underneath. Even the solemnity of Alec's deposit there by his parents was broken by Old Flybuttons' short and unexpected bursts of laughter like nutmeg on a grater.

'Of course, he's very highly strung,' Edith explained, after Robin had given the bronchial case-history.

Alec wondered again what 'highly strung' meant. He imagined himself as a wooden marionette, the sort you found in your Christmas stocking, which you suddenly jerked rigid by a thick string running through its head. In maturity, he felt this self-assessment of his nature fairly correct.

'Highly strung, eh?' said Old Flybuttons gloomily. 'I expect the good air and regular life will do him the world of good. Eh? Ha, ha! It's done wonders for more delicate boys. Eh? Eh? What? Ha, ha, ha!'

Old Flybuttons was always laughing. Sometimes the noise rang from his own quarters through the silenced dormitories after nightfall. At others it burst from him while elucidating obscure Biblical points on the blackboard, or announcing the next hymn from his *Ancient and Modern*. As all the boys could imitate it sometimes it ran like hysteria round an unsupervised classroom, everyone crowing like startled cockatoos until suppressed by the arrival of a master and desperate punishment. Alec felt it all livened the place up.

In his second week at the school Alec stole a carrot.

The appetizing qualities of the famous air failed to affect him, largely through the school food, though adequate, not always being edible. It was mostly carbohydrate in the form of bread brushed with margarine, potatoes roasted in their jackets and occasionally much of their soil, rice pudding as a matter of course, and dried butter beans providing an unexpected dash of protein with a dead maggot or two. There was the treat of fish on Fridays, and a boiled egg on Sunday morning before church, though if a boy got a bad one it was just his luck, for they were never provided with spares.

Alec noticed the sturdy red shoulders of a row of carrots in the headmaster's garden on his way to football. He was alone. He uprooted one, wiped it on his jersey, and ate it. Nothing ever tasted so wonderful to him again.

As he cunningly replaced the feathery top he was observed by the headmaster's scrawny wife washing her hair in the bathroom. After tea he found himself summoned to the study. It was his first entry to the manor house since the day of his arrival. With its pretty flint-walled garden, which Robin and Edith agreed provided the correct English background to Alec's maturing, it was as inaccessible to the boys as Buckingham Palace.

'Trevose, you stole a carrot.' Old Flybuttons swivelled his chair from his roll-topped desk the better to eye the sinner. Even without the headmaster in it Alec felt the study an intimidating enough place, full of forbidding shelves of religious books and photographs of disagreeable-looking religious gentlemen. This brilliant detection left him speechless. 'Eh? What?' asked Flybuttons. 'Ha, ha!'

Alec joined the merriment with a timid smile.

'What's funny about it, young man? Are you making mock of me? You broke the eighth commandment,' the headmaster declared, raising the offence from a matter of mere carrots. 'Get over the arm of that chair. Ha, ha, ha, ha, ha!'

From a corner cupboard, of whose terrible contents Alec had been advised with relish by his schoolfellows, Old Flybuttons selected a stout bamboo cane and beat him six times. That evening Alec discovered the headmaster's laugh was a nervous affliction striking him in moments of tension, like stammering. It was his first disillusionment with human nature.

The establishment had long ago abandoned trying to convince the outside world it resembled a public school and, possibly aware of being as doomed to extinction as Dotheboys Hall, was wearying of trying to convince itself. The masters changed often and in mysterious circumstances, the big boys bullied the smaller boys, and the smaller boys dismembered live blue-bottles. Alec suffered immediately from the bullying, through innocence about those terror-striking gatherings of the whole school after some untraceable offence like carving the desks or silently passing flatus during prayers, when 'owning up' was demanded, in default of which justice would be spread impartially over everybody. Failing to see why all should lose a half-holiday through a few rude words on the wall, Alec piped up the name of the culprit. He discovered painfully 'sneaking' was a hideous crime, even worse than 'swotting', and like all under-sized people having to be quick on the uptake he avoided both for the rest of his life.

Of the two elderly masters who stood rocklike amid the ebb and flow of staff, one was badly addicted to beer, which was never overlooked by the heartlessly keen perception of small boys when it showed in his breath or behaviour. The other was badly addicted to washing the smaller boys on their weekly bath-night with the school's rough yellow soap, all over. Alec's asthma brought him into continual contact with the school matron, who was also the school cook, and some relative of the headmaster's wife. She was thought by the boys incredibly ancient, though he reflected afterwards the poor woman could hardly have been past thirty. He also reflected on the terrible frustrations and neuroses which must have raged within her. She dosed Alec with his cough mixture in her room behind the kitchen which always smelt of hot ironing, often keeping him for a chat, sitting untidily in her chair and fascinating him with glimpses of thick worsted stockings and now and then even green bloomers and hefty pink suspenders. She once asked laughingly if he thought she had nice legs, and rewarded his confusion with a pat on the cheek and a toffee. He had a mysterious attraction for women right from the start.

The school had its sex-scandals, though as Old Flybuttons' daughters grew with adolescence into objects of ridicule

175

rather than distant desire these were of a homosexual or auto-sexual nature. Discovery led to a ceremonial beating, presided over by the headmaster before the highly appreciative eyes of the whole school. As the years passed these became Flybuttons' only appearances, along with prayers on Sunday night. He had a taste for hymns penned by Victorian divines dwelling heavily on Those Who Have Gone Before, Little Mounds in the Church-yard, and similar reminders of the extreme unreliability of the human frame and medical science. He gave long sermons on sin, which seemed to cover everything, and was an enthusiastic prayer for people, not only such standing targets as the leaders of Church and State, but boys incapacitated with quite minor ailments whom he brought undeservedly to the attention of the Almighty. An epidemic would put him in such a good mood he might even distribute afterwards from a tin of chocolate biscuits. With all this religion and caning, Alec supposed the place formed his character as well as anywhere else.

He occupied the most underprivileged social class in the school, of boys left 'in sole charge', their parents having sailed away in P. and O.s to rule, police, or defend the British Empire. Even the holidays were spent at school—poor compensation for letters with excitingly coloured stamps. Either through pro-longed lack of contact with their kin or prolonged over-contact with each other these boys became the awkward squad, stealing freely and using quite horrible language, though one boy usually brightened things up with some highly diverting fits. To keep them out of mischief, Old Flybuttons held classes three mornings a week, right through the summer. When Alec finally qualified in medicine he told himself that he might not have had a particularly good education, but he had had an awful lot of it.

Alec was lucky in escaping occasionally to his grandmother in Ramsgate, or to his uncle the barrister's clerk, who with in-creasing prosperity had moved two stops down the Southern Railway to a jerry-built villa in the even more bosky-sounding suburb of Elmstead Woods. The barrister's clerk didn't care for Alec much. There was some financial arrangement with Robin over his upkeep, and like all Robin's financial arrangements it was on the mean side. Now and then he had a few days with his uncle Graham, spells of long-awaited and unbelievable luxury, though his cousin Desmond still punched him. But at least he was spared the pressing anxieties of the world in the early thirties. Of Hitler, Mussolini, or even Don Bradman he was privileged to know little, Old Flybuttons refusing his boys newspapers on the grounds that everything they reported was sinful. In this Alec afterwards agreed he was probably right.

One summer day in 1933 Old Flybuttons summoned Alec to his study.

'Er, Trevose—' He gave a short laugh. 'Trevose, I have some news for you.'

He laughed again. Alec decided at least it couldn't be a beating.

'Trevose—ha, ha! I have some news of an extremely serious nature. Bad news, in fact. Ha, ha, ha! Eh? Eh? What? Trevose, your father has died. Ha, ha, ha, ha, ha, ha!'

27

GRAHAM WAS STARTLED by his brother's death, however half-expected. The two men had never enjoyed anything in common—if they excluded Edith—but Robin dead like Robin alive preached a moral lesson. Graham realized that time was no longer grains of sand under youthful flying feet, but rather dangerous grains of gunpowder to be used in blasting your path and liable to blow up in your face any minute. He got the news by telegram in a cottage he had bought to replace the Marylebone flat, overlooking the sea at Swanage in Dorset, which gave him the excuse to get away at week-ends and paint.

He was there with a girl called Jeannine, who embodied his first adventure since Maria's attempted suicide. The shame of that, or anyway the fright, had condemned him to three years' chastity. His relationship with Jeannine was admirably workmanlike. He never saw her from one week-end to the other, each Monday morning giving her the means to 'buy something nice', an arrangement which struck her as perfectly genteel through the transactions being completed by cheque rather than hard cash. And now, Graham told himself, as they drove back to London with the depressing telegram in his pocket, Edith would be coming home as an attractive widow of thirty-three. She had already been his fiancée, his mistress, and his sister-in-law, and this further relationship filled him with some disquiet.

She appeared early in 1934 from Elmstead Woods with young Alec, the sunburn above her black dress grotesque in the

London weather. Graham was then earning and spending a good deal of money. He had a new Bentley, and had moved from the leafy avenues of Primrose Hill to a house in fashionable Queen Street, Mayfair. He had a cook, two maids, a house-keeper, and a pointedly ugly governess for Desmond, who had grown as tall as himself and in a year was leaving for a public school of enormous expense, antiquity, and incomprehensible traditions.

'Yes, it was ever so sudden,' said Edith. They were taking tea in Graham's upstairs drawing-room, Alec in his best grey flannel suit and highly-polished black boots, which he was idly kicking against the expensive furniture. 'He'd been having these headaches, but I don't think he ever let on how bad they were, not really. Then one evening he had the stroke. And that was that.'

She folded her hands in her lap. She had the same expression she wore beside the grate that stormy afternoon in Hampstead.

'I should have stopped him going out East again,' Graham reproached himself.

'It wasn't for you to tell him, Graham. Besides, you had worries enough yourself at the time, didn't you? Maria, and that. It was me who should have put my foot down, I suppose. But he wanted to go back. He was only happy out East. In a funny sort of way it made him glad, thinking he was giving up his health like he'd given up everything else.'

Graham shrugged his shoulders. He supposed malignant hypertension would have been equally fatal in London.

'Here are a few of his things. I think he wanted you to have them.'

She produced from her black handbag a crumpled manila envelope containing some cuff-links, a set of pearl dress-studs, and a gold pocket watch. Graham slowly wound it up. He remembered Robin buying it, as a fittingly dignified instrument for taking pulses the day he qualified.

'Well!' Edith straightened herself. Graham saw Robin as a harrowing subject was to be dropped. 'How's Maria getting along?'

179

He laid the envelope aside. 'She has her ups and downs, you know. She's rather on the sick side at the moment.'

'Poor soul.' Edith reached for her teacup, which was of the best china, from Harrods. 'Would she like me to go up and see her?'

'Of course! She'd love it. But what about yourself?' Graham enquired pressingly. 'What are you going to do, back in England alone like this?'

'Oh, I'll manage,' she replied gaily. 'I shall find a position. Perhaps companion to some lady. I can nurse, remember, and Robin taught me lots of medical things. And I haven't forgotten my typewriting.'

Graham found this declaration of independence encouraging. He had feared Edith would impose herself for board and lodging, and there was no telling where that might lead to. Besides, he was living above his income as it was, and tax still stood at Snowden's crisis level of five shillings in the pound. But he was always amazed at the concrete robustness of her personality, weathering stormy tides which would have washed his own away in rubble. As he inclined his head enquiringly in the direction of her son she declared, 'I want Alec to be a doctor, you know. Like you and his father. He's terribly brainy and awfully sweet, honest,' she assured him.

'Yes, I'm sure he is,' said Graham. He surveyed this prospective entrant to the profession, the embodiment of Edith's transferred self-betterment, who had abandoned kicking his chair for playing with his yo-yo. She abruptly put down her teacup. 'Alec, darling, go outside a minute. I want to talk to your Uncle Graham.'

The boy obediently made for the door leading to the hall. Graham wondered uneasily what she wanted to talk to Uncle Graham about.

'I'm sure Alec would make a wonderful doctor,' Edith started. 'It's in the blood, isn't it? I'd love him to take it up. But I couldn't do it myself, of course. Not the expense. Robin left so little, and the pension's pitiful. I thought you might help, you see. Only a loan. He'd pay it back once he grew up and started earning. Lots of the students do, don't they? That's what Robin told me. It's a terrible liberty, I know. I hope you don't mind me even asking. It would have been different, of course, if only the professor hadn't met that woman.'

Graham felt this something of a tall order. A medical education would cost hundreds of pounds.

'I'm only sponging on you for old times' sake,' Edith added in a subdued voice.

Old times! Graham thought. The span of my early idiocies. He saw the professor's bed-knob again, rolling over the lino. But of course he was genuinely fond of Edith—much more than had he actually married her. The ideal lifetime's relationship with a woman, perhaps.

'Of course, I'm not expecting you to make up your mind here and now, Graham.'

'But I have. I'll do it,' Graham decided impulsively. Despite his selfishness, he was generous to the point of stupidity. He had been kind to less worthy women over necklaces and bracelets, and you couldn't heartlessly pawn a medical degree afterwards. 'I've set up a settlement affair for Desmond, and I expect Alec can be tacked on somehow. We'll go to my solicitors and get a document signed, sealed, and delivered. As soon as you like.'

'Oh, Graham!' She got up and came near to him. 'It's my only hope left in the world—suddenly come true.'

'Let's not mention it again. It's all cut and dried.' Emotional thanks always embarrassed him, whether for the gift of money or a new face. 'I only ask you to keep it a secret from the lad. I'd hate to have him treat me like Father Christmas.'

It occurred to him that Desmond might not be entirely pleased at sharing his inheritance. But his son was anyway well provided for—which was about the limit of Graham's interest in him at the time. He was too busy, and anyway what were schools and governesses so handsomely paid for?

'Graham, you're a darling.' He saw she was near to crying and about to kiss him, both of which he found gratifying, but they were interrupted by the maid throwing the door open even without knocking and exclaiming that 'the doctor' must see madam at once. His wife had been in the bathroom for hours washing herself, and the water was starting to come down the stairs.

For a year after her suicide attempt Maria had been quite gay. She was getting up, going out, even speaking of rejoining her committees. The dose of chloral hydrate seemed to have acted as a mental aperient. Then the assassin of depression started stalking again in the shadows of her life. This time Graham invoked a psychiatrist. He had felt earlier that he knew Maria's mind better than anybody, but events had plainly proved him wrong. Besides, now he had nothing to hide. After Cramphorn's gossiping, everyone in Blackfriars knew he had a half-mad wife.

Maria had been against the idea. She detested sharing her troubles with an outsider, it seemed yet another manifestation of weakness. But the psychiatrist himself—Dr Dency, youngish, fair-haired, thin, long-fingered and effeminate, a delicate watch-chain of little gold rods spread across his double-breasted dove-grey waistcoat—won her confidence with professional expertness. Another argument which influenced Graham was of such practitioners becoming not only fashionable but almost respectable. Dr Dency had recently been installed in a brand-new department at Blackfriars itself, to the outraged annoyance of Mr Cramphorn, who believed that all mental conditions from the feminine vapours to frank schizophrenia were curable by the removal of a sufficient number of abdominal organs.

Maria's washing was a recent affliction. She had started repeatedly washing her hands, but now her whole body after the slightest contact with other humans or even the chairs and tables they touched. A spill from her meals or even a speck of dust falling in the sunlight sent her in anguish to the wash-basin, where she muttered and followed a strange ritual inexplicable even to Graham's eyes. When, after Edith's visit, the water started coming downstairs quite regularly he felt it time to summon Dr Dency again. The psychiatrist diagnosed an obsessional state and prescribed one of the powerful new sedatives derived from barbituric acid. He told Graham solemnly to keep the tablets locked up in his study, and to issue them one at a time.

Maria became more depressed. She lay in bed all day staring blankly ahead of her, constantly smoothing the turned-over strip of sheet with her skinny hands. One evening Graham knocked over the flower-vase on her bedside table, uncovering a cache of misshapen veronal tablets under its hollow base. For a week she had been holding every dose under her tongue until he had quit the bedroom.

'You mustn't!' he said angrily. 'You *mustn't* try again. This time you might pull it off.'

Maria dumbly eyed her uncovered secret.

'I don't think I'd be silly again,' she said faintly.

'Then what did you collect them for, damn it?'

'I don't know. I don't know, Graham.' She stared round in confusion. 'I wanted to leave a door open. In case.'

'In case of what? Of what? Tell me!'

'In case I was left alone.'

'Of course you won't be left alone.' He scooped up the half-sucked tablets. 'I promised you, didn't I?'

'Oh, yes, you promised.' Her voice became even fainter. 'That's how I know you still love me, don't I? Even if I am ... even if I am silly sometimes.'

Afterwards Graham inspected her mouth following every dose, like a child. But her fears of being abandoned became intolerable whenever he left the house. It was interfering with his practice. The servants were threatening to leave. Desmond was becoming frightened. He summoned the psychiatrist again. Almost casually Dr Dency mentioned, 'Have you thought about a home?'

'I couldn't possibly do that to her,' Graham objected at once.

'It would be justified by the suicide risk alone, you know, Graham. You can't be your wife's policeman for ever.'

'No, no, it's out of the question.'

After a week, he began to wonder if it might not be such a bad idea after all. She would be well looked after. It would stop wrecking his home and his work. It would be better for Desmond. It would be an enormous responsibility off his shoulders. But to be left among strangers was something she dreaded, and deliberately submitting her to it would be quite inhuman. On the other hand, it would be terribly convenient. He supposed it all came down to the old question—did he love Maria or not?

He thought about it for another week. Then he asked the psychiatrist. Dr Dency's long fingers played with the gold bars of his watchchain. 'I don't think love for your wife really has anything to do with the decision, Graham,' he advised in his soft voice. 'You're suffering feelings of guilt towards Maria, that's all. You've something of the same anxiety neurosis, you know. Luckily, you're able to compensate extremely well.'

'But I *do* love her. Well, I suppose so. Anyway, I must surely have loved her once? When I married her?'

'If I may say so, you have difficulty distinguishing your moods from your emotions. But none of us must be the slave of either.'

'What are you trying to tell me? That I'm hoping to convince myself I still love Maria simply to expunge the guilt I feel over various things I've done against her?'

'Yes,' said Dr Dency.

'Well, where shall we put her?' asked Graham.

Modern psychiatry could really be most helpful.

The psychiatrist recommended a discreet institution amid charming scenery in Sussex, where mildly deranged gentlefolk were housed in the comfort to which they were accustomed. Graham went down with Desmond to see her one week-end a month. The others he generally spent at the cottage with Jeannine. He left a standing order with a local greengrocer to send his wife a large basket of fresh fruit, regularly every Saturday morning.

28

IT HAD BEEN an exhausting three months, and Graham was glad to throw himself into the arms of the transatlantic liner stewards for five days' spoon-feeding to Southampton. He was travelling far too much. He had brought plastic surgery to the colonies with lectures in Kenya and Tanganyika, he had been received warmly in Prague if less so in Berlin, to Swedes and Danes his name was as familiar from the newspapers as Mr Eden's, his enlightenment of Madrid was frustrated only by the Civil War. The Dominions had done him proud, but the United States had outshone the world in enthusiasm and hospitality. In San Francisco he had driven ceremoniously across the amazing new Golden Gate bridge, in New Orleans he had lived in Edwardian luxury amid a regiment of negro servants, New York he had so enjoyed he promised to return for the World's Fair the following year. In Washington he had been introduced to the President, smiling in his wheel-chair, and in Los Angeles he had been introduced to Ginger Rogers. His only regrets were missing a return passage on the brand-new *Queen Mary*, and disappointing the many who asked, after a few moments' conversation, if he personally knew Mrs Simpson.

In August 1938 the sea promised to be calm, he would sit wrapped in a rug on a steamer-chair, smoking Camel cigarettes and reflecting on life in general. There was plenty to reflect about, with Hitler and Mussolini on the rampage. Graham felt the world was starting to move too quickly for him. Perhaps at forty-three he was already like members of his club—he had joined one of the best in St James's—despairing old gentlemen with minds shaped by the more elegant moulds of the past. But at least his private life was undemandingly simple.

Jeannine had been swallowed up by marriage years ago. Then came Annie, a lively young spark, neither well-off nor intelligent, who had half-starved herself to see him as a private patient for a scar on her chin, overgrown with an ugly growth of keloid tissue after a burn from her bathroom geyser. She was what Maria would have called 'a working woman', a shop-girl selling art books in Charing Cross Road. This common interest led Graham to the shop and her later to the cottage in Dorset. He found she had a profound curiosity in copulation, questioning him lengthily about such technicalities as erections and emissions, orgasms and ovulations, and even impregnations and insufflations. He felt she never mastered his explanations, but that hardly mattered. Annie may have been weak on the theory, but he awarded her top marks in the practical. It occurred to him sometimes his conduct with Annie, strictly speaking, was professionally infamous. He had admittedly operated on the girl, but he felt this could hardly be construed as a doctor-patient relationship, as though he were her family physician in charge of her health from one year to another. And anyway, he told himself, the scar had been an extremely small one.

When Annie drifted away, Graham found his booming private practice left him hardly time or energy to find her replacement. To be free of any entanglement was in a way refreshing, like relief from some chronic itch. He had nothing to love but his work, and his work was rewarding him more kindly than any woman. As for Edith, she had returned to square one and was typing for a Gray's Inn solicitor. Maria was well, even putting on weight, and got her basket of fruit every Saturday.

Graham tucked in the rug of his steamer-chair and opened Margaret Mitchell's *Gone With the Wind*, which he felt would outlast a voyage even to China. No more entanglements, no more excitements, just work and the riskless relaxation of painting.

He had no idea Stella Garrod was aboard the liner until the cocktail party in the captain's cabin. He hadn't intended to go, hearing from more seasoned passengers it would be a tedious affair, but he always had difficulty refusing invitations to go anywhere. The captain received him in gold braid and stiff shirt, an amazingly small man, Graham thought, to command so large a ship. The other guests, he presumed business people, were at first soberly dull and then drunkenly duller. He was trying to leave when Stella Garrod arrived—or exploded into the cabin like a shell from some passing battle-cruiser.

She was late. She was always late. To a star of stage and films, time is something to be calculated by others from her own celestial movements.

'My God, I'm sorry, it's really awful of me, I'd no idea of the hour.' She set the little captain awash with gushing apologies. 'The day flies like a dream when you've absolutely nothing to do from morning to night. *Je regrette mille fois, mon cher capitaine, je suis désolée.* Yes, gin, champagne makes me violently ill.' She shuddered as a second steward approached with a tray, caviar apparently inducing similar pathology. 'This weather! So hot and stuffy. My God, I wish I was a seagull! How wonderful to spread your wings and soar all the way across the ocean. Haven't you got Camels? I only smoke Camels. *Merci.*'

The thanks were directed to Graham's cigarette-case. She didn't even look at him, though he inspected her closely enough. She was almost as beautiful as her photographs, which you came across everywhere, even in gentlemen's lavatories. She seemed shorter off the screen. She wore a black chiffon-and-lace dress with a design of pink and gold flowers in sprays, seeming to clasp the gentle contours of her bosom and pelvis as eagerly as half the world apparently wished to. Her blonde hair fell in a jumble of curls over each ear, her lower lip was full, the eyes under geometrically precise arches of mascara she kept half-shut. Graham wondered if she thought it more alluring, or if she possibly suffered from some form of facial palsy.

187

As the little captain introduced his guests Stella Garrod greeted them all warmly—indeed, affectionately—though Graham saw she never bothered to notice their names or even their faces. She seemed to hear neither what anyone said to her nor what she was saying herself. She was totally self-centred. After a few puffs she crushed out her cigarette, immediately demanding another. She hardly touched her cocktail. As she chattered, her little hand, brilliant with diamonds and nail-polish, flicked out to illustrate the points of stories about Ivor Novello, C. B. Cochran, Clark Gable, Alexander Korda and others who crowded round her to exclude the daylight of the normal world. She's really amazingly nervous, thought Graham. He supposed her self-possession on the stage had the same professional quality of his own self-possession in the operating theatre. Actresses were interesting people. He wished he knew more of them. But quite damnably they all seemed to take their faces to Archie McIndoe.

After twenty minutes the performance was over. As the captain and the businessmen swept aside for the star's exit, Graham mentioned on an impulse, 'I believe I know a friend of yours—Lady Pocock.'

'Oh, God! Pat Pocock.' She paused, patting her blonde curls. 'But nobody recognizes her these days, my dear. She got herself a new nose for the Coronation.'

Graham smiled. 'I know. I made it.'

'*You* did? Then you're a beauty doctor? How terribly exciting.' Recognition dawned in the pale green eyes under her lazy lids. 'This week in *Life*—it was you, wasn't it? Pages and pages, quite sensational publicity. I was livid with envy.'

She disappeared, leaving behind a pungent perfume, like the exhaust from some beautiful racing-car.

Stella Garrod ate alone in her stateroom with her secretary, which she told herself was *triste, mais très nécessaire*. If she lost her remoteness she was on her way to losing her all. Besides, people on ships were unbearable, and anyway she had decided to spend the voyage in a bad temper. Her play had expired in the heat of a New York summer, unmourned, its obituaries written

188

at its birth. She had missed the chance of a part in the new Bridie show opening at home in London. The film industry was in a state of jitters because it feared a war, which she felt crossly was really no concern of hers. The script her agent had sent from London was hopeless—the man was impossible, for all he cared she would end up that Christmas playing in pantomime. Her new secretary, an English girl she had hired in New York, was impossible too, and would be fired promptly on arrival. Her mood was not lightened by remembering the shipping company, in reverence of her publicity value, was carrying the pair of them half-fare.

But even the remotest of film stars needs exercise. The next evening Graham found her on deck, trailing a flimsy scarf and wearing sunglasses, leaning in sulky contemplation over the rail.

'Aren't ships ghastly?' she began before he could reintroduce himself. He leant beside her, resting a brown-and-white buckskin shoe on the metalwork. 'They feed you like animals to keep you quiet, the decks resemble the boardwalk at Atlantic City, and the people are just as horrible. It's my twentieth crossing—I think so. I've lost count. Five days gone from my life. A hundred days altogether. Just think! Couldn't you give me a drug or something, Doctor? To keep me insensible till we landed? So you made Pat Pocock her new nose?' she went on without pausing. 'Well, there was plenty of room for improvement.' She wrinkled her own. 'You've got to be a doctor, have you? Just for that sort of business?'

'It's a rather more drastic procedure than a shampoo and set, you know.'

'Everyone seems to be having their noses bobbed these days. Or their faces lifted. I suppose that's your line of country, too?'

He nodded. 'A more desperate operation. To revive past glories rather than embellish present ones.'

'Where do you operate, Doctor? In London or New York?'

'In London. Mainly at the Cavendish Clinic. And at hospital, of course. Blackfriars. On the charity patients.'

'Tell me some other operations you do,' she invited. 'I can take it. I'm tough, you know. You've got to be in this business.'

Resting his arms on the teak rail, Graham gave her a brief and undisturbing, if self-flattering, sketch of his work. He had the valuable quality of lecturing interestingly and acceptably to the lay public, which he had discovered in himself that afternoon at Half Moon Street. She listened in silence, and he ventured to end with, 'At least you, Miss Garrod, are spared the necessity of my attentions.'

She gave a laugh. She seemed to be mocking him. Then she fell silent, looking towards the stern, watching the evening sun dowse itself with amazing swiftness in the sea. 'Come with me,' she said abruptly.

Graham followed her. It was rather peculiar, but she was a peculiar woman. They took the lift down four decks and made their way along the main alleyway, fringed with its ferns in little pots, towards her stateroom. As she still said nothing Graham speculated on the reasons for the sudden invitation, all of which seemed flattering or even exciting. The door of the suite was opened by the English girl, red in the face and hot, having discovered her secretarial duties included washing and ironing Miss Garrod's underwear. She was curtly dismissed to the bedroom. The actress turned to face Graham, pulling up the curls from her right ear. 'Well, Doctor?' Her expression was laughingly mischievous. 'What do you think of that?'

The ear was twisted and deformed, hardly more than a few blebs of scarlet flesh.

'That surprises you, Doctor? The studio can give me a false one.' She let the hair drop into place. 'Marvellous the movies, nothing is beyond them. But now they say hair's going up. Perhaps it'll be the ruin of me, like the talkies were the ruin of half Hollywood.'

She reached for a cigarette.

'But that must have been a tremendous handicap,' Graham burst out. He was moved to pity. A dying man or a crippled child left him unaffected, but marred beauty always touched him.

'Yes, I suppose it was a hindrance,' she agreed offhandedly.

'Wouldn't you like me to do something about it? I could, you know. I could give you an ear just like the healthy one.'

She exhaled smoke from her open mouth. 'How?'

'May I have another look?' She acquiesced. 'Gillies has an operation—you must have heard of him? He uses cartilage from the ear of the patient's mother.'

'My mother's dead.'

'Well, I'm dubious about moving tissue from one person to another, anyway.' He inspected the deformity. 'I'd take a slip from one of your rib cartilages as a basic strut. Skin-grafting and moulding would complete the job. I'd make a sandwich of tissue, skin on the outside, cartilage in the middle, you understand. The lobe and a lot of the outer rim are intact. It would be done in stages, the whole business spread over six or nine months—'

'Impossible! Six months away from the limelight and I'd be forgotten.'

'But you wouldn't be out of action longer than a week at a time. If you were filming it would be quite easy to fit in, surely? I could get you into the Cavendish the day we docked.'

'How much would it cost?'

'Three hundred guineas.'

'My God! I could buy a car for that.' She had a sharp grasp of the value of money.

'But you *must* let me do it,' he pleaded. 'I shall never be able to see your picture again without thinking of it, aching to do something about it. You shouldn't have let me into the secret,' he added reproachfully.

'Oh, life's too complicated. Particularly just now. Everyone has to replan their whole existence after another of Hitler's speeches.' She stubbed out her partly smoked cigarette. She wondered if there was something in the idea. The operation could hardly be more fuss and trouble than an abortion. She supposed the doctor was clever enough—after all, he had been in *Life*. 'Maybe it's an investment for the future? Any man's

191

flattered now to be seen with the famous, fantastic Stella Garrod. Who'd make love to a one-eared old hag?'

Graham nodded understandingly.

She lit another cigarette. 'I'll think about it.'

'Will you promise? Let me know before we dock. You could leave absolutely all the arrangements to me.' He smiled. 'I'd even make sure you didn't back out.'

'I never back out. Once my mind is made up *les jeux sont faits*.'

Leaving the stateroom, Graham remembered something John Bickley had once said—'Never trust a woman who quotes French', though adding over his drink, 'Unless, of course, the dear girl happens to be a Frenchwoman.'

29

GRAHAM'S FIRST DISTRACTION in London was a flaming row with Tom Raleigh.

'What have you been doing all these cases for?' he demanded. 'Look at this ... four rhinoplasties, reconstruction of eyelids, face-lift ... two face-lifts ... three face-lifts. You know perfectly well what the arrangement is. I do the cosmetic operations and you can have your pick of the reconstructive work. It's not particularly loyal of you to take advantage once my back's turned.'

Graham scattered the pile of folders angrily over his desk. He had moved from his Japanese surroundings in Queen Anne Street to a consulting room at the new clinic at Cavendish Square, in which he had made a shrewd investment while it was still a tangle of girders in the sky—a tangle inducing many doubtful shakes of heads behind Harley Street windows. It wasn't the sort of clinic illuminating the earnest dreams of the socialists, with their far-fetched ideas of lighting beacons of free healing throughout the land and pinning patients' bills on the taxpayer. It was as luxurious as the Dorchester Hotel, though naturally the service was more expensive. The operating theatres on the top floor had the most modern American stainless-steel fittings, and coffee was served to the surgeons in silver pots. The consulting rooms on the lower one were decorated in the latest style, the furniture shinily tubular, the lights in severe glass globes with their dregs of parboiled flies, the clocks dispensing with strict accuracy in favour of strict angularity. Graham had one of the largest rooms, and the rent was enormous.

Tom Raleigh opened and closed his small fists behind his back. He had become a partner in the practice when the flood of private cases rose too high for Graham to stem by himself. Graham had picked Tom because he was easy to get along with —he never argued, never complained, and took the blame for everything. He allowed the young man twenty per cent of the profits, though, like the Saracen, had demanded a sweetener to start with. Graham often wondered how the poor little devil raised the money. The poor little devil had forsworn smoking, drinking, and holidays, sacked the housemaid, and mortgaged the modest roof under which his wife and three children lived in permanent hope and temporary forbearance.

'I didn't think you'd mind, Graham,' he said timidly. 'The private waiting-list was getting enormous.'

'Of course I mind! Breaking the spirit of our partnership is far more repugnant than breaking the letter. That's how I see it, if you don't.'

Tom started obediently gathering up the scattered folders. 'I'll tell you why I really did those cases. Because I don't think I'm getting enough experience.'

'My God, you're getting the best experience in the world! I've given you a free enough hand at St Sebastian's and Blackfriars, haven't I? I could have picked up fifty young fellows in America to fill the job instead of you. Think of that next time you're feeling so cocky. Of course I must handle all the cosmetic work, in private, at any rate. There's a perfectly good reason. I'm much better at it than you are.'

Graham lay back in his tubular desk chair, folding his arms across his smart double-breasted chalk-stripe grey suit. Tom went on, sounding casual, 'I've been thinking everything over while you were away, Graham, and I want to leave you.'

'Oh?' Graham sat up. 'So *that's* why you've really been doing all these cosmetic operations? Getting yourself a nice little reputation among the patients' friends and doctors while I was out of the way. I understand.'

'No, no, it wasn't like that at all.' Tom twisted his little hands.

He looked more like a mole than ever, a mole dragged at last into the highly uncomfortable daylight.

'All right, if you want to set up shop on your own go ahead,' said Graham impulsively. 'We'll split asunder. Get the lawyers to scribble something on a piece of paper.'

'Of course, I realize I shall lose my investment—'

'I wouldn't load my conscience with a pound of *your* flesh,' Graham told him airily. 'God knows what you're going to live on, anyway. This is the toughest specialty in the world. I cracked my way into the ring, but I'm damned if I'm going to help you to. That's your affair. I'm just upset by your gross ingratitude, that's all.'

'Listen, Graham—' Tom leant over the desk, his teeth showing and his eyes blazing. Graham looked startled. An angry mole is an unusual sight. 'Do you remember that paper you published on mandibular fractures? Who did the work?' He tapped his tubby chest. 'I did. Whose name appeared on it? Yours. Do you remember those hare-lips you talked about to the Paediatric Society? Whose cases were they? Who did the operations? And who got the credit? Why, you won't even let me give a lecture on my own! I can't understand why you're jealous of me. I've never done anything to harm you, never got in your way.'

'Jealous of *you?*' Graham was outraged. 'Don't be so bloody stupid. You might as well say Carnera was jealous of a fly-weight.'

Tom's anger sputtered out like a match, leaving him with black remorse. 'I'm sorry, Graham. I shouldn't have lost my temper like that. You've been very good to me, and I recognize it—I hope you'll believe that.' Graham said nothing. 'After all, I've been working with you now one way or another the best part of ten years. The last thing I wish is to let you down. I'll certainly stay in the practice until you want to see the back of me.'

Graham looked at his watch. 'It is now eleven fifteen, a.m. Shall we say twelve noon?'

Tom Raleigh pursed his lips. Slowly he gathered up five or

195

six files of notes. Without saying anything else he left the consulting room.

Graham sat at the desk in a temper, worsened by the suspicion that Tom had been perfectly right. Of course he'd been jealous of him. He couldn't help it, he had to be the cock of the walk. He had even been quite jealous of his son Desmond one afternoon before leaving for America, when the housemaid came complaining of seduction attempted with an enthusiasm bordering on rape. He swept the files from his desk into a heap on the floor. He would start from scratch, train up somebody else. Spiritless little Tom had been mentally enervating, anyway. He remembered he wanted a bed that night in the Clinic for Stella Garrod. Now he would have to arrange it himself, which would be a dreadful bore. Anyway, he had to hurry to Blackfriars. He had a long-standing assignation with Lilly.

He arrived at the hospital to find everyone talking about the coming war. Fresh from the secure remoteness of America he was astounded by this mental attitude—people seemed not only to expect the fighting to start, but to have little conversation for anything else.

'Scaremongering,' he dismissed it to John Bickley in the anaesthetic room of the Arlott Wing. 'The Americans don't think anything will come of it. Over there you can take a properly balanced view.'

'So you reckon Hitler's bluffing?' asked John cheerfully. He slowly opened the ether valve of the anaesthetic machine as his patient slid into unconsciousness with nitrous oxide gas.

'Of course he is,' Graham assured him. 'He couldn't possibly start a war over Czechoslovakia. He's no money, no supplies, and all his doctors are in Hampstead.'

He was gratified to find everyone excited to see him back—his new registrar, the houseman he still shared with orthopaedics, his theatre sister, even the pair of nurses scurrying in the background with long-handled Cheadle's forceps plucking sterile instruments from steaming water. Graham could be infuriating while operating, his usual charm ousted by concentration on his work. But he always apologized afterwards, and anyway he was their 'Chief'—a light-fingered wizard to be proud of, a possession and honoured commander. As John Bickley trundled the patient in he said, 'Let's hope this is our final go at Lilly. We'll be glad to see the last of each other.'

'The last pedicle certainly took like a dream.'

'I suppose she's still drinking?'

'Judging by the amount of ether I've had to push into her, yes.'

Graham inspected the face, shoulders, and chest in front of him. There seemed nothing of the original left. Lilly was a drunk—middle-aged, fat, and ugly to start with—and like many drunks destined at some time or other to fall into her sitting-room fire. When she appeared in Blackfriars three years earlier, charred black from the waist upwards, the general surgeons so despaired of her they simply put her in a side room to die. Graham heard about her casually over lunch and asked if he might see her, a request which Mr Doxy, her surgeon in charge, thought typically pushful. But he agreed. After all, she was beyond reclaim by any practitioner on earth and in a matter of hours would have the choice of any in Heaven.

Graham moved Lilly to his own wards and set to work. Since Maria's hospitalization Graham had interested himself in the reparative side of plastic surgery with the enthusiasm of Haileybury, if not his exclusiveness. He was still too fond of the easy fees of vanity. He somehow kept Lilly alive with transfusions and oxygen, then started grafting skin from her plump legs to her raw burns. The more times he operated the more he became obsessed with her case. It was a severe technical exercise, and only he was capable of it. He was proud of the healing body, as he was proud of the burnt children he repaired at Blackfriars and St Sebastian's for no money and scant professional renown. As for the woman herself, he thought little about her. The surgery of burns interested him a great deal and burnt patients very little.

He cut a paper-thin oblong of skin from Lilly's thigh and stitched it to a still untreated area under her chin. The final result he thought spectacular. His pieces had grown into place, his scars were beautifully faint, at least she had a recognizable face and was alive and drinking. 'I'll quite miss her,' he told John Bickley as he put the dressings on. 'She's become to me a regular mental exercise, like the stockbroker's daily crossword puzzle.'

'Don't speak too soon, Graham. She can still fall in the fire again.'

'Human nature,' murmured Graham. 'The more I see of people the more I sense in them the seeds of their own destruction. We bring half the miseries of this world on ourselves, whether we're obsessed at escaping from the shape of our nose or from life in general.'

As he was walking with the anaesthetist from the Arlott Wing for a late lunch in the hospital refectory, Graham said, 'I've come back from America with a new ambition.'

'Let me guess. No, I can't. You're the man who has everything. To buy a string of racehorses and win the Derby?'

'To become President of the Royal College of Surgeons.' John raised his eyebrows. 'That's the one thing I *haven't* got—recognition in the profession. Mention me to any woman over a dinner-table in London or New York and she'd say, "You mean the face doctor?" But how do I stand in the eyes of the general surgeons, toiling away among their ribbons of gut and cobbling up whatever they decide in their majesty to yank out? Nowhere. Plastic surgeons are trivial men, comic-cuts characters.'

'So are anaesthetists.'

'To my modest mind the work I do here on cleft palates, allowing children to grow up without a terrible deformity in their speech, is just as worthy as theirs, allowing them to grow up without a deformity in their guts. What girl can face adolescence sanely with a cleft lip? How about those burns? I've taught myself more about burns than anyone in London. I've saved limbs and lives. If I have to perform an amputation I'm depressed for a week. The general boys do one without thinking twice. And they all dismiss me as a sort of beauty specialist, Elizabeth Arden with a knife.'

'They envy your glamour with the public, Graham. *Life*

magazine, and all that. They're all exhibitionists themselves—
they wouldn't become surgeons otherwise. Though I agree, they
don't waste any chance to get nasty behind your back.'

' "And what is fame? A gilded butt, for ever pierced with the
arrows of malignancy",' sighed Graham. 'Do you know who
said that?'

'No?'

'Edward Jenner. He also invented vaccination. But I've made
up my mind I'm standing for the committee of the College next
year. That'll shake the boys up a bit. I even think I can pull it
off. I've got friends enough to push me. I've grasped the technique of electioneering. I'm going to rely on you to accomplish
some subtle canvassing for me.'

'I'll do anything I can, and willingly. But it's a tough proposition. The competition's terrible.'

'Nonsense.' Graham laughed. 'If I can turn the bulbous-
nosed daughter of a stockbroker into a classical beauty under
the hour, I can do anything.' They reached the stairs to the
refectory in the basement of the main hospital building. 'By the
way, I'd like you to dope a case for me in the Cavendish
tomorrow morning at eight. Female by the name of Stella
Garrod.' John stared at him. 'I crossed on the boat with her.
It's a first-stage reconstruction of the auricle. Yes, you may well
look surprised. Keep it under your hat, there's a good lad. She's
coming into the Cavendish this evening, if you want to have a
look at her.'

'I most certainly *do* want to have a look at her!'

Graham laughed. 'I don't think she'll destroy even your
illusions.'

At eight the next morning the mouth the world yearned to
kiss was blocked with a stout red-rubber tube, through which
John Bickley was delivering his anaesthetic. Graham was encouraged to find he had more tissue to play with than he
expected. The lobe was normal, the shrivelled upper part of the
ear lying more or less in its right position. He could do the first
two stages in one. He cut a strip of cartilage from a rib, and on
a small sterile block of wood in the corner of the operating

theatre fashioned it into a flat plate the size and shape of her normal ear. Then he cut a semi-circle of skin behind the malformed one, slipped the plate of cartilage inside and sewed up the incision with his usual fine, close stitches. Once the wound had healed and the transplanted cartilage was living healthy in its new site, like the corporal's nose of long ago, the plate with its covering of skin could be raised away from the side of her head. Unless, of course, the lot went septic . . . Graham's hands sweated inside his gloves at the thought.

'This is enough to put me off the pictures for good,' said John Bickley.

30

THE CAVENDISH CLINIC was as understanding in providing its distinguished patients with secrecy as with publicity. Three days later Stella Garrod was smuggled back to her flat in Brook Street, near Grosvenor Square. Graham called to remove the stitches after ten days more, the dressings were abandoned a week later. At the end of September her new secretary telephoned him. Yes, Miss Garrod was perfectly fit, and delighted with the operation. She was taking a party to the first night of a new musical the following Thursday. She would be thrilled if Mr Trevose could join them.

They met in Stella's flat for cocktails. There were about a dozen guests, including Lady Pocock, accompanied not by Lord Pocock but an exquisitely brilliantined young man whom Graham supposed his handiwork had attracted. It was a bad evening for a party. The Prime Minister was in Munich and the peace of Europe, for so long as fragile as the Crystal Palace, now looked like following that structure in rapid conflagration. There were actually trenches in Hyde Park—it was serious. Everyone had a gas-mask, even Miss Stella Garrod. The forty-four anti-aircraft guns possessed by the country were bared in public, to influence the will of their protégés if not their prospective enemies. The eagles' wings of the German Air Force shadowed streets and minds everywhere across the face of Europe.

If the musical comedy was to be a distraction from such alarming times, it failed sadly. Even Graham found the show dull, and he had the advantage of no ear for music. Stella Garrod was in a bad mood from the start. A playwright, an old bed-companion of hers, was supposed to be with them and had failed not only to appear but to apologize. Only the cascade of boos descending on the cast with the curtain put her in a better temper. She insisted on taking them to one of the most expensive restaurants in London for supper, which Graham found more exciting. It was splendid to sit among stage people, to hear their chatter, even to impress such worldly creatures with his own calling. He wondered vaguely if the party might get in the newspapers, and what Haileybury would say. About one o'clock the guests started drifting away, and Graham found himself presented with the bill. It was enormous. He looked round hopefully, but no-one seemed inclined to dispossess him. He took out his cheque-book and fountain-pen, feeling it rather a blatant imposition. Why, it ran away with the profits of his hostess's operation.

In the lobby of the restaurant he found her in a sable coat, and on an impulse offered her a lift home. He explained he lived more or less round the corner.

'But of course, you're very kind,' she told him. 'And I detest taxis, you never know who's been in them.'

He drove his Bentley to Brook Street. She yawned and said casually, 'Come in.'

The flat was empty, the sitting-room as they had left it, full of ash and empty glasses. She yawned again. 'Wasn't it a putrid show?'

'I've seen better, certainly.'

'Do you want a drink?'

'No, thank you. Not so late. I'm operating at nine.'

She yawned a third time. Graham stood in the middle of the carpet, his hands clasped behind his back, feeling foolish.

'*Alors? Nous nous amuserons en faisant l'amour?*'

'I beg your pardon?' asked Graham, whose French was not very good.

She gave a laugh and, starting to sing a tune from the show, made her way to the bedroom, throwing the sable wrap on the floor. The playwright had failed her, and she thought no evening complete without a sexual finale.

Graham found her at the dressing-table, taking off her jewellery.

'Didn't you say you had a wife?' She was looking at herself in the mirror. 'Or is she dead?'

'Virtually. She's in a home for chronic invalids.'

'Oh, I'm sorry,' she consoled him offhandedly. 'Yes, I imagined you weren't attached to a woman.'

'Why do you say that?'

'Oh, I don't know . . .' She kicked off her shoes and started to strip her silk stockings. 'You're too polite, too considerate. A man who lives with one woman soon takes all women for granted. Did you have any children?'

'Yes, a son.' Graham slipped off his dinner-jacket. The calmness of the scene startled him. The pair of them might have been married for years. 'He's seventeen.'

She let her dress drop on the floor, and kicked it aside with her bare foot. 'Is *he* interested in women?'

He started undoing his dress-studs. 'I'm afraid rather too much for a boy of his age,' he smiled. 'Now he's left school I suppose he's nothing else to think about. That's one reason why I'm sending him away for a year in Switzerland.'

'Much better! On the Continent they bring up young men to see girls as a necessity instead of an occasional treat.' She pulled the hair from her ear. 'Well, Doctor—you can admire your handiwork.'

The wound was healing beautifully.

When Graham woke up it was pitch dark. Where was he? Ah, yes . . . He looked at his wrist-watch.

My God!

Five past nine.

He leapt up. Light seeped round the edges of the heavy curtains. He snatched one aside. Brook Street was busy with the traffic of an autumn morning. Under the canopy of the four-poster bed Stella Garrod stirred lazily.

'What's the matter, darling?' She focused her sleepy eyes, trying hard to remember who he was.

'I should be at the hospital,' he said frantically.

It came back to her. He looked quite different without his clothes on.

'Darling, do forgive me,' he apologized briskly. He leant across the bed to kiss her. 'I'll ring you later in the day.'

She smiled, and apparently went to sleep again. He looked round for his clothes.

My God!

A dress suit.

There was no escape. He could hardly telephone his house and have Desmond bring across his day things. If he turned up the collar, perhaps no-one would notice. He scrambled into the black trousers. Stella Garrod started to snore, quite loudly.

He tiptoed from the bedroom. The sitting-room was harsh with light. The mess had been cleared away. At a desk in the corner sat a mannish-looking short-haired woman of about thirty, in tweeds and thick horn-rimmed glasses, smoking a cigarette in a holder and snipping cuttings from the morning papers.

'We're saved,' said the woman. She held up the front page of the *Express*, decorated with the five enormous letters PEACE and an exclamation mark. 'He's flying home today, it says. Umbrella and all.'

Graham stared at her blankly, clutching the jacket round his throat.

'Like some coffee?' she asked.

'No . . . no, thank you.' He felt he should give some explanation of himself. 'Miss Garrod's still asleep', was all that came to mind.

'She likes her lie-in when she can get it.' The secretary tipped ash from her holder. 'She deserves it, poor dear, and that's a fact.'

'I've got to get going,' mumbled Graham.

'See you again sometime.'

'Yes . . . yes, of course.' He sincerely hoped not.

His car was outside. He would explain at home he'd been caught in some revels to do with this peace business in Munich. He'd explain at Blackfriars that . . . oh, God, what *would* he explain? He wished he had time for a bath. He must have a bite of breakfast somehow. Then he suddenly remembered the restaurant bill as well. A disastrous evening altogether.

Or was it?

That afternoon Graham stopped in Bond Street to buy a diamond and sapphire brooch. He sent it to Stella with a note saying he would die if he didn't see her. Even the secretary was softened towards him by the obvious cost.

He suddenly remembered he had been home over a month, and hadn't yet been down to Sussex to see Maria.

31

ERIC HAILEYBURY LED what he considered to be the life of a gentleman. He had a small, square, stone-built house off the Upper Richmond Road, amid a tidy garden where even the laurel bushes seemed to have been dusted daily against the London grime. He was forty-six, and still unmarried. There had been shadowy affairs, the most promising with a lady almoner at King Alfred's, whom he had taken once or twice to substantial and sober feasts at the Trocadero. But he forbore inviting her to browse with him on more settled pastures. Marriage meant sexual responsibility, which he was not prepared to shoulder. He didn't like the idea. He failed to see the attraction of submitting part of himself to a dark female tube surrounded by writhing muscles and other tubes of unpleasantly excretory function. It might not be the common view, but there it was. He settled for the housekeeping of his younger sister, who was devoted to him. She was eager for men normally enough, but was obliged sadly to restrict their advances to her dreams, through her close resemblance to his lanky, bony, big-handed self.

Haileybury drove a ten-horse-power Morris, never smoked, drank just a little wine, enjoyed a frugal board, and entertained himself three or four times a summer watching Henry Wood conduct the Proms at the Queen's Hall or Hendren and young Compton bat at Lord's. Where Graham expressed his creative urge in painting, Haileybury made model railway engines. Nothing soothed him like standing at his lathe in his shirt-sleeves, breathing the sweet smell of warm lubricating oil and crunching underfoot metal shavings. He had scores of models, from Stephenson's Rocket to the Coronation Scot, each executed with the same precision as his operations. They were all round the house, and his sister thought they took a lot of dusting.

As Graham observed, with the passage of years such abstemiousness was bound to set its mark on any man. Haileybury grew thinner, the tendons of his neck showing through the skin above his stiff white collars like hawsers under canvas. His outlook was becoming equally desiccated. His lectures suffocated his audiences with torrents of carefully graded facts to the point of occasional unconsciousness. His doctrine of plastic surgery remained as austere as ever, enshrined in the shining if profitless principles of reconstructive operations for congenital defects, burns, or accidents.

Cosmetic surgery he thought devilish handiwork. If we disliked the faces bestowed on us by Nature they were but trials to test us, to be borne with the cheerfulness summoned up by more horrible defects, not changed like an ill-fitting suit of clothes. He argued with Graham at every turn. 'So we may say, Trevose,' he remarked as Graham demonstrated a successful nasal reconstruction on a young Jewess with theatrical ambitions, 'you have turned the lady into not only a thing of beauty but a goy for ever.' It was the one joke of his life.

The only opinion he shared with Graham was on the impossibility of war. He had been to Germany for his holidays, walking across the Thüringer Wald from Weimar to Coburg, and the people were the most sensible, decent, hospitable, and clean you could meet anywhere. But when the olive branch planted with such ceremony at Munich bore only withered leaves of disillusionment, even Haileybury became troubled. He certainly didn't relish a war. He'd seen too much of its dregs with the Saracen. But to find himself again in uniform, with a rank unbelievable to the dapper young lieutenant of the Ramsgate face hospital . . . Anyway, his letter from the

Army had to be kept secret, and so therefore had his excitement. Meanwhile, it led him into a good deal of self-questioning and self-doubt, tempered by some unusual self-deception.

One Saturday afternoon in May 1939, when a gentlemanly British mission was skirting the barren diplomatic pastures of Europe by leisurely taking ship to parley with the ruffianly leaders in Moscow, Haileybury sat in the living-room of his house with an unexpected visitor. When the man had written begging an appointment Haileybury felt the meeting might be a demanding one, and he was discovering that he had guessed right.

'Why precisely did you come to me?' he asked dryly.

Lord Cazalay nervously brushed the bar of black moustache on his fat, red face. He glanced evasively round the room, seeming to meet everywhere model railway engines. It must be like living in a workshop. People were becoming most peculiar in England these days.

Since his father made his trap-door exit from the political stage Maria's elder brother had lived on the fringe of the Pyrenees in Pau, but after succeeding to the title rumblings of wars and a vague call to clear his family name had brought him home. He was shocked to find how the crash of the Cazalays had been totally forgotten. People were far more interested in dog-racing and Mickey Mouse. He approached a publishing firm in Paternoster Row, seized such papers his father had felt prudent to leave behind in dozens of black tin boxes at his solicitors', and started work with desk, pen, and paper. He was starting to confess the vindication of his father might after all be a task beyond him, but the people in Paternoster Row were understanding. They felt it might be a task beyond anyone.

'I came to you because you are a medical man, Mr Haileybury,' Lord Cazalay replied carefully. 'I could have initiated action myself, I suppose—my solicitors say as much—but I should doubtless find myself tied in knots by you professional gentlemen. Anyway, to my mind, it's essentially a matter as between doctors.'

He sat back in his armchair, regarding Haileybury with his bulging cod's eyes.

'I see,' said Haileybury.

'The business is utterly tragic,' Lord Cazalay went on more fiercely. 'I wept when I first saw her. Wept! I don't mind admitting it. Why, she used to be one of the loveliest women in London. And not so long ago. Even twenty years isn't a lifetime. What is she now? A wreck of a human being, aged beyond her years, locked up like a madwoman. Of course she isn't mad! She's as sane as you or I. There's certainly no insanity in *our* family, believe you me.'

Haileybury said nothing. From his professional training he knew the lunatic of the family is always held as the victim of unhappy circumstances rather than of unhappy heredity.

'Everything's the fault of that swine Trevose, Mr Haileybury. He wrecked my sister's health. He's been damnably callous towards her. I knew the man was a rotter when I first set eyes on him.'

Haileybury turned over his Lordship's letter on the low brass-topped table before him. 'It's only fair to say I always heard Trevose was most attentive to his wife.'

Haileybury was the most dangerous sort of enemy, the righteous one.

'Quite frankly, I can't believe that.' Lord Cazalay brushed his moustache again. 'The trouble lay in his being attentive to a good many other ladies as well. I've made it my business to find out.'

'I believe there was some scandal with his secretary. However regrettable, hardly the first in Harley Street. I doubt if the affair was a burden on Trevose's conscience. You can hardly expect it to become a burden on mine.'

'What about this Stella Garrod woman?' Lord Cazalay demanded aggressively. 'You know, the actress. For months now he's been running after her like a little dog. It's disgusting. My sister might just as well be dead and buried, instead of shut away in her prime. And this is the point.' He tapped the brass table with his pudgy forefinger. 'He has operated on this woman Garrod. I don't know what for, some sort of face-lifting I should imagine. That's irregular, isn't it? Most irregular. It would get him in deep water with the authorities. He would be struck off. Struck off!'

Lord Cazalay's fat, high-coloured cheeks quivered. He wanted Graham's blood. But less from brotherly love of Maria than from the memory of past family glories embodied in her shrivelled and witless frame. He could not revenge himself upon the whole world, so one man must make do instead.

Haileybury placed his bony fingers together and blew softly on the nails. 'Why did you come to *me*?' he repeated, most irritatingly.

'Because the man's a damn scoundrel and a disgrace to your profession.' This not seeming to satisfy his host, Lord Cazalay added in a more subdued voice, 'And my solicitors tell me you have known him some years.'

'Your solicitors also told you that I disliked him intensely?' The visitor shifted his fat buttocks uneasily in the chair.

'They imagined my standing in the profession would lend irresistible weight to a complaint before the General Medical Council? And doubtless perhaps that I would assist with the expense?'

'There would be no question of your being out of pocket,' said Lord Cazalay uncomfortably.

Haileybury rose. 'Very well, Lord Cazalay. I should like to give the matter some thought.'

'Certainly, certainly.' He was anxious to leave Haileybury's presence as soon as politely possible. 'Perhaps you would kindly telephone my London flat in due course?'

'I think I should prefer to communicate with your solicitors.'

Haileybury took time making up his mind. He did not want anything to misfire and make him look in the slightest foolish.

He would have to prepare the ground carefully. Professional misconduct must be uncovered and punished whoever the culprit, whether Trevose or some less flashy practitioner. It was the duty of any honest doctor. But he told himself duty must never be tainted by pleasure from personal antagonism.

Besides, from ten minutes' acquaintance he had come to dislike Lord Cazalay even more.

In the middle of June he called at Tom Raleigh's new consulting room in Welbeck Street. He found the young man eager to receive him. Tom was wildly hoping the visit might bring the offer of superfluous cases, of a partnership even. In summer medical practice in fashionable London dropped like the country streams, but in the summer of 1939 it seemed likely to dry up completely. People simply weren't being ill any more. Where the doctors had failed to budge minds from the ailments of a lifetime the dictators had succeeded. Tom Raleigh had decided to spend even August in Town in hope of a good case or two dropping from some richer holidaymaking surgeon's table. He would take his family away in September, when the beaches were less crowded and anyway it was cheaper. He was assuredly revelling in the luxury of freedom from Graham, but he was finding it the most expensive one of his life.

Haileybury sat down and asked at once, 'May I be permitted to enquire the present nature of your relations with Trevose?'

Tom clenched and unclenched his little fists nervously. 'Why do you ask?'

'Would you permit me to explain that after I have heard your reply?'

'My relations with Graham don't exist. We might be two strangers. When we meet he simply ignores me.'

'Then would you be prepared to give me some information in confidence about his private affairs? Information which only you can know?'

Tom hesitated. 'I can't say I'm very keen. Whatever our differences, I worked with him for a good while. He was fair enough to me in many ways. I've got to admit it.'

'I accept that. But this is less a matter of concern to you and me than to the profession as a whole. I will tell you briefly what I wish to know. One, is he conducting an affair with the actress, Stella Garrod? Two, has he operated upon her?'

'It's common enough knowledge he did an auroplasty on

her in the Clinic. I suppose it's also common knowledge he's going about with her. I think there's even been pictures in the papers. But . . . well, how do I know if there's any more intimate connection?'

'Contrary to widespread belief—' Haileybury smiled faintly. 'Possibly a dangerously widespread belief, the actual "misconduct" of a professional man need not be as the word is so euphemistically misused in our courts. Mere association can be enough. Anyway, we all know Trevose, don't we? I doubt if he lets grass grow under him. No more in his private life than in his professional one.'

Tom clasped his hands tightly in front of him. He had spent so much of his life kneeling at Graham's feet he was becoming ankylosed in that posture. Supposing the man *were* hauled before the G.M.C., to be executed as a doctor in full view of the public? It was all he deserved. Besides—another thought struck him. Some of the cases now flowing into Graham's hands would be diverted into his own. An attractive prospect. They could afford to engage the maid again.

'Yes, of course he's going to bed with this woman,' he told Haileybury quickly. 'I often pass her flat in Brook Street. It's on my way home. His car's parked there at all hours. Anyway, he's been boasting about it to John Bickley. It's all in keeping. First there was his secretary, then some girl who did our photographic work, and another with a French name . . . yes, and another he operated on, excision of a keloid scar on the chin, I remember it well.'

Haileybury nodded. 'Would you be prepared to give evidence to this effect?'

Tom hesitated again. 'Yes. I would.' He paused. 'Though have you considered the effect on his wife? She's a sick woman already. What if all this came out?'

'From other enquiries I must tell you with regret that his wife is no longer able to understand anything in the papers.'

'Oh. I see. I'm sorry she's worse.' Tom gave a wry smile. 'If it's of any interest, she too was one of his patients before Trevose married her.'

Haileybury fell silent. 'No,' he decided. 'I think in that case it would be permissible.'

He had been gone twenty minutes before Tom finally made up his mind the last remark wasn't a joke.

32

HAILEYBURY FOUND HIMSELF so distracted by the prospect of new, alarming, but exciting responsibilities that all summer went before Graham's misdeeds were reduced to lawyers' language, typed on broad sheets of best quality paper and bundled with red tape, to be dispatched with his compliments to the Registrar of the General Medical Council in Hallam Street. The Registrar would doubtless pass the bundle to the Council's own lawyers for such action as they thought fit, about which Haileybury affected indifference. He was simply making his complaint in proper form, he was doing his duty. But before the torpedo could be fired to wreck Graham's career two matters had to be settled. The first was Lord Cazalay's contribution to the solicitors' costs, over which the son was showing the slipperiness of the father. The second was telling Graham frankly what the deadly red-taped bundle contained. To Haileybury's mind this was only fair.

He called one evening in August, unannounced. The door at Queen Street was opened by a maid. In the hall was a dark, good-looking young man in grey flannels and a Donegal jacket. Haileybury noticed with distaste the fellow was wearing suède shoes.

'My father will be down in a few moments, sir,' Desmond greeted him affably. 'He's just changing.'

In the drawing-room was another young man, short, peaky, spindly, and pale.

'Can I get you anything to drink?' asked Desmond. 'Cocktail, whisky and soda, that sort of thing?'

'No, thank you.' Haileybury felt shocked at being offered alcoholic refreshment by a youth, particularly with such familiarity—even condescension, damn it! But what could you expect of Trevose's son? He sat on the sofa with his hat on his knees. It was the same one he had worn for the selection committee fifteen years before.

'Well, sir, do you think there's going to be a war?' asked Desmond genially, spreading his legs before the fireplace and sticking his hands in his pockets.

'I fancy not. Mr Chamberlain is a more capable diplomatist than many give him credit for.'

'Everyone in Switzerland thinks there's going to be one. I'm just back, you know. They're pretty shrewd about things out there.' He rubbed thumb and forefinger together. 'Cash. The Swiss have a delicate sensibility for it, quite as touching as the Italians for art or the French for cooking and women. The bankers think war is inevitable.'

Haileybury did not look pleased with this correction.

'Did you know the Lufthansa plane still comes into Croydon regularly from Germany?' Desmond continued informatively. 'With a different pilot every trip. You understand? Familiarization with the route. Pretty significant, if you ask me.'

Haileybury's education in the knavish tricks of the Germans was interrupted by the other young man producing an apparatus with a rubber bulb from his pocket and noisily spraying his throat. 'My cousin Alec.' Desmond introduced him as an afterthought. 'He gets asthma.'

'A distressing complaint,' said Haileybury.

Graham hurried in, wearing his dinner-jacket. 'I'm sorry to leave you at the mercy of these two scamps. Desmond, can't you amuse yourself somewhere? Go to the pictures.'

'But I saw all the new pictures in Geneva.'

'Then go and have a meal, or something.' He took a pound note from his wallet. 'You can borrow the car.'

Desmond's eyes brightened. 'Gosh, Dad, can I? Come on, Alec. We'll have a spin in the country. Good evening, sir,' he added cheerfully to Haileybury.

He left the room whistling 'Jeepers Creepers'. Alec followed with mixed feelings. To drive a Bentley car was sophistication of undreamable brilliance, and he writhed in the painful dumb envy of adolescence. But he fell in as usual with Desmond's plans. Besides, a spin in the open air might possibly relieve his attack of asthma.

'What can I do for you?' Graham asked briefly as the door shut.

Haileybury shot the cuffs of his blue serge suit. 'I have something extremely disagreeable to say.'

Graham shrugged his shoulders. He was not discomfited. Haileybury nearly always seemed to have something disagreeable to say.

'I will come directly to the point, Trevose. It's about Miss Stella Garrod. I believe you know her personally?'

So that's it, thought Graham. 'I am extremely proud of my acquaintance with Miss Garrod. What of it? Perhaps you'd like me to get her autograph?'

'I'm afraid my mission doesn't lend itself to levity.' Haileybury drummed his fingers on the brim of his hat. 'I understand she is also one of your patients?'

'And why should I impart secrets about my practice to you?'

'I have it on good authority you *did* operate on the lady,' Haileybury persisted. 'And on equal authority that your relationship is somewhat deeper than ordinary friendship.'

'Oh, hell, man!' Graham lost his temper. 'What right have you got sticking your nose into my personal affairs? It's pure bloody cheek, that's all.'

'I have the right of a fellow practitioner, in affairs of this sort.'

'What do you think I am?' Graham started to shout. 'Some tuppenny-hapenny g.p. mixed up with an oversexed housewife? Some sordid little doctor snared in a suburban divorce suit? Be your age, man! Miss Garrod is an actress, famous, known throughout the world. You can take it from me she is perfectly capable of looking after herself. Without the assistance of the G.M.C., a body I doubt she's ever heard of.'

'The principle is precisely the same,' Haileybury told him calmly.

'Oh, rubbish! All right, I did operate on her. Well, then? I did my job and now it's finished. I'm not responsible for her welfare. I'm not her personal doctor. Good God, if you had your way I'd be debarred from talking to half the attractive women in London. Anyway, she's no husband, nothing. Nobody's objecting. Nobody except you.'

'You stood in professional relationship to this woman—'

'Will you please stop calling her "this woman"? You make her sound like a barmaid. You seem to overlook she's reached far higher in her own profession than you in yours.'

Haileybury rose. 'I wouldn't presume to know about such values. I merely called out of courtesy. I am making a complaint about your conduct to the G.M.C.'

'Oh, complain to whom you like. The Lord Chief Justice, the Bench of Bishops if you feel like it. But please leave me in peace.'

'I wish you would be fair both to yourself and to me, Trevose.' Haileybury was starting to sound irritated. 'You must take this seriously. It is not simply myself who is complaining. Others are prepared to come forward with evidence.'

'By others you mean Tom Raleigh, I suppose?' Haileybury's silence gave Graham the answer. 'All right, do your worst. I'll brief the best counsel in London, and have you looking a pack of fools.'

'I have no objection to looking foolish if I am doing something unpleasant through a sense of duty.'

'Duty? Jealousy, you mean. Yes, jealousy. You've always been jealous of me, Haileybury, jealous of my practice, jealous of my income, jealous of my social standing. And now you're jealous of Stella Garrod. If you can't catch up with me, you'll have me struck off. That's the plan, isn't it?'

For the first time in their relationship Haileybury lost his temper. 'How dare you say that to me! Of course I'm not jealous of you. I despise you. I've despised you since the day I met you. You'd do anything for money. You've neither morals,

217

principles, nor charity. What have you done with this skill you're so proud of? Made a lot of old women look a couple of years younger. If you can't get anything for money you sell your self-respect for it. As easily as a whore sells her body.'

He fell silent. He wondered vaguely how he came to be talking of whores. It was not a word he recalled using before. 'If you will excuse me, Trevose,' he ended quietly, 'I shall leave.'

Graham said nothing. Haileybury bowed, half-turned to add a word, and left.

Haileybury's tactlessness seemed to operate even on the unconscious level. He could have chosen no worse evening for his visit. Graham had become infatuated with a woman, for the first time in his life, at the age of forty-four. She was admittedly a Titania, a sorceress enslaving men from one end of the earth to the other with the most potent weapon of all—their own dreams. She had enticed him easily into her own supernatural world, unreal in its careless extravagance over everything from material luxuries to human emotions.

At first it had rather tickled Stella Garrod to have a medical man in tow, particularly such a fashionable one. But she became bored with him, as she regularly became bored with her secretaries, her agents, her lovers, and herself. Then she took a fancy to a young Canadian actor with a small part in her film at Mr Rank's new studios at Pinewood. But Graham so infested her flat by then she was forced to make do with the Canadian's, and nothing embittered her against Graham so sharply as finding herself on a cheap bed amid cheap furniture, looking up at a sloping roof with a cracked and dirty skylight somewhere in Bayswater. She decided firmly to get rid of Graham. Thank God the ear business was finished! She wrote saying she never wanted to see him again in her life.

Aghast and disbelieving, Graham cascaded her with letters, flowers, and presents, delivered by the uniformed Corps of Commissionaires, an unlikely body of cupids. When the young Canadian's film part finished he made speedily back to Canada, convinced of the coming war and having no relish for being blown to bits in his bed, even with Stella Garrod in it. She relented, and admitted Graham once more. But an old friend appeared, a tall, rich Swede with colourless hair and eyes, engaged in the futile unofficial diplomacy scurrying that summer behind the skirting-boards of Europe's chancelleries. Graham was casually pushed out again. The night of Haileybury's confrontation he had managed to wear Stella down by self-pity and Commissionaires to agreeing he might take her to the theatre. He was so numbed with worry over her keeping her word he hardly felt the keenness of Haileybury's threat at all.

Immediately his visitor left, Graham took a taxi to Brook Street. He rang the bell of Stella's flat. As he already half-feared, nothing happened. He hammered on the door. He shouted through the letter-box. Hurrying back to the street, he saw all the flat windows were shut and dark. He stood on the pavement, cursing the woman. He found a telephone box and dialled her number. No reply. He banged down the telephone and stood outside with his hands in the pockets of his dress trousers.

He wondered what to do. He couldn't walk the streets—that would be undignified. It would be unbearable alone at home. He couldn't face his club, full of men talking blusteringly about the international crisis. He would look foolish trying to trace Stella through any of her friends, and it was futile, she would have tipped them off. He noticed a public-house in a mews across the street. He went into the saloon bar, and demanded a double whisky. He hadn't been in such a place for twenty years, since he was courting Edith.

He sat on a wooden stool in the corner of the bar, and drank several more whiskies. He supposed Stella was with some other man. After all, she was a diagnosable nymphomaniac. But he didn't care, as long as she favoured him once in a while. He had never bothered to consider his ethical position before that evening. There now crept upon him the worry that Haileybury might be right. To the General Medical Council one woman's body was the same as another's, whether she were a housewife, a hussy, or a harlot. And he had unquestionably stood in a 'professional relationship' to her. Supposing he were really struck off? An idea struck him like a second blow. He was going to be ruined.

Stella had been an appallingly expensive luxury. That summer his practice had dwindled alarmingly, like everyone else's. He was already in debt. There was his house, his income-tax, Desmond—and, oh God! Puny Alec. He could hardly go back on his word to Edith. And Maria! What would happen to Maria if Haileybury made him walk the plank into chilly liquidation? He supposed the municipal asylums were these days quite comfortable. He put his head in his hands and groaned loudly, disturbing the barmaid.

When the public-house shut Graham went unsteadily back to Brook Street. Stella's flat was still dark. He suffered the further humiliation of having to identify himself to a policeman. He went back to Queen Street and lay on his bed in his clothes. Why couldn't a doctor be like other men, he wondered restlessly, wearing one face for his work and another for his fun? A managing director could sleep with whomever he cared and still get knighted. He almost wanted to scream in the torture of exasperation. He wondered where Stella was at that moment. He pictured her as he knew her in bed, with a faceless man. Some twist of his visual imagery supplied the unknown copulator with the look of Haileybury. For a minute it made him quite cheerful again.

Then he wondered what Desmond and Alec were up to. His son's driving was getting dangerously fast.

33

'OF COURSE, I was delivered by my own father,' Alec remarked. 'That might make some difference.'

Desmond didn't seem to hear him. With a contented smile he was driving the Bentley saloon at eighty miles an hour along the Barnet by-pass. At eighteen he was a splendid driver. He was also highly intelligent, spoke fluent French and German, quoted Voltaire, knew how to order wine, whispered jokes which Alec had to pretend he understood, was a skilful cricketer, dressed well, and could dance the Continental.

'Difference to what?' Desmond asked, his eyes on the road.

'To this asthma business.'

'Oh, that. No, I shouldn't think so, Wheezy. Any hereditary influences, joyful or woeful, must have been exerted rather earlier in the proceedings.'

'I mean from the psychological point of view.'

'I don't think anyone's made a psychological study of children delivered by their fathers. I expect they're mostly the offspring of cranks and Esquimaux and people like that.'

It had been a miserable summer for Alec's chest. He wondered if it were the fault of his psychology or of the arid London air, but he fancied the basic trouble was girls.

His uncle Graham had engineered his release from the school in Kent, which Alec had grown into with the resigned docility of a long-term prisoner. Having agreed secretly to grub-stake the budding healer, Graham felt he must take some responsibility for the mechanics of his transformation into a doctor from a hopelessly undersized, painfully introverted, and noisily asthmatical fatherless schoolboy. The school horrified Graham as an educational monstrosity. The boy would never pass his First M.B., nor even his 'Little-Go' entrance examination—particularly in Latin, a subject beyond the preceptorial skill of Old Flybuttons' establishment but cherished by Cambridge as fondly as its other medieval relics. He decided to place Alec at Mr Turton's in Kensington, a 'crammer', highly regarded for preparing even the most feeble-minded sons of the aristocracy for Oxford and Cambridge, the Army and Navy, and the Church, so that in all five they did as little damage as possible.

At Alec's school girls were not conceded to exist, Old Flybuttons considering them to be sinful. All impure thoughts—and any boy's thoughts about girls were held by him to be impure, probably quite rightly—had on his strict orders to be wiped from the mind at once. He allowed that this psychological manœuvre might at times present difficulties, when a sympathetic adult might be approached for guidance. Alec had once started confessing impure thoughts to Graham, but found his uncle baffled, alarmed, and uncooperative. In the free-and-easy atmosphere of the examination factory run by Mr Turton girls were everywhere, not schoolchildren but young ladies, some with quite considerable bosoms. Alec had no idea what to do with them. His shy confusion acted only as a stimulus to flirtation. One forward hussy lured him into the stationery cupboard and actually invited him to kiss her. He had rushed away in panic, knocking over a stone jar of Stephens' ink, which made a terrible mess and cost him five shillings. He felt ruefully that Desmond might have managed the encounter more successfully. He thought his cousin as sophisticated as an emerald bracelet, and envied him desperately.

'Let's go into this dump and have a drink,' said Desmond, pulling up.

The dump was a large modern building of Tudorish aspect, which Desmond explained was a roadhouse. They went into the long bright cocktail lounge, where Desmond ordered a pair of light ales and started teasing the pretty girl behind the bar. The school with the big bills and mysterious traditions had given him quite a number of manners and enormous self-assurance. The year he had just spent in Geneva, at a costly establishment of international outlook, had added such things as philosophy, languages, carpentry, Swedish exercises, a European polish, and a beguiling line in conversation. It was all most impressive, particularly to barmaids.

'This asthma really is tedious.' Alec climbed on to the red-leather and chromium stool beside him. 'I've tried everything by now. I even sent for some pills advertised "To stop an attack within five minutes". I sat down with my watch and swallowed one, but nothing happened. I was terribly disappointed. I've just taken to smoking medicinal herbs.'

'That's the ghastly stink in your bedroom, is it?' exclaimed Desmond. 'I thought you'd set your pillow on fire.'

Alec had been staying in Queen Street most of August since Desmond's return, Graham hoping the companionship would keep his son's mind, or anyway his hands, off the housemaids. Desmond himself had confessed bland neutrality to the invitation. His cousin might be a pathetic little wet, but he could luxuriate in showing off before him. Otherwise, he treated him with easygoing, polite, and total disdain, the heritage of the public-school Englishman.

'I'm sorry about the smell,' Alec apologized. 'I won't smoke them again. They contain stramonium, I think it says on the label.'

'Oh, you mustn't suffer for my sake. Smoke on. But can't we talk about something else? We always seem to be discussing your asthma. Let's talk about Cambridge.'

'I envy you going up in October. Look at me—almost the same age, and a whole year's beastly cramming to do at Turton's. Even if it gets me there in the end.'

'You'll get in all right, Wheezy. Anyone with a clean collar, the right accent, and enough money can get into Cambridge. They're not particular about brains.' Before the Second World War higher education, like motoring, was more free-and-easy,

223

more the prerogative of the better-off and more fun. 'Anyway, they're not frightfully choosy at Latimer.'

'I suppose not,' Alec admitted.

Latimer College had been picked for Alec through its connection with his father's old missionary society. It awarded the sons of such dignitaries its lowest rates, as well as its most uninhabitable sets of rooms. Desmond had a whole year before passed all four parts of the Cambridge First M.B., in basic biology, physics, and chemistry of both sorts, inorganic and organic, to be accepted by Lady Clarice Hall. This was a small college lying between Clare and King's, with delightful gardens running down to the Backs, an expensive standard of living, and an air of self-sufficiency confusable with snobbishness.

Desmond lit a cigarette. 'I'll probably stay on at Cambridge to take a Part Two in the Natural Science Tripos, you know. Before going to hospital.'

'That's awfully difficult, isn't it?'

'Yes. I shan't even try unless I get a First in Part One.'

'You really think you will?' asked Alec admiringly.

'I don't see why not,' Desmond told him airily. He already had his career planned. 'It'll be useful for taking a scholarship to Blackfriars for the clinical work.'

Alec laughed. 'You don't need the money.'

'No, but the kudos is good. Everything helps. I'm going to get on the staff at Blackfriars one day, like the old man. You wait and see.'

Alec hesitated. 'You're pretty sure of yourself, aren't you?'

Desmond looked offended. He objected to Wheezy daring to be cocky while enjoying his own company. 'No, I've just got an idea of where I'm going, that's all.'

'But supposing you came unstuck? You might plough, or get sent down.'

'Now you're getting stupid,' said Desmond shortly.

'I'm glad enough just to be going to Cambridge. It must have been a terrible sacrifice for my father, saving up. They pay them hardly anything as missionaries.'

Desmond narrowed his eyes. Cocky Wheezy must be slapped down. 'You don't really believe that, do you?'

'Believe what?'

'Do you know *who's* paying for your education? I am.'

Alec stared at him. 'I don't understand?'

'It comes to the same thing. My settlement's being raided for the cash. Father fixed it all up. Oh, I don't mind. After all, you are my only cousin, and it wasn't your fault your old man died broke.'

The brightly-lit bar flickered in Alec's eyes. This was terribly confusing, even more than the girls at Mr Turton's. 'But Desmond, I . . . I can't believe you.'

'Ask my old man if you don't.'

'But what made your father do that? Why didn't he tell me?'

Desmond smirked. 'You don't know your own family history. I've smelt out a thing or two. Your ma was on the point of marrying my old man when your own dad stepped in and whisked her off.'

'But I never knew!'

'Didn't you? Aunt Edith must be coy about it, I suppose. So you see, Wheezy, she might have been *my* mother. How do you think we'd have got on? I've hardly had the chance to find out with my real one. She's been ill so long.'

'You know, I . . . I *still* can't believe you, Desmond. I really can't.'

'Ask your ma about it some time.' Desmond gave another smirk. 'I gather my old man was an even gayer dog in his youth. She might have some interesting tales to tell.'

But it was all too much for young Alec. He developed another attack of asthma. It was the second of his disillusionments in life.

34

GRAHAM WAS IN the bath when the war started.

In the last weeks of August the mighty gods sent their dreadful heralds to astonish the citizens of London, like the citizens of Rome before Caesar's assassination. Though no lioness whelped in the streets (those in the Zoo were proscribed to be shot if released by bombing), there were mountains of sandbags, sticky paper dazzlingly criss-crossing shop windows, trenches again in the parks, and the forty-four anti-aircraft guns on show, with perhaps a few more. Strange signs like ARP, HQ, AFS, or WD appeared as prodromal spots for the massive rash of initials to come. For three nights the country had been at its darkest since the Stone Age. Silver balloons, as cuddly as Walt Disney's cartoons, lay close-hauled to their lorries in open spaces, with, it said in the evening newspapers, a notice or two, 'The crew have orders to shoot the next person asking when the balloon goes up.'

The balloon did go up.

Graham had slept late, and felt Mr Chamberlain on the wireless too harrowing to face. During the past fortnight it had dawned upon him there really was going to be a war, as suddenly as it dawned upon him sometimes that a patient was going to die. He felt wearily irritated by the prospect. After all, it was quite soon after the termination of the one to end war. He supposed they'd be living again in the dour world of sickening casualty lists, hospital blues, the Defence of the Realm Act, rallies in Trafalgar Square, spy scares, U-boats, girls on munitions, and patriotic middle-aged ladies. There would be terrible air-raids, of course, like the ones in Spain, but otherwise it would be much the same. This view of the Second World War was shared by almost everyone who had lived through the First, including the Allied generals.

Graham's feeling of detachment was increased by his being alone in the house. Cook and maids had sped home for such a momentous and potentially dangerous week-end. The rising tide of events had swept a million and a half schoolchildren out of London, and he decided that Desmond too should go to the cottage in Dorset. Desmond had objected on the ground that this was funking. Unlike his father in 1914 he knew already that he had escaped the firing-line, medical students being classified among the 'reserved occupations' and forbidden to bear arms as strictly as aliens, miners and middle-aged ploughmen. Graham told him to take Alec for company, and pointed out the fun of looking after themselves. They could go swimming as much as they wished—or as much as Desmond wished, Alec's respiratory deficiencies having left him strictly a land animal. They could even amuse themselves with the local inns, if not with the local girls. Desmond decided evacuation might not be such a bad idea after all. And Alec would be someone to bait, though he really was a bit of a drip, and sharing a bedroom his wheezing at night would be dreadfully noisy.

But war took second place in Graham's mind to Stella and Haileybury. A man with severe enough toothache hardly heeds an earthquake. He had reported Haileybury's threat to his solicitors, and his solicitors were discouraging. If a complaint were made to the General Medical Council it seemed the Council must act, as surely as a steaming railway engine must puff at the shift of the requisite lever. They suggested briefing counsel specializing in doctors' misdemeanours and Graham agreed, though it irritated him calling a man who had saved from erasure back-street abortionists, drug-takers, drunks, canvassers, and the hapless foils of outraged husbands. He went home and counted up his material assets, which were laughable. He kept telephoning Stella, but without reply. He started

227

waking at night with epigastric pain, and wondered if he were worrying himself into a duodenal ulcer.

He was still in his bath when the doorbell rang. That Sunday morning it might mean all manner of tremendous things—an Air Raid Warden to inspect his curtains, an armed party searching for spies, a dispatch rider with a summons to some mysterious headquarters. He briefly towelled himself and slipped on a crimson silk dressing-gown. The ringing had become supplemented by knocking. He remembered guiltily a shotgun and pair of binoculars in his wardrobe, possession of either, he felt, making him liable to imprisonment for the duration.

He opened the door.

'Oh!' exclaimed Edith. 'You're up late. On a morning like this, too. I thought you'd be at the hospital standing by.'

'Sunday morning's Sunday morning, war or peace,' Graham smiled.

'Have the boys gone? Alec *never* gets anything right over the phone. I brought some of his things.'

Graham had seen little of Edith in the five years since her repatriation in weeds. He had grown rich (though extravagant) and famous (though professionally despised), while she had shrunk into the humble uniformity of the barrister's clerk's villa at Elmstead Woods. Her unchanging poverty kept them apart as effectively as Robin in her last days of spinsterhood at Hampstead. They met now and then to discuss Alec, and each Christmas she sent him a card with a tender inscription, generally in verse. She was now undisguisedly what Maria would have called a 'working woman', though dressed smartly enough in a new serge coat and skirt, with lace-up black shoes and a little round hat with frills round it. Her hair was still blonde, clearly with assistance, and in too thin curls round the back. She was holding a small fibre attaché case, the sort you got in Marks & Spencer's.

'Come in,' invited Graham eagerly. He was glad to see Edith, or anybody. He hated loneliness like pain. 'I must apologize for my—'

He stopped. They stared at each other across the doorstep. A new note sounded in their lives. The sirens started the first

228

chorus of their five years' oratorio. For a second, Graham felt
fear tug at his intestines. The moment with which the country
had been obsessed for half a decade had finally come. Field-
Marshal Goering had arrived, with expected German prompti-
tude, to lay the place in ruins.

'Oh, dear!' said Edith. 'I've forgotten my gas-mask.'

'The cook left hers behind, and I expect it'll fit,' Graham
reassured her hastily. As they went into the sitting-room the din
growled away. 'What do you suppose we'd better do? Fill a
bucket with water, or something like that?'

Graham looked into Queen Street. It was deserted, as it
generally was on Sunday mornings. A fat policeman appeared
and cycled the length of it, blowing his whistle. At his hip was a
military gas-mask, on his head a steel helmet, tied front and
back a cardboard notice saying in black letters TAKE COVER.

'What did we do in the last war?' Graham asked Edith.

'At Ramsgate we opened all the windows. My dad said it let
the blast through.'

Graham acted on this suggestion. 'Shouldn't we lie on the
floor?'

'Yes, perhaps we ought.'

'Under the table, I should think. In case the roof collapses.'

Together they lay solemnly under the small table, which was
genuine Chippendale.

'I can't hear anything,' said Edith.

'I expect they fly higher now than they used to.'

'I don't think you ever used to hear the Zeppelins at all. You
could see them sometimes if they caught them in the search-
lights. Great big silver cigars in the sky. They looked so harmless, quite pretty really, I used to think.'

'Yes, I remember the one they shot down in Potters Bar. I saw
it all from Hampstead.'

'They gave the pilot a V.C., didn't they? He must have been
awfully brave.'

Graham became aware that nothing seemed to be happening.
'They may have turned them back at the coast.'

'It may be a false alarm.'

229

'Oh, I shouldn't think so. They say our defences are very efficient.'

They stayed under the table. Edith started to giggle. 'I never thought I'd find myself lying on the floor with you this morning, Graham.'

He grinned. 'Perhaps it's an ill war which blows no good?'

'Oh, go on with you! Don't be daft.'

The sirens sang again. Field-Marshal Goering had apparently got lost. Both stood up, looking foolish. 'I expect you'd like a drink after that,' he suggested.

He gave her a brandy and soda and shut the windows. Air-raid precautions were uncomfortably draughty.

'Well, Graham. War or no war, how's the world treating you?'

'By and large extremely badly.' He poured himself a small drink to keep her company. When she asked his troubles he refused at first to enlighten or entertain her with the details. But he found himself telling her about Stella Garrod, of meeting her on the boat, refashioning her ear, falling in love with her, then Haileybury's onslaught. 'I suppose I've been a fool,' he concluded self-pityingly. 'I've always been too eager, too impulsive, too unthinking where women come into it. Haven't I?' he asked her lamely.

'No, I wouldn't say that, Graham.' She put down her empty glass. 'You're fond of women, of course. So fond you let them do what they like with you.'

'Perhaps that's my only attraction to them?'

After a pause she said, 'I'm sorry, Graham. You *are* in a bit of a mess, aren't you?'

'I'm not beaten till the G.M.C.'s pronounced its verdict. I'm going to make a fight for it. It's all ridiculously old-fashioned, the whole conception of medical ethics. But it's the pillorying I can't stand.' He shuddered. 'Everything that happened between me and Stella will be trotted out and paraded in front of the public as though I were a criminal in the dock of the Old Bailey.'

'What happens if you *do* get struck off?'

230

'God knows! Join the Army as a private, I suppose.'

'If I can help, Graham . . . I've got a little bit of money, what Robin left mostly—'

'Let's not talk about such gloomy subjects.' He got up abruptly. 'Anyway, we'll probably all be blown to Heaven shortly, G.M.C. and all.' He was suddenly aware of being naked under his dressing-gown. Supposing the Air Raid Warden called? It would look terribly compromising. 'I must go and dress, but do stay for lunch,' he invited. 'I expect there's something in the fridge.'

When he came down in his week-end tweeds he found Edith in the cook's apron roasting a chicken. After all, she explained, even in a war you have to eat. He laid the dining-room table, a task he had not performed since his suburban days in Primrose Hill, finding it most enjoyable. The telephone rang.

'Mr Trevose speaking.'

'One moment. I have the Controller for you.'

The girl left him in baffled silence. The Controller of what? 'Controller'—wasn't that a piece of machinery? Perhaps the girl had the wrong number, and some essential ingredient of a tank or anti-aircraft battery—

'Mr Trevose? We were disappointed you weren't at the Ministry at noon.'

The voice was cultured, courteous, and plainly nettled. It was the voice of the Civil Service, frustrated in winning the war. Like the sirens', Graham was to hear more of it than he bargained for.

'Which Ministry?' he asked innocently.

'The Ministry of Health, of course. Surely you have all the documents?'

'My secretary's been rather overwhelmed of late.'

'It was priority.' The Controller sounded hurt. 'Perhaps it was not too serious. The meeting was cancelled at the last minute, and will be at noon tomorrow instead.'

Graham thanked him. He went to the cellar for a bottle of wine. Feeling hock out of place on such a day, he brought up a bottle of champagne. It was going to be a party.

They finished lunch at three in the afternoon, and had some more brandy. They had been talking so much about the old days in Hampstead, Graham suggested suddenly they go to look at the professor's house. Desmond had taken the car to Dorset, but they could go by Tube as they used to. Anyway, the Tube would be a useful place if the Germans came back again after their own lunch. Red in the face and giggling, Edith agreed. He gave her the cook's gas-mask, and they set out with the square cardboard boxes dangling from their shoulders. Edith said they could put you in prison otherwise.

Graham hadn't seen his old home for ten years. His step-mother had gone to seek the professor in Heaven, and Sibyl gone to seek a husband in Southsea. The place looked well enough kept, though the garden had been paved over and a shoddy garage set up. A row of bells beside the familiar front door told him the place had become flats, which he found depressing. It was like the ghost of Henry the Eighth returning to find the crowds swarming over Hampton Court. They stood inside the front gate, pointing out the windows, remembering the rooms and sometimes what happened in them. The profes-sor's bedroom, Graham recalled, was round the back. After a few minutes the front door opened and a fat man in a check suit and horn-rimmed glasses said, 'Yes?'

'Are you the occupier?' asked Graham.

The man looked dubious. 'Of the ground-floor flat, certainly.'

'We're from the Ministry of Health. Didn't you get my documents? They were priority.'

The householder shifted his feet. The atmosphere was thick with such ominous requests, the most law-abiding citizen in danger of prosecution and social ignominy for impeding the march so bravely begun that morning towards eventual victory.

'We have to requisition some property in this area,' Graham told him. 'May we look round?'

So demoralized at the prospect of being turned homeless into the black-out, the man hastily threw open the door. Inside, the decorations had been brought up to date, which Graham felt on the whole an improvement. His father's study was hardly recog-

232

nizable, with the afternoon sunlight flowing unimpeded through the windows. The grate before which he had found himself dispossessed of Edith was the same. The breakfast-room was still shabby, if in a different way, and still filled with books. Graham gathered their involuntary host was an academic like his father, with an interest in early English, which compensated him in some measure for the flats. 'Thank you,' said Graham curtly at the door. 'You'll be hearing from us.'

'I hope I shall have plenty of notice. If you're moving me, I mean.' The man looked agitated. 'I'm supposed to stay at my post. The rest of my university department has been evacuated to Bangor.'

'You shouldn't have said that,' Graham told him sternly. 'Walls have ears.'

'Oh, Graham!' Edith clasped his arm as they walked down the hill towards the Tube station. 'I could hardly keep a straight face! You *are* daft.'

He laughed, and said, 'Well, there isn't much to smile about at the moment, is there?'

There certainly wasn't. He blessed the unknown scholar of early English for taking his mind off Haileybury and the impending bankruptcy which made even the war a shade trivial.

Graham had put her in such a good mood Edith decided to stay to supper. They opened another bottle of champagne.

'You can't go home alone in the black-out,' he told her.

'Why not? I've got my torch. The trains are still running.'

'But supposing the sirens go again?'

'Perhaps they won't.'

'No, I won't allow it! You've got to stay here.'

She looked at him in alarm. 'But what about my sister?'

'You can ring them up to say you're safe and sound.'

'They're not on the phone.'

'Surely one of the neighbours is? They must get messages.'

'You can't go disturbing our neighbours, Graham. Everyone's got enough worry as it is.'

'Nonsense! Everyone's bursting with a sense of civic duty.

233

The country's upside down, people must be passing messages right, left and centre. You've got to stay here.'

Edith became startlingly aware that Graham was putting a most peculiar proposition to her. After all these years! And Robin, too. No, it was daft, really daft, quite unhealthy in fact. 'Oh, Graham!' she said reproachfully.

He sat on the edge of her chair and put his arm round her tightly. He had formed the idea over lunch. Spurned by Stella, hounded by Haileybury, his professional and financial ruin preventable only by his prior blowing to pieces by a German bomb, he desperately wanted consolation. Besides, it would be fun doing it again with Edith. He really was extremely fond of her. And he couldn't possibly sleep alone in the house, not on the first night of the war. It would be far too depressing.

'No, Graham,' she said. 'No, it's not right.'

'Edith, darling . . . why ever not? Don't you want to? It must have been awfully long since you . . .'

She had to admit it had been. So long she had almost forgotten how nice it was.

'But we *couldn't*, Graham! Not you and me. I'd feel like . . . like my own ghost as a girl, looking at myself, shocked to death. It's unnatural.'

'I can't imagine anything more natural,' he said lightly. 'Do you remember the professor's bed-knob?'

She laughed. 'Oh, Graham, you're awful!'

'Come on!' he insisted, as eagerly as dragging her from her typewriter twenty years before.

'*No*, Graham!'

'But Edith, my angel. Just think. Tomorrow morning we might both of us be dead.'

In the end it was this argument which prevailed. During the next five and a half years a whole army of women surrendered to it.

'What about precautions?' she remembered as they got into bed, after carefully pulling the black-out curtains.

'Surely we don't have to worry?'

'Yes, we jolly well do!' She sounded offended. 'I'm not forty yet, if you please. I see something every month, as regular as the morning milk.'

He kissed her. 'When was the milkman's last delivery?'

'It finished yesterday.'

'Then we can take a risk on it.'

'Oh, Graham! You're sure it's going to be all right?'

'I'm the doctor,' he told her authoritatively.

She acquiesced. She always took doctor's orders, all her life.

35

THEY BOTH WOKE early. Graham had to visit Blackfriars and
Edith had to go to the Temple, where her solicitor was busy
moving shop to Ascot. Graham was putting on his jacket when
the door-bell rang. Motioning Edith into the bedroom, he went
down to the hall.

At first he didn't recognize the caller outside. He wore a
military hat, with a red band round it. At his hip was the
canvas case of a gas-mask. He had gloves, and some sort of cane.
The trench-coat was possibly the same he had worn to call at
Primrose Hill.

'Trevose, I must ask you to forgive my coming without warning,' Haileybury apologized. 'Like everyone else, I am severely
put to it these days. I am just on my way to the War Office.'

The astonishing transformation left Graham dumb. He
opened the door silently. Haileybury removed cap and trench-
coat, revealing a Sam Browne, red tabs and assorted brassware
on his shoulders which Graham interpreted as at least a
brigadier's. The man Graham had despised for twenty years
had with a change of clothes become one of his country's *élite*.
Nothing brought home to him so keenly that Britain was truly
at war.

'Come in.' Graham led his military visitor into the drawing-
room. 'I must apologize for the mess. I let my staff go to the
country.'

'So, Trevose, it has come to pass.'

Haileybury stood rigidly in the middle of the room. Even his face looked different. The outfit seemed to have taken over the man. His eyes blazed, his thin cheeks glowed above his khaki collar and tie, his expression suggested the martyr escaping from earthly torments into the congenial comfort of Heaven. Now he commanded more men and material than he had dared to dream, he saw the petty struggles and frustrations of his life as but preparations for this second call to arms. The past had become irrelevant, something to be inspected that morning with sad amusement, like one's passport. He was prepared to wipe the slate clean, to start again in the new framework of society— on which he perched at the top, as anyone could tell from his apparel.

'Will you have a cigarette?' asked Graham.

Haileybury slowly shook his head. 'Trevose, we both lost our tempers the other evening.'

'It wasn't a particularly pleasant encounter for me. I can't say if it was for you.'

'No, it wasn't pleasant at all. You know I wouldn't relish bringing down a man I have known so long? A colleague in the same specialty? Surely not! I hope you wouldn't think *that* of me. I was only doing my duty.'

'Yes, I'm sure you were,' Graham said briefly. He lit a cigarette himself.

'We are at war.' Haileybury stared glumly at his splendidly polished brown shoes. 'It is a stupid thing for the world to bring on itself. But I have never enjoyed a particularly high opinion of the intelligence of mankind in the mass. It is here, and we must do our best. We need every pair of skilled hands available.' He produced a red-taped bundle of papers which Graham had noticed bulging his immaculate jacket. Throwing it carelessly on the table, he added, 'That is the evidence I gathered of your doings, Trevose. You might like to look through it in your own interests. I shan't be sending it to the G.M.C. I should think the matter will end here.'

Graham took care not to change his expression. He picked up the bundle and looked at it idly. Haileybury fixed him with pale blue eyes.

237

'You were partly right in what you said the other night, Trevose. I don't envy your riches. I don't envy your practice among famous and smart people. I don't envy your ways in the world of fashion. But I do envy your skill. I've had to apply myself, to strain myself, stretch my own abilities to the limit, just to achieve half that you do so easily and so successfully. I've always envied that. Even when we worked for the Saracen. I've never been man enough to admit it to you. Or to myself for that matter.'

This dry confession made Graham feel highly uncomfortable. It was as though Haileybury had removed his splendid new uniform trousers in public. 'I've found plenty to admire in your work myself,' Graham told him.

Haileybury seemed to dismiss this as an unlikely platitude. Picking up his trench-coat, he said, 'I expect we shall be seeing a good deal of each other in the months to come, Trevose.'

'Yes, I expect we shall.' Why, in God's name? Graham asked himself.

'I take it you will be joining the Emergency Medical Service? The Ministry seem to have left your unit a little late.'

'I don't know what I'm going to do. As I'm told, like everyone else, I suppose.'

'An excellent precept.' Haileybury paused with one arm in his coat sleeve. 'By the way, you don't still want the services of Raleigh, do you?'

Graham looked up. 'No, the partnership was dissolved months ago.'

'I know that. But had you wanted him as your assistant in the E.M.S. I could get him left in civvy street. Otherwise the Central Medical War Committee will call him up.'

Graham flicked the ash off his cigarette. 'No. I don't want him at all. Call him up if you like. He'll probably make an excellent medical officer. He never questioned an order.'

'Very well, Trevose.' On the doorstep, Haileybury saluted. Graham saw outside a dun-coloured car with a uniformed girl at the wheel. 'If I can be of any help to you at all, please telephone me at the War Office. Room two-six-three.'

238

'Thank you.' Graham suspected the invitation was less a kindness than a temptation to demonstrate authority. The girl in A.T.S. uniform opened the car door with a salute. 'If I may give you a tip, I should avoid seeing more of Miss Garrod than strictly necessary. Things looked pretty black for you, believe me.'

'Who I see or who I do not see is entirely my affair.'

Haileybury gave a cold smile. 'Ah, Trevose, you don't change.'

He entered the car. The girl, who Graham noticed was remarkably ugly, released her salute and climbed behind the wheel. As the car drove down Queen Street he could see Haileybury in the back, as upright as a totem pole.

Graham went back into the house and slammed the door. His feelings were mixed. Relief—incredible relief, he wasn't to be ruined after all. Fury, gratitude, and black ingratitude to Haileybury. He could express them only by sitting on the sofa and laughing almost hysterically. He was still laughing minutes later when Edith appeared.

'Graham, love!' She looked alarmed. 'What's the joke?'

'Oh, nothing very much.' He wiped his eyes on his handkerchief. It would be too trying to tell her the details. They might show him as snivelling before an adversary. 'A stupid man called Haileybury whom I've known for donkey's years has just appeared all dressed up as a general.'

'Lieutenant Haileybury?' asked Edith. He stared at her in surprise. The connection had been thrown from his mind long ago. 'Yes, Lieutenant Haileybury, by God! The scourge of the face hospital and peeping-tom of the summerhouse.'

'Well, fancy!' exclaimed Edith. 'You, me, and Lieutenant Haileybury. Just like old times, isn't it?'

'Yes, just like old times,' he reflected. He paused. 'But I've had a lot of fun in between, haven't I?'

'Too much, Graham, if you ask me. That's your trouble, you naughty boy.'

He took both her hands. His worries had mostly driven off with Haileybury, but Stella could still be elusive. 'How about coming back here again tonight?'

'Definitely *not!*' She sounded firm. 'Graham, you are a fool, aren't you? You don't want to get tangled up with me all over again, surely?'

Of course, she was perfectly right, he told himself. He didn't want to in the slightest. It had caused enough bother the last time.

'I just didn't want you to think, Edith my dear, our bit of fun last night represented the limits of my feeling for you.'

'Oh, I'd never think that. After all, look what you're doing for Alec. Now where on earth's my hat? War or not, it's Monday morning and I've to get to work.'

'You'll be all right out at Ascot. A good spot to spend the war. I suppose you've somewhere to stay?'

'Yes, they're fixing up billets. I'll send you a postcard.'

'I'll come out and see you,' he suggested heartily. 'It'll be a change from London. They might even start up the races again one day.'

'If we haven't had to eat all the horses. Ta ta, love.'

She had hardly left the house before he picked up the telephone and dialled the number of Stella Garrod's flat. This time there was an answer. It was the secretary he had first encountered on leaving her bedroom, who explained that Miss Garrod had left unexpectedly three days previously on an American liner to New York. No, she didn't know when Miss Garrod might be back. But it would be quite soon. She had extensive plans for entertaining the troops. Mr Trevose could always contact her through her agent in New York.

So that seems that! Graham thought. He lit a cigarette. For a while, at any rate. He wondered suddenly if the woman was a bitch, anyway. At least Edith had offered to send him a postcard.

Miss Garrod stayed in the United States for the next six years. Her enthusiastic work in the Bundles for Britain campaign won warm commendation from the Embassy in Washington.

36

BLACKFRIARS HOSPITAL HAD become a weird place. Its wards which had nursed the London sick since the Great Plague stood empty, its staff and students were evacuated to the country, its noble buildings muffled with sandbags and slabs of fresh concrete. Only the shored-up basement was alive. Down there, some more or less bombproof and gasproof emergency theatres and resuscitation wards were staffed by a handful of surgeons, to patch up as best they could the torrent of casualties expected in the first few days of the war from the air-raids. By the end of a month, they were worked off their feet patching up the torrent of totally unexpected ones from the black-out.

Towards the middle of October Graham wandered down the sandbagged entrance in the vague hope he might find something to do. He doubted it. Nobody seemed to want him at all. The 'pair of skilled hands' Haileybury had so condescendingly restored to professional life were idle. His private practice having disappeared with the other frivolities of peace, he felt totally useless, a failure, a man adrift beyond the currents of life. In Graham Trevose this unusual state produced some intensely painful thinking.

His sense of relief from professional death in Haileybury's hands had grown with reflection, until he could hardly bear to think of the episode at all. And Haileybury's motives for the reprieve began to obsess him. There was a war, and doctors were needed because men and women would be killed and maimed—men and women, not 'cases'. It occurred to him

241

chillingly these casualties might include Desmond. Who knew how long the war would last, with his son swept up as a regimental medical officer and sent to the front like his brother? It struck him bitterly his relationship with Desmond was wrong. He had of course handsomely supplied the young man's material wants, and prided himself on being more an elder brother than a father. But that wasn't the point. Adolescents didn't want elder brothers, they needed fathers. What did Desmond think of him? A source of comfort without affection and amiability without authority. Feelings of inadequacy and failure drenched him as uncomfortably as after Maria's suicide attempt. It was all most humbling, and most of all there was no-one to blame but himself—not even Haileybury.

But if only someone would order him to do *something*. He might be able to cut a more commanding figure not only in Desmond's eyes, but in his own. Haileybury proclaimed himself of enormous value to his country in the war simply by walking about in his new get-up. Graham Trevose the expert surgeon seemed as little use as Graham Trevose the sickly student in the last one. He had telephoned the Ministry of Health several times, but nobody now seemed to know who he was. He felt wearily his bad character left him totally unfitted for employment by His Majesty. He supposed he deserved it. He had even telephoned Haileybury, to be told the man was away at some secret destination, which filled him with envy. Graham was to be one of the first to rediscover the deadliness of war's shattering a man's fine opinion of himself, if Hitler was to be one of the last.

Among the timber props in a corner of the basement casualty reception room Graham noticed some screens. Idly he looked behind them. A form on a stretcher covered by a sheet. A corpse. The first casualty of the war? For some reason he drew the covering aside and found himself facing his own handiwork. Lilly was dead.

'Was she one of your patients, sir?' A young houseman in a short white jacket, whom Graham had never seen in his life, appeared at his elbow.

'More like an old friend,' he said morosely. He dropped the

sheet into place. 'I worked on her for the best part of three years. What happened?'

'She's a B.I.D., sir. They found her in the fireplace at home. There was no sign of life when they brought her in.'

'Much burning?'

The young man shook his head. 'I put the cause of death as inhaled vomit. We'll see at the p.m.'

'I suppose she was drunk.' Graham sighed. 'If I had spent a little of my time trying to cure her drinking instead of trying to cure her burns I shouldn't see three whole years' work wasted. What's your name?' he asked abruptly.

'Fordyce, sir.'

'What do you think of me, Mr Fordyce?' The houseman looked uneasy. 'What does *my* name suggest to *you*? An exponent of surgery needing a high degree of skill, patience, and imagination? Or a quack? A man who makes new noses for ugly girls and lifts the faces of decrepit actresses? Am I a remoulder of scraggy bosoms, or the person who knows more about the treatment of third-degree burns than anyone in the country? Well? What do you say, Mr Fordyce?'

The houseman felt more uncomfortable. But the plastic boys were as mad as hatters, everyone knew that.

'I think you're a very skilful surgeon, sir.'

'Why do you say that?'

'Well . . . because you're on at Blackfriars, sir.'

Graham gave a loud laugh in the presence of the dead. 'Mr Fordyce, you have the right idea. Stick to it, and you'll find yourself on at Blackfriars as well. I'm alone, abandoned by my friends, my loves, my family, my patients, and my profession. Nobody wants me, Mr Fordyce. Because I'm really a charlatan, a quack, a moneymaker, a beautifier of human objects who don't deserve to look a whit less horrible than they do. True beauty is in the heart, Mr Fordyce. Here.' He struck his chest. 'Psychiatrists and priests might produce it. *I* can't. Not that I give a damn any longer about tarting up some hag who's willing to pay enough for the job. I was more interested in this old drunk under the sheet than in any of them.'

243

'Yes, sir,' said the houseman. They really were lunatics in the plastic unit, he decided. Worse than the psychiatrists.

'And all that's left of Lilly is a large number of beautifully healed scars. Hardly a trace, most of them. What the hell's the use of a skill like that in wartime? Sweet F.A.! They'll cobble up the soldiers' faces and give them a pension, like they did last time. Nobody's interested in getting wounds and burns looking perfect. Nobody's interested in re-creating the faces of young men who were bursting with sex-appeal one minute and burnt objects of horror the next. *I* could do it, but nobody's asked me. Nobody's going to. This war will turn me into a total nonentity. I'm too good at my job to be any use to my country, that's all.'

He was never so wrong in his life, even when he asked Edith to marry him.

A nurse appeared behind the houseman's shoulder. 'Mr Trevose,' she said breathlessly, 'there's an urgent telephone call. It's from the Ministry of Health.'

'Tell them I've gone home,' he ordered. He couldn't speak to idiots in ministries just then. Lilly's death had quite upset him. He had overlooked for years there were persons attached to his beautiful workmanship. It was a frustrating moment to make the discovery. Graham Trevose at last wanted to help humanity, and nobody was going to let him.

He did make a call later that morning, to Maria's nursing home in Sussex. It was perfectly in order, they told him. Despite the war her basket of fruit would arrive as usual every Saturday.

Book II

Surgeon
At
Arms

1

HE COULDN'T BELIEVE IT.

It was outrageous, ridiculous, but frightening, like finding the Houses of Parliament in the middle of Salisbury Plain, stumbling into St Peter's Square round a corner in Wimbledon, or coming across the Taj Mahal amid the alleys of the City. The front was magnificent. The portico presented a decorated frieze, four stout pale columns of Portland stone, and all the exuberant self-confidence of a Victorian London railway terminus. Behind rose a flattish dome, topped by four minarets, two of them emitting smoke. Then the building seriously got down to business. Its slate-roofed, double-storied, mean-windowed blocks spread in a fan, sticking their ugly fingers into an empty countryside wearing the ragged robes of autumn. All round ran an eight-foot-high wall, topped with unfriendly-looking broken glass. Everything was in yellow brick, which in the pale afternoon sunshine gave the place the look of being constructed from a million bars of Sunlight soap.

But the grounds were magnificent. Lawns, shrubberies, orchards, flowerbeds, and kitchen gardens were laid out neatly on each side of the long winding driveway, all tended with care befitting a palace. He supposed they must have had an embarrassing surplus of labour. There was a Gothic chapel, with a magnificent clock which had scattered unnecessary hours for a century. There were more modern outbuildings with larger windows, and even more modern corrugated iron Nissen huts with no windows at all. There were signs everywhere. One directed CASUALTIES to some more workmanlike entrance in the rear, another SHELTER directly into the earth, a smart new blue-and-gold board where he parked his car announced MINISTRY OF HEALTH—EMERGENCY MEDICAL SERVICE— SMITHERS BOTHAM SECTOR HOSPITAL.

It still struck him as a most peculiar name.

The entrance hall beyond the portico was a disappointment, dark and poky, painted in official spinach green and mustard yellow. Behind a small counter sat an old man with a blue uniform and sadly drooping moustaches, to whom he announced himself, 'I'm Mr Graham Trevose. I'd like to see Captain Pile, please.'

The old man looked at Graham Trevose wearily. For ten years he had sat behind that counter, hardly molested from morning to night, contemplating his pension. But now there were changes everywhere, he'd hardly time to get through his *Daily Mirror*. 'From Blackfriars Hospital, sir?' he asked.

Graham nodded.

'Have you an appointment?'

'For two o'clock.'

As the doorman turned to a small switchboard beside him Graham unbuttoned his fawn overcoat, felt for his gold case, and lit a cigarette. He noticed the hall led to a dim, narrow concrete corridor, stretching apparently to infinity. His eye fell on two doors with big brass keyholes and bolts but no handles. A terrible place to find yourself in, mad or sane. He shuddered.

Smithers Botham was a mental hospital, 'The Asylum' to the villagers, despite the term having been tactfully dropped about the time alienists mysteriously turned themselves into psychiatrists. It sprawled across the sunward slopes of the Downs south of London, which in that autumn of 1939 had lost to the safety of the countryside everything the nation held most precious— the schoolchildren, the expectant mothers, the contents of the National Gallery, the B.B.C., and the Admiralty.

The moment which had dominated British politics for five years—the arrival of the German Air Force to bomb the capital —seemed most regrettably at last about to occur. The Govern-

248

ment confidently expected half a million air-raid casualties in the first week of the war, and something had to be done about patching them up. So the great London hospitals, too, rose stiffly from sites they had occupied for centuries, and shifted to the Home Counties in fleets of converted Green Line buses, doctors, nurses, students, instruments, beds, bed-pans, and all. Blackfriars Hospital, which had tended the sick beside the Thames since the Great Plague, was displaced to Smithers Botham, the others found secure homes in similar nineteenth-century mental institutions scattered so conveniently round the metropolis. The Government could never have kept Londoners healthy through the blitz without these vast and ugly buildings. The bread cast on the broad waters of Victorian compassion was washed ashore in the nick of time.

The Smithers Botham mental doctors, themselves dispatched with the rightful inmates to Scotland, had watched the war approach more bitterly than even Mr Chamberlain. The upper reaches of prewar medicine had many agreeable backwaters, none pleasanter than a job in such a place. They enjoyed free houses in the grounds, free vegetables piled daily on their kitchen tables, even free laundry—which was always beautifully turned out, laundrywork being thought a useful occupation for madwomen. Their main vexations were their own colleagues, who could be difficult, many doctors of unreliable personality choosing to escape from the harsh world behind the same walls as their patients. But their duties were delightfully light, the treatment of mental illness at the time being as passive as the treatment of criminals, consisting mainly in keeping both classes locked well away from public view.

Now the Smithers Botham gymnasium was partitioned into a row of operating theatres, where long-established cats snoozed in the warmth of the sterilizers or disported themselves among the beams above. New laboratories were fashioned from damp little outhouses, where sometimes toads came hopping round the test-tubes. The long bleak wards, re-equipped and refilled with rows of empty beds, after ten weeks of war still yawned hungrily for the half-million casualties, while bats flicked up and down the corridors at dusk, scaring the night nurses. The evacuated Blackfriars staff fitted in as best they could, the matron numbering among the first horrors of war her charges having to sleep without their usual collective chastity belt of spiked railings. But there were unlooked-for rural compensations—fresh air, a croquet lawn, tennis courts, even a cricket pitch, where the more athletic housemen took their exercise in the mornings and the more amorous ones took their girl-friends at night. And everyone agreed the flap would be over by Christmas, in spring they'd be home again in London.

Graham Trevose looked at his wristwatch. Ten past two. 'I suppose Captain Pile knows I'm waiting?'

'He's very busy just now, sir.'

'My own time's not exactly valueless, you know,' Graham told him, not as unkindly as he might.

The old man looked wearier than ever. 'There's a war on, sir.'

Graham winced. He always did at the expression which had come to excuse any incompetence or incivility. Instead of replying he sat resignedly on a short wooden bench, eyeing a red-and-white poster telling him his cheerfulness, his courage, and his resolution would give them victory. In a spot like Smithers Botham, he felt he was going to need all three.

2

GRAHAM TREVOSE was odd man out, as usual.

The Second World War found the British Government prepared to take a more tolerant view of many things than during the First. Conscientious objectors were allowed to fight fires in preference to the enemy, soldiers' mistresses (if reasonably permanent) were given an allowance, and where the cure for hysteria in British soldiers at Ypres was a British bullet, by Dunkirk 'psychological exhaustion' had become entirely respectable. The Government had a particular new enthusiasm for plastic surgery. Men with faces smashed on the Somme were, if lucky, returned home looking grotesque, and if unlucky, either died or recovered so splendidly they were sent back to present another target. Then Harold Gillies created with the basic elements of surgery and the penetrating eye of an artist his brandnew science of facial repair, though until the Armistice his notion of returning casualties to the world looking roughly like human beings attracted derision from many senior officers, to whom it was a matter of supreme indifference if a man got his face shot off or his backside.

But the Government's enthusiasm outran its supply of trained plastic surgeons, who were as scarce as trained pilots. Apart from Graham Trevose, there were only four, installed in special new units round London. Gillies, being the senior man, insisted on first choice and went to Basingstoke in Hampshire (it was convenient for his fly-fishing). An unknown surgeon called Archie McIndoe descended on the charming little local

251

hospital at East Grinstead in Sussex. But Graham went nowhere. He had been overlooked, he assumed deliberately.

Graham was a realist. He knew he was dismissed by his profession as a 'beauty doctor', a trivial practitioner, a refurbisher of distraught débutantes who had inherited daddy's nose along with his money. He had admittedly specialized in offering hope to young actresses who saw their names one day in lights, or to old actresses for whom the lights were starting to dim. He had erased the scars of hunting accidents from the cheeks as neatly as those of dissipation from below the eyes, and the 'Trevose nose' was famous in London society—a little too famous: women were starting to recognize its distinctive handiwork across crowded cocktail parties. Perhaps he had made and spent too much money, lived too fashionably. Perhaps his private life unfitted him for employment by His Majesty. He had recently had a close shave from the General Medical Council over the famous 'infamous conduct'. Or perhaps, he told himself wearily, some stupid clerk in the Ministry had simply mislaid his file.

When the war was a month old, before he had set eyes on Smithers Botham, Graham was surprised by a telephone call inviting him to meet Brigadier Haileybury at his club the following evening. Before the war, Haileybury, too, had been a civilian plastic surgeon, and the pair had for twenty years lived in mutual dislike. It was a dignified but deadly feud, and like all feuds afforded the onlookers much innocent amusement. But Graham accepted the invitation. He had nothing else to do. And it would be the first time that he could remember Haileybury buying him a drink.

The newly created brigadier was already waiting. Of all the man's virtues, Graham found his strict punctuality the most regularly irritating.

'Well, Trevose, you're looking fit.'

'That's very kind. So are you.'

'I'm finding it difficult to get enough exercise, sitting all day behind a desk.' Haileybury held an administrative job in the Army medical services. He had a flair for organizing people. 'Shall we find a quiet corner in the morning room?'

Haileybury ordered sherry. He was a tall, thin, bald, grace-less man with large red hands more fitting a stevedore than a surgeon, wearing an immaculate uniform with red tabs. 'I've just seen Tom Raleigh,' he stated.

'Oh, Tom.' Tom Raleigh was a young plastic surgeon, Graham's partner until the arrangement was disrupted through the Trevose temperament, which was almost as famous in London as the nose.

'You know he's been called up for the R.A.M.C.? I could have had him left in civvy street had you wanted his services. But you'll remember, when I enquired, you turned the idea down very flatly indeed.'

Graham did remember. He'd learned Tom had supplied evi-dence leading to that close shave with the General Medical Council. A stroke of treachery he was disinclined to overlook. But he said only, '*His* services? No one seems to find any use for my own.'

'I assure you that you're misinformed, Trevose,' Haileybury said hastily. 'I admit there was some hesitation. . . .' He stopped. Under the circumstances, it seemed best not to recall the past. 'Anyway, you'll shortly have your chance to join the civilian Emergency Medical Service. I thought that something really should be done about you.'

The condescension grated on Graham, but he said nothing. He was adjusting himself to being a nonentity, while Hailey-bury was now one of the nation's élite, as you could tell from a glance at his clothes.

'But I have something better to offer.'

Graham looked up.

'I have never made a secret of my disagreement with you on many things, Trevose, personal and professional.'

'No, you haven't,' Graham concurred.

Haileybury had passed his civilian years between the wars with a modesty indistinguishable from drabness, his bachelor home in Richmond as plain as his sister's cooking, his few amuse-ments harmless to the point of boredom. Where Graham saw plastic surgery as an exciting art in the most rewarding medium of all, human flesh and blood, to Haileybury it was a science, the calculated repair of injuries and defects rather than interference with the endowments of Nature. He would have been almost as reluctant to reshape an actress's nose as to perform her abortion.

'Neither have I made a secret of my admiration for your workmanship,' Haileybury went on. 'Your surgery on burns at Blackfriars called for far wider recognition.'

'I found it a very interesting branch of plastics.'

'I supposed you didn't publish it because you found the surgery of pretty women even more interesting.'

'That's unfair. It was simply because I hadn't the time.'

'Forgive me. Perhaps it's not the first occasion I've misconstrued your motives.'

'Misconstrued?' Graham smiled. 'Are you being honest with yourself?'

'I think that my next remarks will prove that. I am going to offer you a responsibility which, to be frank, I would offer no-one else.' The brigadier leaned back impressively. 'The responsibility for all facial and related wounds in the Army. Let your mind dwell on it a moment. I can promise you a perfectly free hand. Within the usual limits you will be your own master. I can promise you first-class accommodation and equipment. You can pick your own team. You can organize your own training programme and choose whom you want to train. No one will interfere. I give you my guarantee. Come! Just think. Isn't it a splendid chance to make a second reputation?'

Graham said nothing. His quick mind had fallen on the suggestion like a terrier, worrying the different elements from it.

'Of course, you're already famous,' Haileybury conceded. 'Far more than myself. Everyone in London knows Graham Trevose.'

'By "everyone in London",' Graham suggested, 'I presume you mean the few despised for regularly getting their names in the papers by the many who wish they could?'

Haileybury shrugged his shoulders. 'I'm trying to say this would bring a different sort of fame. It's a chance to get yourself remembered as Gillies was in the last war. Surely that would be reward enough?'

The idea appealed to Graham. He would be making himself known to men who had, at the most, only seen his name in the gossip columns. It suited his exhibitionism, which had saddened his friends in the profession as much as it had enraged his enemies. He would be running his own show, pushing his own ideas, moulding his own assistants. Haileybury would be as good as his word—that was another of his infuriating virtues. Anyway, it would be better than doing nothing.

A thought struck him. 'You mean I'd have to join the Army?'

Haileybury looked surprised. 'That would be inescapable.'

'What rank?'

'Lieutenant-colonel.'

'Is that the best you can do?' Graham asked crossly.

'That's a very high rank.' Haileybury was shocked. 'Quite a number of senior men are coming in as majors.'

'Then it's out of the question.'

Why, he would be subordinate to Haileybury! Even if he, too, became in time a brigadier, the fellow would by then be a general, or some such. He would have to call the bloody man 'Sir'! A grisly thought.

'Totally out of the question,' Graham repeated. 'I was a civilian in the last war and I'd best stay a civilian in this one. I'm not the military type.'

Haileybury sipped his sherry with a pained look. 'Neither are most young men in the country, but they are finding themselves obliged to be.'

'I hope you're not suggesting I lack a sense of duty?'

'I am suggesting nothing of the kind,' said Haileybury patiently. 'If anything, I am suggesting you lack a sense of perspective. I made my offer because I thought, firstly, it was in the best interests of the Army, and secondly, it was in the best interests of yourself. You turned it down with hardly a second thought.'

Graham sat looking surly. Haileybury saw the delicately built-up reconciliation was about to come down with a crash.

'Perhaps I am pressing you too severely,' he retreated. 'I cannot expect you to decide on such a far-reaching matter in a couple of minutes. Please excuse my unreasonableness,' he apologized with unexpected good grace. 'Perhaps you will accept it as evidence of my enthusiasm for your services? Telephone me in a day or two, when you've mulled it over. Here is the number of my extension.'

Haileybury spent the rest of the meeting talking about the disastrous effect of the war on county cricket, a topic Graham found painfully boring.

3

'TREVOSE?' asked Captain Cuthbert Pile of the Royal Army Medical Corps, sitting in his office at Smithers Botham. 'Trevose? Never heard of him. What's he want, Corporal?'

'He's from Blackfriars, sir,' said Corporal Honeyman.

Captain Pile groaned. 'Not another? He doesn't need accommodation, I hope? I'm doing miracles as it is. The Ministry can't expect me to squeeze anyone else into the place. What's his line?'

'He seems to be a plastic surgeon, sir.'

Captain Pile looked horrified. The war had forced acquaintance with fellow-doctors in many outlandish specialities, but the company of professional face-lifters he felt outside the line of duty. '*I* don't want to see him.'

'You made an appointment, sir. For two this afternoon.'

'Oh? Did I?'

'You'll remember the Ministry telephoned, sir. The gentleman has just joined the Emergency Medical Service.'

Captain Pile rummaged busily through the papers covering his broad desk, which commanded a fine view of the sweeping front drive. There was a fire flickering in the oversized marble grate and an overall glow of mahogany-and-leather Victorian comfort. It had been the office of the Smithers Botham medical superintendent, then a consultant psychiatrist in the Army, where he was, in time, to have greater influence and invoke more widespread exasperation than a good many generals.

'Where is this Trevose? In the hall?'

257

'Yes, sir. He would have come to see Annex D, sir.'

'Annex D,' observed Captain Pile sombrely. 'Very well, Corporal, I'd better have a word with him. You go back to your work.'

Corporal Honeyman withdrew to a small adjacent office to continue reading *Lilliput*, which he kept in a desk drawer with his bars of chocolate. He was a willowy young man with thinning, dandruff-laden hair, glasses in circular steel frames, and a battledress which chafed his long neck. He was a sight which depressed Captain Pile deeply. Corporal Honeyman had been a clerk in an estate agent's before joining the Army through love of his country and dislike of living with his mother. The Army found he could use a typewriter, and sent him to Smithers Botham. He felt he would have been tolerably happy there, had it not been for Captain Pile, whom he was coming to care for even less than his mother.

Captain Pile sat reading through some documents, feeling a little wait would put his visitor in his place. His own civilian career had been sadly frustrating. An intolerance of sick humans had led him into various medical administrative jobs, an intolerance of even healthy ones had made all of them short. But in the Army he felt he was fulfilling himself, having command of all Service patients finding themselves in Smithers Botham and charge of the general running of the place. He rose, and inspected himself carefully in the gilt-framed mirror over the mantelpiece. Red-cheeked, dark-moustached, well built, if inclined to be stoutish for the late thirties, he felt he filled his new uniform stylishly. He placed his cap on his well-brillian-tined head, took his gloves, leather-bound stick, and greatcoat, and opened the door on the hall.

'Mr Trevose?' He found the caller slight, pale, and fortyish, with large eyes in a large head, wearing under his overcoat a double-breasted chalk-striped grey flannel suit cut with smart-ness—flashiness, the captain might have said. 'I know nothing whatever about plastic surgery,' he told Graham proudly. 'And frankly I'm too busy to start learning such subjects now. I suppose you make women new noses and that sort of thing?'

'That sort of thing,' said Graham.

'Must be very profitable.'

They went on to the broad front steps, Captain Pile giving a quick glance up and down. There might be a soldier or two about to award him a salute. But there were no soldiers, only a schizophrenic cutting the grass. 'Annex D has been empty for a while,' he explained. 'It's not one of the best wards, but your other people from Blackfriars have bagged those already. I'm afraid you've rather missed the bus.'

They started across the lawn.

Captain Pile unlocked a heavy teak door in another yellow-brick wall with more broken glass on top. Graham's spirits, already sinking under the weight of Smithers Botham's massive ugliness, plunged further. The annex was ghastly. It looked older and bleaker than the rest of the hospital. It was as narrow as a ship, two stories high, a hundred yards long. Slates were missing from the roof, a good many windows were broken, and all of them were backed with stout iron bars. A jumble of small buildings sprouting iron stove-pipes were tacked on one end as an afterthought. The garden had for some seasons clearly been left to its own devices. Even Captain Pile looked faintly apologetic.

Inside was dark, damp, and empty. On the bare floor were sheets of newspaper, streaming toilet rolls, a pile of black-chipped enamel mugs, and other wreckage beyond Graham's powers of identification. Something scampered in the corner. The smell was strange, but predominantly faecal.

'Do you mean human beings actually lived here?' Graham exclaimed. 'And not so very long ago?'

'It's a bit musty,' Captain Pile agreed. 'I gather they used to keep their senile dementias in the place. You can't expect those sort of cases to take much notice of their surroundings.'

Graham eyed a wooden partition dividing the long room, its door swinging ajar. 'What's through there?'

'The night ward. This would be the day room.'

Graham picked his way gloomily through the rubbish to the far end of the annex. Of the tacked-on buildings, one revealed itself as the kitchen, with a stone floor and a black iron range. The second contained some cracked washbasins and three large bath-tubs raised proudly on pedestals in the middle. In the third, Graham found himself facing what appeared to be a row of horse-boxes. He discovered the half-doors opened inwards, to disclose lavatories with no seats and the chains encased in lengths of pipe running from cistern to handle.

'The patients have hanged themselves on the chains,' Captain Pile told him informatively.

Graham stuck his hands in his pockets. After turning down Haileybury's offer he had signed a contract with the Emergency Medical Service, and was committed to install and run a plastic surgery unit at Smithers Botham. Though he was always able to see a new face in the battered and bleeding remains of an accident, as a sculptor can in a lump of stone, it was beyond him to depict the rotting building as a busy, complex, cheerful, sterile centre for healing the wounded.

'That day room would have to be my operating theatre,' he suggested glumly. 'The place must be ripped apart, replumbed, fitted with sinks, sterilizers, electric points. We'll have one ward in the night room and another upstairs. God knows how we'll shift anaesthetized patients up there—fireman's lift, I suppose. I'll want partitions for the anaesthetic room, the surgeons' room, the nurses' room . . . and where am I supposed to fit the photographer's studio, X-ray, somewhere for the dentists? I'll need extractor fans, heating, reinforced ceilings for the lights, doors widening, new windows made. Those horrible iron bars must come off for a start. I want the whole place painted a bright pastel shade. Duck-egg blue, something like that. I'll have gay curtains, white bedside lockers, flowers everywhere, comfortable chairs, radios, the prettiest nurses in the hospital. My patients get depressed enough with themselves, without any encouragement from their surroundings.'

'Duck-egg blue, did you say? murmured Captain Pile, mystified.

'I want those two far tubs in the awful wash-house partitioned off. They'll have to do for the saline bath unit. The kitchen we'll have to equip again from scratch. We'll put locks on the lavatories. I'm far more likely to hang myself on the chain than the patients are. No, no, it's all impossible,' he decided abruptly. 'No one could turn this place into anything but a pigsty. They can burn it to the ground, as far as I'm concerned. They'll have to send me somewhere else.'

Captain Pile grunted. 'Where else had you in mind?'

Graham lit another cigarette. The dreadful man was right, of course. Hospital accommodation was as precious as anti-aircraft guns. It was Smithers Botham or nowhere.

'We'll have to make the most of it, I suppose,' he said resignedly. 'Baron Larrey did wonders for Napoleon's wounded in cowsheds.'

'Well, it's not my pigeon.' The captain was becoming impatient. 'You'll have to take up rebuilding problems direct with the Ministry. Have you seen enough? I've got to get back to the grindstone.'

Graham stopped half-way along the ward. He noticed a door with a cracked glass panel leading to a veranda under a rusty green-painted roof. It reminded him of a similar one in the sanatorium where he had been sent to die as a young man, a war ago. He wondered if that verandah were still there, and who was lying in his place to count the rivets of the roof in the feverish boredom of tuberculosis. As he turned away, another door with a small glass peephole caught his eye. He swung it open. A tiny high barred window disclosed a cubicle lined entirely with black padded leather, even the floor. A padded cell. Graham couldn't recall seeing one before.

'I expect you'll find a use for it,' Captain Pile suggested helpfully.

Graham walked back across the lawn in silence. It was all horribly depressing. But, he reminded himself, it was better than having to say 'Sir' to Haileybury.

4

BY THE FIRST CHRISTMAS the war was still a novelty, something to expose the nation's pettiness rather than its greatness. Olympia housed not Bertram Mills' circus but Germans, Nazis interned with anti-Nazis in scrupulous British fairness. Débutantes put their hands enthusiastically to driving ambulances, and showgirls theirs slightly less so to the udders of cows. Royal Academicians were painting trees to disguise factories, and keepers at the London Zoo were armed, in case bombs sprung the cages, to organize big-game hunting in Regent's Park. In Bloomsbury, the Ministry of Information was emitting propaganda of praiseworthy gentility and over Westphalia the R.A.F. were dropping leaflets in impeccable good taste. Citizens were advised to walk in the blackout with white shirt-tails exposed behind, lighting cigarettes in the street after dark attracted abuse and sometimes prosecution, and for protection against motorists with two dim half-moons for headlights, the ponies of the New Forest were striped with white paint like zebras. The weather was more irksome than the war, the countryside for most of the winter being covered thickly with snow, a fact unmentionable in the papers lest it reach the attention of the enemy.

At Smithers Botham there was a wonderful house-party atmosphere, with snowballing, skating on the pond, and amateur theatricals, like Dingley Dell. The fighting in Finland stimulated the students to inaugurate a sauna bath, rushing naked from their steaming wash-house to roll with wild shouts

262

in the snow in full view of any female who might be passing in the blackout (an extraordinary number always were). The vast wards stayed half-empty, most civilians on the Blackfriars waiting-list being required to hold on a little longer to their hernias and varicosities in contribution to the war-effort. Space must be kept for the half-million casualties, enjoying a stay of execution. Trained hands remained idle. The nurses occupied themselves making and remaking beds, and the housemen occupied themselves making and remaking the nurses.

Five miles away, in the Kentish market town of Maiden Cross, the local hospital was overwhelmed with cases of meningitis, of which there was an epidemic that winter, with a befitting outbreak of German measles. On Christmas Eve an old man was hit by a lorry in Smithers Botham village, and rushed by ambulance to the splendid portico. Captain Pile hastily redirected it to Maiden Cross, admission of such cases to Smithers Botham being against the regulations. The ambulance driver protested, but set off along twisting and slippery roads, and if the old man died on the way the coroner pronounced afterwards he would most likely have done so anyway.

Something more horrifying happened on Boxing Day. A lady visiting her sister hospitalized with a goitre was caught short by her pregnancy, and enthusiastically delivered by an orthopaedic surgeon occupying the operating theatre at the time. But Smithers Botham was not classified by the Ministry for midwifery. No one had the slightest right to be born there. Captain Pile confessed himself greatly distressed by the irregularity. The versatile orthopaedic surgeon apologized, but found himself caught in a baffled correspondence with Whitehall, which continued on and off for the duration of the war.

New Year's Eve fell on a Sunday, and Graham had spent the day as usual at Smithers Botham. There was so much to do. He was astounded how the squad of builders were performing a workmanlike miracle in the annex. Huts were thrown up in the neglected garden, pipes and wires sprouted everywhere, they were even starting to apply the duck-egg blue, and if this turned out nearer royal purple the place was at least beginning

263

to take something of its shape in his mind. He began to gather staff. Tudor Beverley, a young plastic surgeon from Canada whom Graham had met on a lecture-tour, unexpectedly appeared on the Smithers Botham portico and was promptly press-ganged as his first assistant. He even had a few patients, whom he was obliged to operate upon in the main theatres. His first case was the removal of a soldier's tattoo, a splendid emblazonment on his arm dedicated to Florence, who had apparently become unworthy of the honour. Graham pickled it in a jar of spirit, and kept it on the desk of his hut office until the end of the war. He treated a sailor with a jaw fractured while fighting, regrettably not the enemy but another sailor in a pub off Piccadilly. There were a number of smashed-up dispatch riders, the motor-bike at the time striking Graham as the most dangerous weapon in the British Army.

Feeling he should prepare himself as well as the annex, Graham read as many textbooks and papers about wound surgery as he could lay hands on. He listened to Archie McIndoe at the Royal Society of Medicine, and to Sir Harold Gillies more intimately at Basingstoke—and more exhaustingly, Gillies being a forceful and sometimes eccentric exponent of his genius. Graham had resigned himself to the annex being something of a sideshow. The other four plastic units were better housed, better equipped, and better staffed, destined to take most of the work, if the war didn't fizzle out. He even half-regretted not submitting himself to Haileybury. He would at least have had a uniform. He had come to avoid his club in St James's because he felt the members looked askance on his lack of it. Most seemed to possess one, though whatever their martial duties these did not prevent their spending a good deal of time in its comfortable leather armchairs. But he had made his decision, and if it were the wrong one it unhappily wouldn't be his first.

On that New Year's Eve he left his Bentley in a mews garage off Curzon Street and walked the few yards to his house in fashionable Queen Street by the light of his pocket torch (screened by law with two thicknesses of tissue-paper). As he approached his front door he saw a girl standing on the step, her identity solved by an invitation flashed at him by a torch through her mackintosh pocket.

'Do you want to come home with me, darling?' she enquired.

'I'm afraid this is my home, here,' Graham told her politely.

'Oh, sorry. I hope you don't mind?'

He noticed she was young, and very plain. The regulations which forbade the lighting of shop windows threw a kindly shade on goods more immediately for sale, and the West End of London was as alive with seductive murmurs as Prospero's Isle. Graham supposed the girls hadn't enjoyed such a busy time of it since the lightless days of Boswell. He entered the empty house, reflecting sombrely that the difference between many women he knew of easy-going morals and these seedy and undoubtedly infected creatures was exactly the same as between Haileybury and himself. Even Haileybury had done the occasional beautifying job for guineas. But Graham had for the best part of fifteen years sold his services without question to all comers. And what was left? He had been dreadfully extravagant. His contract at Smithers Botham had exchanged an income of thousands for one of hundreds and debarred him from private practice—if he could have found any, plastic surgery suddenly being fashionable no longer, perhaps because the possibility of having one's head blown off ousted any dissatisfaction with the look of it. He was terribly in debt. And the income-tax inspector, as always, clanked across his life like Marley's ghost.

He fixed the blackout in the upstairs drawing-room, switched on the light, and poured a whisky at the corner cocktail cabinet. Usually he drank only to relieve the tedium of other people's company, now he was drinking twice as much to relieve the tedium of his own. His servants had left, a genteel middle-aged woman came in daily from Finchley to clear up his mess, which she referred to as her 'war work'. His son Desmond was in his first year at Cambridge, reading medicine. Unlike the First World War, which emptied the medical schools into the ranks of Kitchener's army, the Second barred medical students from joining the colours as firmly as miners or middle-aged ploughmen. For safety's sake, Graham had sent Desmond to spend Christmas with his cousin Alec, also destined for medicine, Alec's mother Edith then running a guest house for the better class of evacuee in Devon. Graham swirled the whisky round his glass. Edith Trevose had been successively his own fiancée, his sister-in-law, his brother's widow, and his mistress, but despite these disturbing changes in status still his friend. He wondered whether to ring her up, but decided against it. It might start new complications. And anyway, the long-distance telephones were becoming dreadfully unreliable.

He reflected again that he should give up his Queen Street home, store the furniture, and take a room at The Oak inn on the village green at Smithers Botham. He would exchange the Bentley for a Morris, and be patriotic over petrol. It was all an excuse to save money, to live a simpler life, until the fuss was over—as everyone knew from the newspapers, the Germans were already short of everything from shells to shoeleather. He poured himself another drink. Here was Graham Trevose, he thought sadly, the fashionable plastic surgeon, the favourite guest of a thousand smart parties, and nobody even wanted to talk to him. He had always far keener pity for himself than for his patients. He felt loneliness like pain, to exist without a woman's company struck him as hard as solitary confinement. Without the compensation of a caress he became as wretched as a stray dog, to wake at night alone he felt a foretaste of the grave. He'd enjoyed affairs enough before the war, but what was their lasting satisfaction? he asked himself bitterly. As little as a handshake. Now everyone he knew seemed to have disappeared, and if the Germans did arrive that night to blow him to pieces there was hardly anyone to care.

He had a wife, of course, but she was in a home in Sussex, mad for fifteen years.

5

THE HURRICANE had two self-sealing petrol tanks in the wings and another in the fuselage, directly in front of the pilot. On the August Sunday morning when a Messerschmitt 109 caught him over Dungeness he calculated, after a panicky moment wondering if he were alive at all, that he still had a fair chance of eating his dinner that night. As he jettisoned the cockpit hood a stench of petrol struck him. In a second his world was alight. He never remembered how he fell clear. His next recollection was the petrol replaced by a smell even more pungent. It reminded him of something. It was the stink of burning wool, which stuck in your nose when they cleared up after the clip back home.

He didn't remember getting clear of his parachute harness, but he must have managed it somehow because he was free when they reached him. His only worry was whether a Mae West could really keep a man afloat. The sea was dead calm, he felt no pain, no unusual sensation at all. Like everyone else, he'd been flying without goggles and gloves. It made it easier to see the enemy and to handle the controls. He watched with detached interest bits of skin and flesh come away from his hands and forearms, like fragments of roast chicken, and float in the water. A civilian lifeboat picked him up. As two men in black oilskins got him aboard he noticed their faces, and wondered what the hell they were staring at.

It was the same expression on the face of the girl looking down at him. She was in a white apron, a nurse he supposed.

267

Pain, shock, and morphine had by then turned him from a human being to a collection of organs struggling to function together as best they could. He asked where he was, but she didn't seem to understand. He wondered suddenly if he were in France, put in the bag by the Germans. Then she said, 'You're all right. You're in hospital. In Kent, not far from Tunbridge Wells.'

He'd heard of Tunbridge Wells. It struck him as an odd sort of place to find himself in.

He floated on a cloud of euphoria as they were obliged continually to increase his dose of morphine. He didn't know if he'd been lying there for a couple of days or a week, though it was in fact more than a month. Gradually his body seemed to grow some sort of skin against the painful world. A variety of doctors in white coats came to see him, and generally dug about with forceps and probes, most painfully. As he began to notice things again, he saw when they changed his dressings his hands were black, clawed, and wizened. They reminded him of the hands he'd once seen on the body of an aboriginal, brought into the sheep station after lying for months shrivelling in the sun of the outback. He asked for a mirror, but was told the hospital hadn't any to spare. They had been broken by a freak of blast in the bombing, they explained, and glass was in short supply.

His room was small, white-painted, and sunny, looking on to a small garden. He wondered what sort of hospital it was, and if there were any other patients. He certainly saw no sign of them. Over the next few weeks the pain began to ease and the needles became less frequent. One afternoon he noticed there was a mirror right in the room. It was over the washbasin, though they'd covered it with flowered curtain material fixed by strips of sticking-plaster. He crawled out of bed, staggered, and fell. He managed to struggle across the floor, and to tug the flowered covering aside with the point of his elbow. He wondered who he was looking at. The face in the glass was swollen, black, and running with pus. There was no nose, and the eyes stared through a pair of encrusted lids. The door opened and the young nurse came in, scolding him like a naughty child for getting out of bed.

A few mornings later the blue-uniformed sister, a stout and kindly woman, appeared at his bedside with a stranger. He was a civilian, thin, pale, weedy-looking, with a large head and eyes showing too much white.

'Bluey Jardine, isn't it?' began the visitor affably. 'The Australian? I've heard a lot about you. Sorry to make your acquaintance in these particular circumstances.'

The patient looked suspicious. Whenever anyone new appeared in the room, it seemed to mean something unpleasant was going to happen.

'My name's Trevose,' the civilian went on. 'I'm a surgeon who specializes in your sort of trouble. I suppose you know well enough you were pretty badly burnt?'

'Am I going to live?'

'Yes, of course you are. But it'll take a good deal of treatment getting you into shape. We're going to see rather a lot of each other in the immediate future, I'm afraid.' Graham took a bundle of case-notes from the sister. 'You weren't wearing goggles and gloves?'

'I don't reckon so.'

'A sadly common omission,' murmured Graham. With sterile forceps and a kidney-bowl he began picking away the dressings. Another case of 'airman's burn'. If only these chaps would keep their gloves and goggles on, he thought, they'd have at least some sort of protection in the cockpit. The first-aid station had smeared tannic acid jelly all over the raw surfaces, of course. Damnable stuff! Why couldn't the muttonheads at the top issue orders banning it? It would take weeks for him to pick the dried tannic acid crust away, before he could even think about skin-grafting. The hands were terrible. The face was a pretty bad mess too, but that didn't matter so much. A face was a decoration, but you needed hands to live.

'Right, Sister,' Graham decided. 'I'll have this one.' He turned to the man in bed. 'Would you like a change of scene? This hospital, however excellent otherwise, hasn't the facilities for the sort of surgery you need. I run a little show nearer London where we can look after you properly.'

Bluey hesitated and said, 'I reckon I'm in the hands of you quacks now, aren't I?'

'Good. I'll send a car for you tomorrow morning. Do you like ice-cream?'

'I don't mind it.'

'Vanilla or strawberry? I'm afraid there's no chocolate.'

'Vanilla will do me.' Bluey was mystified. Bits of him were burnt to cinders, and they talked about ice-cream. This doctor, whoever he was, seemed an odd bloke.

'We'll be feeding you it till you're sick,' Graham told him cheerfully. 'See you later.'

In the corridor the sister chided Graham with more severity than usual, 'But Mr Trevose! You *did* say you wouldn't kidnap any more patients.'

'This officer will be my last—honestly.'

'It does make life so difficult for us, you know.'

'Of course I do. But leaving Bluey here will make life very much more difficult for *him*. Should the powers that be object—'

'But they *will* object, Mr Trevose.'

Graham grinned. 'Just say I behaved in such an overbearing and arrogant manner you had no alternative but to give in. Say I threatened physical violence if you like. With my reputation they'll believe you.' He patted her amiably on the arm. 'Don't worry, Sister, I'll see there's no trouble. I'll take full responsibility. It's really quite easy. I'm one of the few people at the moment who don't have to give a twopenny damn for the grandest air-marshals, generals, admirals, or anyone.'

She hesitated. She had quite taken to Graham, who had set himself to be resolutely charming towards her. 'You do behave badly sometimes, you know,' she told him gently.

'I behave badly frequently. But it's a change doing so on someone else's behalf instead of my own.'

The following morning Bluey Jardine arrived at Smithers Botham in Graham's second-hand Morris, driven by a green-uniformed W.V.S. worker, with most of him hidden by a tartan rug. It was then October 1940, and the population had found more to worry about than whether to wear their shirt-tails outside their trousers at night. But it had been a lovely summer. The cherry trees had flowered charmingly over the little Gothic mortuary, the patients were kept awake by owls serenading to the crickets' violins, the tomatoes ripened wonderfully along the sunny walls of the main operating theatres (nourished by the unused offerings of patriotic blood-donors). It was difficult at Smithers Botham to believe the Germans might leap from the seas or the skies any moment. The litter of old iron gathered from surrounding fields to make room for growing food was put back again to frustrate enemy gliders. At the portico, the words 'Smithers Botham' were painted from the blue-and-gold notice to baffle Nazi para-chutists dropping on the lawn, doubtless dressed as nuns. The chapel clock was hushed, chimes being classified with sirens, whistles, and football-rattles as the portents of varying sorts of doom. The L.D.V. crawled enthusiastically on their stomachs everywhere, carrying shotguns and threatening with much ferocity anyone moving after dark they disliked the look or sound of.

The vast main wards of Smithers Botham remained almost empty. People heard so often on the B.B.C. of 'hospitals and churches' being hit by bombing all over southern England that these seemed highly dangerous places to find yourself in (whether there was a comparable decline in churchgoing no one bothered to find out). The reluctance of these civilians to present them-selves for long-awaited treatment Graham found a godsend. After Dunkirk, the annex had been alarmingly overcrowded. If he wanted to throw up more huts, he was told they were 'unavailable'—an infuriatingly handy expression of rebuff. If he wanted more beds, he knew where to look. With the amiable connivance of Mr O'Rory, the Blackfriars gynaecologist work-ing at Smithers Botham, Graham sent Tudor Beverley and his houseman to shift some unoccupied ones from O'Rory's wards. When the traffic was interrupted angrily by Captain Pile in the middle of the lawn, Graham drove to Maiden Cross and bought camp beds in the sports' shop. Captain Pile appeared in the annex to object wrathfully, but even he could hardly evict the sleeping patients.

'It's most irregular, Mr. Trevose. You can't just increase the number of beds in the hospital like that.'

'But the men would be terribly uncomfortable on the floor,' Graham pointed out mildly.

Captain Pile went redder than ever. He was having a bad war. His command was admittedly complete over the military patients at Smithers Botham, who on his approach were expected, with the difficulty of saluting smartly from the pillow, to stiffen themselves under the sheets as though they were corpses already. But the civilian doctors from Blackfriars took no notice of him at all. It was most frustrating. The senior ones made clear that the possessors of Fellowships from the grand Royal Colleges could hardly be bossed by a mere Licentiate of the less exacting Society of Apothecaries. The younger ones defaced his signed notices, often quite obscenely, predictably named him 'The Haemorrhoid', and made up rude songs about him which they sang outside his office window. And Trevose he found more maddening than the rest put together.

'If I may say so, your wards give me a great deal of unnecessary trouble,' he continued warmly to Graham. 'You make absolutely no attempt to maintain proper discipline in this annex. Why, you're actually mixing officers with other ranks!'

'Surely this is hardly the moment to insist on the niceties of military etiquette, Captain Pile?'

'But it is *against regulations*! What have you done with those board partitions? I had them sent specially to divide up the wards, officers one side, men the other.'

'I'm keeping them handy. They'll be essential if we get anyone from the women's Services. Though I suppose it would be all right bedding them down among the men, as long as the ladies weren't officers?'

Captain Pile decided to ignore the question. You could never be quite sure with a man like Trevose if he were being serious. 'And what about all this ice-cream? I gather you're getting it from some merchant in Maiden Cross. I must insist the practice stops forthwith. You must know it's quite out of order for anyone except the catering officer to have foodstuffs sent to the hospital?'

Burned men lose protein from the raw surface of their bodies, and Graham had discovered sadly with his own palate that the Smithers Botham diet was miserably mean in such a costly essential. The dishes consisted mostly of porridge, stew, and rice pudding, which, being boiled in the same vats, had interchangeable tastes. Though like an old-fashioned Christmas pudding they occasionally offered keepsakes, a dirty bandage, a broken tooth, once even a well-worn rubber heel. Graham supposed that none of the original inmates was expected to notice what he ate, anyway. During the hot summer he had hit on the idea of ice-cream, telling the manufacturer to cram in as many protein-rich eggs as he could find. But all this seemed too complicated to explain to Captain Pile.

'I eat it all myself,' he said. 'Incidentally, I pay for it from my own pocket.'

'But you buy churns of the stuff!'

'I happen to be particularly fond of ice-cream.'

Captain Pile looked baffled. Trevose was an eccentric, quite off his head. 'Furthermore,' Pile recalled, 'you sent six shirts to the hospital laundry last week. The maximum permitted number is three.'

'Good God,' muttered Graham.

When Bluey arrived at the annex he had no idea what might be in store for him. He had no imagination at all. It was an essential ingredient of his limitless courage. The Ministry of Information, hungry for heroes, had trumpeted him as the Australian 'ace', printing his photograph and his number of enemy kills in the newspapers. He was a rewarding subject, tall, good-looking with dark wavy hair, unmarried, a sportsman splendid at cricket, swimming, and tennis. But a hero has no more likelihood of being pleasant than lesser men. Bluey was pushful, overbearing, and vain, as malicious behind the backs of his superiors as into the faces of anyone unlucky enough to be set below him. Since puberty he had seduced as many girls as he could lay hands on, regarding them all as the fortunate recipients of his passing favour. In the air, he would risk his neck for anyone. On the ground he would lift a finger only for himself. No one in the squadron had much time for Bluey.

'Good morning, Flight-Lieutenant Jardine.' A young nurse with a mature air, holding a board with a clip of notes, approached as he stood at the ward door trying to take it all in. 'We've put you in the far end bed. That's a bit of an honour, you know. It's supposed to be quieter.'

Bluey looked round anxiously. It was certainly a change from the last hospital. The long narrow lower ward of the annex was crammed with beds, though the patients were mostly dressed and lounging about, smoking, laughing, or chatting noisily. They struck him as an odd bunch. The majority were bandaged heavily about the head, some wore slings and plaster casts, others had their hands in bulky dressings like boxing-gloves. The ward radio was at full blast. It always was at Smithers Botham, from early tea to lights out, right through the war. Graham often idly wondered how many people died to the strains of Geraldo.

'Do you want me to turn in?' Bluey asked.

'Not unless you're tired. In the annex we like to keep everyone up and about. Dr Bickley thinks it stops you getting bad chests.'

'Who's Dr Bickley?' asked Bluey warily. You never knew how many of these medical jokers were waiting to have a go at you. 'I'm under Dr Trevose.'

'Dr Bickley's the Gasman. The anaesthetist. You'll meet him later. You can smoke whenever you like, there aren't any rules. Have you got enough cigarettes? The boys'll help you light them.'

'I'm all right.' He wasn't going to feel gratitude towards anybody.

'Is there anything special you like to eat? We'll try to get it, but we can't guarantee results.'

'I'm not particular.'

'Here's Peter.' The nurse smiled. 'He'll look after you. He's the oldest inhabitant.'

The nurse left Bluey with another man in flight lieutenant's uniform, his tunic hanging from his shoulders and his sleeves pinned to the pockets. Bluey inspected him with fascination. His face was mostly hidden in crêpe bandages, but a strange yellowish-pink sausage sprouted from the middle of it. This was fixed to his left wrist, held against his cheek by a plaster cast. His hands were bandaged, but his thumb was free enough to grasp a cigarette in a long holder.

'I'm Peter Thomas,' announced the apparition amiably. 'Welcome to the mausoleum. You're the Australian, aren't you? I remember seeing you in the *Daily Mirror*. If I recollect aright, you were sharing the page with Jane.'

'What do they do to you in this place?'

'Make you look like an advert for Brylcreem.'

Bluey stared round. 'How long before they let you out?'

'Well, it's inclined to be a long job, as possibly you can see for yourself. The Wizz doesn't believe in rushing things.'

'The Wizz?'

'The Wizard. Trevose. He made this elephant's trunk affair. It's a wrist pedicle. It started life as a slice of skin from my belly. The Wizz kept my wrist attached to my navel for weeks, before raising it to higher things. It's all a matter of re-establishing the blood supply before making the next move. You'll soon pick up the lingo. We become very professional here, you know. The pedicle's going to be part of my nose, incidentally.'

The two officers started walking along the line of beds.

'It's noisy,' observed Bluey. 'The place I came from, they shut me up alone in a room.'

'Life is very informal in annex D. Everyone mucks in together, all Services, all ranks. It's the Wizz's idea. Good for morale, he says. Though I rather think he does it to annoy the brass-hats. We had an admiral in here last week. He fell on his face down a ladder. Drunk, doubtless. I don't think he cared for the atmosphere much. The only gentleman enjoying privacy at the moment is a German bastard shut in the padded cell.'

As Bluey stopped short his companion gave a laugh. 'Didn't you know? This used to be a nuthouse. The change isn't always apparent. Which part of Australia do you come from?'

'Outside of Melbourne. My people own a sheep-station. I came over to join up before the war.' His near-lidless eyes stared round. 'Maybe all this means I'm on my way back again?'

'They'll notice a change in you,' said Peter Thomas crisply.

It was a remark in the spirit of annex D. The men had grown a shell of arrogance towards the world which had brought them to such straits. To be pitied was so unbearable, any eye sensed to be softening with compassion fired only an explosion of rudeness. The nurses got used to it—if they didn't, Graham had them shifted to more conventional wards. The elderly hospital padre found his attempts to 'cheer up the poor boys' so unwelcome, his Christian fortitude collapsed beneath him and he avoided the place. Even well-meaning ladies with baskets of gifts saw them accepted without a flicker of gratitude. After all, the patients felt the country owed them more for their pains than a few bars of chocolate.

'I suppose I've caught it pretty badly?' Bluey hazarded.

'Oh, I've seen worse,' Peter Thomas told him with an air of authority.

'When did they get you?'

'I was one of the earliest. I've been in here so long I'm practically one of the staff.'

'What's happening outside? Nobody's told me any news.'

'The Germans seem to be crying off. In daylight, at any rate.'

'That's funny. I thought we'd go on like that. Flying every day till the end of the war.' They stopped at Bluey's bed, the last before the partition dividing off the operating theatre. 'I was just starting to believe in my luck.'

'If you like, I'll see if I can find a newspaper,' Peter Thomas offered helpfully. 'Though the selection isn't very uplifting. There'll probably be a *Daily Press*, which is good for at least one laugh.'

'Thanks. I reckon I've a lot to catch up.'

Bluey sat on his bed and inspected his surroundings. There

was no need for mirrors in annex D. He could see himself in the monstrosities all round him. He suddenly realized he was an outcast, a frightening object, something to make any man wince and any woman run away in horror. For the first time the bitterness of his humiliation swept over him. He wanted to cry in self-pity. But his lachrymal glands were burnt, and even to weep was impossible.

6

BRIGADIER HAILEYBURY was a fair-minded man. He knew Trevose was a prima donna, unwilling or temperamentally unable to fit into any co-ordinated effort, even to win a war. And of course Pile didn't help. The fellow was unbelievably stupid. But the line must be drawn somewhere. Authority must be established. On the morning following Bluey's arrival he appeared at Smithers Botham to make his first inspection of the annex.

He could readily believe Pile's account of indiscipline among Graham's patients. He needed only to recall the notorious laxity of Graham's own life before the war. It would have to be checked, even if it meant a row. Haileybury was aware that he and Graham had quarrelled every second time they met, and recalled uneasily that he himself generally got the worst of it. Trevose had a quick tongue, and a slick way of putting things. But now Haileybury told himself he was dressed in authority—which was neither little, nor, in view of the summer's military disasters, likely to be brief.

He marched across the lawn with Captain Pile, admiring the flower-beds. As the operating theatre now blocked one end of the annex, entrance was between the horse-box lavatories and the kitchen, where twice daily the nurses portioned out food dispatched from the central Smithers Botham kitchens in reputedly heatproof trolleys. As the pair entered, the door of the washroom opened and Graham himself appeared. He was wearing a surgeon's green gown with a gauze mask dangling below his chin, and seemed busy.

'Haileybury, I was delighted to learn of your impending visit,' he began affably. 'I'd been hoping you'd look us up all summer.'

'I'm glad to find you so cheerful, Trevose. No one knows better than myself the difficulties under which you've been obliged to work.'

'I agree, we haven't sufficient equipment, sufficient room, sufficient staff, or a sufficient number of hours in the day, but we manage. I'd like you to see our star turn,' he invited. 'Nurse, give these two gentlemen masks and gowns. Step inside. It's the saline bath unit.'

In a partitioned corner of the wash-house one of the bath-tubs was in use. Sitting up to his waist in water was a man—or so it was to be assumed, the creature being without hair, eye-brows, or nose, the skin of his face and even his eyelids burnt away. There were two nurses working on him in white gowns and rubber gloves. One was moistening the man's head with a trickle of clear solution running from a glass vessel suspended near the ceiling. The other was manipulating a pair of forceps in the stream, picking away plaques of hard black material embedded in the pus and raw tissue. Captain Pile, whose eyes had become used to inspecting official rather than human material, felt his stomach turn over.

'Very interesting,' said Haileybury.

'Somewhat Heath Robinson, but it works,' Graham explained. 'It's got plenty of snags. For one thing, the saline solution in the carboy up there cools too quickly. It's a nuisance for the nurses to keep replacing it.'

'Doubtless,' said Haileybury.

They watched the operation in silence. After a few minutes Graham led them out. 'Why do you do it to them, Haileybury?' he demanded.

Haileybury untied the tapes of his surgeon's gown. 'Do what?'

'Plaster those burns with tannic acid jelly. Do you know what I feel when I look round my wards? No hatred of the

279

Germans. Their fellows are getting even worse treatment, I know that well enough, I lectured there before the war. No, I simply writhe with indignation over the stupidity of my own countrymen.'

'So you think tannic acid is stupid, do you?' Haileybury asked drily.

'I think it's criminal.'

'But you must know perfectly well, Trevose, it happens to be the regulation treatment. And what else would you suggest? That the dressing-stations do nothing in the way of first-aid at all?'

'That's exactly what I do suggest. I'm charitably assuming you treat burns with the equivalent of grannie's cold tea because, one, you can't think of anything better, and two, you want the casualties to feel something's being done for them. Well, something's being done, all right. Medieval mutilation.'

'I really don't think I need comment on that,' said Haileybury wearily. 'Ever since I've known you, you've ruined your advocacy of any cause, worthy or not, with the extravagance of your language.'

Graham suddenly felt angry. 'This situation doesn't need any language at all.' He pointed to the closed door of the washhouse. 'Haven't you eyes to see for yourself? That patient's a pilot officer, observer in a Blenheim, which failed to take off properly for some reason or other. The pilot was burnt to a cinder. By the time that poor devil turned up here his head and neck had skin like an elephant's. You know what it was, don't you? Congealed tannic acid. His hands were worse where he'd tried to pull his blazing clothes off. The fingers were drawn into the palms, webbed together, one black horrible mess. That's his real tragedy. With time and luck I can give him a face which will pass without too much comment in a crowd. But he'll probably never feed or wash himself again, even light his own cigarette. He'll be dependent on someone for the rest of his life. An awful prospect for both parties.'

Haileybury decided to be firm but patient. If the argument was to end in his favour, Trevose needed even more thoughtful

280

handling than usual. 'I can appreciate how you feel involved with these men, Trevose. But you must try and see our arrangements as a whole. The application of tannic acid as a first-aid measure to burns isn't some shot in the dark. It's been most carefully thought out. It is the official procedure. It is *regulation treatment*,' he emphasized.

'Then it's got to be changed. Do you know the first cases I had in here? A pair of naval ratings, picked up after an hour in the sea at Dunkirk. Both were badly burnt in the arms and legs. Both did splendidly. No tannic acid. Just salt solution like I'm using here, Nature's own.'

'Now you're being fanciful.' Haileybury started to sound irritated. 'I'm certainly not going to let you rush all of us into something entirely new.'

'Am I? Send me a lot more burns and make up your mind in six months. I'd like you to pull a few strings for me, by the way,' Graham invited airily. 'The unit's got to be expanded. I shall have to squeeze a second operating table into the theatre somehow. Tudor Beverley can run that himself. He's good enough. I'll need more assistants. And we want more huts desperately. It's like a slum in here.'

'You might reduce your difficulties if you ceased scouring the countryside for extra patients,' Haileybury told him bleakly.

Graham gave a grin. 'You heard about that, did you? It's the Services' own fault. It's weeks before I see some of the cases. They go on a ghastly traipse all over the shop, rotting for weeks in hospitals in Scotland or Wales, miles away. Faulty organization, that's the trouble. I'd like you to do something about that, too, please, and quickly.'

Haileybury became angry despite himself. 'Have you thought of making life easier for yourself and everyone else with some attempt to understand how Service administration works?'

'The only administration I understand is the one which gets me my own way.'

'No one's yet signed for the extra beds shifted here, sir,' interrupted Captain Pile, who was feeling out of it.

'Oh, do be quiet, Captain!' snapped Haileybury. 'Listen,

281

Trevose, I know you're an enthusiast. Often enough, I'll admit, in a perfectly good cause. But you can't expect the Services to make fundamental changes according to your whim of the moment. Please get that into your mind for a start.'

'Do you imagine I haven't thought about these problems just as carefully as you or anyone else? You must issue instructions banning tannic acid.'

'Are you giving *me* orders?'

'Yes.'

Haileybury drew a breath. 'You might have the courtesy to recognize my position, even if you don't respect it.'

'Why should I? It's I who have to handle the patients. Anyway, I know far more about burns than you do.'

'You would seem to have lost nothing of your high opinion of yourself.'

'It's a justifiable opinion,' Graham told him off-handedly.

'As far as I could make out before the war,' Haileybury exclaimed, 'your best skill was concentrated in your cock.' He stopped, looking confused. He could not remember using the expression before. Trevose always seemed to bring out vulgarity in him.

'Then do as you please,' Graham said casually. 'I'll get the tannic acid banned by the R.A.F., at least. You know a Member of Parliament called Fergusson?'

'I've heard of him,' Haileybury admitted surlily.

'He's just collared a job in the Air Ministry. Have you met his wife Sally? Wonderful pair of tits. Guaranteed to stop the conversation at a party. Well, I made them. The couple are pathetically grateful.'

'You mean, you intend to go behind my back?'

'I've no inhibitions about going behind anyone's back if I think it's in a good cause.' Haileybury said nothing. It was all most frustrating. 'You know, I've made so many bad decisions in my life,' Graham told him with returning cheerfulness, 'it's good to find once in a while I've hit on the right one. I mean staying out of uniform.'

'I would offer no view on the rightness or wrongness of that.'

Haileybury looked at him sourly. It seemed he had lost the argument, as usual. He vaguely wondered why. 'As I am here, perhaps you would invite me to look round your wards?' he added as sarcastically as possible.

'Of course.' Graham smiled. 'You know that I am always ready to oblige an old acquaintance in any professional matter whatever.'

Graham opened the door of the ward. It was a terrible thought, he told himself, but he was really quite enjoying the war.

7

'BUT WHY DON'T YOU divorce her, Graham?' asked Denise Bickley. 'I can't understand why you don't divorce her.'

It was a subject which Graham chose to skip away from as quickly as possible. 'I hate having truck with lawyers, I suppose,' he told her. 'They give me the creeps. With their undertakers' clothes and their undertakers' faces, burying all your hopes under a mound of stony possibilities.'

'But unfortunately not at undertakers' rates,' smiled John Bickley, the anaesthetist, across the log fire.

It was a Sunday afternoon in the first week of 1941, when the *Luftwaffe* was bombing the country nightly, the onion had become a fragrant memory, whisky and bananas had vanished with the other flavours of peace, and the war was starting to change from a perilous adventure to a wearisome way of life.

'But you *can* divorce her, you know.' John's wife Denise was chillingly well informed about everything to do with the married state. 'You can these days. The law's been changed.'

Why does the woman continually go paddling in the muddy waters of my soul? Graham asked himself. 'So I understand,' he agreed. 'A. P. Herbert's Act altered everything. Maria's been mad for over five years, so I'm legally at liberty to rid myself of the encumbrance whenever I feel like it. Of course, it was different when I first had her locked up.'

Graham had hoped that putting the situation so starkly might shame Denise into changing the subject, but she per-

284

sisted, 'I'd have thought it worth taking the trouble, if only to get things straight.'

'But how could it make the slightest difference to my life?'

'Supposing you wanted to get married again?' Denise exclaimed.

Graham laughed.

'Well, you never know.'

'I'm forty-six. Hardly the romantic age. Anyway, who's to be the bride?'

'How old must Maria be now?' asked Denise.

'Let me see—she's nine years older than me. Which makes her fifty-five.'

'How's she bearing up? Physically, I mean,' asked John. It was an attempt to turn the conversation. He knew Graham's sensitivities far better than his wife did.

'Her body's extremely well. I went down with Desmond to see her over Christmas. She's put on a lot of weight—they generally do, I gather. But her vital organs are functioning perfectly, though admittedly her blood-pressure's a bit up. Her mind's quite unbalanced, of course. She doesn't know me, sometimes she doesn't know her own nurses. On good days she washes herself. On bad days she wets the bed.'

Denise lit a cigarette and said, 'It must be dreadfully upsetting, seeing her like that.'

'Not particularly. I can hardly be expected to correlate her with the person I married. She was what they called a "society beauty", you know. The only daughter of our popular tub-thumping millionaire, Lord Cazalay.' A lot of things have happened since then, Graham reflected sombrely. Lord Cazalay's gone bust, for a start.

'Graham, may I ask you one thing?' Denise puffed earnestly. 'I'm only trying to help, you do understand that, don't you?'

'Ask anything you like,' said Graham resignedly.

'Do you still love her?'

'I never did.'

'But surely you must have done once?'

'I don't know. I don't know if I've ever been in love with

285

anybody. I fancy I have some sort of inborn immunity to the condition, like some people have for tuberculosis. Or perhaps I just expect too much.'

'But that's a tragedy, Graham! A life without love.'

'Is it? Aren't people over-obsessed with such attitudes? It's all the fault of the pictures and the wireless. Anyway, I've enough satisfaction for one lifetime in my work.'

'That tannic acid row was fun,' laughed John.

Graham's face lit up. He developed an almost schoolboy eagerness when anyone started talking about the annex. 'It was amusing, wasn't it? I told you, if McIndoe and myself made enough fuss in the right places they'd ban it. Fergusson grasped the point at once, luckily. Haileybury was so delightfully furious. He suffers a terrible spasticity of ideas, that man, his mind's as rigid as a plank. In peacetime I never had much use for the bigwigs who impose their authority on the profession, you know that, John. I never realized how gratifying it would be to extend my range in the war.' He looked at his wrist-watch. 'It was a wonderful lunch, Denise, but I must go.'

She looked disappointed and asked, 'Won't you stay for another cup of coffee?' She always did, every Sunday.

'I promised to see Peter Thomas this afternoon. A vital consultation—he's bursting to go on leave. Then I've someone to interview for a job. I'd like an early start in the theatre tomorrow, John,' he added. 'An awful list of oddments has piled up. Tim O'Rory's sending us a newborn baby with a hare lip. It ought to be done as soon as possible, I think, to give the poor little thing a chance to have a go at mother's milk.'

'I'll have the case on the table at eight.'

'I'd be much obliged,' said Graham.

When he had gone, Denise started clearing the dishes and declared, 'I really can't understand about Graham and Maria.'

Her husband, tall, bony, wearing an old jacket and chalk-striped flannels, stretched himself in front of the fire. 'Perhaps he doesn't think a divorce would be in Maria's own interests.'

'I couldn't believe that for a moment,' she said impatiently.

286

'Graham's one of the most selfish men I know. He's totally self-centred about everything, even the war.'

John started refilling his pipe. 'I imagined our Graham had undergone something of a sea change this last year.'

'*I* certainly hadn't noticed it.'

He stuck a spill of newspaper into the fire. Matches were becoming almost as precious as razor-blades. 'Do you think he really is so selfish? The plastic surgery racket was pretty tough in London before the war, you know. If a man didn't push himself, nobody else would take the trouble. Now that it doesn't matter a damn to Graham if he operates on three cases a week or thirty, perhaps he can afford the luxury of indulging his better nature.'

'He hasn't been showing much of it to you lately, has he? In the annex, I mean.'

John shrugged. Never an easy-going colleague, Graham was becoming worse-tempered in the theatre than ever. 'With the amount of work we're getting through, some tension between surgeon and anaesthetist is inevitable.'

Denise picked up the tray. 'If he *did* divorce the woman, it would all be perfectly respectable. He wouldn't have to take a girl for a week-end to Brighton, or anything like that.'

'I rather think you need a permit these days to pass a week-end in Brighton,' John observed mildly.

'Oh, you never take anything seriously,' she complained, disappearing into the kitchen.

Graham usually walked from the Bickleys' cottage back to Smithers Botham, on the double assumption that it did him good and he ought to save his official petrol. He started along the bare country lane wondering how he could get out of these Sunday lunches. Denise's insensitivity was deadly.

She had come into his life on the shoulders of John, a friend of twenty years' standing. John Bickley had given the anaesthetics since Graham was a young house-surgeon making a false start on throat work, in the days when children were submitted to the rape of their tonsils under the oblivion of asphyxia more than anaesthesia. Perhaps Denise was jealous, Graham

287

wondered. The relationship of surgeon and anaesthetist had something in common with marriage. He and John had half a lifetime of shared experience, together having faced the triumphs, failures, and excitements concentrated in the few square feet round an operating table. As Graham had become a fashionable plastic surgeon so John Bickley had become a fashionable 'doper' or 'stuffist', hurrying with his rubber tubes and cylinders from nursing-home to nursing-home on a time-table more complicated than Bradshaw's. The surgeons allowed him ten per cent of the operating fee, so he had to keep in with a good many to keep going. The year before the war he had married Denise, whom he had met at a suburban golf-club. She was tall, slim, blonde, and athletic, and had money. It struck Graham that ever afterwards John occupied himself by keeping in with her.

Graham hadn't liked Denise from the start. She had taken him over, as she had taken over everything else connected with her husband, even his Saturday's golf. It was becoming a complication to their work in the theatre, and Graham wouldn't countenance any complication likely to affect his patients. The Bickleys had found a cottage near Smithers Botham—very luckily, the arrival of Blackfriars having shifted most of the white elephants squatting on local estate agents' books. Having neither children nor evacuees, Denise had first invited Graham to live with them, confessing her astonishment at his tolerating the pub. But he was never a man to lack excuses. She insisted he at least called for Sunday lunch. She had a pressing sense of social duty, devoting much energy to organizing the wives of Blackfriars consultants scattered round the countryside into cosy if meatless dinner parties, into fours of bridge or sets of tennis, and into the knitting of large quantities of Balaclava helmets.

She loved quizzing him about Maria. It seemed to be her Sunday treat. Graham could anyway hardly explain his motives for not divorcing his wife when he didn't know them himself. Perhaps he had no more than a vague reluctance to put down some decrepit animal which once strode vigorously in the sunshine of admiration. Or perhaps, he thought more darkly, his wife was a mother-substitute, his feelings towards her loaded with guilt—but one mustn't take too much notice of the psychiatrists, they told a lot of fairy-tales. Somehow he must see less of Denise, particularly now it looked as though they'd be living in each other's pockets at Smithers Botham for life. Only General Wavell in the Western Desert was providing any encouraging sweeping black arrows on the front-page maps of Lord Arlott's *Daily Press*. Graham wondered glumly if the ebullient Australian newspaper proprietor, whom he had known well enough in peacetime, had foreseen that his task of chirpingly maintaining civilian morale every morning would have reached its present bleak severity.

Reaching his office in the hut outside the annex, Graham changed his shoes, pulled on a white coat, and sent a nurse for Peter Thomas.

'I hope I'm a specimen worthy of display to the outer world,' Peter began cheerfully.

The patient's flesh sausage was by then detached from his wrist, and starting to turn into something like a nose. The rest of his face was a patchwork of skin, too yellow and too shiny, Graham thought, cut from various bits of his body. Graham removed a dressing and saw with satisfaction that some sepsis in the corner of his last graft had healed. 'The sulphanilamide powder seems to have done the trick,' he announced. 'It's saved me the necessity of having to use you as a guinea-pig for penicillin.'

'Penny what?'

'Oh, it's some stuff they invented at Mary's. Their Prof. Fleming found a mould which kept killing off the bugs he was trying to grow in his lab. It must have been very irritating, until he put two and two together. Our medical unit are working on it. It's supposed to be secret, though God knows why. The stuff's as rare as hens' teeth.'

'What's it look like?' asked Peter, with interest.

'Very yellow and sticky, and personally I don't think it's going to be the slightest use.'

Graham took the man's hands. Not much movement yet. Annoying.

'Is that physiotherapy girl bullying you to use your hands, Peter?'

'Quite delightfully so.'

'I think we can risk doing without your company for a couple of months,' Graham decided. He turned to the folder of notes on his desk. 'Then I'm afraid it's back for the next stage.'

'How long, O Wizz, how long?'

'Altogether? The next step shouldn't be too bad. I'll make you some eyebrows from the hair on the nape of your neck. But I've never made a secret that we'll be very old friends by the time we finally part. You're a major construction job.'

'That's an interesting way of putting it.'

'I'm sorry. It must make me sound dreadfully heartless.'

'But that's the secret of your success, Wizz! You've got a ward full of monsters, and you look on us as so many construction jobs. Exactly the right attitude. Surely you know how sickening it is to be pitied?'

Graham nodded. 'Yes, of course I do. But I'm not putting on an act, you know. I've always looked on my patients as construction jobs. I could never have run the sort of practice I had before the war otherwise.'

'You must find us lot rather a come-down after remodelling film stars.'

'Quite the opposite,' said Graham warmly. 'When I came out here I knew I'd have to remodel my operative technique— after all, a land mine makes rather more mess than even the worst car smash. What I didn't know was the extent to which I'd have to remodel myself. What did I do before the war? I lifted a face or reshaped a nose, took out the stitches, collected the fee, and that was that. But I live with you fellows, day and night. You've always got some interesting problem for me to solve, psychological if it isn't surgical.'

Peter laughed. 'You make us sound like a bunch of damn nuisances.'

'On the contrary, you've presented me with an object in life.

You didn't seek out my service, like my patients in peacetime. You'd no choice, the war washed you up on my doorstep. I feel I owe you something.' He laughed, too. 'It's terribly stimulating. And terribly gratifying. This "Wizz" stuff, it's stupid really, I'm only doing my job. But it means more to me than the most gushing praise I ever got for hanging a new pair of tits on an actress. You boys are highly selective in your appreciation of anything.'

'We're exposed to an awful lot of well-meaning hypocrites. We soon learn to pick out the genuine ones.'

'Or perhaps it's just a form of selfishness on my part?' Graham philosophized. 'I like to think of you as worthwhile memorials to my surgery. I've reached a depressing age. I'm beginning to realize I'm at the whim of any passing disease. "Death hath ten thousand several doors for men to take their exits"—a sobering reminder from Webster. But what am I complaining for?' he apologized. 'You've been near enough to getting yourself killed.'

'Yes, and I was terrified. I've vomited in the cockpit. Once, though I kept pretty quiet about it, I accomplished what you would refer to as "defaecation".'

'You'd no hopes of the life hereafter?'

'I preferred to wait and see.'

'I expect you're right. I had a brother once, a medical missionary. He at least departed this life in a spirit of glowing optimism. Do you want some cigarettes?' Graham felt suddenly the conversation was becoming too self-revealing. But now he never had a chance to reveal anything of himself to anybody. 'They're called Sweet Caporals—Canadian, it seems.' He had given up smoking, mainly through the tediousness of queueing, but scrounged what he could for his patients. 'Do you want another book?' He tossed a paperback on his desk, alongside the unfamiliar white packet. In peacetime, he hardly got through a book a year. Now he spent most evenings in his room at The Oak reading. There was nothing like a world war to simplify your life. 'It's *Decline and Fall*, by Evelyn Waugh. Very funny. How's Bluey getting on?' he added.

'Somewhat restless.'

Graham lit the cigarette in Peter's holder. That was bad news. Bluey had to stand at least another dozen operations, and needed all the patience he could muster.

'Though his morale has improved considerably,' Peter added, 'since getting his hands on a supply of rum. God knows where from. He keeps it in his locker, which I presume is strictly against regulations.'

'The annex houses enough trouble without regulations,' Graham said briefly. He looked at his watch. 'Very well, Peter, off you go on leave. Now there should be a female waiting for me. I don't know what she's like—young, old, fat, thin, as ugly as sin or a goddess. She wants to take over as ward sister, God help her.'

Peter looked surprised. 'The Dragon's going?'

'Yes, Sister James has decided to join the Q.A.s and nurse the Army. You can hardly blame her. After the annex she'll find even a pitched battle a rest cure. As the Blackfriars matron has broken off diplomatic relations with me through the disgraceful behaviour of my patients,' he told Peter with a grin, 'I am obliged to find most of my own staff. This one's been recommended by a surgeon I know in a children's hospital. Just about the right background for handling you lot, I'd imagine. Send her in, will you?'

The prospective sister struck Graham as resembling a Botticelli virgin with disastrous dress-sense. She was slight, fair, and transparent-looking, wearing lisle stockings, stout laced black shoes, and a suit of green and very hairy tweed. She had no hat, her hair was in the usual page-boy bob. Big eyes, Graham noticed, a pretty mouth, if rather over-large. No trace of make-up, but a good skin. He decided she didn't look nearly tough enough.

'It's Miss Mills, isn't it?' he asked, as she sat with hands crossed demurely in her lap. 'I'm afraid all I know about you is confined to a telephone conversation with Mr Cavill, and the line was terrible.'

'Yes. Clare Mills. I'm Mr Cavill's staff nurse.'

She had a soft voice, speaking with great deliberation. Graham noticed she had a trick of emphasizing her last syllables. Probably nervousness, he suspected.

'How old are you?'

'Twenty-three.'

How the nursing profession thrusts responsibility on its daughters! Graham reflected. Before the war, they had to be twenty-one and of unspotted character before being allowed to handle the Blackfriars sick at all. But perhaps women were built for it. After all, there was no responsibility like motherhood, and that was liable to catch a girl unawares anytime.

'I'd better make plain from the start that the work here isn't hard, Miss Mills. It's exhausting. I'm an impossible taskmaster. I'm demanding, boorish, and usually most ungrateful. I don't expect loyalty. I expect devotion. I tolerate incompetence badly, and fools not at all. It's a mystery how I manage to keep any assistants in the place. And the patients are much worse than I am. Life can be hell for nursing staff in the annex. Though, to be fair, most of them seem to find it an enjoyable hell.' Graham smiled at her. 'Would you like to end our interview here and now?'

'I should very much like the post, Mr Trevose.'

'Why?'

She hesitated. 'I've always wanted to work on a plastic surgery unit.'

'A strange ambition.'

She paused again, and went on shyly, 'You once operated on a friend of mine, Mr Trevose. She was a girl—seventeen at the time. She had a deformed lip. Her name was Susan Wright.'

Graham tried to remember. It was impossible. He had operated on so many girls. 'I can only hope the operation was a success?'

'Oh, yes!' She suddenly became animated. 'It made an enormous difference to her. Not only physically, I mean, but mentally. She told me all about you, Mr Trevose—how understanding you were, how skilful. Perhaps it gave me the ambition of one day working for you.'

Graham folded his arms. She was terribly young, but old Cavill had praised her warmly enough. She'd be pretty to have about the annex. Perhaps the boys would take pity on her delicate looks, though he doubted it. And she had a neat hand with flattery. A sensible girl. It was a talent which had taken him a long way at the beginning of his career.

'Can you start on Wednesday?' he asked her.

8

BLUEY JARDINE bared the upper half of his left arm with an air of resignation. He knew exactly what was coming to him. It was a Friday morning, following the Sunday when Graham had sent Peter Thomas on leave, which gave Bluey the dubious honour of being the ward's oldest inhabitant. He had then been in the annex four months, and into the theatre eight times. Like everyone else, he had developed a keen interest in the science which was bedevilling him.

The routine of an operation had become as familiar to him as the routine of flying. The injection about to enter his arm was his 'premedication', and he even knew the names of the drugs. There was one hundred-and-fiftieth of a grain of scopolamine, which dried up your mouth and lungs and stopped you bubbling and drowning yourself once you were under. There was a third of a grain of omnopon, which was just another name for morphia, and gave you guts. He twitched as the staff nurse punctured his skin with the syringe. The more needles they stuck into you, the more you came to hate them.

He lay back in bed, wearing long white knitted socks and a short over-laundered cotton nightshirt which fastened with rubber buttons at the back. He didn't seem to be growing as drowsy as usual. Perhaps the injection was losing effect. Only to be expected, he told himself. Once he could get drunk on a bottle of beer, now it needed a couple of crates. He wondered how many more operations the Wizz had in store for him. It never occurred to Bluey that he might ask Graham to stop, to leave him with a half-patched face and makeshift hands, but in peace. He accepted his treatment as something which went on until it reached its natural end, like the war.

As they wheeled him the few yards from the ward to the operating theatre on a trolley he searched the ceiling for a peculiar star-shaped crack, as he always touched the dried kangaroo paw in his tunic pocket before flying. Sometimes when they trundled you out you were dead scared, others you didn't give a damn. He supposed it depended how rough they were on your last visit. Anyway, the operation today was kid's stuff. He'd soon get over it. With luck, he'd be out on the grog again on Saturday night, as usual.

The anaesthetic room, improvised out of flimsy partitions, was hardly big enough to hold the patient, the ward nurse accompanying him, the tall frame of John Bickley, and the anaesthetic trolley gleaming with dials, bottles, piping, and coloured cylinders. Bluey raised his head from the pillow. The Gasman, his long green gown pushed up to his elbows, was holding a large syringe.

'Not another bloody needle?'

'You're a favoured customer, Bluey. No gas this time. I'm sending you off with an injection.'

'Go on?' This was an interesting departure, something to tell the ward afterwards. The anaesthetist rubbed a swab of cold antiseptic on the crook of Bluey's left arm. 'What's the stuff called?'

'Evipan.' John drew back the plunger of his syringe, a swirl of blood telling him the needle lay safely inside the vein. If the injection went by error into the skin of Bluey's elbow there would be an abscess, and a terrible row with Graham. 'There, you didn't even feel the needle, did you? Now count, out loud. . . .'

Bluey reached fifteen, yawned deeply, and fell asleep. John plucked out the syringe, simultaneously freeing Bluey's breathing by holding up his chin. 'This stuff was invented by our friends the Germans,' he told the nurse. 'I ought to use it as a routine. The boys get pretty browned off, being suffocated every time with gas. That can't be much fun when you have to face a dozen operations on the trot.'

Like all specialist anaesthetists, John Bickley brought to his work the artistic touch of an experienced chef. First he held a triangular padded mask tight to Bluey's patchwork face, and concocted a delicately proportioned mixture of oxygen and nitrous oxide gas. Then he moved a lever on a bottle of blue liquid to add a trace of trichlorethylene vapour—a more powerful anaesthetic to deepen Bluey's unconsciousness. John edged across the lever on another bottle to admit the pungent vapour of ether, the main ingredient of the dish. Bluey coughed fiercely. He always did, John reflected. He should insist that Graham stop his patients smoking for at least a week before their operations. But Graham objected that would be bad for morale, and they'd smoke in the lavatories, anyway. Graham objected to almost everything he suggested, it struck John wearily, ever since he had started calling for Sunday lunch.

Two coloured bobbins already danced up thin vertical glass tubes on John's anaesthetic trolley, indicating the volume of oxygen and nitrous oxide flowing to his patient. When he judged the anaesthesia deep enough, he sent a third bobbin spinning by adding carbon dioxide to the mixture. This stimulated Bluey's breathing, until he was heaving away as though finishing some desperate race in his sleep. With economical movements, John laid aside the face-mask, reached for a narrow, stiff, greased, red-rubber tube, and inserted it into the remains of Bluey's right nostril. He edged it inwards gently—an unsuspected nasal polyp would bring blood all over the shop and an even worse row with Graham—listening to the breath-sounds as it slipped behind Bluey's flaccid tongue, then finally through his widely open larynx into his windpipe. It was a technique invented by Harold Gillies' own anaesthetist, Ivan Magill, to deliver the anaesthetic directly into the patient's lungs while leaving his face and mouth as a sterile unoccupied battlefield for the plastic surgeon.

'That looked pretty easy, I must say,' observed the nurse, who like all nurses had long ago ceased to be impressed by her medical overlords. But her remark pleased John. The trick was rather like playing darts in the dark, not easy at all. Only the experience of twenty years made it seem so.

As Bluey himself knew, the operation was to be a simple affair. Graham cut a thin graft of skin from Bluey's thigh with a Thiersch knife like an oversized razor, then stitched it along his chin where a former one had failed to take. Bluey was back in bed within the half hour, struggling to consciousness through dreams about flying, which were always unpleasant but soon forgotten. He woke up deciding he didn't feel as bad as usual. The Gasman's injection was a winner. The next night he'd be fit enough to finish the bottle of rum in his locker, then slip out with half a dozen others to The Oak.

Knowing the habits of his patients, Graham made a point on Saturday nights of taking a bus to the pictures in Maiden Cross. That Saturday he queued to see an American film about the war, in which all the Germans conversed in villainous guttural undertones, all the British officers had Oxford accents, and all their men talked like Sam Weller. The star was Stella Garrod, the woman Graham had made a fool of himself with before the war. He wondered wryly if she ever bothered to think of him. In fact, she spoke fondly and often of her affair with the little London surgeon, immorality with Englishmen having, after Dunkirk, considerable kudos in Hollywood.

When Graham reached home on the last bus the pub was already closed, but Bluey and his companions had been disinclined to finish the evening. They had staggered down the Smithers Botham drive singing *Cats on the Rooftops*, and the night being moonlit someone noticed a collection of builders' materials stacked outside Captain Pile's office under the gleaming portico. Bluey gave a whoop as he found a tin of paint and a brush. A porter appeared through the complicated blackout screening the front door to investigate, but identifying denizens of the annex retreated instantly. Bluey painted across the portico a single word in large letters, one on each of the four columns. Then they went singing and laughing back to the annex and bed. The night nurses were used to it.

Early the next morning Mrs Sedgewick-Smith came down the hospital drive, hurrying to a long-standing appointment with the elderly padre. Mrs Sedgewick-Smith was the wife of a stockbroker who commanded the local Home Guard, and before the war had filled the vacuum of her life by fussing over the mental patients at Smithers Botham, or as many of them as remained socially presentable. She had organized whist drives, jumble sales, demure dances, and extremely amateur theatricals, invited the inmates for tea or for outings in her Rolls, all of which she bracketed as 'giving the poor things a nice little break'. The war presented even more poor things as targets for her deadly solicitude. She had installed herself as unofficial welfare officer at Smithers Botham, and was beginning to hope the war would go on long enough for somebody to give her a medal for it.

She saw the word.

She was horribly shocked. It was not a word which could possibly appear in print, but she had of course overheard it, from workmen, soldiers, lunatics, and the like. She had always imagined it spelt with a 'ph', like 'phutt'. To see it splashed in black paint across the portico was absolutely outrageous. And on a Sunday morning, too. She would have to find Captain Pile.

Captain Pile occupied a comfortable villa in the grounds, where he managed to live in unmilitary domesticity with his wife and two children. He was in his braces, enjoying his breakfast. He put on his tunic and inspected the word officially. Though he used it frequently himself, he had to affect an air of disgust as pained as his informant's. Mrs Sedgewick-Smith must be humoured at all costs. She was a powerful lady at Smithers Botham, the dispenser of valuable grace and favours, mostly unobtainable off the ration.

When Graham arrived at the annex at nine for an informal Sunday ward-round with his new sister, his spirits fell as he noticed Miss Mills in close conversation at the ward door with Captain Pile. He caught sight of Mrs Sedgewick-Smith, and they dropped further. He had often noticed her fluttering in and out of the Tudor house across the village green, but hearing she

299

was a professional busybody had taken pains to avoid her. Besides, she was thick with Denise Bickley, and probably knew far more about his personal affairs than she deserved.

'Good morning,' Graham greeted the visitors politely. 'Anything I can do for you?'

'I'm afraid a most serious matter has arisen, Mr Trevose,' Captain Pile told him solemnly.

Oh God, this is going to be a bore, Graham thought.

'I expect you've seen the main entrance this morning?' the Captain added.

'No, I came here direct, through the orchard.'

'A word—a most offensive word—has been written across it in paint. Mrs Sedgewick-Smith was most disturbed to see it.'

'I'm sorry about that. But—I know the annex has a bad name —why hold my patients responsible?'

'For the simple reason they were seen by the night-porter. Flight Lieutenant Jardine and some others.'

Graham nodded slowly. That's encouraging, he thought, Bluey's getting enough function in his hands to wield a paint brush. 'Then I can only apologize most sincerely to both you and Mrs Sedgewick-Smith.'

'You realize they'd been drinking?'

'Had they? I don't mind that. I even encourage it,' Graham explained mildly. 'It's a matter of pride to my anaesthetist if they feel capable of taking a few drinks after his attentions.' Seeing the captain's irritated expression he continued, 'You see, I want these men to live a normal life. Or as normal as they can manage. I want them to think of an operation as something as casual as a visit to the dentist, not the upheaval of a lifetime.'

'That's all very well,' the captain told him testily, 'but you have to maintain discipline—'

'I'll talk to them,' said Graham firmly. 'I promise. Isn't that enough? It won't happen again.'

'No, that is *not* enough, Mr Trevose. You cannot simply take the affair into your own hands. It is my duty to see that appropriate action is taken.'

'Listen, Captain,' said Graham briskly, 'I alone am responsible for these patients. Neither you nor the Army nor anyone else has the first idea how to cope with them. Will you kindly understand that?'

His patience suddenly broke and he felt angry. In peacetime he had been a somebody, the friend of rich and influential men, a doctor with a name almost as familiar to the general public as Lord Horder's. Now he was being lectured by some hack in a uniform which passed as a substitute for intelligence.

'Can't you see? These men aren't invalids.' Graham's outstretched arm indicated the ward, where the patients were lying in bed reading the Sunday papers, trying hard to give the impression they weren't listening. Bluey himself was asleep at the end, snoring loudly. 'Underneath their wounds and scars they're full of life, fit and lusty. They were youngsters with charm and sex-appeal, and what happened? In a few seconds they were turned into objects of horror. Then they were locked up in this converted madhouse. And that's not to be their fate for a week, or a month, or even a year. When the war's over and everyone's back in their comfortable little slots these patients of mine will still be coming up for another graft, another pedicle, another operation of some sort. How are they going to face that miserable prospect if they can't run wild now and then?'

Captain Pile tried to say something, but Graham went on, 'Do you know what happened in the last war? When I first heard of plastic surgery I was a patient myself in a sanatorium. There was a plastic unit billeted in half the wards. Every afternoon, under King's Regulations, the men had to be marched by an N.C.O. round the countryside for exercise. You can imagine the effect. People weren't so well educated then, were more superstitious. You'd have thought an army of ghouls was advancing on them. They locked their doors, covered their windows, and hid their children. So the Army confined the poor fellows to hospital, with nothing to look at but each other—an inspired piece of morale-building. I don't want any of that nonsense in this war. There's one thing my patients ask from the world, and only one. To be treated as normal individuals. Oh, I know it's difficult, they're freaks. But the effort isn't much to ask.'

'I think Mr Trevose is perfectly right,' announced Mrs Sedgewick-Smith.

Captain Pile spun round. The unexpected desertion of his ally appalled him. Trevose was a difficult customer at the best of times, and that morning he needed all the support he could muster. She stood tugging the hem of her tweed jacket and staring at Graham with large grey eyes. She must have been quite a good-looking girl, Graham thought. Even now, I could do her face a power of good.

'After all,' continued Mrs Sedgewick-Smith crisply, 'there are no children roaming the hospital. And the rest of us surely know that expression exists.'

'Exactly,' said Graham.

Mrs Sedgewick-Smith had undergone a change of heart. She had been dying to meet Graham for eighteen months. He was *the* Graham Trevose, the man you once saw in the *Tatler*, the surgeon one or two of her friends could talk about, quite breathlessly. Now she saw him at close quarters she realized he had a distinction, a dignity, an authority, an air about him which Captain Pile despite his uniform so sadly lacked. In short, Graham Trevose was a *gentleman*. And, war or no war, the ladies and gentlemen of England had to stand shoulder to shoulder together.

'We mustn't wallow in our indignation,' she continued calmly, 'and I'm sure the paint can very easily be cleaned off. Mr Trevose, I appreciate every word that you have said. Isn't there anything I can do for your patients? To give them a nice little break?'

'There most certainly is. And it isn't very much. Just ask them to tea, invite along some girls, and talk about the weather.'

'This is nothing to do with a breach of discipline,' Captain Pile broke in furiously.

'Surely, Captain, if Nelson could turn a blind eye you can?' asked Mrs Sedgewick-Smith tartly. 'There are so many regulations these days, none of us can avoid breaking one or two, can we?'

Captain Pile fell silent. He had been rather afraid of this turn in the conversation. Regularly every Friday Mrs Sedgewick-Smith brought him half a dozen eggs from her hens, in a card-board box labelled as Red Cross library books. A side of bacon had once been smuggled into his house, wrapped in a sheet to resemble the laundry. There had been pots of gooseberry jam, pounds of sugar, even a few ounces of butter. It would be sad if the flow ceased. Captain Pile was extremely fond of egg and bacon for his breakfast. It was a testing decision. Should he pawn his military honour for a handful of eggs?

'I suppose if you don't feel inclined to press the matter, Mrs Sedgewick-Smith, I—'

'Extremely sensible of you,' she said quickly. She turned to Graham with a smile. 'Mr Trevose, I do hope you can drop in for a little drink some evening? I'm sure my husband can find something in the cupboard.'

Graham promised. The bargain struck him as cheap at the price.

When Graham finally started his ward-round, he said to Sister Mills, 'I'm sorry about that. It doesn't happen every Sunday morning.'

'Oh, what a pity.' She smiled. 'I thought you were terribly impressive, Mr Trevose. Though I can't for the life of me see what all the fuss was about.'

'Neither can I,' said Graham. It suddenly occurred to him he didn't even know what the word was.

9

THE HOSTESS opened her own front door. In peacetime, as she was half-tempted to explain, there would have been a maid in a lace apron. 'I'm so glad you could come,' Mrs Sedgewick-Smith greeted them brightly.

Bluey and the half-dozen others who had courted disgrace on the Saturday night found themselves standing on Mrs Sedgewick-Smith's doorstep the following Monday afternoon. Graham had conscripted them as a punishment. The outing had not struck them as at all attractive. Tea didn't promise much fun, and an invitation from the local grand lady had an intolerable air of condescension about it. But if the Wizz told them to go, go they must. Even Bluey agreed a bloke would do anything to please the Wizz.

'Hello, Missus,' announced Bluey. 'Here's the Home for the Sick and Crippled. Frankenstein's monsters' annual outing.'

Mrs Sedgewick-Smith gave an uncertain smile. But years of intense social struggle with the wives of other stockbrokers had tempered her conviviality like steel. She hesitated only a second before continuing, 'But *do* come in. Quite a charming afternoon for the time of year, isn't it?'

Bluey led his companions into the hall. He stared round. Graham had warned him to be on his best behaviour, but he was determined to keep the social balance tilted in his favour.

'Old place you've got here, Missus.'

'Oh, yes! Parts of it go back to Henry the Eighth.'

Bluey sniffed. 'Smells like it.'

There was an awkward silence as the patients stood grinning at their hostess, like mischievous children with Hallowe'en masks. I must treat them as normal people, she reminded herself, as perfectly normal people. Like the charming young men who used to call before the war for tennis. And surely if they were officers they must also be gentlemen? Even the one with sergeant's stripes on his sleeve was aircrew, and as things went at the time socially acceptable. Her loss for something to say was relieved by the oak door of the sitting-room opening, to emit a slight girl in a yellow-and-white flowered dress, with rigidly outstretched hand and a rigidly fixed smile.

'My youngest daughter Stephanie,' said Mrs Sedgewick-Smith, on a note of enthusiasm.

'Spiffing to meet you,' said Stephanie, hand still outstretched.

Stephanie was at an age which should have changed her from a grub in boarding-school uniform to flutter gaily amid the dances and parties of the 'season'. As it was, she was trying to decide whether to start as a probationer nurse at Smithers Botham or to make Sten guns in the shadow factory at Maiden Cross. But Graham had prescribed girls, and girls being like everything else in short supply, Mrs Sedgewick-Smith had patriotically concluded that Stephanie must do.

'You should have warned us, Missus, you'd a houseful of beautiful women,' said Bluey sarcastically.

'You mustn't say things like that,' smiled her mother. 'You'll turn her head.'

Stephanie went pink. 'Oh, *Mummy!*'

'You must forgive my daughter for being a little shy,' Mrs Sedgewick-Smith apologized uneasily. 'You see, she doesn't have much chance to meet young men these days. The war has quite ruined our social life.'

'It's ruined a lot of things,' said Bluey.

They went into the timbered drawing-room. There was a small fire, an eggless cake, and meat-paste sandwiches spread with margarine—Mrs Sedgewick-Smith considered raiding the butter-ration as carrying compassion too far. She fiddled anxiously amid the teacups, aware that her guests were going to be terribly difficult to entertain. Of course, one couldn't—or at least mustn't—blame the poor things for being rather peculiar. She hoped it wouldn't have any lasting effect on Stephanie, who was sitting on a low chair with the arresting habit of repeatedly crossing her legs then nervously tugging her hem over the knee of her lisle stockings. Her mother had instructed her sternly to treat the guests as perfectly normal. Her boarding-school had instructed her even more sternly how to carry such things through. As she chatted haltingly it amused Bluey to see her struggling to pretend they were ordinary-looking individuals. She'd be a virgin for sure, he decided, though might make a satisfactory bang if touched up enough first.

'Why don't you come back to Australia with me after the war, Stephanie?'

'I'd love to, really! Honestly, I would. I've heard it's a super place.'

'It's not bad. All the good things are free—surfing, lying on the beach, Sunday picnics, riding round the station. Australia's got space. You can get lost in it. There's no one to bother you. No one to stare at you.'

He stopped, realizing he had unthinkingly let show the raw edge of his feelings. The sergeant, whom Bluey always irritated, took advantage of the silence to compliment Mrs Sedgewick-Smith on the sandwiches.

'I'm so glad you like them. I made the paste myself, you know, from leftovers. I got the recipe from a magazine—the food facts are so helpful these days, aren't they? I would have done you a carrot flan as well, but of course that needs a lemon jelly for the glazing, and there just isn't *one* in the shops.'

Food at the time was starting to replace sex as the basis of most adult conversation.

'You're quite right about your daughter,' the sergeant continued. 'It's hard to miss the enjoyments of youth. You can't store them away like your pretty frocks for use after the war. They won't fit any more.'

Mrs Sedgewick-Smith gave a faintly puzzled smile. Behind

the bandages was he young or old? Serious or mocking? Just a sergeant, or a gentleman?

'There's an exact moment in life for your first taste of wine and of love,' the sergeant went on. 'You'll always remember it, and never succeed in recapturing the flavour of either.'

'You know, I think I read something like that in a book,' exclaimed Mrs Sedgewick-Smith.

'Probably one of mine,' said the sergeant, who had been desperate to make some such remark. Before the war he had written a couple of novels, which though noticed kindly by James Agate had not been noticed by his present companions at all. Mrs Sedgewick-Smith, a three-volume-a-week woman with Boot's, became agreeably flustered to find herself in the company of a man of letters. It also kept Bluey out of the conversation, which continued at a genteel literary level until they had finished the last pale dry crumbs of the tasteless cake. Then Bluey, resentful at his ousting from the centre of attention, demanded abruptly, 'Where is it?'

'I beg your pardon?' said Mrs Sedgewick-Smith.

'The doings. I want to go. Tea runs through me like a dose of salts.'

'You mean the smallest room?' his hostess interpreted coyly. She rose helpfully. 'I'll show you the way.'

'I'll need some assistance with the buttons.'

'Oh,' said Mrs Sedgewick-Smith.

Bluey fixed Stephanie with his eye. 'Perhaps the young lady will oblige?'

'The young lady will certainly not oblige,' snapped her mother.

'Didn't she say she was thinking of being a nurse?' asked Bluey innocently. 'The nurses do it for us in the annex.'

Mrs Sedgewick-Smith looked round desperately. None of the others gave any indication of volunteering. They found the situation only something to grin about. The literary sergeant might have saved her embarrassment, but he was damned if he were going to handle Bluey's private parts. Mrs. Sedgewick-Smith drew herself up. It was too bad. Even the lunatics hadn't

307

offered such problems. 'If you will come with me, I shall do all that is necessary.'

'Good on you,' said Bluey amiably. He hadn't really expected to get away with Stephanie. Well, it might be funny watching the old bag fumbling with him. She didn't look as if anyone had put a prick in her hand for a good many years. It was only the embarrassment he could provoke in others which made bearable his humiliation at needing such attention at all.

'I'm sorry, but it's a social disability I rather overlooked,' Graham laughed when Mrs Sedgewick-Smith explained the predicament the next morning. 'Those buttons are a terrible obstacle for the boys' hands. But I really can't think what to do, apart from sending them out in kilts.'

Mrs Sedgewick-Smith hesitated. She wanted to edge away from the subject as soon as possible, but persevered bravely, 'I don't know if you would welcome a suggestion, Mr Trevose. But when my husband came home from America before the war, he was wearing a suit . . . equipped with a zip-fastener.'

'Yes, of course.' Graham snapped his fingers. 'I remember seeing them there myself. It's a sound idea. If only, of course, I can get a supply of zips.'

It struck him that a beleaguered country could hardly be expected to continue manufacturing such metallic frivolities. There were certainly none in the shops at Maiden Cross. You probably needed as much influence to lay your hands on some zip-fasteners as to lay them on a case of Scotch or a few gallons of petrol. But he had still one friend who might be expected to perform miracles, and the provision of patients' flies was a minor miracle indeed. Graham telephoned the *Daily Press* office in Fleet Street, and found himself asked up to lunch.

Graham had a standing invitation to visit Lord Arlott, but hadn't taken advantage of it partly because he was too busy at the annex, and partly because of a vague desire to keep his pre-war life disconnected from his new one. At seventy, Valentine Arlott continued to conduct his newspaper with undiminished energy and interference. He was a small, lively man in rimless glasses, the fiery red hair which Graham well remembered long ago turned grey, but his Australian accent was as fierce as ever, to be dimmed or intensified according to how it suited to illuminate a particular argument. The *Press* was continuing in the Second War its policy of the First, bringing the exploits of Lord Arlott's countrymen repeatedly and enthusiastically to the attention of the British public. Its office was by then more or less roofless, weatherproofed by tarpaulins, standing amid buildings apparently gnawed by giant rats, or simply replaced by holes in the ground, or revealing themselves on a second glance as blackened shells like burnt-out fireworks. Graham found Lord Arlott had installed himself in a shored-up room in the basement, which he had fitted out like a military headquarters with telephones of various colours, charts, and large maps, all of great complexity. Val Arlott liked to spread the notion that the *Press* could manipulate any national movement of importance, from which he saw no reason to exclude the war.

'Zip-fasteners?' Val exclaimed, Graham coming to the point of his visit at once. His thick grey eyebrows shot up. 'What the hell would you want those for?'

Graham explained.

'Sounds like a good cause,' said Val. 'Fix it up, Geoff, will you?'

'Certainly, Val.'

There was a third person in the basement room, whom from the humility with which he conducted himself Graham passed off as some sort of secretary. He was startled to discover a little later that the man was the paper's editor.

'Well, Graham—how are you going along?' Val Arlott leaned back in his swivel-chair, smiling but eyeing Graham with a shrewdness he turned impartially on prime ministers and messenger boys. 'By God, you're looking fit. And ten years younger.'

Graham laughed. 'It's the simple country life. Think what a fortune it would have cost to enjoy before the war.'

'Don't you get bored?'

'Not much. I just work and sleep.'

'You must notice the change—patching up our national heroes instead of our national beauties.'

'I do. It's much more gratifying.'

'I suppose it should be gratifying to me, too. I'm the one who gave you your start, aren't I?'

'Of course—no Val Arlott, no Graham Trevose.'

In the nineteen-twenties Val had run a crusade in the *Press* to install not only London's first plastic surgery unit in near-by Blackfriars Hospital, but its first plastic surgeon embodied in Graham Trevose. Graham's father-in-law had owned half the paper, which stimulated the benevolence. But Val's interest had quickly turned to some other campaign for lightening the burden of humanity—the opening of cinemas on Sundays, if Graham remembered aright.

'Making much money?' asked Val.

'No, but there's nothing to spend it on.'

'That's true. Not these days.'

'You must have had a pretty bad time of it up here in London,' observed Graham.

'It certainly hasn't been a picnic. Any bombing down your way?'

'Our only casualty has been a cow. I think they mistook us for Biggin Hill.'

'Now the bastards are turning their attention to the provinces. Swansea had a nasty time of it last night.'

'Is the damage serious?' It warmed Graham to talk again to someone important, a man who not only knew the inside story of the war but who, from the look of the room at least, might even affect the turn of the plot. 'I mean, taking the country as a whole.'

'It could be worse. They get the railways running again pretty smartly, and production all round has been hit much less than we feared. The U-boats are a stickier problem, between you and me. But civilian morale has stood up to it. It might have gone the other way, you know. Could have been panic, demands for peace. He confided in me he's genuinely relieved about that.'

'Who is?' asked Graham.

Val Arlott seemed surprised at the question. 'Churchill.' His look turned to annoyance as Graham gave a laugh. 'What's funny?'

'Nothing, Val, nothing.' The Captain Piles and Mrs Sedgewick-Smiths of Graham's new world shrank into their true inconsequence. 'I don't move in such circles, I'm afraid.'

'Geoff, fix up some drinks, will you?' ordered Val Arlott.

'Certainly, Val.'

When they were alone, Val asked Graham, 'How's your wife taking the war?'

'Maria wouldn't begin to understand. The clock of her mind stopped somewhere in the thirties.'

'I ran into her brother the other day.'

'The second Lord Cazalay?'

'Yes, God help us. There was some unpleasantness between the pair of you, I gather?'

'Yes. Cazalay and that fellow Haileybury were in it together, trying to get me struck off.'

'You mean about the actress? What's her name—Stella Garrod?'

Graham nodded. 'I'll concede that Haileybury moved against me through his usual high-mindedness or his hypocrisy—I've never really decided which it is. But I can't understand why Cazalay started him off. Through spite, I suppose.'

'Did you know he's got himself some sort of job in the censorship? Through the title, doubtless. I can't think of any other qualifications.'

'I wouldn't trust him even to deliver the morning post,' Graham said sourly.

'Yes, they're twisters, the Cazalays, all of them,' Val said amiably. 'Though it was sad about the father. To be reviled and ruined after enjoying power is bad enough. To face death in exile is heartbreaking. Even the sick rabbit can crawl back to its own burrow. I suppose it can all be forgotten now. Even the muddiest little eddies in our history have been submerged by the tidal wave. Not that I came out of the Cazalay crash badly,' he continued more cheerfully. 'I picked up his share of this paper dirt cheap. I suppose you've some pretty little girl tucked away there in the country?' he added.

'No.'

'You've turned over a new leaf? I don't believe it.'

'Let's say I haven't time. I'm worked off my feet, you know. I've a hell of a lot of worry. Particularly over one of your compatriots—Bluey Jardine.'

Val frowned. 'I wondered what had happened to him. He just dropped out of the news. Badly smashed up?'

'With patience on both sides and a couple of years I'll get him looking human.'

'Poor bastard.' Val rubbed his chin. 'How about our doing a story on your little show? I'd like to remind people about Bluey.'

Graham looked doubtful. 'Would anyone be interested? Plenty of men have suffered worse. And my boys aren't particularly pretty objects to come across in your morning paper.'

'Yes, people *would* be interested,' said Val decisively. 'We could send down Martha Raymond. Do you know Martha?'

'She wrote a bitterly unkind story about me and Stella Garrod in your gossip column before the war.'

Val shrugged his shoulders. 'These things happen. She's a game kid.'

Martha Raymond's physical courage matching the flintiness of her mind, she was then scaling cliffs with the newly raised Commandos, defusing unexploded parachute mines with the Royal Engineers, flying in the empty bomb-bay of Wellingtons with the R.A.F., or diving into the waters of Weymouth harbour with the Navy, all for the enlightenment and entertainment of Val Arlott's readers. But Graham wondered if even she would be game enough to drag a story from his patients.

'Geoff, what's Martha doing?' Val asked, as the editor reappeared.

'On an Army cookery course, Val.'

'Fix her to meet Graham when she's free.'

'Certainly, Val.'

'I hope my boys won't resent her,' said Graham doubtfully. 'They can be prickly with strangers.'

'Martha's a real professional, Graham. She can get round anyone. Like you.'

'Then I only hope the zips arrive first,' Graham added. 'Otherwise Bluey might feel inclined to provide the girl with rather too colourful copy.'

10

'I SEE GRAHAM's getting up to his old tricks again,' remarked Denise Bickley, putting down her coffee cup.

'Eh? What's that? Old tricks? What old tricks?' Her host, Mr Claude Cramphorn, F.R.C.S., paused in lighting his pipe. 'He had plenty of them, as far as my memory serves.'

'Didn't you see this morning's *Press*, Crampers?'

Mr Cramphorn shook his head.

'There was an enormous article by some woman about the annex. Pictures and all. As a matter of fact,' she added casually, 'I happened to cut it out.'

Denise felt in her handbag and produced a strip of grey wartime newsprint, which she handed to her husband beside her on the sofa. 'It's wildly inaccurate, of course,' smiled John Bickley, passing the cutting on. 'The newspapers never seem to get anything right.'

Mr Cramphorn took it with a grunt. He was a fiery little surgeon given to pepper-and-salt suits, brown boots, half-moon glasses, briskly puffed pipes, and clipped sentences, a bachelor who had retired from the consultant staff of Blackfriars before the war to a farm which by chance lay within sight of the minarets of Smithers Botham. Nobody seemed to know how old he was, but no ageing general dug out to sit behind a ministry desk accepted his invitation to reactivity as eagerly as Mr Cramphorn—if he had ever been invited at all. When overlooked by the authorities at the beginning of the war, unlike Graham, who was inclined to take a neurotic view of every-

314

thing, Mr Cramphorn had simply ignored the slight. He had appeared on the Smithers Botham portico puffing his pipe, rubbing his hands, and declaring, 'Work to do? I'm willing and ready. Boys to teach? I'll teach 'em?' He marched in, discovered his old ward sister, herself recalled from helping a cousin run a boarding house at Bexhill, appropriated a dozen of the empty beds, and set up shop.

Mr Cramphorn did teach very well, the surgery of the First World War. He had lived through all the fashions. From the twenties, with short skirts and the surgical vogue of removing as many internal organs as possible compatible with the continuance of life, through the thirties with their padded shoulders and the enthusiastic tacking of floating kidneys, spleens, colons, and the like the more firmly into place, to the forties with their slacks and headscarves and 'septic foci'. Nobody knew exactly what these malevolent foci did, nor even what they were, but Mr Cramphorn removed them just the same.

It never crossed his mind to explain his methods to his patients, whom he treated as a well-mannered squire his tenants. To Mr Cramphorn a hospital was a charitable institution, and a man begging bread at your door had no business enquiring the ability of your baker. For a disgruntled sufferer to threaten litigation was to him as unthinkable as for his gardener to threaten joining his dinner-table. He was an individualist, and like the British generals facing up to the aeroplane, distrustful of such comparatively new-fangled devices as asepsis coming between himself and the pure exercise of his art. His gloved fingers often strayed absently during operations to the pocket of his pepper-and-salt trousers under his gown, to produce a large yellow handkerchief on which he would blow his nose. He frequently puffed his pipe over the scrubbing-up basin, laying it aside with his freshly sterilized hand. But whatever operation he performed, whatever its chances of doing good or ill (they stood about fifty-fifty), it was a superb piece of surgical handicraft. Mr Cramphorn was a real professional.

'H'm,' said Mr Cramphorn, finishing reading the cutting. He

315

liked the company of good-looking women, and had asked the Bickleys across that April evening for dinner. He had bagged a couple of precious rabbits, though he often complained the war had quite ruined the shooting. 'What d'you think of that, Pomfrey?'

He passed the cutting to the fourth sharer of the feast, a Blackfriars physician at Smithers Botham, Dr Paul Pomfrey, who observed mildly, 'I do hope it's nothing disgraceful.'

Dr Pomfrey was a distinguished elderly neurologist, a collector of butterflies, a player of the 'cello, an addict of crossword puzzles, his mind too fine a key to unlock such current mysteries as ration books, identity cards, and stirrup-pumps. He was under Mr Cramphorn's thumb through living with him. When the war started, Mr Cramphorn instructed his housekeeper to open his doors to the expectant mothers who arrived from London, much fortified by vicars and vitamins, but his brisk behaviour so induced fears of premature labour, the women were replaced by evacuee children—according to himself the nastiest available, through the billeting officer's personal spite. These guests, too, Mr Cramphorn was shortly relieved of, after insisting on treating their nits in the sheep-dip. Dr Pomfrey was conscripted to fill the spare room, and so put an end to such rude intrusions into a professional man's privacy.

'Oh dear,' added Dr Pomfrey, reading. 'We did have so much trouble with young Trevose at Blackfriars before the war. He always seemed to be getting into the papers. People must have gained the impression that plastic surgery was the only work our hospital was capable of.'

'It doesn't actually mention Graham by name,' said John, coming to his surgeon's defence.

'He'd be much too fly for that,' laughed Mr Cramphorn, puffing briskly.

' "This wonderful work",' Dr Pomfrey read out hollowly, "is being performed by the brilliant plastic surgery expert who gave hope and beauty to stage and society in London before the war". I suppose that would sink in with a good many people—eh, Crampers?'

'Of course, Graham *is* doing wonderful work,' admitted Denise. 'But I don't see why he should take all the credit. John comes home utterly exhausted most nights. Don't you, darling? And Tudor Beverley's rushed off his feet. Besides, there're plenty of others in the hospital who deserve being taken notice of. Quite as much as Graham. They haven't his flair for publicity, that's all. I met Babs Twelvetrees while I was buying the rations this morning, and she was dreadfully upset.'

She was the wife of Mr Alan Twelvetrees, a young Black-friars consultant surgeon who had been invalided out of the Royal Army Medical Corps. He had expected to be treated at Smithers Botham as a returning hero, but was disconcerted to find himself resented as an intruder who hadn't suffered the earlier disorganization and inconveniences, to be given the worst wards, the surliest sisters, and the most awkward hours for operating.

'Graham didn't instigate the article,' John pointed out. 'The paper suggested it. They're always looking for odd corners of the war to write up. It's good for morale, I suppose, the more people read of what's being done.'

'You know perfectly well Graham would go to any lengths to get himself known,' his wife told him briskly.

'Mustn't give a dog a bad name, my dear,' Mr Cramphorn told her. 'Otherwise you can't blame him if he bites you.'

'I don't think Graham would bite anyone, Crampers,' she said. 'Of course he's utterly charming and such fun, and John and I love him. But he is so dreadfully weak. Look at those awful women who had him round their little fingers.'

'What do you think I should do, Crampers?' asked Dr Pomfrey helplessly. He asked Mr Cramphorn's opinion on every-thing. He was more under his thumb than ever at the time, through the surgeon teaching him to drive, which he performed as he operated, very fast and impatient of obstacles. After Dr Pomfrey's chauffeur had been called up the motor-car pre-sented him with severer difficulties than the most elusive neurological diagnosis, the physician driving across lawns and flower-beds, on the wrong side of the road, and frequently within inches of Captain Pile. 'Perhaps you'd care to take it up with Graham?' he suggested hopefully.

'Not me,' said Mr Cramphorn. He disliked being drawn into the animosities of others. He had enough in the hospital of his own, complaining almost daily to Captain Pile about the quality of everything from the operating equipment to the food, and appearing regularly in his office with the shepherd's pie. 'Why don't you have a friendly word in his ear, John? You're nearest to him.'

John Bickley tried to find an excuse, but Dr Pomfrey looked at his watch and hastily switched on the wireless. The nine o'clock news brought an end to the conversation, as it did to almost every other in the country.

John had his friendly word with Graham in the annex the following morning. His wife had insisted on it. But Graham only laughed and said, 'Well, I half expected something like this. Who's kicking up the fuss?'

'Pomfrey, in his own sort of way. And a few of the others.'

'Twelvetrees, I'll bet?' John said nothing. 'Will they never learn? Things are so different now. There's no one to benefit except the boys. It cheered them up, someone taking an interest in them, particularly a pretty girl. Though God knows I deserve some sort of encouragement. I haven't had much since the war started.'

'I know all that, of course, Graham. But you must be aware how sticky the others can be about publicity.'

'I don't give a damn.' They were standing outside the wash-house, and Graham started towards the ward. 'I cared little enough in peacetime what my professional brethren thought of me. Now I don't care at all. Anyway, they've a nice surprise in store. As a result of the article, that American fellow's coming down—what's his name, always being photographed in a tin hat coming out of shelters? Hugo Kirkham. His stuff's syndicated right across the States, and they aren't coy over there about hushing up the doctors' names. A nice little flutter that'll cause when the cuttings get back here.' Graham began to sound annoyed. 'I'm not trying to attract attention to myself. I'm trying to attract attention to the annex, which is quite a different thing.'

Anxious to change the conversation, John asked, 'Are you going to have a look at that fellow with the post-operative chest?'

'Later, old man, if that's all right?' Graham excused himself hastily. 'I've got to have a word with sister.'

Sister Mills occupied a partitioned office the size of a largish cupboard beside the ward door. She had been on the unit for three months, and Graham was astounded at her success. She seemed to have the right touch with unruly patients. There was less drunkenness, less swearing, fewer nurses asking for transfers. Even Bluey seemed to be behaving himself. Graham felt smugly gratified at the perspicacity of his choice. On the mornings when he wasn't operating, he exercised his prerogative as 'The Chief' by taking with her a cup of the tasteless khaki liquid passing at Smithers Botham for coffee. He was not usually one for fraternizing with his nursing staff. He generally treated them brusquely, partly through fussiness over the smallest details of treatment, and partly as a defence reaction. For the sake of his patients he tried to fill his wards with the prettiest girls going, and though some of them fired his imagination, particularly in his present monkish existence, he was careful to avoid any entanglements. He didn't care to foul his own doorstep. Besides, he was something of a sexual snob. The man who before the war had got himself into bed with Stella Garrod might find the joys of common-or-garden girls something of a come-down. And anyway, he told himself sharply, he was getting far too old for them.

'You look in a mood,' Sister Mills smiled, as Graham squeezed himself into the spare chair.

'It's a passing irritation. Some of the others are grousing about that article yesterday. They still can't forgive me for getting my name in the papers before the war.'

She handed him a thick chipped cup and said, 'Yes, I remember reading some of the things they said about you.'

'I hope they were nice things. Many of them weren't. But you must have been only an impressionable schoolgirl at the time.'

It always put him in a better humour talking to Sister Mills. And he noticed she had become less solemn, less nervous of him. A sympathetic ear was a luxury when he was expected to bear the troubles of everyone in the annex.

'My father was always interested in your activities,' she told him.

'Is he a doctor?' He had never asked about her background before.

'No, he's a commercial artist. Not a particularly successful one, I'm afraid to say. Now he's working for the Ministry of Aircraft Production.'

'I used to paint at week-ends before the war. I don't think I was much good at it. I used to delude myself it was based on the same principles as my surgery. But it isn't. My job's more like plumbing, really. Whatever the look of the result, everything's got to join up the right way underneath.'

'Your own father was at Blackfriars, wasn't he?'

'Yes, the formidable old boy was the professor of anatomy,' Graham said fondly. 'He wrote an erudite volume about the synovial membranes, so erudite that only about fifty people in the country understood it. We've always been doctors of a sort. My grandfather was a semi-educated bonesetter. My great-grandfather wasn't educated at all, but an out-and-out quack. He left a fortune. He could diagnose everything known to medical science, and a good deal that wasn't, by merely inspecting the patient's urine in a flask. What's called a piss-prophet.'

She smiled. 'Quite a weight of medical tradition to carry.'

'The family business, I suppose. My son Desmond's going in for it. You must meet him when he comes down from Cambridge. He stays with me at the pub, and I let him mess about here trying his hand at being anything from assistant anaesthetist to theatre porter. You'll like him. He's a charmer.'

'I'm sure I shall. I'll look forward to it.'

Graham fell silent. He had a vague uneasiness about men-

320

tioning Desmond. 'The fuss about the newspaper will soon blow over,' he went on.

'*We*'re proud of you on the unit, anyway.'

' "The Wizz".' He laughed and got up. 'If I'm making a reputation I'd better live up to it, by doing some work. I've got to see a pneumonia John Bickley's inflicted. The fellow uses far too much ether.'

Despite his protestations, the realist in Graham admitted readily enough that he enjoyed recapturing the glory of print. He was an exhibitionist in a neurotically self-effacing profession, and finding himself so long in a surgical backwater where nobody was inclined to wander had been galling. But it was more gratifying still to find the article reviving Val Arlott's twenty-years-old interest in plastic surgery. He telephoned asking if Graham lacked equipment, promising to jolt action out of the authorities. The longed-for extra huts seemed at last likely to appear. Val even suggested a fund to provide the annex with 'comforts'—an excellent idea, Graham thought, it would keep the place in the public eye for months. But the best news of all was Peter Thomas becoming engaged to marry one of the nurses. He still looked a mess, but there he was, to marry in the merry month of May. It put up morale in the annex wonderfully. If a girl could sleep with Peter Thomas looking like that, Bluey declared, then he was off to pick up a bloody harem.

The wedding was to be at Chelsea registry office on May the twelfth, a Monday. On the Saturday night London had its last bad raid of the war, and an unexpected guest, Rudolph Hess, floated by parachute into Scotland. While the Deputy Führer's fractured ankle was being attended by a British military doctor, a younger German flier, steadfastly doing his duty above the Thames, made a mistake in his bomb-aiming and blew most of Blackfriars Hospital to pieces. Luckily, the casualties were light, the patients being at Smithers Botham and the wooden props in the basement being stronger than everyone gloomily believed. But the firemen were still working thirty-six hours later, when Graham stood with a carnation in his buttonhole

321

soulfully inspecting the wreckage before making across battered London to the registry office. The Arlott Wing, where he had worked before the war, had simply disappeared. The rest of the building, which he could remember standing in apparently unshakeable dignity when his father had shown it off as a childhood treat, was a hardly recognizable ruin. But the pavements were still busy. The bowler hat was still worn. The tramlines still ran down the Embankment. London had shrugged off fire and plague before. The smashed eighteenth-century masonry was a shame, but what was the loss of the most splendid building, he asked himself, compared with that of the most miserable of lives?

'Graham—'

He turned. He didn't recognize her for a moment. She was small and gingery, with a scarf round her head, staring at him.

'Sheila Raleigh—' he held out his hand, smiling. 'How's Tom?'

'Didn't you hear? He was killed.' He looked blank, hand outstretched and untaken. She bit her lip. 'In Greece. He was one of the last.'

'Sheila, what can I say—'

'Don't say anything, Graham. Please don't.'

'But Sheila, I'm so dreadfully sorry. It's a terrible shock. I mean, Tom was my houseman, my registrar, my partner. We worked together for ten years. He was such a wonderful chap.'

'Then why didn't you keep him?' she demanded savagely. 'If you'd wanted, he'd be safe with you now in the country. But you didn't. You rejected him. Because you really hated him. Because you were jealous of him. Because he wasn't of use to you any more. That's the truth, isn't it? Now you know exactly what you've done.'

For a moment Graham could say nothing. 'How can you accuse me of that?' he managed to ask weakly. 'It isn't right, you know. It just isn't true at all. Honestly, I'm heartbroken at the news. Surely there's something I can do to help? For the children? Isn't there anything? If there's some sort of assistance I can give, financial assistance—'

'I wouldn't take a penny from a murderer.'

She shrugged her shoulders, turned, and abruptly walked off. Graham watched her disappear, picking her way among the fire-hoses.

The wedding was to Graham as joyless as a funeral. He found it impossible to be even faintly amiable afterwards. He pleaded work, and drove straight back to Smithers Botham. He knew that everything Sheila said was perfectly correct. To come face to face with his old self was harrowing. Things had so changed. Or had they? His egotism and jealousy, which had cost poor Tom his partnership and then his life, he supposed must still be in his system somewhere. Perhaps he was merely redirecting them to temporarily more acceptable ends, like some thug given a rifle and praised for killing Germans? Was it too much to hope he really was becoming a better sort of man? How could he tell? There was no one near enough to ask.

At Smithers Botham he made for his office. He had to find some work, anything to occupy himself, to stop his self-inflicted mental wounds. He paused in the doorway, surprised to find Sister Mills at his desk. Then he remembered he'd asked her to collect case reports of something—what was it? Maxillary fractures. He was about to ask her to go when she noticed his face and jumped up, exclaiming, 'What's the matter? Was it something in the blitz?'

He shut the door behind him.

'I killed a man,' he said wearily. 'Unwittingly and indirectly, but I killed him. Tom Raleigh— did I ever mention him? He was my partner. We had a row. He should have been working with me out here on the unit. I wouldn't take him. So instead, he was killed in Greece.'

He sat in a chair by the desk.

'I'm so sorry,' said Sister Mills quietly. 'It must have been terrible news.'

'Particularly as I got it from his widow. Who knew exactly what the facts were.' He stretched out his legs. 'She told me what she thought of me. She was perfectly right. To her, I

323

couldn't be anything but the vilest and wickedest creature in the world.'

'She'd be feeling emotional. She let her tongue run away with her.'

'I'd like to think so. But my whole life before the war doesn't stand much examination.'

'Doesn't it? You brought a lot of happiness to people.'

'At a price.'

'Well, why not?' she asked simply. 'What is the price of happiness?'

'Anyway, I didn't give a damn about the happiness. Only the guineas.'

'That's quite impossible to believe. Not after all I've seen here.'

He sat staring in front of him. Then he noticed she was crying.

'I must apologize.' He got up abruptly. 'All these troubles I've brought back are upsetting you. I shouldn't have mentioned them. I've no right asking you to share them.'

'I'm crying for you,' she told him. 'You're so much the nicest person in the world, and you fight so terribly hard against it.'

Then he had her in his arms, and she was kissing him with a passion even he found exciting.

Meanwhile, Mrs Sedgewick-Smith was holding another of her regular Monday afternoon tea-parties. She had told Stephanie severely that she mustn't keep crossing her legs like that. After all, she was really getting quite a big girl.

11

ON SUNDAY MORNINGS Graham would lie in bed, reading the papers, *Picture Post*, the *Strand Magazine*, a novel, anything unconnected with the annex. It was only the bad doctor, he reflected, who killed himself to cure his patients.

By that November Sunday of 1942 the posters in the Smithers Botham entrance hall had changed from the ringing warning YOUR FREEDOM IS IN PERIL to the more sophisticated COUGHS AND SNEEZES SPREAD DISEASES and IS YOUR JOURNEY REALLY NECESSARY? The place was by then more than simply a hospital. It was another of the countless closed communities stretching across the globe from Spitzbergen to the Falklands, all more interested in themselves than in the war which had fathered them. There was always something going on there. The fashion of the times provided the staff with bountiful opportunity for self-expression, self-examination, and self-instruction, with dramatics and debating, brains trusts of varying trustworthiness, lectures on everything from Britain's War Aims to Milk Production, plus E.N.S.A., A.B.C.A., and I.T.M.A. Conversation in the long corridors never lacked an interesting case or an interesting scandal. The housemen continued to entertain the nurses. The matron continued to entertain doubts.

The war had swept a remarkable assortment of illnesses and injuries into the vast wards. It was an Aladdin's cave of clinical medicine, if only the students had bothered to rub the lamp of learning. There were special units for surgery of the head, the chest, the limbs, and the arteries, created not through the benevolence of some millionaire but through the malevolence of Adolf Hitler. Its beds contained Free French, Free Poles, Free Norwegians, Free Dutch, Free Czechs, and unfree Germans (who made model patients, there being nothing like several years' Nazi indoctrination for fitting in with the ideas of an old-fashioned British ward sister). Captain Pile was still there, and still a captain. Corporal Honeyman was still there, and still a corporal. Dr Pomfrey, after a baffled half-hour with his car at full throttle, unaware that his rear bumper was enmeshed in the stout railings of the coal store, had decided to settle for a second-hand bicycle. But to anyone who read the newspapers, Smithers Botham in 1942 was the place where a man called Graham Trevose performed his miracles.

The annex was no longer a sideshow but one of the busiest surgical units in the country. The huts in the grounds had doubled and the staff had trebled. Graham was receiving more patients from the R.A.F. than he could handle. His work had attracted surgeons—and journalists with their photographers—from every Allied nation, even the Russians. Women in fish-queues could talk to each other about Graham Trevose. Every morning brought a letter or two, generally badly written and spelt, with a few shillings towards the comforts fund. Graham thought this the most rewarding recognition of all. And it had all started because he had gone to Val Arlott seeking some zips for trousers.

An unaccustomed sound crept across the misty morning. Church bells in the distance. For more than two years these accompaniments of Christian joys and sorrows had been silenced, reserved by the Government to herald not the coming of the Lord but of the German armies.

'Listen.' Graham slipped his hands between his head and the pillow. 'I remember in the last war they rang the bells after Cambrai. It was when we used tanks for the first time, and broke the German lines. In a week or two we were back where we started, of course. It always seemed the case in those days. Let's hope this Alamein affair is more permanent.'

Clare Mills slipped her hand into the jacket of his pyjamas, which were pure silk, prewar, made to measure in Jermyn Street. The poor lamb really was terribly thin. It was like being in bed with a skeleton beside you. 'Happy?'

'This is probably a terrible confession, but the war's been the happiest time of my life.'

'Is it so terrible?' she asked gently. 'Surely the misery needn't go undiluted?'

'I suppose happiness is a well-insulated state of mind. Most of the boys are perfectly happy, and God knows they haven't got much to justify it. Even Bluey seems happy enough these days.'

'Perhaps he's found a new girl-friend.' She ran her hand down Graham's chest. It was so smooth, the ribs standing out like the black notes on a piano. No wonder he'd once suffered from tuberculosis.

'Why do I attract you?' he asked.

She pouted thoughtfully. 'You're different. From any other surgeon.'

'Different from old Cramphorn, you mean?'

Clare laughed. 'You're gentle, you're amusing, you're kind, you understand women. And I love you. Besides, you had a tremendous build-up. I'd read so much about you. It's like being with a star you've only seen on the flicks.'

'Don't tell me I've got to match up to Clark Gable?' he asked, though feeling flattered.

She touched his small hard nipple with the tip of her fore finger. 'Tell me why I attract *you*.'

'You're a good housewife.'

'I thought that was it.'

'Do you realize, darling, this is the first time in my life I've had a home I could call my own? I mean a place where I could do as I pleased, without it being run by a lot of servants. Where I didn't feel I had to put on a show, to impress the world with my importance.' He looked round the room, which was hardly big enough to take the bed. The beige wallpaper had galleons sailing across it, a fumed-oak dressing table was squeezed into a corner, there were faded pink curtains, an angular hanging mirror, and a coloured print of Tower Bridge, pre-blitz. They lived in a bungalow, rented furnished in the country some ten miles from Smithers Botham, with four small rooms and a kitchen, a bath with an alarming geyser, and the name of 'Cosy Cot'.

Graham felt he would have been happy with Clare even living in a Nissen hut. She shared his new liking for books and for the concerts on the wireless. She cooked agreeably and mended his clothes with her painstaking nurse's stitches. He had enjoyed himself teaching her to dress properly, pulling her out of those awful tweeds and putting her into frocks, though the fun had been officially dimmed by the coming of clothes' rationing. She was the most adoring woman he had known, which he sometimes wryly reflected accounted for their harmony. They had always the annex to fall back on as a common interest, Graham insisting she continued with her job, declaring the ward would fall into anarchy otherwise. As for their other common interest, Graham decided she enjoyed a greater talent than any woman he had met for copulation, with all its ancillaries, which he was apt to describe as 'novelties'.

As the church bells died away he said, 'You've given me something to live for, darling. A unique gift.'

'You always had your work.'

'Only a fool or a saint lives for his vocation. Do you know, before you came along I was the prey to horrible and gloomy thoughts. Doom, impending death, extinction. Most uncomfortable. Such things don't even enter my mind now. You've exorcised the ghosts. Perhaps the magic charm is finding myself with a girl of your age. Or perhaps it's just the flattery.'

She gently kissed his unshaven cheek. 'It isn't flattery.'

'Is the distinction important? At my age, flattery's a workable substitute for love.'

'Now you're being silly.'

'Yes, I hope I am.' He looked up at the ceiling, which had a large crack running across it. 'Do you think we should have another week at that place in Wales?'

'They were awfully awkward about our identity cards.'

'They might have grown more accustomed to such irregularities by now.'

He had taken her to a village hotel, remembered from before the war, for what he liked to remember as their honeymoon. Their first sudden contact in the office, the day he had met Sheila Raleigh, he told himself was like the unexpected symptom of some smouldering disease. He had been attracted to Clare almost since setting eyes on her. But he was immediately disconcerted to discover there was another—a Royal Marine lieutenant, stationed in India, to whom she was unofficially pledged. Graham declared to himself hastily that any monkey business was out of the question. Her lieutenant was abroad in the service of his country, like the Crusades, exactly the same principle. A man of his own standing couldn't possibly stoop to such things. But he wondered how strong the psychological chastity belt was. It might be fun to try the luck. In the end it sprang open with an ease which surprised both of them, the severest difficulty being the locale. His house in Mayfair was bomb-damaged beyond habitation, and he could hardly smuggle Clare upstairs in the pub like one of the students. It occurred to him he hadn't taken a holiday since the war started. Afterwards, she declared she couldn't possibly go back to the nurses' home. In a place like Smithers Botham, everyone would know of their adventure. The other sisters were unkindly enough already, and anyway had a tendency to kiss each other good-night. They moved into Cosy Cot, and she wrote to her Royal Marine, a dreaded epistle known as a 'Dear John'.

The rest of the Smithers Botham staff thought sharing a bungalow with your ward sister rather rich, even for Graham. He didn't care. It never occurred to him to ask if Clare did. Denise Bickley was particularly outraged, about which Graham cared even less. In peacetime, Graham's goodwill represented a large slice of her husband's income, and Graham reflected grimly the war couldn't go on for ever. As for Clare's parents, who lived in Bristol, they were gratified to learn from her letters that their daughter had moved from the hospital to comfortable and apparently altogether satisfactory lodgings.

'Why don't we have our own celebration of the victory in the Desert?' Graham asked her from the pillow. 'We're alone in the house, no one's likely to call and disturb us.'

Clare laughed and got out of bed, throwing back her blonde hair and starting to take off her red-and-yellow spotted cotton pyjamas. She really had an admirable figure, Graham reflected. Her breasts were wonderful. He couldn't have made anything better himself.

'Must I keep using this toothpaste stuff?' she asked, squatting to insert her diaphragm.

'My God, yes,' said Graham hastily. 'It's terribly risky without the spermicidal jelly. All that cap does is to hold it round the cervix.'

'It's awfully messy.'

'You can't have everything, my love,' he told her, a shade primly.

'And I shall have to keep it in half the day, won't I? It'll give me backache.'

'I'll sit rubbing it with Sloan's liniment.'

She laughed again, and came back to him.

In the sexual line Graham was, as Haileybury would have put it, an enthusiast. After all, he told himself, he had a deep knowledge of the apparatus concerned, and he might as well put the information to fullest use. He often recalled with satisfaction Balzac's exhortation for no man to marry before dissecting at least one female pelvis. But he could never bring himself to feel the business more than 'a sneeze in the loins'. It was only a reflex, centred in the humblest lower segments of the spinal cord, transmitted across the pelvic basin by fibres hiding under their Latinized name 'the nerve of shame'. Even a real sneeze was a more cerebral occurrence, conducted by fine-sounding aristocratic nerves springing out of the brain itself. Of course, women took a different view. However many men sneezed in their loins, they invested it with some mystical significance. He supposed it was mainly through their fear of appearing tarts.

'You look sad,' she said teasingly afterwards.

330

'Do I? It's physiological after an orgasm. Isn't there a classical tag? Though the single one I can remember is *calor, rubor, tumor, dolor,* and that's only inflammation.'

She ran the tip of her finger round his umbilicus. 'That's a strange thing we have.'

'It's only a cicatrix, a scar.'

'What's inside it?'

'Nothing. The remains of the blood-vessels which fed us before we were born.'

'It's quite pretty, really, like a flower. A budding rose.'

'Most are like cabbages.'

Her hand slipped down to his penis, off duty in the at-ease position. 'It's full of tissue like a sponge, isn't it? I remember from our anatomy lectures. It was awfully funny, the sister-tutor was a terribly dried-up old thing. She told us all about an erection, with diagrams on the blackboard, as though she was talking about the moon. She could never have seen one in her life.'

'It's a really most interesting organ. The arteries dilate enormously, quite unlike any others in the body.'

'It must be fascinating to have one.'

'According to the psychiatrists, all women think so. Penis-envy. Though quite where that interesting discovery gets us, I don't know.'

'Did all your women want one?' He felt this reference, under the circumstances, in rather bad taste, and said nothing. 'Have you had an awful lot of women, Graham?'

'You know I'm a married man.' As she gave a small pout he went on, 'My sex life with Maria pretty well ended with the honeymoon. You could hardly blame me for seeking out others, particularly when she went off her head. But none of them meant anything, not one.'

'Not even Stella Garrod?'

'Particularly Stella Garrod.'

'How about Edith?'

'That's rather going into ancient history,' he said quickly.

'Graham, darling, perhaps I'd better give up the annex.'

331

'Unthinkable!'

'Staff-nurse Jones could easily take over. She's awfully good with the boys.'

'But why this sudden change of heart? I thought you liked the work. You'd get bored all day here.'

'I haven't used the toothpaste once or twice. I didn't think it would matter. I haven't seen anything now for a fortnight. Of course, it may be perfectly all right. Just a delayed period.'

His large eyes stared at her across the pillow.

'If it isn't all right, will you be pleased?' she asked timidly. 'No, don't answer. Wait till we know.' She kissed him and got out of bed abruptly. 'It's Sunday. That means fried eggs for lunch. Something lovely to look forward to, isn't it?'

12

TO FIND HIMSELF confronted with fatherhood on a second occasion filled Graham with the same numb shock as on the first, almost exactly twenty-two years previously. With Maria, their sexual endeavours were so beset with difficulties he somehow felt her reproductive system too inefficient for conception. With Clare, he had put a touching faith in science. As usual, the human element had let him down. It was the same in the annex, when they got a run of infection after the nurses forgot to sterilize the needles properly in carbolic.

Monday was Mr Tim O'Rory's day at Smithers Botham. Graham caught the gynaecologist at lunch in the medical officers' mess and invited him for a stroll on the lawn.

'It's Clare,' he said, once out of earshot. 'I think she's pregnant.'

'Well, now,' said Mr O'Rory. A thick-set, dark-haired, red-faced, humorous Irishman, he looked kindly on feminine failings through his heavily rimmed glasses and seemed to find them an endless source of innocent merriment. 'And what gives rise to this little suspicion?'

'She's a fortnight overdue. She's always been as regular as clockwork before. Of course, it might be a chill, something like that, mightn't it?'

'Sitting on a damp park bench, doctor?' Mr O'Rory chuckled. 'Maybe so.'

'You don't think that's a possibility?'

'You know my low mind, Graham. Any woman outside a

nunnery, who misses a period between the ages of fifteen and fifty, must be assumed pregnant until proved otherwise. And I'm not so sure about the nunnery these days, either.'

Graham was in no mood for professional pleasantries. 'Can you do a test in the lab?' he asked irritatedly.

'I will certainly invoke the assistance of a small frog, Graham, if you want. I'll be needing a specimen of the lady's urine.'

'I've got one in the car.'

'But don't get too alarmed,' Mr O'Rory added amiably. 'The lady may have made a mistake in her dates. It's remarkable how unreliable the feminine gender is at its fundamental calculations.'

The telephone at Cosy Cot rang the following evening.

'That was Tim,' said Graham, putting down the receiver. 'It's on.'

Clare turned her eyes back to her sewing. Graham stuck his hands in his pockets and stood in the middle of the small sitting-room, which was filled with books, medical journals, files of notes, photographs of his patients, and had a coloured picture of Bubbles over the fireplace.

'It's wonderful news, isn't it?' he declared.

She looked up again. 'Are you sure you want it?'

'But of course I do! As long as you do?'

'More than anything.'

Graham perched on the edge of her chair and put his arm round her tightly. So, he thought, one of my wriggling little spermatozoa has threshed with its hair-like tail across the black mucoid depths of Clare's pelvis, to sink itself joyfully into the speck of jelly comprising her ovum. The stark object of the most fashionable wedding, with all its elaborate trimmings of an ecclesiastical, legal, floral, and emotional nature, had been simply achieved. No trouble at all. The human race really did surround itself with a lot of fuss over its reproduction. Clare wondered what he was going to say. At least he'd declared he wanted the child, she thought. She didn't dare to question whether he really meant it. Living with Graham, she rarely dared to question whether he really meant anything.

334

'There'll be a terrible lot of practical details to settle,' Graham announced.

He immediately threw himself vigorously into solving the varied problems set by the new pregnancy. He decided Clare must leave the annex at once. Staff-nurse Jones could enjoy unexpected promotion, he must find someone to succeed the girl as staff-nurse. Appointments must be made with Mr O'Rory. Specimens must be collected. A woman must be sought to help in the bungalow. They would go away for the holiday in Wales, it would do Clare good. Her ration-book must be exchanged at the Food Office for a pregnant woman's green one. Extra milk and vitamins must be applied for, with a dozen Government forms. Pregnancy struck Graham as a highly complicated item of official business. It had been so much simpler last time. Which reminded him, he really must do something about Maria.

Graham had been meaning to do something about Maria for over a year. But there had always seemed a last-minute snag. Whenever he steeled himself to start instructing his lawyers there was somehow a rush of work in the annex, keeping his mind occupied for weeks. The solicitors had anyway been bombed out of the City, and re-established themselves at some inaccessible address near Southend-on-Sea. There seemed then no urgency. Clare appeared perfectly content with their arrangement. Graham couldn't see how ten minutes in a registry office would make the slightest difference to the pair of them. Or perhaps, he sometimes suspected, he still had his lingering reluctance about disowning Maria, for good. Or perhaps . . . perhaps he was afraid of committing himself wholly to Clare? It was too difficult to think about, and the problems of the annex came first. Clare certainly raised the topic of a divorce. He felt it only to be expected, but she never harped on it for long. It never occurred to Graham that she saw how much it distressed him, nor that her silence was the expression of her terror of losing him.

But now the solicitors were written to. A divorce was imperative, the wheels of the law must be geared to the rapid

335

process of reproductive physiology. The solicitors wrote back with a promise of doing their best, explaining the Court would doubtless be sympathetic, but there were innumerable difficulties in wartime. He fixed a visit to Southend for the end of the month. He also agreed at last to see Clare's parents in Bristol. It was a glum prospect, even his charm might not prove an antidote to all unpleasantness, particularly as Mr Mills was hardly older than himself. Besides, a journey in the crowded, slow, and foodless wartime trains would be terrible.

First of all he must put matters to his son Desmond.

Something seemed to have gone wrong with Desmond. At Cambridge he had taken a fair degree in Part I of his Tripos, stayed on a year to breathe the rarefied academic atmosphere of the Part II, and done rather badly. From a gay if self-centred schoolboy he was turning into a reticent and solemn young man, wearing a dignity as unfitting for his years as a middle-age spread. He was even something of a prig. When he had left Cambridge that summer to start his three years' clinical course at Smithers Botham, Graham had assumed he would move in with them at Cosy Cot. But Desmond was reluctant. He suggested it might somehow hold him up to ridicule, particularly in the eyes of his cousin Alec, Edith's child, who was arriving to study at Smithers Botham the same autumn. Desmond arranged to live in the hospital itself, as one of the dozen-strong students' 'Emergency Squad' under the direct orders of Captain Pile—though for what emergency this squad was held in readiness, and how it would tackle it when it arose, everyone had long ago forgotten.

Graham dismissed all this as the self-dramatization to which the young were so distressingly liable. Desmond had probably been mixing with the wrong sort of people at college. Though perhaps the son's disinterest was partly the father's fault, Graham admitted. He had never taken overmuch care in Desmond's upbringing. Before the war he was too busy making money and amusing himself. During it he was too busy with the annex. Anyway, the lad seemed to step along confidently enough by himself. But now there was another factor. The war would certainly be grinding along in 1945, when Desmond was due to qualify, to sweep him with the others into the medical branches of the Forces. Why, he might even find himself under the orders of Haileybury! Somehow, Graham determined, he must get the young man into the Navy.

Graham set the scene of Desmond's enlightenment carefully. He had anyway been remiss about standing the boy treats. He made the effort of booking a couple of stalls for *Blithe Spirit*— as Russians were then being bombed instead of Britons, a seat in a London theatre was as hard to come by as a seat in a long-distance express. After the show they went to an Italian restaurant in Soho. In the first black nights of the war Graham had sometimes cheered himself up there by toasting Allied victory in Chianti at the insistence of the proprietor, who by 1942 had been caged up for a couple of years in the Isle of Man. But the elderly head waiter remembered him, and even laid the establishment open to immediate prosecution by letting them consume not only soup and chicken but a slice of fish as well.

Over the meal, they talked about their work. Now Desmond was growing up in medicine, Graham could enjoy the singular satisfaction of a medical parent in watching his child emerge as a professional colleague. They met often enough at Smithers Botham on perfectly easy terms, though coming to talk less of personal things than their cases, or to dissect the characters, abilities, and errors of the other consultants.

'Anything interesting in the annex at the moment, Dad?' Desmond asked across their corner table in the restaurant.

'A lot of oddments. The by-products of the war, mostly. There's a man from the Desert who gave himself a rub-down with petrol—they're short of water, you understand. Then the idiot lit a cigarette. He was an awful mess. There's a naval rating who was working in the engine-room of a destroyer when some fool turned on the superheated steam. Tragic cases. There's not much glory in being run over by your own tank. Anyway, war's a horrible business.'

'Are you getting sick of it?'

'I've never had time to pause and think. I suppose when I get back to bobbing noses, it'll be a relief knowing the patients' real suffering is only in the pocket.' Graham added after a moment, 'Sometimes it's difficult for me to realize our present highly abnormal form of life won't go on for ever. I suppose the same goes for all our generals.'

'Do you expect a lot of changes after the war?'

'I can tell you one.' Graham picked up his small glass of sloe gin, doing wartime duty for cognac. 'I'm going to obtain a divorce from your mother.'

Desmond considered this for some moments. 'That comes as something of a surprise, I must say. After all this time.'

'But surely my decision doesn't mean much to you, does it?' Graham asked, rather over-anxiously. 'Your mother's been ill for so long. You were only a child when she first had to go into hospital. You can hardly remember her when she was . . . well, as she used to be.'

Desmond said nothing. Graham wondered what Maria would be like had she kept her wits and her money. Doing something energetic in the war, doubtless. She was always the busy type.

'She's a complete wreck of her former self,' Graham added. 'Only I can appreciate the change.'

'She's not in very good shape, admittedly.'

'That's a mild way of putting it, Desmond. I assure you it makes not the slightest difference to your mother if I remain her husband or not. The whole conception of marriage is far beyond her ability to grasp. She's certified, you understand—certified as insane. Of course, I'll see she's looked after. Just as I do now. She'll stay in that home in comfort until the end of her days.'

'But *why*, Dad?' Desmond looked more solemn than ever. 'Why this sudden decision?'

'Because I'm going to marry Clare. Surely you must have expected that?'

'No. Not really. I didn't think you felt it necessary.'

'It's decidedly necessary,' said Graham, nettled by the remark. 'Clare's pregnant.'

Desmond stared at him.

'It's going to call for a measure of mental readjustment in both of us,' Graham continued. 'But it's a demonstrable fact.

The embryo has been created. Your baby half-brother or sister already exists, ectoderm, endoderm, mesoderm, yolk-sac, amnion, the lot. Two or three millimetres long, snug in the mucosa of Clare's uterus. We can't get away from that.'

'What's Alec going to say?'

'Why do you always bother what Alec's going to say?' Graham asked irritably.

'He's always trying to get some sort of hold over me. He's got a nasty tongue when he likes.'

'I'm sure you can cope with Alec.'

'It's bad enough his taking my money.'

'I'm certainly not going into that again now,' Graham told him promptly. 'If the cost of his education is coming from your trust fund, it was the least I could do for both the family and for Aunt Edith.'

Alec's father, the medical missionary, had maintained that the rewards of his vocation were to be found not in this world but the next, where presumably he had been enjoying them for seven years since dying, flat broke, in Malaya.

'Anyway, it's only a loan,' Graham pointed out. 'Alec's supposed to pay it all back once he's qualified. In the end you'll be no worse off.'

'What do you suppose Aunt Edith is going to say about your marrying again?'

Graham raised his eyebrows. That delicate little complication hadn't occurred to him. 'Desmond, I'm afraid I've got to go ahead with this divorce. I hope you'll come to see it as the right step.'

'I only see it as being rather hard on mother.'

'That's ridiculous.' Graham became angry. 'You know perfectly well most of the time your mother hasn't even the first idea who I am.'

'Still, she is my mother. I feel sorry for her.'

He really had little affection for his mother. But he was desperately frightened about doing the 'wrong thing'. He was becoming aware of inner forces which could drive him along the same devious paths as his father, and *that* must be avoided

339

at all costs. Graham's life had already made his son an easy target for ridicule, not only from Alec but from any of the other students disposed to a bit of ragging. For security he must fly into conventionality.

'Now you're just being pompous,' said Graham curtly. Desmond turned red, and Graham rebuked himself. He'd been too savage. Desmond was really very young, and confused with the ways of the world. Just as he had been himself at the same age. 'Come, Desmond,' he added more kindly. 'Try and adjust yourself. Clare won't be more to you than a stepmother in name. She'll be terribly tactful. I promise you that. You'll come to like her tremendously.'

Desmond hesitated, and said, 'I think I prefer to make up my own mind about people, Dad.'

Graham called for the bill. Desmond really could be terribly difficult when he wanted. Just like Maria.

Everyone at Smithers Botham seemed to know about the baby from its conception. Graham had confided in John Bickley, and he supposed Denise had spread the news with enthusiasm. Crampers had grunted something at him—congratulatory, Graham hoped. Even Captain Pile had made the point of repeating that no woman whatever was permitted to give birth within the hospital's glass-topped walls. Graham didn't care about the notoriety. He rather enjoyed it. He told himself more forcibly every day he was delighted with their child. A young life, something to perpetuate himself right to the end of the century, was an anodyne for any painfully intruding ideas about death and extinction. He could have no possible reservations about it whatever, he decided. And it would be wonderful for Clare. He treated her with the greatest tenderness, physical and mental. As for the effect on the mother-to-be of her circumstances in general, and her standing in the eyes of everybody at Smithers Botham in particular, it never crossed his mind to enquire.

All this happened in the busy fortnight following the Sunday when they rang the church bells. Then he had a letter from the Ministry terminating his contract at the annex.

13

'I WANT TO SEE Brigadier Haileybury,' said Graham to the sergeant in the hall. 'My name's Trevose. I'm a surgeon. The brigadier knows me well.'

'Have you an appointment, sir?'

'No. But I'm aware that he's in the building and I don't intend to leave until he gives me an interview.'

The sergeant looked uneasy. The wild-eyed civilian seemed an unlikely crony of the austere brigadier. 'If you'll wait here, sir, I can but pass on your message.'

'Please do.'

He left Graham alone in the hall, which like the inside of all requisitioned houses had bare walls and floor, was furnished with trestle-tables and fire-extinguishers, and had the decorations badly knocked about. Haileybury now held sway in a country mansion fronting the River Itchen south of Winchester, in preparation for the 'Second Front', Graham supposed, whenever that might be established. Within a minute the sergeant came clattering down the oak staircase, announcing that the brigadier would be delighted to receive his visitor at once.

The office upstairs was large, warm, and bright, overlooking the river, where in season Haileybury amused himself fishing for trout. There was a neat, busy-looking desk, filing cabinets, maps and charts on the wall. A lieutenant with twined-serpent R.A.M.C. badges, who hovered in attendance, was gently waved from the presence.

Haileybury extended his large red hand. 'An unexpected pleasure, Trevose.'

'Is it so unexpected?'

The brigadier pursed his lips. 'Won't you sit down?'

Graham took a small hard chair and began, 'Haileybury, do you know the one thing the powers-that-be in this war could do with me? They couldn't court-martial me. They couldn't put me in jail. They couldn't even tell me off. The only way they could save themselves the nuisance of my existence was to sack me. They have.'

Haileybury put his finger-tips together and blew on them, rather noisily.

'You're perfectly aware of that, of course,' Graham added accusingly.

'It has come to my ears.'

'Why did you do it? Why did you throw me out?'

Haileybury looked shocked. 'I?'

'I've a certain right to know, you must admit.'

'But, my dear fellow, I couldn't possibly be responsible for your dismissal. That would be a civilian matter, quite outside my province.'

'In all the years we've been squabbling, Haileybury, you've invariably done two things that I often enough have not. Told the truth and been honest.'

There was a silence. 'I see,' said Haileybury.

He got up, crossed silently to a filing cabinet, and still without speaking removed a folder.

'Your suspicions are correct, Trevose, I must agree,' he admitted, sitting down. 'Though only partly correct. I certainly made representations to the proper authorities. And I can hardly pretend otherwise than that my views were bound to carry some weight.'

He opened the file. My God! thought Graham, he's more of my cuttings than I've collected myself. He imagined Haileybury painstakingly snipping each one out, muttering to himself and shaking his head sorrowfully.

'Very well, the annex has been getting some publicity,' said

342

Graham. 'And what of it? It's cheered the patients up. It's encouraged my staff to keep working flat out. It's given the civilian population something to feel proud of. Hasn't it put up the morale of your own men? At least they know there's a unit to look after them efficiently, if they get their faces smashed up. It's made a hell of a difference in the R.A.F., I happen to know for a fact.'

'That isn't the point,' said Haileybury.

'You don't imagine it's done me any personal good, do you?' demanded Graham irritably. 'I've neither the desire nor the need to push my own interests. I'm only concerned with those of my patients.'

'I think we know each other's views on these matters too well for the need of repetition. I will only emphasize that mine have remained quite unchanged by the war.'

'Oh, you're stupid, ridiculous, blind, smug. Of course I can't help getting into the papers. I'm part of the scene. Nobody objects if General Montgomery or Vera Lynn or whoever you like gets photographed for the front pages, do they?'

'I think you're putting it rather extravagantly, Trevose.'

'Then tell me why you're getting me kicked out? No, don't bother. I know. Through spite, that's all.'

Haileybury drew a deep breath. 'You must be perfectly aware,' he said calmly, 'that there has been a great weight of complaint. However understandable your enthusiasm—perhaps even commendable—you have rather created the impression . . . well, the impression that nobody else in our profession is doing anything for the war at all. It has all been brought very sharply to the notice of the Ministry and the Service departments. And to myself personally.'

'By whom?' Twelvetrees at Smithers Botham, Graham thought, perhaps even Crampers.

'You might prefer me not to name names. The last time I unwittingly did so, I understand it led to a good deal of remorse on your part.'

The reference to Tom Raleigh made Graham shift uneasily in the chair. He continued in a more subdued voice, 'You

343

might at least tell me why the Ministry should have chosen this particular moment to pounce. It couldn't have come at a more awkward time for me personally.'

Haileybury reflected that most times were awkward for Trevose personally. 'I fancy people had to decide when matters had gone a little too far,' he declared. He paused and added, 'As I have been frank, will you perhaps let me make my motives clear?'

Graham nodded curtly.

'I assure you there was no suggestion of spite on my part. Surely you don't really think that of me? Not in your heart? There was no spite on anybody's part. But medicine is entering upon difficult times. You must know that, if only from the newspapers. When we raise our eyes from the war, what do we see? The future of our profession is in the balance. The politicos are concocting a large number of recipes for cooking our goose, believe you me. There's talk of forcing us into some sort of State health scheme—pure socialism.' Haileybury seemed to shudder. 'That would never do. We should lose our professional freedom. We should become mere civil servants, with the Government our taskmaster. The doctor–patient relationship, as we have known it for centuries, would be lost for ever.'

'All that's nothing to do with me.'

'But it is.' Haileybury leaned forward earnestly, his eyes shining. 'We shall have to fight these people. Fight them at every turn. And what shall be our weapons? We shall need every scrap of dignity, of integrity, of professional correctitude that we can muster. We must make it plain to the public that we stand above the ordinary commercial motives of life, that we seek no vainglory for ourselves, that we have no thought but for the welfare of our patients. None of us must falter—or appear to falter—from the rigorous discipline we have imposed on ourselves. None of us! We must fight not as individuals, but as a profession. Oh, politicians are slippery people, Trevose. I know. I've had dealings with plenty of them. We mustn't give them the smallest stick to beat us with.'

Graham replied by holding his hands before his face. 'So that is why these must be lost to the country like a torpedoed munition ship?'

'You're taking too dramatic a view, as usual,' said Haileybury shortly. 'Your unit will continue as before. That Canadian Tudor Beverley is a perfectly sound man. You should be the first to admit that none of us are indispensable. If I may say so, in peacetime you had rather a procession of assistants. Anyway, you remain on the staff of Blackfriars. Some beds will be found for you, either at Smithers Botham or elsewhere. Perhaps the Ministry of Pensions would have something to offer. You might like to know that I have made a point of assuring myself you wouldn't be left in the cold.'

'I am not going to treat a single casualty outside the unit that I have built up.'

'Then I fear you will find little else to do. Women are not given much to having their faces remodelled these days.'

'You're wrong.' Graham got up. 'Once released from my contract, I'm allowed to take on as much private practice as I can handle. Right? Well, women are continuing to give a great deal of thought to the new area I'm treating. I've been working with O'Rory at Smithers Botham on a reconstruction procedure for congenital absence of the vagina. It isn't a particularly unusual condition, you know. The operation's extremely interesting. You dissect the pelvic tissues from below, then put in a skin-graft on a mould. Sometimes it takes, sometimes it doesn't. You have to cut the graft extra thin or you'll get a crop of hair, which would be highly uncomfortable for all concerned. So, Haileybury. You don't want me. Nobody does. I shall therefore spend the rest of the war making new pussies.'

Without another word he clattered down the oak staircase and out to his Morris. The sergeant stared after him anxiously. Whatever had happened, it seemed likely to put the brigadier in one of his moods.

Graham wanted to leave the annex as soon as possible. Tudor Beverley and his staff offered to resign *en bloc*, but Graham wouldn't hear of it. Desmond, who seemed more shocked by his father's dismissal than by his second stab at paternity, suggested he withdraw from the Blackfriars medical school—the ridicule was liable to break out afresh, he suspected inwardly. Graham told him not to be stupid. His patients suggested getting up a petition, but Graham knew that official minds couldn't be swayed by even a snowstorm of paper. Anyway, he was suddenly weary of battling with authority. He'd lost, and he wanted to leave the field, just as soon as he could tidy up his work.

Clare was wonderful. Her practical mind stood rock-like amid their sea of troubles. She decided they would move somewhere for the span of her pregnancy, perhaps up to Scotland. They could enjoy a wonderful holiday until the baby was born —Graham had no need to start work, they'd saved a bit, and she'd a little money of her own. The divorce could surely be left in the hands of the solicitors. Graham agreed with everything. He felt he wanted the child desperately. It would be an achievement, a symbol of defiance, something to show for his existence. Without a regular achievement of some sort, he doubted if he could live at all.

Then they killed Bluey.

It was stupid, unnecessary, almost criminal. A couple of years of Graham's surgery had the Australian looking more or less like a human being. Better still, his hands were mending splendidly. He had a pair of new thumbs made from chips of his hip-bone, he could light cigarettes, hold a tankard, even fondle a girl. A small operation was still needed to trim the inside of his lip. John Bickley again gave an injection, and slipped the rubber tube into his windpipe. To stop the blood from Graham's incision trickling into his patient's lungs, John packed the back of Bluey's throat with a length of oiled bandage. It was common practice, performed on the patients every operating day. Afterwards, John drew out the tube and forgot the bandage. They wheeled Bluey back to bed. The nurse who found him dusky and straining to breathe wasted away his life trying artificial respiration. John was summoned, and instantly ripped out the bandage which was suffocating him. But it was too late. Two years in hospital had so enfeebled Bluey that the survivor of a blazing Hurricane succumbed to lack of oxygen as readily as a baby.

346

John went back to the theatre and told Graham. The surgeon dropped his instruments, left the operation to Tudor Beverley, and strode out to sit alone in his office. John hesitated. He had better face him. At the end of the case he followed Graham to the hut, and found him in tears.

'It was a terrible mistake,' John admitted at once. 'I just don't know how it happened.'

Graham said nothing.

'I'm always so careful about the throat-packs, Graham—you know I am. I've had nightmares about leaving one in. I've been half afraid something like this might come about, ever since the unit started.'

Graham wearily moved the glass bottle containing the soldier's tattoo. 'And after all the poor devil went through,' he muttered.

'I can't begin to say how sorry I am.' Graham again made no response. 'But it's awfully difficult, you know, with two tables in the theatre. Without any proper assistants. I've told the nurses time and time again to feel for the throat-pack at the first sign of trouble afterwards. The nurse in charge of Bluey was new. She let us down.'

'If you're going to make excuses, don't shift the blame on to some poor girl who at the moment is too frightened to speak.'

'I'm not making excuses,' said John patiently. 'I'm only putting the facts.'

'Whose responsibility is it?'

John shrugged. 'Of course, mine. Ultimately, as the anaes-thetist in charge of the case. I'm not denying that.'

'Of course you're making excuses,' Graham told him angrily. 'You're always making excuses, whenever you make a mess of it with a patient. If you give a perivenal injection, the vein was abnormal. If you break a needle, it was a faulty one. If your oxygen cylinder runs out, you told the orderly to change it. I only hope you'll find the coroner a more sympathetic listener.'

'I'm perfectly prepared to answer whatever the coroner feels like asking me,' John retaliated. 'I've nothing to hide.'

Graham made an impatient gesture. 'Oh, you'll come out of the inquest with your skin. Unavoidable mistake, pressure of work, patient's difficult airway. You'll continue with your job here as though nothing had happened. *I* shan't even be here to inconvenience you. You and Denise can go on putting out poisonous gossip about me, as much as you care. That probably helped to get me sacked, if you looked into it.'

'It's not fair to say that, Graham,' John told him patiently.

'It may not be, but it's the truth and you know it. Denise doesn't like me. She never has.'

'If Denise has sometimes been . . . well, indiscreet,' John admitted, 'she's been careful nothing could go further. Not outside the hospital. But now you're talking as if we were sworn enemies. Of course we're not. You're imagining things. Haven't we been friends, you and I, close friends, for years? Ever since the E.N.T. days? We've been through enough together, God knows. We've lost patients before.' He hesitated. 'We've even covered up for each other before. I wouldn't like to think that, however tragic, this incident meant the end of our personal relationship.'

'Be that as it may, but never in your life will you give another anaesthetic for me,' Graham told him angrily. 'At this particular moment, I doubt if that strikes you as much of a penalty. I'm down, I know it. But I won't stay down. When the war's over there'll be fifty anaesthetists in London breaking their necks chasing after my work. I'm going to make my fortune again. And this time you won't get ten per cent of it. Now please leave me in peace.'

That night, Clare woke with pain in her back. When she looked, she saw there was some vaginal bleeding. Graham telephoned Mr O'Rory. Then he carried her outside in a blanket, tucked her into the back of the Morris, and drove the ten miles to Smithers Botham. The gynaecologist was already waiting, greeting them with some mild joke about plastic surgeons working at the right end to avoid calls from their sleep. He put Clare into his ward, tipping up the foot of her bed on wooden blocks. He surrounded her with hot-water bottles, ordered an injection of morphine, prescribed doses of bromide, and added well-polished reassurance.

'Is she aborting?' asked Graham, outside the ward.

'Well, now, it's a threatened abortion,' Mr O'Rory said amiably. 'It's just eight weeks since the end of the lady's last menstrual period. So it wouldn't be an unheard-of occurrence at such a time, would it?'

'Could anything have caused it?' Graham asked anxiously. 'Mental distress, that sort of thing? You know what worry we've been having.'

'Oh, these things happen, they just happen. To tell the truth, none of us knows really why.'

'What's the chance of saving the foetus?'

'I'd say quite good. Yes, quite good. Though the lady will have to take life with queenly ease for quite a while afterwards.'

'That's nothing to bother about, nothing at all. . . .'

'And anyway,' smiled the gynaecologist, 'the lady isn't necessarily destined to repeat the performance on a second occasion, is she? If all is lost, there's plenty more where that one came from. Eh, Graham?'

Graham began to wonder if he really liked Tim O'Rory after all.

The bleeding went on. The following day Mr O'Rory shook his head and said he feared the lady must visit his operating theatre. They gave Clare another dose of morphine and wheeled her along the cold concrete corridor. Mr O'Rory's anaesthetist administered gas and trichloroethylene, they stuck her legs in the air, Mr O'Rory settled himself comfortably on a metal stool between them, and with a curette removed Graham's latest achievement for good.

Graham spent the night alone in the bungalow. Depression was no stranger at his side, but he had never known such misery before. Everything was running against him. When he told John Bickley that he wouldn't stay down he'd meant it. But for the first time he now sensed he was finished for good. He'd never recover professionally. Not when everyone could point to him as the man who was sacked in the war. The child was lost,

349

and in such straits they'd be insane to start another. He wondered if Clare would stay with him. He had really little to offer her, and at her age she must surely expect something rewarding from life. It never occurred to Graham how much she might love him for himself. He always expected to take so much from others, he sometimes felt obliged to offer more than he possibly could.

Haileybury would not have been surprised at this mental turmoil. He knew Graham's moods well enough. He was unaware of the pregnancy, and only faintly aware of Clare, whom he had dismissed as another of Graham's pick-ups. The following morning a car arrived at his mansion, containing a general. Haileybury knew the general well. They had been to the same public school, they belonged to the same London club, before the war they had been off golfing and mountaineering together. The general marched up to his office, saying nothing. He laid on Haileybury's desk a slip of typewritten paper, which declared simply,

Pray, why has one of our most famous and able doctors been dismissed his post? The news of his work has vastly heartened men and women in all the Allied Services. He will be reinstated immediately. I wish to know who is responsible.

Haileybury gave a deep sigh. It was useless to fight Trevose. When they both got to Heaven he was bound to get God on his side.

'Abortion?' said Mr Cramphorn to Denise Bickley at Smithers Botham. 'I'll bet Graham did it himself. With a knitting-needle.'

14

IT WAS A GLORIOUS AFTERNOON. The sun streaked the water
with gold and warmed the grassy slope where twenty-two-year-
old Alec Trevose lay with his face roofed by Sir Robert Muir's
Textbook of Pathology, all 991 pages of it. The slope ran down to a
white-painted hotel which had once housed holidaymakers at
Southsea, near Portsmouth, but was now a makeshift hospital.
Both sea and sky were for once free of men and their machinery,
except for an approaching landing-craft, its silver balloon
floating nonchalantly overhead, bringing smashed vehicles
and possibly smashed humans back from Normandy. By mid-
July both the weather and the progress of the invasion had
improved noticeably. Montgomery had liberated Caen, the
Americans had started moving down the eastward side of the
Cherbourg Peninsula, and the coloured-headed pins stuck into
maps on the walls of homes all over the country began to lose
their faintly worrying immobility.

Beside Alec on the grass was his sports jacket with leather
patches on the elbows, a frayed Blackfriars tie, and a semi-stiff
collar. He had cast off his shoes, and his big toes poked through
the holes in his socks. His striped shirt was open to display his
thin chest—he suffered from asthma, an awkward complaint,
liable to grip him in moments of emotion, sexual or otherwise.
Alec often put down the asthma to some obscure psychological
effect of having been delivered by his own father, the medical
missionary, in the Malayan jungle several hundred miles from
alternative professional attention. It was the first of many uncomfortable things which seemed to happen to him.

351

While his cousin Desmond had gone to a splendid public school, he had attended an odd establishment for the education of the sons of other missionaries, to be reared in a strong atmosphere of piety, chastisement, and carbolic soap. Even the cost of his education was being met by his Uncle Graham (or his cousin, Desmond, however you looked at it), though his bills were thankfully met by anonymous lawyers. He had started the telescoped medical course at Cambridge when the war was a year old. It wasn't much fun, he reflected, with no one to talk to except potential doctors, engineers, and clergymen, all three professions being thought essential by the Government to ensure eventual victory. But he had seen Cambridge as it should be seen, with King's Chapel shining in the pure moonlight like an iceberg, Great Court at Trinity a mystery of stones and shadows, Clare College running lightless to the river as a silver screen, the alleys returned to their rightful medieval blackness. It was Cambridge as Newton and Milton had seen it. His tutor was an ancient cleric in a purple stock encrusted with the memorials to countless college soups, who wore both gown and air-raid warden's helmet during alerts, taking seriously his responsibility for the physical as well as the moral safety of his pupils. The science dons had mostly disappeared to concoct new devilment for the enemy. On the whole, Alec thought the University rather superior about the war. It had lived through plenty before with fitting scientific detachment. The church clock still stood at ten to three, and for most of the time honey was off the ration.

That sunny afternoon by the sea he was still officially studying clinical medicine at Smithers Botham, where he had occupied almost a dozen lodgings in the surrounding countryside. However agreeable his hosts, however tasty the Woolton pie, however hot the officially permitted few inches of bathwater, Alec was always convinced of being happier at the next stop. It was a strange restlessness which applied to his hobbies, his friends, his enthusiasm for the various subjects he studied, and his views of life in general. He had finally asked his uncle Graham to get him into the Emergency Squad. He felt he got on rather well with his uncle Graham. Physically they were much alike. Alec supposed when the family genes had been shuffled at their separate conceptions, they had drawn much the same hand.

The Emergency Squad at Smithers Botham occupied a low two-storey block which in peacetime had housed the better-class lunatic, who could afford to pay for his own incarceration. It was comfortable enough, it saved paying rent, and you could always risk smuggling in a girl. The Squad's existence was at last justified on D-Day, when they were abruptly dispatched by lorry across the face of signpostless England to the converted hotel at Southsea, which they found in charge of a Polish civilian doctor who was unable to speak much English, and who seemed uncertain if they were a party of top-flight specialists from London or the men come to mend the boiler. No one knew what cases the hospital was created to take, because none ever appeared. Everyone seemed to have forgotten about them. Their only contact with authority was Brigadier Haileybury, who one afternoon had arrived unheralded to inspect them. 'I believe I know you, don't I?' he had asked Desmond.

'Yes, sir. We met once before the war. In my father's place in London. My name's Trevose.'

Haileybury nodded. 'Your father is certainly making a name for himself.'

'Deservedly, I hope, sir?'

'Of that I have no doubt. I hope you inherit a share of his remarkable talents, young man. You could look forward to a brilliant career.'

The brigadier disappeared. They all noticed he had a wonderfully pretty A.T.S. driver.

Alec slid the pathology textbook from his nose, aware that someone was approaching up the slope. It was Desmond, dressed in a grey flannel suit. His cousin sat down silently beside him, picked a stalk of grass, and stuck the end between his teeth.

'Anything doing in the wards?' Alec asked.

353

'No. What are you reading?'

'Muir.'

'I mean this other book,' Desmond picked up an open volume from the grass. He turned the pages frowning, and after a moment read aloud,

> *'Behold me waiting—waiting for the knife.*
> *A little while, and at a leap I storm*
> *The thick, sweet mystery of chloroform,*
> *The drunken dark, the little death-in-life.'*

He tossed the book down and asked, 'What are you reading that sort of stuff for?'

'It's too hot for pathology.'

'It's a rather flamboyant bit of verse, isn't it?'

'No, I don't think so. Doesn't it put a patient's feelings well? God knows how many think the same thing. They aren't articulate enough to express themselves, that's all.'

'Nobody uses chloroform any more,' said Desmond briefly. 'Who wrote it?'

'Henley. When he was in Edinburgh Infirmary, waiting for them to chop his foot off.'

'Why have you taken to poetry?'

'Why not? Don't you realize, we're totally uneducated. All of us. At Blackfriars they simply drown us intellectually in a torrent of facts, mostly extremely dull. What chance have we got to equip ourselves with some knowledge of literature, the arts, philosophy?' he added grandly.

'I daresay.' Desmond bit a piece of grass then spat it away. 'Unfortunately, they don't ask questions on those subjects in the finals.'

'I think we should be more interested in being well-educated doctors than getting through our finals.'

'Oh, this is just another of your crazes,' Desmond dismissed his cousin's cultural ambitions. 'I've got to go back to London this evening.'

'What's this? A night out?'

'No, it's my mother,' Desmond told him with careful casual-

354

ness. 'I've just heard. She's had a stroke. Quite a severe one, I gather.'

'I say, I'm sorry.'

'So am I. But these vascular accidents happen.' Desmond got up. 'Shouldn't you try and find someone to mend your socks?'

It would never do to display emotion, or even concern, especially in front of Alec.

The news telephoned from Sussex that morning was hardly a surprise to Graham. For a year Maria's blood-pressure had been steadily mounting, as she became fatter than ever. He still hadn't divorced her. The plan had somehow been overlooked in the flurry of his reinstatement at the annex. He told Clare—as he told himself—the episode of his sacking must be taken as a warning. For the patients to continue benefiting from his abilities, he must be careful about publicity in the future. A divorce case in the papers certainly wouldn't help his standing in the eyes of the Ministry. Such distressing tangles were perhaps best unravelled after the war, when he was his own master again. Clare agreed. The subject was dropped. So was that of a second excursion into pregnancy. Among any affectionate couple the matters never mentioned are generally the important ones.

Their domestic bliss at Cosy Cot continued. Clare didn't go back to her work at the annex, but stayed at home to look after the house, grow radishes and lettuces in the garden, and cook the rations. They were frequently indebted to Mr Cramphorn, who seemed to have taken to them after Graham's brush with authority, and would appear at the door with a rabbit he had shot, or a pigeon, or a rook, or even a squirrel, which he proclaimed excellent eating if roasted with a strip of bacon, as inclined to be rather dry. The food situation was trying. Graham himself sometimes guiltily brought liquid paraffin from the hospital to eke out the cooking fat, until the Ministry tumbled to this regrettably widespread practice and added the chemical phenolphthalein, which turned the fried fish bright pink.

'What's Maria's prognosis, Graham?' Clare asked.

They were sitting on the handkerchief of a lawn in the garden that evening, waiting for Desmond. Graham had managed to buy a bottle of Pimm's No. 1, which he prepared with great enthusiasm, adding bits of apple, cucumber rind, mint, and even carrot. 'It's difficult to say. She may recover, more or less completely. She may end up with a hemiplegia, half-paralyzed—and dumb, of course, if her speech centre's gone. She may go on having small strokes for months, even years. On the other hand she may develop broncho-pneumonia and die in a week. These patients get bedsores, sepsis, you know. Sometimes they just fade out.'

Clare said nothing. If Maria died, the last obstacle to their marriage would die with her. Well, the last excuse, anyway. Sensing her thoughts, Graham added, 'I should have gone ahead with that divorce.' He reached out and took her hand. 'I know how you feel, and it must be awful. Stepping into a dead woman's shoes.'

'No, I don't feel that at all, darling. Maria's never been more than an abstract quality to me.'

'You should have made me do something about those lawyers.'

'You'd have said I was nagging.' She laughed. 'You might have left me.'

He squeezed her hand and said, 'Don't be silly. You know perfectly well—'

He broke off. A noise. A motor bike in the sky, coming nearer. 'Is that one?' he asked anxiously.

'Yes, I rather think it is.'

'Crampers told me the one which fell in Maiden Cross yesterday killed about twenty people.'

The engine stopped.

'It's a long way off,' he said, still sounding uncomfortable.

They stared at each other. The silence seemed to last for an age. Finally there was an explosion far in the distance.

'Some of them glide on for miles,' Graham observed. The flying-bombs had taken on an ill-natured personality of their own. They were malevolent, winged, fire-spitting beasts, impossible to relate to the busy grey-uniformed squads dispatching them. 'I hope Desmond's all right,' he added in a worried voice.

But Desmond arrived unaware of his peril. He spent the night in the bungalow, setting off early the next morning with Graham in the Morris. The nursing-home where Maria lay ill catered for a more genteel mental sufferer than once found themselves in Smithers Botham. It was a manor house providing seclusion, fresh vegetables from the garden, and nursing which was unfailingly kindly if not particularly skilful. They were received by the matron, a stout, blue-uniformed north-countrywoman, radiating cheerfulness. 'The poor soul's poorly, of that there's no doubt,' she greeted Graham. 'If she went, we'd quite miss her, you know. She's been with us longer than anyone.'

Graham was familiar enough with Maria's room. She had occupied the same one since he had her shut up in the place ten years ago. It was small, bright in the sunshine, with a vase of pink roses beside the bed. Maria was unconscious, breathing noisily. It was too soon after the haemorrhage, which had sprung from a brittle artery amid the microscopic telephone-cables of her brain, to tell the extent of her coming paralysis. Graham noticed she suffered the indignity of a large fly crawling unmolested across her cheek. Her grey hair lay neatly on the pillow in two plaits, each tied with a pink bow, like a schoolgirl's.

Desmond stood in the background, looking solemn. However much he had prepared himself, however often he had observed the same clinical state in others, however little he felt for his insane mother, it was a shock to see her like that. Graham went to the bed and felt her pulse. His fingers slipped down to take her flaccid hand. It reminded him of the night when her troubles had started, when she tried to kill herself with an overdose of sleeping-draught and had been saved by the skill of John Bickley. He suddenly felt himself touched. Now his wife lay under his eyes as a dying wreck, he felt a surge of love for her. It was stronger than any he could remember in his life, even before he had married her.

357

'Isn't her breathing rather obstructed?' he complained mildly.

'The doctor will be along by and by,' the matron told him comfortably. 'Doubtless he'll deal with it.'

Graham nodded. He supposed at that stage it didn't make twopence worth of difference. 'Perhaps you'll ring me at Smithers Botham, Matron, if she takes a turn for the worse?'

'I will that, Mr Trevose.' In the corridor outside she went on cheerfully, 'It's sad, isn't it, your poor wife should be smitten when there're such good news on the wireless this morning.' As Graham looked at her blankly she explained, 'Haven't you heard? They've tried to blow up Hitler with a bomb. The Germans themselves. It won't be long now till it's all over and done with, you mark my words.'

As they drove away, Graham said to Desmond, 'I suppose there're people who ought to know. You'd better try and get hold of your uncle Charles. You can probably find his whereabouts if you telephone Val Arlott's office at the *Press*. Say it's on my behalf. God knows where her other brother's got to.'

'Do you want to speak to Uncle Charles yourself, Dad?'

'I most certainly do not.' Graham drove in silence for a mile. 'So they tried to liquidate *Der Führer*, did they? Perhaps they'll end up with a revolution in Berlin, like last time. It could all be over by Christmas.'

Graham hardly said anything for the rest of the journey. The shadow of death that hung over both Hitler and Maria was bringing to the front of his mind difficult problems.

15

MARIA'S FUNERAL caused a frightful fuss. She lingered a week, regaining consciousness, her hand groping the air, her eyes askew, speechless. During the days she was passive enough, but at nights she grew restless, clawing at her sheets, trying to get out of bed. The nurses were perfectly used to such behaviour. They brought long boards to slot along the sides of her bed, as though she were in her coffin already. On the Thursday morning she had another cerebral haemorrhage, and left life as she had entered it, with a gasp.

When they telephoned Graham at Smithers Botham he shrugged his shoulders. But he was surprised at his inner distress. It is a merciful quality of the human mind never completely to expect the inevitable. There were practical details again. He knew his wife wished to be buried at Biddenden, in more glorious days the Cazalay family's country 'place'. She had told him as much when her life was in danger once before, at the stormy birth of Desmond. But Biddenden was in Kent, and since the opening of the second front a military area. Graham seemed to remember that permits were needed to venture there. He approached Captain Pile, who confessed it outside his authority—though he had taken to Graham since the surgeon had become a national figure, often boasting to his cronies of association with this wonderful work. The undertakers finally sorted things out, and the following Wednesday morning Graham set off in the Morris again with Desmond. They started late, Graham having been called to a soldier brought into the annex from a bad road smash. In an age infested with priorities, he supposed that the dying could claim precedence over the already dead.

Graham remembered the Cazalays' old house well enough. It was a mile or two from Biddenden, near another village with a few houses, a pub, and the church. You first caught sight of it as the road turned on the hill, through a gap in the trees—but the trees had grown. Graham tried to remember the last time he'd been invited to spend a night in its spacious and chilly bedrooms. It was not really an old house, its twisted chimneys, leaded windows, and timbered gables going no farther back than the reign of King Edward the Seventh. It was rather vulgar, really, like the late Lord Cazalay himself. He wondered how the famous glasshouses were, the airfields in the area having been plastered by the Germans generously. As he drove past the lodge gates he saw a notice announcing HEAD-QUARTERS—FORCES AND WORKERS ENTERTAINMENT SERVICE. Well, he supposed, that was carrying on the first Lord Cazalay's tradition.

'Did you ever visit the place?' Graham asked Desmond.

'I don't know. I could hardly remember, could I? I was too young before the family disgrace.'

Graham grunted. He disliked to think of the disgrace spilling on to his own family. He had brought nothing but honour to the Cazalay tree. 'We're late,' he said, as the church came in sight. 'Everyone's gone in.'

They hurried inside, making for the front pew. Graham found himself beside a fat man with the bar of a black moustache across his red face—Maria's brother Charles, the second Lord Cazalay. They inclined their heads gravely. The elderly clergyman rose. A familiar noise intruded into the church, a phut-phut-phut coming steadily nearer. Graham shifted his feet uncomfortably. Now they had moved the anti-aircraft guns to the coast and left the Spitfires and Hurricanes to prowl inshore, most of the flying-bombs were being shot down. It occurred to him they were standing in the middle of the area proscribed by the Air Ministry for exactly this purpose.

The noise grew closer. The clergyman stood with his mouth open. Graham noticed the church windows had already been blown out and boarded up. It would be a strange end, to be buried alive at his wife's funeral. The engine cut out. Silence. Then an explosion which shook the earth under them. The clergyman started the burial service in a tone of deep relief.

It was all mumbo-jumbo, Graham thought. The only difference between a human body alive and a human body dead was that between an engine running and switched off, though the stopped engine didn't inconveniently rot to pieces. There were a surprising number of people in the church, twenty or thirty. Old friends of Maria's, he supposed. Living ghosts, come to clank the rusty chains of their memories in his ears. He hoped the old clergyman would get it all over quickly. He probably would, there was always the chance of another flying-bomb.

As they wheeled Maria out, Graham noticed the route to the graveside passed a row of elaborate memorials to others of the Cazalay family. Though not her father and mother, who had died in the arid air of Venezuela, a destination recommending itself for Lord Cazalay's retirement through its lack of an extradition treaty with Great Britain. As Maria's remains were lowered from sight another flying-bomb came out of the distance. As the engine stopped, heads turned heavenwards in anxiety rather than supplication. It exploded with a distant thump. Graham wondered idly who was unfortunate enough to be underneath it.

'Mr Trevose, you must remember me,' said an old lady in a velvet hat, voice conscientiously hushed.

'Of course I do,' Graham lied.

'I was on the committee of the Sunshine League and the Free Medicine Club with your dear wife, you know.'

The Sunshine League! Well, the war had relieved the rich of the painful necessity of lightening the burdens of the poor. Graham found himself facing a thin old man with two sticks, whom he recognized after a moment as Sir John Blazey. He'd been chairman of the small hospital at Uxbridge which Graham had used as his first step to success in plastic surgery—rather unscrupulously, he supposed. He thought the fellow had died long ago.

'Your wife was a great woman, Trevose.' The old man shook his head reflectively. 'She was quite unsparing in her sense of duty to others. We shall never know how many unfortunate people have had cause to be grateful to her.'

Graham thanked him. He had almost forgotten the Maria of the busy committees, with her picture in the *Illustrated London News* and the *Bystander*. Now the glories of her past began to draw his eye from the shadows of her later poverty and insanity. Well, it's good to know she died a credit to me, he thought. He found himself shaking hands with Val Arlott.

'Why did you come?' Graham asked, looking surprised. 'I didn't notice you in the church.'

'Have you a moment for a stroll?'

They walked together in the country lane outside the church-yard. 'I can't say why I came, exactly,' Val told him. 'I've been wondering. Perhaps it's to make up for missing the burial of her father. I was fond of old Cazalay. In some measure, I suppose I was responsible for his plight.' Graham made an unbelieving gesture. 'It's difficult to know. There are things I might have said or done to check his recklessness. Perhaps I'm suffering unconscious feelings of guilt towards the family. This is my penance. You'd know about such matters, wouldn't you? How are things going?'

'At the annex? We're still busy. Though the excitement's gone. We're an institution now. Like all institutions we've lost the fun of getting greater and grander, we've only the worry of seeing ourselves slipping.'

'I wish I'd done more for you medical people. Particularly now I'm getting so old and infirm. Look at Nuffield—given millions, set up professors, all manner of things.'

'You know they tried to sack me?'

'Yes, I got the P.M. to scotch it.'

Graham looked faintly put out. He had imagined the inter-vention a tribute to his own personality. 'After the war you'll have plenty of room for your charity, I should imagine, Val. These ideas about State medicine and so on, nothing will come of them, surely?'

'Don't you believe it. When the fighting stops we'll get a socialist government.'

'Surely you're not telling me the country's going to reject Churchill?'

'Why not? What stopped us giving in after Dunkirk? Our national streak of perversity.'

Graham looked glum. 'That'll make it tough for me, trying to build up again.'

'You've got a wonderful reputation.'

'I can't eat it.'

'No, but it helps. There'll be a lot of goodies and gongs going after the war, Graham. I don't see why you should be passed by. I take it you'd be agreeable if I put you in for something?'

Graham gave a faint smile. 'Haven't I been too gay a dog to be given an official collar?'

'The war's altered a lot of that. After all, if you're brave enough to win the V.C. nobody gives a damn how many women you've screwed.'

'It's certainly an attractive proposition—' He broke off, listening. 'No, it's only a motor-bike somewhere. Those doodle-bugs are damn scaring. I thought that one in church was going to blow the lot of us up, corpse and all.'

'Don't worry. Duncan Sandys says we've got them licked. Only about one in five get through now.'

'When's the war going to be over?'

'Against the Germans, by Christmas. Against the Japs, in a couple of years. Against the Russians, God knows.'

With this deep and disquieting observation, Val Arlott shook hands, entered his chauffeur-driven car, and made off.

Graham felt he needed a drink.

The other mourners were cramming themselves with some agitation into three or four taxis parked off the lane. His son was standing alone, looking awkward by the lych gate. 'I expect you could do with a stiff one, Desmond, couldn't you?'

363

'Yes, it wouldn't come amiss.'

'We'll try our luck in the pub.'

They walked a quarter-mile down the lane in silence. The funeral had already been displaced from Graham's mind by his talk with Val. Some sort of 'gong'. What sort? They could hardly hand him the O.B.E., like some zealous food official. A K.B.E. would make him Sir Graham, which would sound very pretty. But he doubted if even Val could push him into the pure light of official favour. The bigwigs in the medical profession would certainly have a say in it, and they had always mistrusted him. Someone would be resentful he won his fight over the sacking, and eager to express it practically. And Haileybury would be against him. No, not Haileybury, Graham decided, after a moment's thought. Haileybury was far too stupidly righteous to take the chance of such easy revenge. Anyway, he didn't care. He had never let official honours flicker among the varied ambitions which had burned inside him. He knew medical knights enough, and he thought most of them horribly dreary.

They pushed open the door of the little saloon bar, to hear a loud voice declaring, 'But of course you must have some whisky. Come along, be a good fellow, look out a bottle from under the counter. Don't you understand, I've just been to a funeral?'

Graham hesitated, but it was too late to withdraw. He had never liked Maria's brother. The man had laughed at him as her suitor, paining young Graham with the discovery that in 'society' medical people were seen with the eye of fifty years previously, when the healer was admitted only via the tradesmen's entrance—though Graham had acted afterwards on this brutal realization, most profitably. He was also rather afraid of Charles Cazalay. He had the unscrupulousness of his father, if not the intelligence which made the most of it. He had tried to damage Graham once, and wouldn't hesitate to try again if it suited him.

'Don't you know who I am?' Lord Cazalay continued to the landlord, half-chaffing and half-hectoring. 'You should, you know. I'm Lord Cazalay. I used to live in the house. Before your day. I remember the fellow who kept this place, man called Greensmith. Greensmith would have found something for me, I don't mind telling you. Now run along and see what you can do.'

Overcome either by the materialization of the local legend or the solemnity of his errand, the landlord departed anxiously to search his cellar. Graham approached and said, 'It must be twenty years since we met.'

'Graham, I'm delighted to see you again,' Lord Cazalay greeted him affably. 'I'm sorry it should be on such a sad occasion.'

Graham introduced his son. 'You can't have set eyes on Desmond since he was a baby.'

Lord Cazalay briskly brushed his moustache and remarked, 'He's grown into a fine lad. As you know, I decided to make my home for some years in France.' He lowered his voice respectfully. 'It was very distressing about Maria, Graham. I know how you must feel. Her life was such a waste, shut out of the world so long. It was always a comfort to me that my sister had you to care for her—a medical man.'

'Thank you,' said Graham shortly.

'Well, Graham—you've become more famous than ever. I always seem to be reading about you in the papers.'

'I'm only doing my job. Like a lot of others who don't get noticed.'

'I'm with security, you know.'

'I thought you were censoring civilian letters?'

'It's the same thing,' said Lord Cazalay, looking put out.

The landlord reappeared, holding an unopened bottle of Haig like a newborn baby. As he poured three measures Lord Cazalay went on, 'What are your plans for after the war, Graham?'

'I think it's only courting disappointment making any.'

'I wouldn't say that. It'll be every man for himself and the devil take the hindmost. Like last time. The thing is to get in early, before the mugs. There'll be pickings enough for the right people.'

365

'Where precisely do you intend to pick, if I may ask?'

'Travel.' Lord Cazalay swallowed his whisky and demanded another. 'People have been cooped up here all the war, they'll be bursting to get out and about. There'll be plenty of spare shipping space, Army buses, that sort of thing, if you know where to put your hands on them. I've plenty of valuable contacts in France. I doubt whether they've got into any trouble with the Germans.' He looked at his glass reflectively, and added, 'As a matter of fact, I'm starting a small company. If you're interested, I could let you have a piece of it.'

Graham thought this brazen, even for his brother-in-law. 'You're asking me for money, after having tried to get me publicly disgraced as a professional man?'

Lord Cazalay looked serious, then said, 'Graham, I'm glad you raised that business. It's been on my conscience. I'd been meaning to have a word with you, but with the war, of course, everything's been difficult. It was all a tragic misunderstanding, surely? I was simply wrongly advised. It was a relief to me nothing came of it.'

'It was to me, too.'

'Don't you trust me?' he asked, part humorously and part aggressively.

'I don't think this is quite the occasion to conduct commercial affairs.'

'No, no, perhaps you're right,' Lord Cazalay said quickly.

'Now we must be going. Desmond has to catch a train for Portsmouth.'

'We'll keep in touch,' Lord Cazalay promised. 'Yes, very much in touch.'

They left him with the bottle of whisky, which he seemed about to settle down and finish, on the estimable principle that unexpected blessings needed exploiting to the full.

'WHAT WAS IT LIKE?' asked Clare as Graham got back to the bungalow, having left Desmond at the station in Maiden Cross.

'More harrowing than I imagined.'

'Do you want some tea, darling? You can't have had anything to eat.'

'I don't think I'm hungry, really.'

He sat in an armchair in the sitting-room and picked up the *Daily Press*. He hadn't seen a paper that morning. 'The Russians seem to be doing well,' he observed. He wondered what Val Arlott had meant about a war with the Soviets. They seemed prickly customers, but at least they were on our side, and putting up a far better showing than last time.

'Did you see the brother?'

'Yes.'

'Any trouble?'

'No, he tried to borrow some money off me.'

Clare sat on the arm of his chair. 'I can see it's upset you, Graham.'

'It was all the paraphernalia—dirges, gloomy incantations, that sort of thing. Why should I be disturbed by her death in itself? It was a merciful release, overdue if anything.'

'I never met her, of course. But I thought I knew her. I've so often imagined her lying beside you.'

'That was never particularly successful or pleasurable.'

'What was she like? In her prime?'

Graham tossed the paper down. 'Active. Always busy. A

great do-gooder. On dozens of committees. She was an intelligent woman before her brain gave way. We had a rather cerebral relationship, I suppose. She was dreadfully afraid of her own emotions. The only thing in the world she was afraid of.'

'What made you marry her?'

'Who knows at such distance why they married anyone?'

After a pause she asked, 'When are we going to be married ourselves, Graham?'

'There'll have to be a decent interval, naturally.'

'Of course, I appreciate that.'

'I've got to take some account of the world in general, however much I despise it. There'd be gossip if we got married tomorrow—Crampers, the Bickleys, everyone at Smithers Botham. It would probably get into the papers, certainly into the *Press*. I don't want to invite maliciousness. God knows I've had to suffer enough of it recently.'

She noticed it didn't occur to Graham even to ask her own sentiments. Clare was used to his self-centredness. She had decided there was nothing unkind or even unattractive about it. In some ways it was a virtue. His egotism, more than anything else, had made the annex what it was. If Graham could think of nobody but himself, she felt resignedly, it was perhaps because there was nobody in his acquaintance half as interesting.

'How long?' she asked.

'I really can't say off-hand, Clare. I've had no experience of the situation.'

'Do you mean six weeks or six months? A year? Two years?' For the first time she resolved to press him.

'We must allow the corpse to grow cold.'

'Well, then—six months, say?'

'I should think that would strike everyone as respectable.'

'Shall we decide on January?'

'Yes, in January. The war will be over by then.'

The sitting-room window was open, and a breeze blew some sheets of case-notes from Graham's table on to the floor. She rose to gather them. 'We'll be back in London then, as likely as not,' he told her. 'Mightn't this be the moment to start looking for a flat? My house in Mayfair would cost a fortune to put into shape. I'll need new consulting rooms, too. We might be able to combine both. Harley Street isn't a bad area to live. It's near Regent's Park and not far from the West End.'

She smiled and said, 'It's difficult to imagine myself living in London at all.'

'It'll be wonderful, once things get back to normal. Wonderful for both of us. There's scores of places I'm longing to take you—restaurants, theatres, little clubs I remember. Not all of them can have disappeared in the blitz. There's hundreds of people I want you to meet. This time they'll come back, thank God. It was different after the last war, with those awful blood-baths.'

'You won't do anything like that at all, Graham,' she chided him gently. 'You'll be too busy working.'

'I've worked hard enough during the war. I deserve a bit of relaxation. It's been five years out of my life. Do you realize that by Christmas in 1954 I'll be sixty?'

'That's a long way off. Anyway, I'll be almost forty.'

'Of course, I shall have to make a living, build up from scratch.' He gave a grin. 'I'll have a new wife to impress. I don't really believe these wild schemes for putting doctors under the State will come to anything. Supposing we all went on strike? That's a chilling prospect for the politicians. Things will go on much the same, if you ask me. You can't change England.'

'But what about the annex?'

'I suppose it will cease to exist, or become totally unimportant again, like the R.A.F. itself. I don't know. It's no concern of mine. My job there finishes with the war.'

'But Graham!' she exclaimed. 'I can't believe you could give up the annex, just like that. You created it. It's filled your thoughts, day and night. You'd be aimless without it. You can't have just lost interest in it.'

'But it's a phase in my life. Don't you see, Clare? We've all grown so used to the war we've forgotten it's a highly abnormal form of existence. I've been lotus-eating down here. I've had no

369

worries about making money, nor about what to spend it on. A lot of the others at Smithers Botham haven't the sense to see it the same way. They're stuck in a rut, you'd imagine they thought the war was continuing for ever.' He swept his hand round the sitting-room. 'My God, I'm longing to live in a proper house. Somewhere with my own furniture, decent pictures, eating off plates without cracks in them. None of this bloody rationing, servants to do the dirty work, a bit of style again. Oh, I'll admit it, the war's been stimulating, rewarding, often amusing. But when it's over I want to forget it like an illness. I want to pick up my career again. As far as surgery goes, I'm only approaching my prime.'

She was facing him, leaning against the table, and he saw she had started to cry. Women were unaccountable. 'What's the matter?' he asked, not particularly kindly. 'I haven't said anything wrong, surely?'

'I thought the annex meant everything to you, Graham.'

'It's something I'll look back on with considerable affection.'

'Like me?'

'Why do you say that?' he asked irritably. 'You're being fanciful.'

'I'm not. It's perfectly true. I'm just part of the annex, as far as you're concerned.'

'Now you're being downright silly.'

'You don't want to marry me, do you? You don't want to at all.'

She advanced on him angrily. Graham was startled. All his life he had surrounded himself with submissive people, and it was always unsettling when they turned on him.

'Clare, you're simply saying a lot of irresponsible things which are making you overwrought.'

'I'm saying things which I should have said months ago, years ago. My God, I've been a fool. Do you imagine all this hasn't been boiling in my mind since I came here? Of course you don't want to marry me. You've always had some excuse, something to put it off. Even when you got me pregnant you didn't want me as your wife. You were scared stiff at the thought. You didn't want that child either. You were as pleased as Punch when I aborted. That's the truth, isn't it?'

He stood up. 'Of course it wasn't the truth,' he told her crossly. 'I did everything I could to save it, didn't I? I was upset when we lost it, dreadfully upset. Do you think I don't know my own mind?'

'No, you don't know it at all, Graham. That's your trouble. There're plenty of wonderful things about you, and you don't recognize them. There are plenty of horrible things about you too, and you don't recognize those either. Or you won't bring yourself to face them, which is the worse for you.'

'So you're suggesting I'm going to turn you out after the war, like some camp-follower?'

'It won't come to that. We can't go on with this play-acting any longer. We've got to split up.'

'You can't mean that?' He was alarmed at this practical turn in the conversation.

'It'll only get worse if I stay.' She looked down at the threadbare carpet and went on more calmly, 'I haven't made up my mind just this minute, Graham. I decided . . . oh, months ago, I don't know when. Perhaps I didn't decide at all. It just crept up on me.'

'Clare—' He approached her, but she pushed him away. 'Supposing I said I'd marry you tomorrow?'

'No, it wouldn't do. It wouldn't work. We'd be in a worse mess than ever. Once you got back to London you'd want to be rid of me. I'm not your type. You don't love me. I don't think you could love anyone. Your attitude to women is like your attitude to the boys in the annex. So many 'construction jobs', as you say. You overlook that I've got the right to any feelings at all.'

Graham stuck his hands in his pockets. It was all most distressing. He hated emotional scenes. Perhaps they were both upset with the business of Maria. Clare would be over it tomorrow. 'Why did you take up with me in the first place?' he asked, a shade resentfully. 'You knew enough about me, about my past affairs?'

371

'Every woman's a heroine, I suppose. She expects to succeed where others have succumbed.'

'Possibly.' They stood looking at each other. 'You can't mean it?' he asked more quietly. 'About going away?'

'Yes, I do. I'll get a job somewhere.'

'Let's discuss it again tomorrow, when we're ourselves.'

'No,' she told him. 'There's nothing else to say.'

A week later Clare left the bungalow and Graham took a room in a London hotel, explaining to everyone at Smithers Botham that this temporary change in domestic arrangements was necessitated by his searching for a flat. The pair had parted politely, even amicably. A continued emotional tempest would have worn out both of them, and they were old enough to take such things sensibly. In the end, Graham was rather pleased. He would miss Clare, of course, but she was right. She was a simple, kindly girl, but not at all the sort to stand beside the fashionable plastic surgeon, Graham Trevose, now returning like the exiled European governments to his rightful dominions. A marriage would have been a disaster. And supposing this 'gong' materialized? Lady Trevose? Decidedly not. To fill *that* rôle he wanted someone far more intelligent, more versed in the ways of the world, more socially adept, someone of better family than the seedy commercial artist's.

Someone like Maria? he thought.

Yes, someone like Maria.

Maria in death, like Maria in life, always came out top in the end.

17

BY CHRISTMAS, when the fighting should have been over, the German armies broke through at the Ardennes for the second time in the war. Luckily for the Allies, the weather cleared and they could bomb them to pieces on the twisting hilly roads— which they would have saved themselves a great deal of trouble by doing in 1940, if only they'd had any aeroplanes. In London the flying-bombs were replaced by rockets, which perplexed and affronted the Government, as Lord Cherwell had worked out most carefully they were too expensive for the Germans to use. The rockets particularly harassed Alec Trevose, who was doing his two months' midwifery training at a sandbagged lying-in hospital in north London. Every time one fell the noise sent half a dozen local women into labour, and it was no fun finding your way through blacked-out back streets on a bicycle, loaded like a mule with bags of instruments and dressings, suspected by policemen of being some sort of saboteur, and wondering if the next unheralded missile had your number on it.

Alec didn't like midwifery. He was beginning to see himself as an intellectual, a man of culture, and childbirth was an extremely uncultured pursuit for all concerned. Alec hated the babies. He hated the midwife in charge of him, a sparse-bosomed Scotswoman with a vinegary tongue. She in turn seemed to hate him, and indeed men in general, which he felt was reasonable from her toilsome occupation. Only the jovial Mr O'Rory brought levity to the solemn reproductive circus

373

with his visits twice a week. He was a Catholic, and therefore unable to perform abortions—though he stretched a point when they were natural, like Clare's miscarriage, and passed the others to his houseman, back-seat driving over his right shoulder. Female sterilization was for him, he confessed, quite out of the question. He would perform the operation to the crucial point, then demand genially of his assistant, 'Just tie a a knot in those two ligatures round the Fallopian tubes, my boy, there's a good fellow. My religion doesn't allow me to do that sort of thing at all.'

Alec rather took to Mr O'Rory. He felt he had the cultured approach.

In the spring the Nazi magnificos suddenly appeared in the papers as haggard and anxious old men, shuffling about in baggy civilian suits. It induced feelings of freakishness rather than triumph. To anyone of Alec Trevose's age, a world empty of Hitler and Mussolini was as strange as one without Mickey Mouse and Donald Duck. Himmler bit the cyanide capsule in his tooth, and vomited himself to death over the trousers of a British officer. If nobody really knew what had happened to Hitler, nobody really cared. There were rejoicings in British streets, of a seemly nature. The Government, in a burst of official relaxation, allowed the citizenry to use binoculars again. If the population were restrained by the scarcity of hard liquor from getting lit up when the lights went up in London, at least they had some sort of fling before the authorities switched them off again through shortage of fuel. On the June day when the world inaugurated the United Nations in San Francisco and so abolished war for ever—for the second occasion in a quarter of a century—both Alec and Desmond found they had qualified as doctors.

Alec quickly found that qualification, like marriage, brought more problems than it settled. His first difficulty was to win a resident post at Smithers Botham. Failing to get a 'house job' in your mother hospital was like being expelled from school, it stuck for life. Besides, he was going to specialize. All the students were going to specialize, their teachers (who were specialists) having freely laced their instruction with their opinion of family doctors as dangerous fumbling ignoramuses. But specialize in what? Psychiatry, Alec decided. It was intellectual, and you never got your hands messy. There was no psychiatric houseman, so as a first step he must land a house physician's appointment. But unfortunately for Alec the jobs had come to be decided solely by Mr Cramphorn, who dominated the selection committee. His methods were simple. He would look through the list of applicants, grunting, and strike out with his gold pencil all coloured students, Jews, those with un-English sounding names, any he had taken a dislike to, and any he had for some reason never heard of. And Mr Cramphorn had taken a fierce dislike to the Trevose family. He thought Graham's treatment of Clare outrageous, and after he had lavished his rabbits on her, too. Desmond, he admitted grudgingly, must be given a job, as the son of a Blackfriars consultant. If that unspoken rule lapsed the whole structure of the hospital might tumble, and there were changes enough in the wind already. But Alec could be sacrificed. In the end, Mr Cramphorn compromised by making Alec the resident anaesthetist, this speciality, Mr Cramphorn believed, being reserved for those unfitted for the practice of medicine at all.

Alec had never administered an anaesthetic in his life, but luckily John Bickley was an indulgent master. He was used to getting the duds. John had been working for Mr Cramphorn and Mr Twelvetrees in the general theatres of Smithers Botham itself since his row with Graham, who often enough had wished him back. But he was not a man to relent on his own rashness. Alec was scared of Mr Cramphorn, but discovered that he treated his anaesthetist exactly as he treated his prewar chauffeur, an underling expected to do his job and keep out of the conversation. Otherwise his new occupation seemed, like the war, ninety per cent boredom and ten per cent panic. He started bringing books into the theatre, reading them hidden in the sterile towels screening the unconscious patient's head. Having a quick mind he could demolish even a Victorian novel in two or three operating sessions. Alec was never sure of the effect of his anaesthetics on his patients, but he felt they were improving his own mind considerably. He was becoming more intellectual and cultured than ever. Desmond meanwhile performed the duties of a house-surgeon, with much correctitude and distinction.

Alec's second problem was his political allegiance. The general election of July 1945 was a nervous experience for the medical profession. Like Henry the Eighth's monks, the doctors quivered, half in indignation and half in fright, as schemes for their official disposal reached their ears. The hospitals were apparently to be grabbed, not only inefficient little institutions maintained by ladies selling paper flags, but those as proud as Blackfriars itself, even though it most regrettably existed at the time only as a pile of rubble with pretty wild flowers growing on it. It would all wreck the 'doctor–patient relationship', everyone declared at Smithers Botham, and though nobody knew exactly what this meant, it was a telling phrase with a ringing note to it, and anyway a substitute for whistling to keep your spirits up.

How should he cast the first vote of his life? Alec wondered. The newspapers seemed poor instruments of political education. The cartoons at least made the issue simple, between bad bald men in top hats and good clean-cut ones in overalls. 'The People' came into it a good deal. Alec rather distrusted The People, who were sadly unintellectual, indeed somewhat dim. Sensitive to the doctors' vote, the local candidates presented themselves on successive nights in the Smithers Botham assembly hall. The Conservative was plump and confident, and based his persuasion on the fact that the Cabinet were a very decent set of chaps (he had been to school with many of them). The Labour man was hollow-chested and nervously respectful, and based his persuasion on the fact that someone was rude to him in a Labour Exchange during the thirties. Mr Cramphorn clapped the first oration to the echo, and walked out of the second.

Alec decided to support Labour, because he learned Desmond was voting Tory. In the end he was too busy in the operating theatre to reach the polls, and the hollow-chested man won handsomely. Mr Cramphorn stayed at home for a week's sulk.

But worse was in store. He appeared in the theatre at the beginning of August white and trembling. 'They sang the *Red Flag*,' he muttered. 'Actually in the House of Commons! Good God! Some woman danced in the benches. It's the end.' But it wasn't. The next day a patient addressed him as 'Mate'. Mate! To Mr Cramphorn, who had given a lifetime to the curing of the poor, who felt the deepest concern for their ills and pains, just like the old Tsars of Russia for their serfs. Social order and sanity were sliding everywhere. They would be swinging from the lamp-posts next. He stayed at home for a month, and his housekeeper sent a message to say he was very poorly.

Alec's next concern was finding his mother about to become a G.I. bride.

Edith Trevose had spent the war in a small Devon seaside town, in a guest-house whose rooms were furnished for a fortnight's summer endurance at the most, but had been occupied since 1939 by elderly middle-class guests from London who complained increasingly about the food, the cooking, the war in general, and each other. Edith had been a typist with a Gray's Inn solicitor, but decided to help a friend run the place as her 'war work'. She was still pretty, and the sun of her affections, which had dawned upon Graham and shone through the noonday of her life on his brother, now glowed upon her son Alec, and was crossed by the first long restful shadows of the menopause. Edith had a split social position in the town. However much she tried to disguise it from herself, in the boarding-house she was taken as a servant. When twice a week she lent a hand in the small local hospital, she was respected by everyone as the widow of a medical missionary and the sister-in-law of Graham Trevose himself. Edith bore the discrepancy cheerfully. She had put up with more disagreeable places in life than the guest-house, and always reflected that the irritations of others, like their illnesses, though painful to witness could hardly kill her.

In the summer of 1943 something happened to change the town's face more alarmingly than the war itself. Strange uniforms, strange vehicles, and strange habits became evident everywhere. The Americans poured from a near-by camp to amuse themselves, having to draw less on their supplies of cash (which were said to be limitless) than on those of their native enthusiasm and optimism. Strange soft-packaged cigarettes, chocolate bars, chewing-gum, and tinned beer circulated everywhere, and the girls' hair-styles improved sensationally. The Americans had glamour, in a land which was short of it outside the overpacked cinemas. All were assumed to come from spacious and labour-saving apartments in Manhattan, though most lived in towns even sleepier than a Devon village, and knew of their hosts only from their official guide-book, which told them not to say 'bloody', that the British could take any amount of aerial bombardment, and were deeply grateful for all the dried egg.

Edith met Hal White at the hospital. He was a doctor, a captain, about her own age, thin, with a large Adam's apple, glasses like Glenn Miller's, and given to long periods of deliberation before opening his mouth about anything. He offered her a packet of Life Savers and asked her to a dance. Edith hesitated. Jennifer, the girl who helped in the kitchen, might be there. Hal explained it was an officers only affair, and she accepted. She loved dancing. It would be really quite fun to be taken out by a man again. And of course he was a doctor, and therefore a gentleman.

The dance was exactly like a thousand others in the kingdom that Saturday night. The local recreation hall was crowded, dirty and ill-kept, with French chalk sprinkled hopefully over a rough floor with painted lines for badminton courts. The decorations were posters urging the merrymakers to dig or save for victory, and that careless talk cost lives. At one end was a trestle table where for half an hour or so they sold gin and lime, and afterwards beer, which everyone hoped would last the evening. Half a dozen G.I.s on the stage were playing with startling professionalism. Hal and Edith danced to *Paper Doll* and *Sentimental Journey*, and she thought him amazingly light on his feet. He said he lived in Yonkers and was a widower. They tried to hokey-cokey, which Edith thought silly, really, but quite fun. Hal explained he had knocked around the world

378

a good deal, mostly doing medical jobs with construction companies, for a long stretch in Singapore. Edith exclaimed she knew Singapore well. They cheerfully explored the graveyards of their memories, exhuming a body or two to see if it were a mutual friend.

For the last year of the war they saw each other regularly. Hal brought her a good deal of Spam, *Life* magazine, and some nylons—her eyes shone as she smoothed the wonderfully sheer material with her fingers. When he asked her to marry him she was amazed. Marriage simply hadn't entered into her scheme of things. Illness and death, yes, but widowhood had become a settled way of life, to be borne as patiently as residence in the Malayan jungle or in the Devon guest-house. Yet she realized that she belonged to the dread class of 'distressed gentlefolk'. What would she do after the war? She was frightfully poor, she would have to go typing for solicitors until her fingers became too infirm for the keyboard. Hal was really very kind. And he was a doctor. The emotions of her life had been entwined round doctors, as pliantly as the serpents round Aesculapius' staff. She would have to live in America, but America was the place for self-betterment, everyone said so. The ideal of self-betterment had driven her as a girl from her father's butcher's shop in Ramsgate—to where? After a quarter of a century, to running a boarding-house. It was a chance. Only one thing could she be certain of. It would be her last.

That summer, the inhabitants of two Japanese cities were off-handedly incinerated, and the war was over. A week later Lease Lend was cut off, equally off-handedly. It occurred only to Lord Keynes that the country was broke, and the millennium which so agitated Mr Cramphorn would have to be financed by a loan of American money. So the country, like Edith, escaped from the possibility of German mastership to the certainty of American, with as much excitement and less thought.

Edith, Hal, and Alec met for the first time in the basement restaurant of the Criterion in Piccadilly. It was a disturbing gathering. Alec seemed to find Edith's lover only funny. She had been worried for months at the peculiar excited flippancy

379

in her son, quite unlike the stolid outlook of his father. She gave him a cheque for a hundred pounds, explaining it was all she could afford, and he must save it to visit her in America, once she was married and transported by the United States Government with eighty thousand other British women. Alec decided to spend it on a car. The medical profession lived at the time in a weird intimacy with the motor trade. Though the petrol ration was small, increased by the new Government so meanly as to arouse the irritation of even the *New Statesman*, doctors, who went on errands of mercy, were allowed more or less as much as they could use, with a bit of fiddling. He'd raise the fare to see his mother when the time came, he decided. He was never able to give a serious thought to the future of anything, particularly when there was fun to be found in the present.

During the rest of the hot summer of 1945 the war began to run down at Smithers Botham as gaily as everywhere else. There still wasn't much to drink, but there was A.F.N. Munich on the radio, the jam ration was said to be going up (incorrectly), and the place was enlivened by the first demobilized medical officers, sent on a six-month course to refit them for gentler practice. Captain Pile was finally demobilized. He went to Olympia for his new suit, and at once returned to Smithers Botham. He had grown to like the country hospital, and the future medical world was filled with half-glimpsed hazards. He had taken the post of medical officer to Smithers Botham as a mental institution, and was charged with preparing its return to normal function whenever Blackfriars could be evicted. As he walked up the long drive from the bus, once again mere Dr Pile, he saw the portico had for a second time been decorated. A Union Jack was spread across the columns, and a painted banner announced, 'Welcome Home Our Heroic Cuthbert'.

18

THE FIRST ANNUAL DINNER of the Annex Club at the beginning of 1947 was predictably a noisy affair. It was held at a restaurant frustrated like all others from doing its best for its diners, by the Government order that only three courses might be served, including the soup. The law took itself seriously, an establishment serving asparagus on a separate plate instead of accompanying the sliver of meat having already incurred prosecution. But the millennium had arrived. The coal mines had been nationalized, the railways and the doctors were next. The rations were reduced, coupons were needed for bread, and cigarettes were as hard to come by as ever.

The club was Peter Thomas's idea. Military units seemed hardly able to await their dispersal before arranging their reunions, so why not the patients who had passed through the annex? Besides, some sort of society was needed to help those who suffered from disability, official meanness, or bad luck. And it would be tragic for the buoyant comradeship of Smithers Botham to be lost without trace in the rough waters of the post-war world. The annex itself still existed, almost as busily as ever, with Tudor Beverley in charge. Graham had left, as he had promised himself, with the end of the war. His status as a Blackfriars consultant entitled him to half a dozen beds in the main wards at Smithers Botham for civilian cases, the arrangement to which Haileybury had tried to condemn him in 1942. But the time for self-sacrifice was past, Graham thought, personal and financial. One day the annex would have to close and Smithers Botham evacuated, he'd be back in the bright new wards of Blackfriars again beside the Thames—though from the permanent look of the hospital's rubble, that day seemed as unlikely to dawn as the one of settled amity across the split face of Europe.

Graham was naturally the club's president. It still gave him a feeling of smugness to see himself described on the printed menu as 'Sir Graham Trevose, K.B.E., D.Sc., F.R.C.S.'. The goodies had been delivered as Val Arlott had promised, and the doctorate of science had been conferred on him at the same time by a provincial university keen on entering into the spirit of the times. He had found himself more proud of the knighthood than he had expected. It was an emblem of something he sought all his life—a recognition that his work was far from trivial, but on a par with that of general surgeons majestically toiling among their sausage-chains of guts. Besides, everyone was terribly nice about it. Haileybury had called specially to congratulate him, almost with tears in his eyes. It was a well-deserved honour, he explained, not only for the surgeon and for the annex, but for the speciality of plastic surgery, to which he was himself about to return. Graham knew that Haileybury, of all his wellwishers, meant every word. He also knew the intense self-discipline which had brought the man to face him, for the first time since their meeting beside the River Itchen. He would know Graham well enough to sense the risk of a cutting rebuff. But Graham told himself the time for wounding was over, and reconciliation was in fashion.

'Thank you,' Graham said solemnly, shaking hands. 'Thank you . . . Eric.'

Haileybury swallowed. 'It is a real pleasure to congratulate you . . . Graham.'

It was the first time they had used each other's Christian names. In a world which could address old Cramphorn as 'Mate', reflected Graham, such relaxations were plainly overdue.

At the dinner, Peter Thomas proposed a toast to 'The Wizz'. Graham replied. Shortly afterwards the patients started singing, something innocuous at first, *Macnamara's Band*, moving on to *Cats on the Rooftops*, an enduring favourite, then the *Ball of Kirriemuir*. Graham knew this always ended in argument, and sometimes in fisticuffs, over such points as the Minister's Wife Who Felt Unweel coming before The Swishing of the Pricks in the Haystacks, or the other way round. When Peter Thomas put a glass of beer on his head to play The Muffin Man, Graham thought it time to withdraw. He leant over to touch John Bickley, two places away. 'I fancy we're a little old for this, old man,' he smiled. 'Shall we see if there's the chance of a taxi?'

The two stood in dinner jackets and overcoats, surveying the ill-lit street from the door of the restaurant without much hope. It was bitterly cold, and snow had paralyzed the country more effectively than the *Luftwaffe*. There was a scarcity of coal, new shoes were on the ration, a warming tot of whisky was a luxury, and the Government had banned even greyhound racing to save electricity on the hares.

'What a bloody night,' muttered Graham. 'I should have brought the car.'

'What are you driving now?' They had spoken little since the incident of Bluey, and since Graham had left the annex hardly met at all.

'I've got a prewar Bentley. A peculiar beast with a fabric body, but it goes like a clock. I bought it from some spiv in the street, who wanted spot cash. God knows where the thing came from, probably stolen for all I know.'

They found a taxi and Graham asked John back for a nightcap. He had a large flat in the Marylebone Road, convenient for his new consulting room in Wimpole Street. John found it furnished stylishly with Graham's stored belongings. There was brandy on the sideboard, a bowl of fruit, even a box of chocolates. Graham seemed to have climbed back on to the lap of luxury.

'I suppose I'm allowed to switch on the electric fire?' Graham removed his overcoat. 'I can never remember what the permitted hours are.'

'Don't they just cut your current off?'

Graham grinned. 'I'm on the same cable as the Welbeck Hospital, so I'm spared.'

'You always did have all the luck.' As Graham poured him a drink, John added, 'It was quite a party tonight.'

'It's good to find the boys enjoying themselves. Though I could see that Tudor Beverley's got a deal of work to do on some of them. But at least it's a club where we can feel glad the membership won't be increasing.'

'It was good of you to ask me along.'

Graham looked surprised. 'But of course you had to be there. We couldn't do without "The Gasman", surely?'

' "The Gasman", if you'll recall, Graham, was requested not to call.'

Graham gave a short laugh. 'The famous Trevose temperament. Do you still hold it against me? I was upset at the time, all sorts of things were pressing on me. After all, they were trying to get rid of *me*, and damn near succeeded.' They took the comfortable armchairs on each side of the fire. The three bars gave a welcome glow. The central heating was off, and the block of flats as inhospitable as an iceberg. 'I know I've been a bastard often enough in my life,' Graham continued. 'As you get older you begin to see yourself properly. It was my temperament which wrecked our partnership. It wrecked my partnership with Tom Raleigh. It wrecked a lot of other relationships in my life. But I couldn't help it. If I'd managed psychologically to emasculate myself, I'd have had no drive to achieve anything at all.'

Graham sipped his drink in silence. The reference to tempestuous partnerships set John wondering about his host's present arrangements for sexual relaxation. He generally had some of a sort, though John had picked up no gossip round the nursing-homes of the West End. He wondered if the fellow were getting past it. By way of a probe, he asked, 'Do you live in this palace all alone?'

Graham nodded. 'It's too big, but I had to take what I could. The squatters were in downstairs, you know.'

'You were lucky to get your hands on it.'

'London's a peculiar place just now. Everyone knows some-one who can obtain the unobtainable. This austerity's a bore, isn't it? I certainly didn't expect it after the war. I thought everything would more or less click back into place again. I must have been mad.'

'You weren't the only one. The Tory party suffered the same insanity.'

'I suppose I'm amusing myself. Though the people you meet are peculiar. Not at all like before the war. I wonder what happened to them all.'

'Haven't they gone to Kenya and Rhodesia and such places?'

'I'd rather put up with things here. I'm not doing badly, you know,' Graham told him defiantly. 'The plastic game's as tough as ever, if not tougher. But I'm well and truly inside the magic circle now.' He smiled. 'The new handle helps, I suppose, "Sir Graham" and all that. The outsiders have a thin time of it, trying to break in. I'm certainly not going to help them. I suffered enough myself, and nobody was inclined to give *me* a leg-up.'

'Aren't you afraid of what Bevan's going to do?'

'Not really. The scheme won't touch us consultants much. We might even be better off—after all, we'll get paid for the work we do free in hospital. The g.p.s will get the dirty end of the stick, and that's too bad. The B.M.A. have spotted that, of course, that's why they're kicking up such a shindy. They're the g.p.s' trade union. The Royal Colleges, who represent people like me, are coming round to Bevan's line of thinking. The letter from the three presidents last month certainly seemed to indicate something like that. You see, Bevan's split the profession. Cunning blighter. I rather admire the man. If I'd gone into politics, which God forbid, I should have modelled myself on him. He knows what he wants, and can be perfectly charming as he invariably gets it. How are *you* doing, John?'

'Very busy. I've Smithers Botham, the Cavendish Clinic, half a dozen hospitals scattered round London. I'd almost forgotten I was on the staff of half of them.'

'I missed you badly at the annex, I don't mind admitting it.'

385

'Nice of you to do so now,' John said drily.

'That Australian we got was all right as a stuffist, but the anaesthetist's the stage-manager of the operating unit. With you, everything went so smoothly.' The vague idea of staging a reconciliation with John, already in Graham's mind before the dinner, now struck him as urgent. After all, he had a real affection for the man, they had been professional brothers-in-arms for the best part of thirty years. 'How's Denise?' he asked.

'She's been a bit off colour, recently. Nothing definite. One of the physicians had a look at her. Trying to run a home these days is enough to get any woman down.'

Graham hesitated, and added, 'If you'd like to get away, I've a villa you could borrow in the south of France. At Roquebrune, up above Monte Carlo.'

John raised his eyebrows. 'How on earth did you get the currency?'

Graham laughed. 'Oh, there are ways and means. I bought it a month ago—very reasonably, once I got hold of the francs. I don't think one should take these restrictions too seriously. After all, there are so many of them, if we observed the letter of all the laws we wouldn't be able to stray from our front-doors.'

'It's a very kind offer, Graham, but I don't know when we'll have a chance to take you up on it.'

'I've hardly had a chance myself. I'm sending Sheila Raleigh down there next month—you know, Tom Raleigh's widow. She needs a holiday. I've given her the job of secretary to this Annex Club. There's an awful lot of work to do, quite a lot of money in the kitty It's a way for me to make amends. If I have any amends to make.' Graham finished his drink. 'It was sad about Tom. It shook me badly at the time. Too much so, per-haps. I felt somehow I was responsible. But how could I have been? I must have been feeling oversensitive in those days. Anyway, Sheila's getting married again this summer, some fellow out of the Navy. Do you want another drink?'

'No, I must get home, I'm afraid.' John rose. 'I promised Denise I wouldn't arrive back in too alarming a condition.'

'Do you think you'll find a taxi?'

'I'll walk. We're not far away, across the Park.'

'John, I wonder if you'd like to take over my anaesthetic work again?'

John paused, getting into his overcoat. This will prove, Graham thought, if he holds everything against me still.

'It's good of you, Graham, but I'm afraid my time for private work is absolutely booked.'

'Too bad,' murmured Graham.

He *does* hold it against me, Graham told himself. And quite badly. Probably Denise is behind it.

'Perhaps when things become more organized we can team up again?' Graham suggested vaguely.

'Yes, perhaps we can,' said John.

Graham closed the door behind his guest. He stood alone in the middle of the room. Something was disturbing him. He looked round, then sprang towards the mantelpiece and seized the ornamental clock. He looked at it foolishly for a moment, and carried it out to the kitchen. He had let it run down, and the woman who cleaned the flat must have rewound it. He hated clocks. Tick tock, tick tock. Every one a click along the ratchet towards extinction. Such thoughts came upon him often now that he lived alone. He sat down heavily in the armchair, telling himself he was really becoming dreadfully neurotic. Perhaps it was all to do with the symptoms of the male menopause.

19

THE PARTY was in Grosvenor Square, in a block of flats occupied mainly by Americans left over from the war, the only class of people in the country who could afford the rent. Lord Cazalay occupied the penthouse which covered most of the top floor. Graham admitted that his brother-in-law seemed to be making a success of his life. Despite the currency restrictions, the travel business appeared to be prospering, and he claimed to have his fingers in all manner of tasty pies. He always treated Graham with the warmest affability. Graham did not deceive himself this was through fraternal love, or remorse for past malevolence. Sir Graham Trevose was a useful name to keep around him. Graham didn't object overmuch. If you wanted such things as whisky, beefsteaks, suit lengths, or villas on the Riviera, you couldn't be squeamish over the company you kept.

'Graham, I'm delighted you could come.' Lord Cazalay pushed his way through the noisy crowd of guests. 'I hope you got over that dinner last night. I read about it in the papers.'

'I left before they started breaking the place up.'

'Very wise. It must be gratifying to know you've got these young men in such good spirits again.'

'I only did my best,' Graham told him modestly. 'Some of them would still give a girl a nasty scare on a dark night.'

'Champagne? I was rather lucky to get this consignment across the Channel. There's someone I'd like you to meet.'

Lord Cazalay led Graham across the room, putting his arm

round his shoulders, to demonstrate either affection or possession, Graham wasn't sure.

'Fred, this is Sir Graham. I know you'll be glad to meet him.' Graham found himself facing a short, square man with a leathery face, smoking a pipe. 'This is Fred Butcher,' Lord Cazalay introduced him. 'You know, from the War Office.'

Graham recognized one of the Ministers who had been swept to breathtaking heights by the flood of electoral popularity, to be left sitting forlornly on his isolated peak as the tide abruptly turned. He was a rather colourless public figure, a fair-minded, hard-working, trade union official with a valuable flair for bedding down lambs with lions. Graham wondered how he got on with the more peppery generals.

'Glad to meet you, Sir Graham. Heard a lot about you during the war, of course.'

'Perhaps too much?' Graham asked. 'That's some people's view.'

'Every word was deserved, I'm sure of that.' He relit his pipe and added, 'You know a surgeon called Mr Haileybury, I believe?'

'Extremely well.'

'He got me to speak at a luncheon the other week. About this burns hospital, and that. He seems a great one for the idea, does Mr Haileybury.'

'Personally, I think he's got something of a bee in his bonnet about it.'

'Maybe so,' said the politician guardedly.

Graham had heard of Haileybury's plan only second-hand. It seemed that Haileybury, once reconciled to the Government's cosseting the nation's health to a greater extent than providing clean water and drains, had turned himself into a crusader for the new scheme. He suddenly woke up to its offering an outlet for his qualities of administration, sadly frustrated once he put away his uniform. He was particularly taken with the idea of establishing a hospital in London for burns and accidents, arguing that the experience gained during the war should not be dispersed, but concentrated under one roof and passed to

389

visiting surgeons from countries which had regrettably been spared the opportunity for such practice. The Ministry of Health was sympathetic to Haileybury, but doubtful. They had to find the money to put roofs on the old hospitals before digging the foundations of new ones.

Graham had a dozen questions he would like to have asked the Minister about the fuel crisis. But politicians, like medical men, must learn to keep their counsel, and he found himself talking instead about the restarting of international football. Then Lord Cazalay reappeared and said, 'Fred, I must tear Sir Graham away. There's someone else I'd particularly like him to have a word with.'

As Graham allowed himself to be led across the room, Lord Cazalay asked, 'Isn't Liz coming? I thought you were giving us the pleasure of looking at her?'

'She's meeting me here. The curtain at her show doesn't ring down till after ten.'

'That's splendid news. Graham, this is Arthur King. A very close friend of mine.'

Arthur King struck Graham as resembling a worried ferret. He was a youngish man, certainly not over thirty, with thinning fair hair and sidewhiskers. He wore a smart blue double-breasted suit with over-emphasis on the lapels, a dark striped shirt, and a plain grey tie with a diamond pin stuck in it. His green eyes had an expression of continual anxiety in them, and if he had ever learned to smile he seemed to have forgotten the knack.

'Pleased to meet you,' said Arthur King.

'Of course, you'll know all about Sir Graham's work in the war,' Lord Cazalay said affably.

'Yes, I read about it in the papers.' He inspected Graham anxiously. 'You fixed all them pilots up with new faces, didn't you? Must be a clever feller.'

Graham nodded. To have his work praised by a Minister of the Crown was one thing. Approbation from a man who might have left his fruit-barrow at the door was less welcome. Still, he told himself, society was changing, you had to take people as they came, if you played the snob you got nowhere.

'You'll remember, Arthur, that Sir Graham has an interest in our travel business.'

'Smart lad. Going like a bomb, that little company. It's only the beginning, mind. Once these bloody restrictions come off, the market'll be wide open.'

'I hope I'll see something back for my money,' said Graham, for the sake of making conversation. 'It isn't much fun paying it all away in taxes.'

'Oh, taxes,' said Arthur King, contemptuously. 'There's another little idea of ours. Shall we tell him, Charles?'

'Television,' said Lord Cazalay.

'There's not much future in that surely?' Graham looked surprised. 'Nobody will be able to afford the sets.'

'Another ten years and there'll be one in every home,' said Arthur King confidently. 'Just like the toilet.'

Graham's instruction in the mysteries of commerce was interrupted by the arrival of Liz.

Liz was an actress. Not a particularly well-known one—indeed, discovery of her name generally called for a fairly close reading of the programme. She was in one of the postwar revues, with a small part which hardly justified her style of living. She had an enviable knack of getting to know the people who mattered, and an even more valuable one of dropping them before they ceased to. She was a big woman, red-haired, with enormous teeth. Graham supposed she must be well past forty. He had met her a few weeks before, in the dressing-room of an actor whose noble features had illuminated the musical-comedy stage for some decades, and now, with his assistance, seemed likely to continue lightening it for some decades more. Graham had begun to move among theatrical people, even adopting some of their little affectations. It pleased him to see himself as part of their scene, to understand their momentously whispered trivial gossip. He found Liz heavy going, but a man must have a companion, and he was never one to play the monk.

391

'Graham darling, how wonderful.' Liz embraced him warmly, simultaneously managing to take a glass from her host. 'And Arthur, bless you, how nice. Thank you so much for all those lovely nylons. You *are* clever. They're divine.'

'Glad you liked them,' said Arthur briefly.

'Graham, tell me *all* you've been up to,' she invited, though they had parted less than forty-eight hours before.

'I went to a party with a lot of my old patients.'

'Those poor boys! They must look so peculiar, all together.'

'They do, but they've given up thinking about it, which was the object of the exercise.'

'How on earth could they manage to give up thinking about themselves? I should feel dreadful, quite an outcast, if I had the merest scar.'

'They manage it because I always made the effort of having people treat them like normal human beings, not as something out of a circus.'

Liz gave a faint smile. He looked in danger of being serious again. He really was a dreadful bore when he got serious. If he went on mixing with all these awful deformed creatures, he really shouldn't bother everyone by insisting on talking about them in quite repulsive detail.

'Let's go and grab something to eat,' Liz suggested. 'I think they've even got lobster.'

After ten minutes she said to him, 'You *are* grumpy tonight, I must say. What's the matter?'

'Oh, nothing.' An uneasiness had settled on him. These people really were rather dreadful, he told himself. Though why should he complain? There was wine, lobster, and bright company, all hard to come by. 'Shall we go on?' he asked her abruptly. 'To a nightclub or somewhere?'

'But darling! I've only just arrived.'

'I'm feeling restless.'

'Oh, all right, then. You do carry on peculiarly sometimes, darling, don't you?'

'Yes, I know I do. Very peculiarly. All my life. It's a bit late in the day to change my habits, I'm afraid.'

'I see you're in your *interesting* mood,' she told him. It was too bad, but she had to put up with it. He seemed very wealthy.

The nightclub, like a dozen others sprouting after the war, was in a basement near Piccadilly. Graham signed an order for a bottle of gin, which was supposed to be sealed and reproduced at the guest's next visit, but somehow never was. There was a rumba band and they danced for a few minutes on the overcrowded floor. 'Let's go home,' said Graham. 'This place is suffocating.'

'Darling, what's wrong with you tonight? You can hardly wait to get at it.'

'You're right. I can't. I feel like it.'

'I don't know!' She laughed. 'You're worse than any of the young ones.'

'The young ones don't need consoling.'

She ruffled the hair in the nape of his neck, which he was allowing to grow rather long. 'What do you need consoling about? You've got everything.'

'I've got nothing. Nothing that counts.'

'Now you *are* being interesting. I can't see anything you lack.'

'A human being, the most precious commodity of all.'

'What about me? Aren't I human?'

'Shall we go?'

'Oh, all right, darling. Though don't rush at me like a bull when we get in, will you?'

When they reached the flat she insisted on taking her time, to put him in his place. 'Can't we have a drink?'

'Yes, of course.'

As he poured out the gin she took a cigarette and remarked, 'That's a pretty picture.'

'Yes, it is pretty. That's its trouble. There's no feeling underneath.'

'Who did it?'

'I did. Before the war.'

'Really?' She looked surprised. 'I didn't know you were an artist. I mean, apart from making people faces. I suppose that's much the same thing, isn't it?'

'I *am* an artist. Rather than a surgeon. I am an artist obliged to conform with the discipline of a surgeon's life.'

'That doesn't seem to worry you,' she laughed.

'It does, quite often. For most of my life I've fought against the rigidity and stuffiness of the medical profession. Now I'm not so sure. It's rewarding, being set apart, being someone special. Even if it's only through your own rules, many of which can be extremely silly. I suppose it was the war which changed my mind, though I didn't realize it at the time.'

'Please, darling, don't go on about the war again.'

'I'm sorry. I'm really trying to forget it, but it keeps coming back, more and more.' He sipped his drink and reflected, 'It was really the only worthwhile time in my life, out at that annex place.'

She stubbed out her fresh cigarette. 'Come along, darling, shall we get on with it?' she invited. Anything to stop him talking about the war.

Graham had taken to copulating with the light on. He found it more amusing, and anyway had read somewhere that turning out the light was a suburban habit. Liz, possibly worn out by her exertions on the stage, fell asleep almost immediately afterwards. He lay for a long time looking up at the ceiling. She really was a ghastly female. She was fat, and her breasts fell away to the sides of her chest like a pair of half-filled sandbags. Still, she had a kind heart and she was always available, valuable and infrequent attributes in any female. He would be generous writing her cheque in the morning. He must have been rather difficult to tolerate that evening. His life was all wrong, all completely wrong. But he didn't see much prospect of setting it right, even if he had the remotest idea what the right sort of life for himself should be.

20

THE SAME EVENING Desmond Trevose was entertaining his cousin Alec to dinner at high table in his Cambridge college.

Desmond had spent six months at Smithers Botham as Mr Twelvetrees' house-surgeon, and a further year as his registrar, which substituted for service in the thinning ranks of the Army. He was a good house-surgeon, competent and thoughtful, skilful enough with his hands as assistant in the theatre. But he was not really a success.

He was too cold, too brusque with the patients. He had no sense of human relationships. This was admittedly not a necessity for the effective, or even successful, medical man. Many renowned surgeons have been abominably rude. Others like Mr Cramphorn regarded hospital patients as simple-minded supplicants, unable to grasp such intellectual matters as the nature of the disease which irked them, which having a Latin name could only be discussed, if at all, by educated gentlemen. But the mood of the patients, like the mood of the nation, was becoming restless with smug authority. Medicine had advanced during the war as strikingly as aeronautics, the hospital doctor found himself turning into an applied scientist, yet the more he could do for his patients the less they seemed to regard him. It was baffling, not only for Mr Cramphorn. But the patients were only daring to express what they had expected from their medical attendants all along—to be their friend in health, their ally in sickness, and their companion in death, a relationship previously accorded only to those among them with a fee in their pockets.

Early in 1947 Desmond applied for a research scholarship at his old college, to study anatomy. It was in the blood. *The Synovial Membranes*, the anatomical thesis by his grandfather the professor, published in the year of Desmond's birth, lay on the desk in his college rooms. The old boy had a few sound ideas, Desmond decided, though the bulk of the book was nonsense. But the synovial membranes, lining the joints of the body, might be worth a second look, and he had decided to spend a year taking it.

He had asked Alec to dinner through no feelings of duty or affection. After living with him for a year in the medical officers' mess at Smithers Botham, Desmond had allowed the lifelong tepidity of his feelings towards his cousin to cool into frosty dislike. But having him up for the night seemed the only way to pin him down. Desmond wanted his money back, and Alec showed reluctance even to discuss such ungentlemanly a subject.

'I hope you won't find that guest room too chilly,' said Desmond, standing before dinner amid the beams of his own sitting-room. 'Did my gyp light a fire? I expect he'll give you a hot-water bottle.'

'Don't I need a gown, or something?'

'Guests at dinner aren't required to wear them,' Desmond told him solemnly. 'What have you got there?'

'Gin.' Alec produced the bottle from inside his jacket. 'A brand I've never heard of, it's probably full of methyl alcohol, enough to turn you blind. Not to worry. I was damn lucky to get it. I thought it would be an acceptable present.'

'I'd rather not risk it, if you don't mind,' said Desmond warily. 'I've got some reasonable college sherry.'

'You won't mind if I drink the stuff?' Alec had brought the bottle only with this intention. Desmond was a mean host. 'Do you remember the trouble we had buying booze at Smithers Botham? That ghastly grocer with his wine counter.' Alec poured half a tumbler of gin, which he started to sip neat. 'It was a kindly Act of God which landed him on us with a strangulated hernia. Afterwards I believe he genuinely tried to do his best for his medical customers. He was dead scared he might find himself in our hands again.'

'Everyone drank far too much at Smithers Botham.'

'You know, I loved the place. A lot of people were browned off with it, but not me. I suppose it was because you could get away with anything. No stuffiness. Do you remember that party when some fellow kept insisting on lighting his own flatus with a match? It was quite sensational. Amused the girls terribly.'

'Aren't you drinking rather a lot yourself, Alec?'

'I expect I'm an alcoholic. My present employment is enough to make me one.' Alec had left Smithers Botham for a hospital in the north of England, where he was anaesthetic registrar. 'It's a ghastly hole. The town's all trains. They seem to go clanking and hooting everywhere, into tunnels, across viaducts, holding up all the traffic at level crossings. The hospital's dreadful. Not a gentleman in the place. All the residents are Irishmen, Indians, Scotsmen, those sort of people. No intellectual conversation. Anyway, drinking seems to do my asthma good.'

Desmond put his hands behind his back and pursed his lips. 'I thought you might have given conventional treatment a chance first.'

'But I did.' Alec finished his gin and poured himself another. Desmond began to feel worried. His cousin had become dreadfully unreliable socially, and it would never do upsetting the dignity of the dons' dining table. 'I was skin-tested, and they told me I was allergic to grasses—crested dog's-tail, sheep's fescue, bird's foot trefoil. Whoever could imagine things with such lovely names doing anyone the slightest harm? It's ridiculous.'

'That's not a very reasonable attitude towards medicine, is it?'

'Well, medicine's only a branch of zoology. We mustn't take ourselves too seriously. But I let them fill me up with grass extracts. They didn't do the slightest good. Did you know I went to a psychiatrist at Smithers Botham?'

'There was a rumour to that effect.' Desmond gave a faint smile. 'Nobody seemed to think it particularly surprising.'

'Of course I kept quiet about it. For a Blackfriars houseman, visiting a psychiatrist would be far more shameful than visiting a prostitute. I went to see old Dency. He said I suffered from *Haltlosigkeit*.' Desmond frowned. 'It means an irresponsible, aimless personality, with no perseverance, no will-power, no concentration, and no particular interests. An optimistic hysteric who lives for the present and refuses to learn from experience. I looked it all up. Possibly he's right. It's apparently due to maternal over-indulgence in early childhood.'

'How is your mother?' Desmond asked.

'She seems happy enough in the States. I suppose it's nice to warm your feet on the small of a man's back again, even at her age. And even with a cold fish like her husband. I always thought Americans noisy and fun-loving, like the ones we used to see lounging about Piccadilly and spitting on the pavement. She's a peculiar woman, my mother. It's odd, the particular severity one judges one's parents with as one grows up. Must be fundamental. Some species eat theirs. Dency looked after *your* mother, didn't he?'

Desmond nodded. He supposed the reminder was vaguely ill-intentioned.

'Do you think he's a pansy?' Alec asked. 'He kept patting me, like the geography master at school.'

'He's got a certain effeminacy of manner,' admitted Desmond awkwardly. Homosexuality was not a subject to be mentioned, even in private.

'Are *you* a pansy, Desmond?'

Desmond went red. 'How dare you ask such a thing?'

'I've often wondered. You're not particularly interested in girls. I don't believe you've ever had one, have you? Even at a Smithers Botham party, where maidenheads popped like the balloons.'

'I can hardly afford to get involved with women,' said

398

Desmond defensively. 'I'll be here for a year, maybe two, hardly paid at all. Only my keep and an honorarium. I can't expect to sponge on my father at my age.'

'You asked me here to get your money back, didn't you?'

'Yes,' said Desmond.

'You haven't got a hope, old cock.'

Desmond stuck his hands in his pockets and asked angrily, 'Why don't you make some attempt to behave honourably about it? It's a debt. It's on paper. You'd never have qualified at all without it.'

'In good time, all in good time,' said Alec amiably. 'At the moment I've rather a lot of expenses. I'm going to get married.' Desmond stared at him. 'To Felicity, only daughter of Air Marshal Sir Giles Perrins, K.C.B., D.S.O., D.F.C. And bar. Very grand, you see.'

'I don't believe you.'

'Come, Desmond. The only asset I've got is a strange sex appeal. Don't deny me that.'

'I still don't believe you. How on earth would you meet her?'

'At some sort of social to do with my present hospital. She was a W.A.A.F. I asked her and she said yes. Remarkably straightforward. I'm seeing her in Town tomorrow. She's just been demobbed.'

Desmond digested this. 'What can I say? I hope you'll be very happy.'

'Thank you.'

A bell started to ring. Desmond picked up his gown. 'It's time for hall.'

'So you see, Desmond, I shall shortly be in a position to pay you off. I should imagine the dowry will be considerable. They're stinking rich. For the moment, patience.'

As Alec reached for his gin-bottle again, Desmond said testily, 'You haven't time for another.'

'But I must, Desmond, I *must*. I have a pathological fear of meeting strangers. Don't worry, I shan't be sick into the soup, or anything like that.'

399

Alec was not sick into the soup, but he broke a wine glass, talked continuously and extremely loudly, and told obscene stories. Desmond recognized his invitation as a terrible mistake. He wondered for the first time if his cousin really were a psychopath, a manic-depressive, something like that. He certainly suffered the most alarming swings of mood. At other times he could be solitary, silent, gloomy, and savage. The only course was to get him safely to bed in the college's guest-room. Further discussion about the money must wait until the morning.

But in the morning Alec had gone.

He woke in the dark, had no notion of the time, found his watch was stopped, and felt possessed with the idea of going down to London. The college porter let him out and he started his car. He hadn't even shaved. It was light when he reached Felicity's house in Chelsea. There were few people about. He remembered it was Sunday. He rang the bell. Nothing happened. He stood back from the door and started to shout. A grizzled head appeared at an upstairs window. He recognized Air Marshal Sir Giles Perrins, K.C.B., D.S.O., D.F.C. and bar.

'What the hell do you think you're up to?' demanded the householder.

'I've come to see Felicity.'

'Oh, it's you. Well, clear off. Neither Felicity nor anyone here wants to set eyes on you again.'

'I demand to see my future wife.'

'For God's sake, man! Get away, will you? You know perfectly well my daughter wishes to have nothing whatever to do with you.'

'Felicity agreed to marry me.'

'Please, please be reasonable. You're just causing trouble for yourself and all of us. Felicity never said anything of the kind. You know that as well as I do.'

'You're deliberately keeping her from me.'

'Do go away, there's a good chap. You're disturbing the neighbourhood. It's terribly early.'

'I demand admittance.'

'Oh, clear off, you stupid little bastard.'

'How dare you speak to me like that! I am a healer, I demand the respect to which I am entitled.'

There was a milk-bottle on the step. Alec picked it up and threw it into the closed downstairs window. He thought the crash sounded very satisfactory.

The rest of his morning was confused. There were policemen, the Air Marshal, even Felicity in the background, in her dressing-gown. People kept holding him down. They were persecuting him terribly. They wouldn't listen, however much he tried to explain. There was another man, very worried. He was a doctor, he explained. 'Now calm down, old man, calm down,' he implored. 'Look what a mess you've made of this sitting-room.'

'I didn't make the mess,' Alec protested violently. 'They made it, they're trying to discredit me. It's all a plot. What's that?' he demanded.

'It's only a syringe. I think you'd benefit from a sedative.'

'You're trying to poison me.'

'No, I'm not. You'll recognize the need for it yourself when you recover.'

'Recover? I'm not ill. Everyone's against me. Oh God, everyone's always against me.'

Alec suddenly felt he couldn't be bothered with these unpleasant persons any longer. Drowsiness overcame him. He'd had a tiring few hours, he had to agree. People seemed to be moving him. He let them have their way. He'd let them persecute him. He'd lost the will to resist. He was lying on his back, moving along. In something, a car. Surely not an ambulance, he wasn't in the slightest ill. He was still on his back, in the fresh air again. His surroundings struck him as familiar. The flat dome, the smoke-belching minarets, the magnificent portico. Smithers Botham. They wheeled him to the block which had quartered the Emergency Squad, one of the first sections of the hospital returned to rightful use.

'Hello, Alec.'

401

He looked up. It was Dr Dency, long fingers playing with the little gold bars of his watch-chain as usual.

'Don't worry, Alec. We'll look after you. You'll be all right here.'

'Home again,' said Alec simply. 'Yes, I always liked this place.'

21

'I'M SORRY I'M LATE,' Graham apologized. 'I had to go out to Smithers Botham. My nephew Alec was admitted there yesterday.'

'I'm sorry to hear that,' said Haileybury. 'Nothing serious, I hope?'

'No, not too alarming. He's in the psychiatric block as a voluntary patient. Dency's looking after him. Alec's landed himself in a bit of trouble. He's been behaving rather oddly recently, I must say. I expect they'll get him straightened out. I gather they've some new drugs coming in for this manic-depressive business, which should help the poor fellow.'

'Nevertheless, it must be very disturbing for you.'

'It is.' Graham sat down. 'I thought we had enough mental illness in the family with my wife. God knows where Alec inherited it from. Though his father could be peculiar enough when he liked. Missionary or not, there were one or two stories about him I shouldn't care to repeat.'

'No, no, of course not,' said Haileybury hastily.

'Anyway, every family's got one or two mad ones in it, if you look closely enough. Not that Alec's certifiable, anything like that. He just needs watching for a while. He's grown into a peculiar young man all round. And I'm more or less responsible for him, with his mother in America. At least, I promised her as much. She's a pleasant woman. You've never met her?'

Haileybury gave a faint smile. 'Indeed I have, Graham. You seem to forget she was our secretary at the plastic hospital near Ramsgate in 1918.'

Graham laughed. 'I could be forgiven for the lapse, surely? Water has poured over the dam with frightening speed since then. Then you'll also remember I was having a violent love affair with her at the time?'

'I don't think we need go into that now,' said Haileybury amiably.

He's mellowing pleasantly with the years, Graham thought. In those days of far-off passion, he tried to lose me my first chance of a decent job over it. He isn't a bad fellow, really. At least he isn't a hypocrite. As most doctors are obliged to be—half the time for the good of their patients, and the other half for the good of themselves.

'What can I do for you, Eric?' he asked.

They were sitting in Haileybury's club, in the same corner of the morning-room as at the beginning of the war. Haileybury was wearing his usual plain blue suit. Graham could never remember him in anything else. It was early evening, and Haileybury signalled the club waiter to buy Graham a drink for the second time in his life.

'I gather you met Butcher the other evening?' Haileybury asked.

'I bumped into him at a party.'

'I also gather he said something to you about my scheme for a national burns unit?' Graham nodded. 'Would you like to hear more about it? If you don't, if you think it might bore you, if it's a notion you couldn't feel interested in, do please say so. We'll just drop the subject, have a gossip instead. I shan't be in the slightest offended. I've talked about it to so many people, I can't expect all of them to share my enthusiasm.'

'I should be very interested indeed. I suppose I must by now have handled more burns than most people.'

Haileybury nodded slowly. To Graham's surprise he produced a briefcase and laid it on the table. A man like Haileybury would not encumber himself with a showy accessory unless he felt most strongly about its contents. Haileybury extracted some papers.

'These are my ideas reduced to writing. You may like to take

404

them and study them at leisure.' Graham found himself with a thick bundle of closely typed foolscap. 'Since I first talked to Butcher I have raised my sights somewhat. With the Government, the more you ask for the more you get. I see it as a centre devoted to the surgery of accidents in its widest sense. Motor accidents, accidents in the home, industrial accidents. This last, I think, gives me the most confidence of success. It strongly appeals to the trade-union element in the Government. Nobody's really bothered to specialize in the surgery of industry before. To my mind, the need is just as pressing as specializing in the surgery of war.'

'I'm sure you're right.'

'I understand that Bevan himself is very keen on the idea.'

'But when's it all going to materialize?' Graham asked. 'After all, the Government's already committed to taking the profession by the ears and shaking it out of all recognition in the next few months. It's supposed to be building health centres everywhere like luxury cinemas. It's got half the hospitals in the country damaged by air-raids, and the other half falling to bits anyway. When are they going to create your shining new palace? I'm sure the idea will come to something one fine day, Eric, but I'm afraid you and Nye Bevan and I shan't be here to attend the opening ceremony.'

'It already exists,' said Haileybury quietly.

The waiter brought their drinks. As he retired, Haileybury added, 'It exists less than twenty miles from where we are sitting. To be precise, near Iver, in Buckinghamshire. Extremely convenient for London.'

Graham frowned. He couldn't recall such a place. 'Has some genie waved the magic wand?'

'No, but the Americans have. They built a hospital there during the war. It took them, I believe, a matter of some weeks. They are not a people for procrastination. Now the Americans are going home, the building stands there stripped and empty. There seems no obstacle to our taking it over. It is a perfectly adequate structure, single-storey wards, room for five hundred beds. The design of the operating theatres is quite remarkable.

There are one or two peculiar features—a soda-fountain, for instance—which can easily be removed. I gather the price will be nominal, particularly if we call it the "Franklin D. Roosevelt Hospital", something of that nature.'

'That sounds a pleasant windfall,' said Graham thoughtfully. 'What would you want me to do? Serve on some committee to raise funds for the equipment?'

'I would want you to head the staff.'

Graham looked up. He had imagined that Haileybury's interest in the hospital came at least partly from the glory of running it himself. 'But what about you?'

Haileybury shrugged his shoulders. 'You would be the better man.'

'Aren't you rather carrying modesty to extremes?' Graham found himself faintly irritated by Haileybury's honesty. It was something of an affront. 'You're the one who's preached for years that plastic surgery was essentially the surgery of repair. As for me, I'm a beauty-doctor, a face-faker.'

'And that, if I may say so, is a rather over-modest view of your work during the war.'

'I thought you imagined my work during the war was grabbing publicity?'

'I did imagine it at the time,' Haileybury told him frankly, 'but I was wrong. I didn't understand the importance of the cosmetic work you were doing. I make all the apologies you feel you deserve. It was difficult, confined to administrative tasks. I was too far from individual patients. I came to appreciate only late in the war how much you did for morale.' He tapped the table with his long forefinger. 'And that is what we need in this new place of mine. Someone to make plain that those mutilated by the hazards of peace can be treated as effectively as those mutilated by the hazards of war.'

'But Eric! This is an enormous job you're asking me to take on. There're all manner of questions for me to decide first.'

'At least the financial question will decide itself. As director, you would draw the appropriate consultant's salary in the new health service. Plus a merit award, doubtless, if that part of the scheme goes through.'

'But what time have I for such responsibilities? Don't forget I've a busy private practice.'

'I regret that private practice would not enter into it. The post would be full-time. You know how strongly the Government feels on such points.'

'Then I'm afraid it's out of the question.'

'Do you know, Graham, it's the second time you have used that expression to me sitting exactly in this spot?'

Graham smiled. 'I'm sorry. I much appreciate the honour you've paid me, but I must look to my own interests. I've landed myself with a hell of a lot of debts, to be paid off somehow before I'm too old to work at all. I'd love to accept, Eric, the idea's got tremendous attraction, it would be like the annex all over again. But I'm afraid it's just not on.'

'Last time, I made the mistake of pressing you for a decision. I shall not repeat it. There is plenty of time—months, perhaps a year, perhaps two. Any moment you feel inclined to discuss the matter further, lift a telephone. Will you promise?'

'Very well,' Graham told him amicably. 'I'll keep it constantly before me. Should I undergo a change of heart you'll hear at once.'

'Excellent. Now let us drop the subject and talk about something else. Very sad, don't you think, Graham, the prospects for the coming county cricket season?'

Graham quickly put the offer out of mind. A salaried post, he decided, would be far more suitable for a man of modest tastes like Haileybury himself. But even Haileybury indulged in a little private practice. He did operations every Saturday morning in a small hospital near the Crystal Palace, which during the war had somehow fallen under the domination of his own in London, King Alfred's, and afterwards never escaped. It had few private beds, the theatres were antiquated, but the nursing was sound and the general atmosphere Haileybury found agreeably modest. John Bickley was a consultant to the hospital and generally gave Haileybury's anaesthetics, though regretting that Haileybury didn't take the same wide view of operating fees as Graham.

The following Saturday, as Haileybury was finishing the repair of a child's cleft palate, he observed to John, 'I saw Trevose the other day.'

'Yes, I ran into him only last week. He seems to be doing as well as ever.'

'He's full of bounce, certainly. With Trevose that generally indicates a stuffed wallet.'

'Did you think him cheerful? I felt he was rather miserable with himself.'

Haileybury inserted the final stitches in the child's mouth. 'He's a man of moods,' he observed drily. 'And that nephew of his has gone off his head.'

John frowned under his surgical cap. 'Alec was my junior assistant. He was something of a queer fish, I must say.'

'That goes for all the Trevose family, doesn't it? They don't make life easy for themselves.'

'Perhaps you're right.' John disconnected the long corrugated rubber tube of his anaesthetic apparatus. 'Alec's mother will be upset. She had high hopes for him. Saw him as a second Horder, I believe.'

'Well, he might achieve it yet. Some of our most eminent brethren have been somewhat unbalanced. It's a matter of survival until they reach the position where nobody dare mention it.'

John removed the throat-pack and the thin, wire-stiffened armoured Magill tube from the child's windpipe. 'I think I'll go back to the ward with this one.'

'All is well, I trust?' asked Haileybury sharply.

'Yes, perfectly. But you can never be sure of anything at all in this game.'

In the children's ward at the end of the corridor he passed his patient to the care of the staff-nurse, and asked, 'Where's Sister?'

'In her office, Dr Bickley.'

John knocked on the door by the ward entrance and went in.

Clare Mills looked up from her desk. 'Hello!' She smiled. 'Quite a stranger.'

'I was bringing back that palate.' He popped a cigarette over his sagging mask and lit it. 'I had a chat with Graham last Saturday night.'

Clare raised her eyebrows. At first she said nothing, but moved some notes on her desk. 'And how is he?'

'He's wearing well. And he seemed to be enjoying life. Or trying to convince himself that he was.'

'I'm glad he's all right.'

'Do you ever hear from him?'

'Oh, no! I would never have expected that. Not with Graham.'

'He didn't mention you at all,' John volunteered.

'I wouldn't have expected that, either. Once anyone's left his orbit he likes to cut them out completely. To forget about them, as though they'd never existed.'

'Even you, who tried to save him from himself?'

'I wasn't conscious of doing so at the time, but I suppose that's true.'

'It's all part of his selfishness, I suppose. Rejecting even those who've helped him, once they're no more use.'

'I don't think so. Not entirely. We can understand his trying to spare himself the pain of sad memories. He inflicts enough on himself. Anyway, he doesn't know where I am,' she added more briskly. 'He doesn't even know if I'm still in the country.'

'Do you want to see him again?'

She looked at him hard for a moment and said, 'What's the point?'

John nodded understandingly and asked, 'Have you any plans—for getting married, that sort of thing? Anyone in mind? I hope you don't mind my asking, Clare. I've come to feel something of an uncle to you.'

She smiled again. 'A very useful uncle. You found me this job.'

'I felt I wanted to do something for you. If you remember, we were both suffering from the Trevose temperament rather severely at the time.'

409

'Perhaps it was all something to do with war-weariness.'

'You haven't answered my question.'

'No, I haven't anyone in mind. I don't suppose I shall. I've got my work.'

'At which you're extremely efficient.'

'Thank you. Everyone regards me as a dedicated and completely sexless ward sister. There're plenty of them about. The backbone of any hospital. The whole system would fall to bits without such women. When I was in training, I often wondered exactly what created them. Now I know.'

'That sounds a gloomy prognosis for yourself.'

'Perhaps someone will turn up. You never know. Otherwise I shall sister on, until I'm pensioned off and go to live in a seaside boarding-house.'

'But don't you bear any resentment? Towards Graham?'

'How can one bear any resentment towards a maladjusted child?'

'I daresay you're right,' John told her.

22

THE GOVERNMENT was out of luck. The worst snowfall of the century was followed by the worst floods that could be remembered at all. The cascade began in the middle of March 1947, the rivers spilt disastrously across the countryside, swamping the roads and railways, drowning the sheep, ruining the potato crop and countless carpets. Two years after victory the people who had given blood, toil, tears, and sweat were left standing in queues holding damp ration-books.

The postwar disgruntlement which affected everyone began to depress Graham. He was starting to confess himself bored and disgusted with his brother-in-law and his cronies. The girl Liz was really a shocking creature, though he felt disinclined to ditch her with no replacement in sight. Perhaps there never would be, he reflected. He was becoming a shade elderly to play the rake. He would have liked to stay at the villa after Sheila Raleigh came home, he craved for luxury and sunshine, but he had too much private work in London. There seemed to be a dammed-up demand for plastic surgery, as for other prewar luxuries like chocolates and cars, and plastic surgery was readily obtainable for your money. And at least, he reflected, he passed most of his time in hospitals and nursing homes, where it was warm and there was plenty of hot water.

He was still living alone, and trying to reconcile himself to it. To make his evenings more bearable he started to write a textbook on the surgery of burns. He had never written much before, though he felt that if he could paint he was equipped with the

411

right sort of mental muscles for self-expression. He turned out a trunkful of notes from the annex, sorted them into bundles, and started work with his portable typewriter. Progress was slow. As he read his scribbled pages, he found himself drawn back to the atmosphere of the bungalow where he had jotted most of them down. He found the composition becoming dominated by Clare. He remembered exactly what she was saying or doing when he had drawn up some particular account of a patient or an operation. It disturbed him. He had thought about her often enough since they separated, but he told himself she was in the past, finished and done with, like Edith. He determined to put her resolutely out of his mind. It was the only way. Anyway, if he didn't, the book would never be finished.

He was working alone one evening towards the end of March when the telephone rang. It was Lord Cazalay.

'I say, Graham, are you still at home? We were expecting you tonight.'

'I'm sorry, but I couldn't make it.' Another one of his damn parties. 'Didn't you get the message? I asked the Clinic to phone you.'

'Some signal got through to me, but I didn't take it seriously.' Lord Cazalay sounded offended. 'You remember you particularly promised to come.'

'I've got an urgent case coming in, I'm afraid. You'll have to excuse me.'

This pretext being unanswerable, Lord Cazalay added, 'I wonder if I could have a word with you fairly soon? It's a matter of some importance.'

Graham gave a grunt. He probably wants more money out of me, he thought. Money is the only matter of importance that he knows. 'I'm dreadfully booked up this week, Charles, professionally.'

'Surely you can spare a moment? It's rather pressing. How about lunch tomorrow at my club?'

'It's a miserable confession, but my lunch is always a sandwich between cases.'

'Can't I call tomorrow evening? About seven?'

'All right, I'll make a point of being here,' Graham told him, giving in.

'I'm much obliged. By the way, you'll make sure we're undisturbed, I take it? It's extremely confidential.'

'I'm nearly always on my own,' Graham assured him.

In the next morning's paper he saw that Fred Butcher had resigned from the Government. He wondered why. He had seemed from brief acquaintance a likeable, down-to-earth sort of fellow. He couldn't be bothered to read the story running down the column. Politics was a bore, and the newspapers only made up fairy-stories. When someone mentioned the incident in the theatre of the Cavendish Clinic during Graham's first case, he said, 'Yes, I met the chap the other day. Seemed a very solid citizen.'

'*Did* you?' asked his young assistant, looking up.

'What's the matter?' Graham was surprised at the tone. 'Is he in disgrace, or something? I supposed he'd resigned on some lofty point of political principle.'

'Reading between the lines, he's in the cart. Something very peculiar about Army contracts. A number of old Army wireless sets seem to have gone sadly astray.'

'Who on earth would want an old Army wireless set?'

'People want anything these days. In Germany you could refurnish your house with a few hundred cigarettes.'

'I suppose so,' said Graham sombrely. 'Everyone seems to be on the make. There's a spiv in all of us.'

Lord Cazalay arrived promptly at seven. With him was the ferret-faced Arthur. Graham invited them in cordially. If they had some proposition for him, he had already decided to reject it. But at least he could politely offer them a whisky. After all, it had come via Lord Cazalay.

For a while Lord Cazalay talked about the obstacles to making money in the postwar world, a subject he seemed inclined to leave with more impatience than usual. Arthur sat sipping whisky nervously and said nothing. After a few minutes Lord Cazalay declared, 'Graham, I've found you a new patient.' He inclined his head. 'Arthur here.'

Graham looked at the ferrety man with mild interest. 'What's the trouble?' he asked.

'I'd like you to fix my face up, Sir Graham.'

'But you haven't any scars or blemishes that I can see.'

'I'd just like you to change it a bit. Like you did to the pilots during the war.'

Lord Cazalay gave a harsh laugh. 'Plenty of room for improvement, eh, Graham?'

Graham put his finger-tips together and gave the proffered features a more careful inspection. It wasn't a bad face. The nose was too pointed and the jaw underslung, but not to the point of unsightliness. But he appreciated, even if he still never understood, the psychological forces urging patients towards him. A crooked nose or a dropping eyelid, passing more or less unnoticed by the world, could incite any amount of self-torture. He remembered a youth during the war with a leg withered from polio. All the frustrations of his life were ascribed to his leg. He implored one of the general surgeons to chop it off, to cast it from his life altogether, replace it with one of the splendid artificial ones they were designing for the wounded. The surgeon obliged. Six months later the young man committed suicide. We must all find something to blame, Graham thought, even if it's a bit of ourselves.

'Of course, you realize that a cosmetic operation, like any operation, carries a risk?' Graham explained, as he did to every patient. Arthur nodded. 'Nor is it free from pain and bother. Some can be distinctly uncomfortable for weeks afterwards. And even I can't guarantee a perfectly successful result.'

'The bill will be rather painful too, I fancy,' said Lord Cazalay, laughing again.

'I wouldn't conceal that, either,' said Graham.

'You'd be looked after, Sir Graham,' Arthur assured him solemnly. 'Rely on me for that.'

'As this is turning into a consultation, I'll have to ask you to leave us, Charles,' Graham explained to his brother-in-law. 'It's rather irregular to conduct one with an audience.'

414

Arthur looked at Graham imploringly and asked, 'Can't he stay? He's a friend.'

'Oh, very well, if you wish,' Graham conceded testily. 'In what particular way do you want your appearance changed?'

'I just want it changed. I'm not fussy.'

Graham frowned. 'But what's the object? What is it that distresses you about your looks?'

'I want it changed for business reasons.'

Graham looked at Lord Cazalay. 'What's going on?'

'Graham, do you have to ask so many questions?'

Graham paused. 'I'm sorry, Mr King, but I'm afraid I can't take you as my patient.'

Lord Cazalay glared angrily. 'Look here, Graham, you're being ridiculous.'

'I apologize if it strikes you that way. But I couldn't possibly operate on a patient without satisfying myself over the reasons. Some of them are pretty obscure, admittedly, but at least they hold water. I'm inclined to think there's something behind all this. I'd prefer not to ask about it. There're plenty of other plastic surgeons in London. You can always try your luck elsewhere.'

Lord Cazalay brushed his moustache, 'I'm sorry you're being so unco-operative. Perhaps you'll think again.'

'Why don't we tell him the truth?' suggested Arthur, as if struck by a novel thought. As Lord Cazalay made no reply, he went on, 'Look, Sir Graham—I'm in a bit of trouble.'

'We're all in a bit of trouble,' muttered Lord Cazalay.

'You saw in the papers this morning about Fred Butcher?' Arthur continued. 'It's the beginning of something. People have been nosing about where they shouldn't, making trouble. Mind, I've always acted in good faith, always. But you've got to cut a few corners these days. I'll have to lie low for a bit. I thought if you changed my face it would all be a bit easier to avoid the publicity.'

Graham sat staring at him. 'You mean, you're a crook and you want me to alter your appearance to escape your just deserts?' As neither visitor said anything, he continued, 'Well,

415

I shan't play the outraged citizen. I've had a few requests of a similar nature in my time. I'll only tell you the whole idea is reprehensible, and ask you to leave at once.'

'I'll make it well worth your while, honest I will,' Arthur repeated hopefully.

Graham got up. 'You could never do that, Mr King.'

'Just a moment,' Lord Cazalay interrupted. 'We're none of us shining with innocence. You seem to have forgotten the few favours I've done you. That foreign currency for your villa. It would look pretty nasty if it came into court, wouldn't it? They'd hand out a stiff sentence for a fiddle on that scale. You'd go to jail, wouldn't you? And your medical authorities would have a few words to say about the matter, too. They'd hardly let you go on practising after that.'

'You mean you're blackmailing me?' demanded Graham.

'Blackmail? I don't know what that means. Business is run on a system of favours done and granted. Persuasion is necessary from time to time.'

'Get out.'

'I'm not going to let you take this high-and-mighty line,' Lord Cazalay continued more confidently. 'For your own good, Graham. You won't do yourself any harm, tidying up Arthur. You get dozens of people coming to have their faces altered, you said so yourself. You aren't to know he's in any trouble. Not yet. In a week or two it'll be a different matter. You're going to do this, my boy. I'm not given to idle threats. You've known my family long enough to realize that we get what we want. Either you do something for Arthur, or the details of your little currency transactions end up on the desk of the Director of Public Prosecutions.'

'Get out,' Graham repeated.

'No, I shan't get out. Sit down and think it over. I'll give you five minutes.'

23

GRAHAM WAS STARTLED how old Denise looked. Then he remembered she had been ill. As she opened the front door she stared at him with surprise, quickly trying to find a smile.

'Could I see John?' Graham asked at once. 'The Clinic told me he'd gone home.'

'Yes, of course, Graham. Come in. How are you keeping?'

'Oh, pretty well.'

'The weather's ghastly, isn't it?'

'Yes, ghastly.'

'And all this dreadful austerity we're supposed to put up with.'

'Yes, yes,' said Graham.

He came into the cold hall of the Bickleys' flat overlooking Regent's Park. It was barely an hour since his confrontation with Lord Cazalay.

John was in the sitting-room, reading the evening paper and tickling the dog. He stood up as Graham entered, saying amiably enough, 'An unexpected pleasure. Or have you come for a contribution towards the damage the boys did to that restaurant?'

'I won't stay a moment.' Still in his overcoat, Graham looked pointedly at Denise.

'Would you like a cup of coffee or something?' she asked with great reluctance.

'Please. That would be very kind.' As the door shut he turned to John and said, 'I wonder if you'd stuff a case for me? To-morrow morning.'

John knocked his pipe on the fireplace. 'I expect I could squeeze it in, if it's early enough. Has everyone else let you down?'

'It's a special case.' Graham hesitated. 'It calls for a great deal of discretion. I'm going to do it at that little nursing-home place out at Ealing.'

'Graham!' John laughed. 'Don't tell me you're branching into the abortion racket?' Seeing Graham's troubled expression, he added seriously, 'But what is it? Some actress with a secret scar? Stella Garrod all over again?'

'Oh, it's a much nastier business than the Stella Garrod affair. I've got myself in a bit of a mess.'

John raised his eyebrows. Hardly the first time. At Graham's age, he really should start to learn. Perhaps Clare was right about the maladjusted child.

'A woman, you mean?'

'No, not this time.'

Graham explained about Arthur King.

'I see,' said John calmly when he had finished. 'So you're going to do the case?'

'I've no alternative, have I? I was a fool having anything to do with that Cazalay bastard. He tried to bring me down once before. This time he's going to make a proper job of it.'

'But if you do it, and the fact comes out in the papers, it's going to look pretty nasty for you.'

'Perhaps nothing will come out.'

'These things generally do.'

Graham looked more uneasy, and said, 'It isn't the first time, you know. Before the war I did a couple of patients like this. I had my doubts about them, but didn't delve very deeply. I just blinded myself to the fact they were a pair of crooks. I was disgusted at myself afterwards. I don't want to repeat the experience, quite apart from risking my neck. But if I don't . . . why the hell did I buy that villa, anyway? I've never had a chance to use it.'

'I don't think I can really give the anaesthetic for you, Graham.'

'No, I didn't expect you would. It was selfish of me to ask. I wanted the moral support, I think, that's all. I'll see what I can do under local. Probably I can manage more than I expect. We get spoiled, with good general anaesthetics always available from experts like you. Some of our more unfortunate brethren manage to run a flourishing practice in cosmetic work under locals. The ones who get themselves struck off for advertising.'

'Won't you take my advice and not touch this case, Graham?'

'You mean to substitute the certainty of trouble with the law for the possibility?'

'It's two sorts of trouble. The operation would spoil everything you gained for yourself during the war.'

'What did I gain? A knighthood. For services to publicity.'

'You know that's not true.'

'Not completely so, perhaps. But it's near enough to the mark.'

'I was speaking to Clare about you two or three weeks ago,' John remarked unexpectedly.

Graham looked at him sharply. 'I thought she'd disappeared off the face of the earth?'

'She's at the Kenworth. Children's ward sister. I do a list there once a week.'

Graham made a wry expression. 'How is she?'

'Very well. She likes her job.' John paused and added, 'Do you want to see her again?'

'She'd hardly want to set eyes on *me*,' Graham told him impatiently.

'I'm certain she would.'

'No, that's ridiculous. Not after the way I treated her.'

'Is it ridiculous? You'd know. You've had more experience of women than me.'

Graham stuck his hands in his trouser pockets and started pacing the room. 'Everything's wrong, isn't it? You see things differently as you go through life, and often enough you realize all the time you've been seeing them wrong. When I was young

419

I could view the way ahead, and I tramped up it not caring overmuch how I muddied my boots. Things didn't go all that smoothly—Maria, all that fuss. But I got where I wanted. In the war, I didn't really want anything for myself and I was happy. Now I'm trying to worship my old gods, but they don't represent anything any more. They're like native idols discovered in some jungle. Incomprehensible, frightening to look at, make you wonder at the simplicity of the people who venerated them. I'd got no proper sense of values. The war imposed one on me.'

'Graham, you're making yourself sound a horrible type,' smiled John.

'Well, I am. Though let's hope it's not because I can't help it, but because I try to be.'

'Because you think it's smart?'

Graham shrugged. 'I can't even contemplate meeting Clare again. Not at this particular crisis in my life.'

'She might be glad to help you. She did during several others.'

'I suppose she loved me.'

'You loved her, surely?'

'Deep down, I told myself I didn't. It was the same with every woman I've got mixed up with. I never wanted to give myself to them completely. At the age when you can face these things, it's too late to rectify them.'

Denise appeared with the coffee.

'Graham wanted to discuss a case he's doing tomorrow, darling,' John explained.

'I'm not doing it,' said Graham briefly. 'I've decided it's inoperable.'

He'd forgotten about Denise and her coffee. He then had to sit down and make conversation of some sort while he drank it, and she always made dreadful coffee, anyway.

24

HAILEYBURY HAD HARDLY SHAVED when Graham arrived the next morning at his house in Richmond. His sister, who had seen six years' service in the A.T.S., had returned to offer the same dutiful devotion to her brother as to her King. She showed Graham in to the cold sitting-room, which was filled with models of railway engines. Graham sat in his overcoat, looking at them in puzzlement. He supposed Haileybury had constructed them all with his own hands. A strange secret for a man to have.

'I'm sorry to keep you waiting, Graham.' Haileybury appeared in his usual blue suit.

'And I'm sorry to have telephoned for an appointment so early. But I have some news. I have decided to accept your kind offer of a job.'

Haileybury inclined his head silently. 'That is good news indeed. It is all I will say, but I think you will understand how I feel. The new project is very near to my heart.'

'On one condition.'

'I'm sure any reasonable condition can easily be met.'

'I don't know if this one can. The condition is that I stay out of jail.' Haileybury looked at him blankly, wondering if he were joking. 'I've been involved in some currency deals. About five thousand pounds' worth of French francs. If it comes to light, I've had it. I've reason to expect it might.'

Haileybury put the tips of his fingers together and blew on them. The noise still irritated Graham.

'I see.'

'It's all mixed up with Cazalay and your unfortunate friend Fred Butcher. You know a fine rumpus is blowing up?'

'I see,' Haileybury repeated.

'Of course, the very fact I've misbehaved might be enough for you to withdraw your offer. I'd quite understand that.'

'Could you explain the details?'

'I gave Cazalay a cheque for five thousand pounds and he gave me the francs. He wants me to do a job on one of his little crooks to stop the police recognizing him. I won't. It's as simple as that. So Cazalay will cook my goose.'

'But what on earth were you doing with all this foreign money?'

'Oh, I haven't it hidden in a biscuit-tin, bricked up in the chimney, anything like that. I never actually handled it. Cazalay bought me a house in France.'

'I see,' said Haileybury again.

Graham rose. 'That's the situation, Eric. If I don't land in abject disgrace over the next few weeks I presume you'll take me on?'

Haileybury made an accommodating gesture. 'I'm only sorry you should find yourself in such a predicament.'

'It isn't my first,' Graham told him. 'But, whichever way it goes, it will be my last.'

He couldn't face operating or seeing patients. He rang Smithers Botham and a couple of nursing-homes, putting his day's work off, excusing himself with illness. He walked the shabby streets of London, hardly noticing where his feet took him. He found himself in Piccadilly, not far from Half Moon Street, and turned towards the Cazalay family's old town house. A hole in the ground. As he started walking northwards the rain began to fall. It was the same route he had taken thirty years before, tramping home through a thunderstorm to his father's home in Hampstead after he had first met Maria. On that walk he had decided three things—to become a plastic surgeon, to grow rich, and, more immediately, to ditch his fiancée Edith. He had done all three, and ended up with nothing but the prospect of prison. He plodded on. It wasn't so easy to walk these days. Well, your arteries and joints had to grow stiff some time, it was inevitable. At least you were saved the effort of struggling against it, as he'd had to struggle against tuberculosis in his youth.

He decided to make for the house in Hampstead. It was still standing, but horribly dilapidated. It had been turned into flats before the war, now there seemed to be a dozen families living in it, with washing forgotten and soaking in the front garden. The professor would hardly have countenanced that, Graham told himself. He wondered what his father would have to say of his misdeeds, personal and professional. Perhaps the old boy would have the chance to give him a celestial wigging soon. He had rather let down the family. Even the piss-prophet didn't get himself locked up.

He looked at his watch, and was surprised to find it almost six in the evening. He made for Hampstead Tube station, where he bought an evening paper. The storm had broken. The police were looking for Arthur and for Lord Cazalay, neither of whom could be found. Graham wondered if Cazalay had gone to Venezuela, too. But the stop press revealed he had gone no farther than Newhaven, where he was assisting the police with their enquiries. Graham stuffed the paper in his overcoat pocket. He would have to face the music, and the grisly concert had begun.

In the hallway of his block of flats a woman approached him.

'Graham! I'm sorry to sit on your doorstep. But I've been trying to get you all day. There's something terribly important you really ought to know.'

Graham recognized Sheila Raleigh. She must have just returned from France. 'I must apologize,' he told her absently. 'I've had rather a lot of things occupying me. It's about the Annex Club, I suppose?'

'No, it isn't.' She looked round. 'Could we have a moment alone?'

'Yes, of course.'

They said nothing until he let her into his flat. He felt she had

423

chosen a damn inconsiderate moment to call. 'I hope you're liking the job?'

'Yes, it's wonderful. I can't thank you enough. Particularly after I said such bitter things to you once.'

'I deserved them.'

'No, you didn't. But you can understand how I felt at the time? I had to blame someone. It all seemed so pointless otherwise.'

Impatient to get rid of her, Graham asked, 'What can I do for you now.'

'It's about your house, Graham. In France.' She sat down, frowning. 'There's something fishy about it. There was a man who came to look at it, just before I left yesterday. A Frenchman, a very nasty piece of work. He arrived in a Citroën with two others, who looked like thugs. Apparently . . . well, apparently you don't own the place at all. Lord Cazalay does. He's been "selling" it to a dozen different people. Oh, Graham, I'm so sorry! It must be awful to have lost all that money.'

25

FOR A WEEK Graham read the morning and evening papers
with eagerness and apprehension. But the Press stayed infuriatingly bare of facts, reassuring or deadly. Lord Cazalay
and ferrety-faced Arthur were remanded in custody by the
Bow Street magistrate on some comparatively trivial charge, a
detective-superintendent implying from the witness box that
all hell was in store for them once it could be properly docu-
mented. The disgraced Fred Butcher was announced by his
distraught secretary as having entered an unnamed nursing-
home for 'nerves'. He had sent his passport to Scotland Yard,
though purely as a matter of courtesy.

   The Tory party, squashed for a couple of years under Mr
Attlee's majority, fell like bluebottles on the festering wound in
the pure-white body of socialism. They even stripped the
friable wrappings from the mummified first Lord Cazalay,
recalling with glee that his disgrace had occurred under the
sway of Ramsay MacDonald. There was a dreadful fuss in the
House of Commons. The Speaker twice suspended the sitting,
leaving the chamber like a despairing headmaster shaming his
boys with a display of dignity. Two more Ministers resigned
(but kept their passports). Then the Government neatly announced an investigatory tribunal to be established, under a
judge of unassailable wisdom and impartiality. The matter was
henceforward *sub judice*, and could not with propriety be raised
in public at all. The House simmered down, the legislators

turning their vigilance to the raising of the school-leaving age to fifteen.

After ten days of uncertainty, paralysing all his activities and most of his thoughts outside his professional ones, Graham ran into John Bickley in the Cavendish Clinic. He had just finished his last case of the afternoon, loosening a Dupuytren's contracture in the palm of a stockbroker (the deformity interfered badly with his shooting). As he pushed open the door of the surgeons' room to change, he found the anaesthetist in his long green theatre gown, packing away rubber masks, tubing, swabs, syringes, and other tools of oblivion into a square black-leather bag.

'That was the best advice anyone's given me in my life,' Graham said at once.

John looked up. 'About not operating on that spiv fellow?' He gave a smile. 'You know, I hadn't the slightest expectation that you'd take it.'

'If I had, I'd be well and truly up the creek by now, wouldn't I? With all this fuss, all these political people getting interested, trying to outdo each other scratching up the dirt. The ridiculous aspect of the whole affair is that I'd nothing to worry about from Cazalay. Nothing at all. He simply swindled me out of my money. He didn't even buy those pernicious francs in the first place.'

'How much did you lose?'

'Five thousand quid.'

John's eyebrows shot up.

'Yes, I'm a mug,' Graham admitted. 'Cazalay might as well have sold me a gold brick or the Eiffel Tower—didn't some bright Frenchman flog it to the Germans for scrap during the war?' He undid a length of bandage round his waist, and slipped the white linen operating trousers from his spindly legs. 'But perhaps it was a reasonable fee to pay for the shock treatment. I've learnt my lesson. Henceforward Trevose sticks to the straight and narrow path.'

'Oh, come, Graham! You're making yourself sound like an old lag, not an ornament to one of our Orders of Chivalry.'

Graham threw his trousers into the corner with an impatient gesture. 'You know what I mean. Well, you ought to. You don't imagine I'm unaware of your going about referring to me as "Flash Harry"?' John laughed. 'By the way, I'm giving up my private practice,' Graham added.

The anaesthetist paused in packing away his apparatus and stared at him. 'You're not serious?'

'I'm perfectly serious. I'm abandoning the private racket for a full-time job. On the new unit Haileybury's always talking about. I'm to be its first Director.'

'But Graham—your whole life's been built round your private work. Everyone in London is green with envy at your reputation. You already get patients sent to you from all over the country. Once things get really back to normal you'll be getting them from all over the bloody world. Surely you can't throw all that away?'

'My life wasn't built round private work during the war, and that was the only time I was happy.' He pulled on his grey suit in silence. As John snapped the two catches of his leather case, Graham continued, 'Perhaps the Government are right to set themselves against fee-paying medicine. It's immoral really, if you look at it carefully. It didn't matter so much even thirty years ago, when the doctor could generally do damn all whether you paid him or not. Besides, I want to think. Perhaps to write. Rushing round nursing homes chasing guineas, you haven't a chance to do either. Perhaps I've an academic streak in me somewhere—don't forget my father was a professor. He left a massive volume on the synovial membranes as his tombstone, which is more than I shall ever achieve.'

'I still can't take you seriously, Graham.'

'Then wait and see. You won't even have to wait long. The appointment's being announced by the Ministry at the beginning of next month. I'll have to resign from Blackfriars, of course, which will be a wrench, though mainly a sentimental one. There doesn't seem the slightest prospect of the place being rebuilt in my own lifetime. And the staff there will all be working for the Government anyway, whether they like it or not.

427

I'm giving up my flat—I've got to economize and I want something smaller, nearer the site, to organize things.' Graham's face suddenly lit up. 'It'll be like those early days at the annex, all over again. Except this time everyone will be on *my* side. I'll only have to snap my fingers for equipment to arrive by the lorryload.'

John stood looking at him, his bony long-fingered hands resting on the top of his case. 'It must have been a sacrifice. Or at least a horribly difficult decision.'

'Not really. Like most of the big steps in my life, I didn't think twice about it.' As John slipped the green gown from his shirt, Graham added as off-handedly as possible, 'You know, I really would rather like to see Clare again.'

'That's the best news you've given me today.'

Graham felt this sounded vaguely condescending, but asked, 'Do you think she'd respond to some sort of social invitation? To dinner, a show, something like that?'

'Why don't you come and find out? I'm just off to the Kenworth to do a case. I know for a fact she's on duty. Are you free?'

Graham hesitated. Then his natural impulsiveness made him say, 'All right. You can give me a lift.' As John picked up his instrument-case he added, 'After all, I've nothing to lose, have I? If I admit to you now that I treated Clare quite disgustingly, it's something which I have only just come to admit to myself.'

'Quite so,' said John.

It suddenly struck him how much Graham was starting to sound like Haileybury.

It was fortunate for the reputation of Sister Mills at the Kenworth Hospital that she had charge of a children's ward. Unlike the adult patients, who had little to do except listen to *Workers' Playtime* through the headphones and intensely observe the personal behaviour of the staff, the youngsters saw nothing remarkable—only some welcome entertainment—in a wide-eyed little man bursting among them, a startled cry from Sister, a whispered conversation, glances between bewildered nurses, a brisk retreat to Sister's office, a slamming of the door. Graham reflected afterwards he could as well have telephoned, but his

428

unexpected appearance was much more dramatic and much more satisfying. In the office, they were far too confused and embarrassed to say very much, nor even to approach within arm's length of each other. Graham told her he must see her, it was desperate—couldn't he even take her to dinner? She demurred, trying to adjust her mind to the situation. But he was never a man to lose the advantage of a woman's hesitation.

'All right,' Clare agreed doubtfully. 'All right, Graham. For old times' sake.'

'That's wonderful! We'll have so much to talk about. It's almost three whole years since we—' He wondered how to put it. 'Went our separate ways.'

She couldn't prevent herself asking, 'Did you miss me?'

'Like an amputated limb. You know how the patients get pain in them, don't you? "A phantom limb." It hurts worse than ever, even if it isn't there.'

She gave a nervous smile and said, 'You mustn't forget the limb's always amputated for the patient's own good.'

There was a pause. Neither of them felt entirely sure where the conversation was leading. Both were relieved for it to be frustrated by a knock on the door and the news that a child due for release, overcome by excitement, had vomited copiously over the newly cleaned floor.

Two evenings later they met. Graham had chosen a restaurant in Soho, whispered among a small and knowing circle as providing with its generous portions not only butter but crisp, white, mysteriously unrationed bread. By then both he and Clare had found time to adjust themselves, and were perfectly charming to each other. They sat in the corner of the small, rose-lighted room, chatting gaily of pointedly inconsequential generalities. Graham had really no precise idea what he was going to propose to her, and hoped he could rely on her delicacy to raise nothing that would make him feel too uncomfortable. He picked up the wine-list and suggested champagne, adding half-humorously, 'This place is terribly black market.'

'Oh, everyone these days knows someone who can get them

something.' Clare smiled. 'Our theatre porter finds us the most lovely nylons—"They dropped off a lorry" is the story. It must have been an extremely large pantechnicon.'

'I'm growing rather tired of all that, you know. I've had some sort of moral conversion. And, like most converts, I was scared into it.' He picked up the evening paper, beside them on the table. Lord Cazalay and Arthur had been charged that morning with a number of offences from bribery of Government officials to possessing unauthorized sweet coupons. To Graham's relief, there was still no mention of currency transactions. 'You've read all about this, I suppose?'

'Is there anyone who hasn't?'

'But I think I can entertain you with some unpublished details.'

Over dinner he gave a frank account of his life since she had walked out of Cosy Cot, with the exception of Liz. In his penitent mood he was half-inclined to throw her in too, but consoled himself that Clare would certainly suspect he had been mixed up with a woman or two, and through natural female pride and vanity imagine them goddesses. If she became increasingly serious and sympathetic, Graham had been smugly confident of as much. His moral weaknesses had always been of as much concern to her as his physical ones, he reflected, and she accepted both with the same resignation. She hadn't changed, he told himself. Though if she had changed towards *him* was a separate question. When he finished the tale she held his hand under the table, and said, 'Poor Graham! You did get yourself in a mess, didn't you?'

'I didn't have you to keep me out of it.'

He started to talk about his new job, a conversation which drifted naturally back to the annex and Smithers Botham. Her eyes began to sparkle, she gripped his hand tighter than ever, and he felt a sudden glow of relief. It was going to be all right. She had forgiven him, they could pick up neatly where they had left off, except this time he really would marry her, just as soon as the little formality could be arranged. He was starting to believe she would go that very night with him to the flat, when she said, 'Graham, it's been simply lovely meeting you. We must have another reunion one day, mustn't we? Perhaps when all this black-market and rationing nonsense is over.'

He looked blank. 'But Clare! Aren't you coming back to me?'

'Don't be silly, Graham.'

'But this time, I mean . . . we'd be married, it would be different.'

'It wouldn't be different in the slightest. As I told you once before, it wouldn't work.'

'You're being ridiculous.' He sounded quite cross. 'Everything was abnormal in those days.'

'Yes, there was a war on.'

'I mean everything about *me*. I was selfish then, foolish, chasing all the wrong things. I've changed. I know I've changed. I've got my sense of values straight. I don't give a damn for the fripperies of life any more.'

'You sound like Sir Stafford Cripps,' she told him.

By the time he reached home Graham was furious. It was beyond him why Clare had refused to fall gratefully into his arms. All this effort to turn himself into a decent human being, he reflected petulantly, would be absolutely wasted if nobody was going to take it seriously. He poured himself a whisky and sat in the armchair. For the first time there stole upon him the black realization that he had lost Clare for good. A solitary life stretched ahead, as bleakly as the concrete corridors at Smithers Botham. And at fifty-one you needed someone beside you, much more desperately than at twenty-one. But there was nobody who cared a damn about him. Only his son Desmond. At least, he presumed so. The young man had more or less given up speaking to him.

The next morning Graham had a letter from Haileybury, confirming his new appointment and inviting him to lunch with some political figures who were enthusiastic over the new hospital. Mr Bevan himself, he added, might possibly be joining them for the coffee. Graham wrote resigning his post as consultant surgeon to Blackfriars. He would devote himself wholly to his new interest. He would have the best part of fifteen years in the place before he retired, and he would leave it as a splendid monument to himself. He would meanwhile live alone and put up with it. After all, he was a widower, not some crabby never-loved bachelor like old Crampers. He wondered vaguely if Crampers were still alive. He doubted it. The Welfare State seemed to have been the death of him.

26

THE POLITICIANS' LUNCH was held in the House of Commons, a fair proportion of which, like a fair proportion of the capital itself, lay in apparently permanent ruins. Graham was interested to see for the first time the inside of the place, though confessing as he was escorted rapidly through the corridors and stairways a feeling of disappointment. The marble floors, the vulgar murals, the pillared corners and vaulted ceilings, the solemn dress-suited attendants, reminded him of somewhere— yes, it was the casino at Monte Carlo. He supposed that both structures had been raised about the same time, and had much in common in their function.

The party gathered in a smallish upstairs room with mullioned leaded windows and an over-abundance of carved pale oak, overlooking the river. Graham at once realized the importance of the affair. Of the thirty-odd men in the room, about half he recognized as top medical people, including Haileybury. Clearly, the Government had taken the new hospital to its heart.

Never a martyr to the self-inflicted tortures of modesty, Graham was flattered to notice the stir his arrival made among the politicos. They would have heard enough of him during the war, he supposed. Or perhaps, he reflected wryly, they were aware of his having married the daughter of the first Lord Cazalay, and his kinship to the rogue at the seat of their present troubles. Graham was coming to detach himself from the man in Brixton prison with more assurance every day. He decided his brother-in-law had enough on his hands without dragging him into the mess—though with a man like that you never could tell. But if anything about himself was exposed by the promised radical surgery of the tribunal, he fancied even the memory of the present feast would induce in his hosts an attack of acute dyspepsia.

Graham found himself sitting next to a young Member of Parliament with junior rank in the Government, though he was vague what, and felt it would be discourteous to reveal such ignorance. Graham was far too self-centred to have much interest in politics, a quality which, combined with his exhibitionism, might have made him a successful politician. He had troubled neither to vote in the recent election, nor even to hear Churchill's broadcast speeches during the war. Like most medical people, he saw mankind less as noble sufferers in adversity than as sadly muddle-headed ignoramuses, to be saved from themselves by well-educated ladies and gentlemen as kindly as possible. With a lazy if reasonable over-simplification, Graham wrote off the Tories as appealing to the populace's natural greed, and the Socialists to its natural envy. If the Government were now trying to organize everyone's life from the cradle to the grave he felt it probably a sound idea, most inhabitants of a growingly complicated world apparently being incapable of even crossing the road with impunity. Long ago, in the days of the first Lord Cazalay, he had grasped that politicians ran to their own rules, as detached from those of everyday life as the rules of some game of cards. You had to let them get up to whatever they wished, running your life as best you could and allowing for their existence like the bacteria contaminating every article you touched.

The young M.P. revealed himself over the soup as a strong enthusiast for the coming National Health Service.

'My father,' he explained forcefully to Graham, 'suffered from bad eyes. He couldn't afford to attend a doctor, or an optician, or anyone qualified for the job. Do you know what he was obliged to do? Go to one of the cheap sixpenny stores, where they had a card affair, with those different-sized letters

434

on it. Right on the counter, among all the tubes of toothpaste. He'd pick up lenses and try them till he found the right ones. Thousands of sufferers from bad eyesight had to do exactly the same. Those cheap stores were providing a valuable social service on behalf of their shareholders, if they but knew it. But it's disgraceful, isn't it, Sir Graham? In future, every citizen will be entitled to a properly fitted pair of spectacles as a right. Just as he's entitled to clean water or the protection of the law.'

'It'll probably be equally expensive,' Graham demurred mildly.

The politician's gesture brushed this aside impatiently. 'Naturally, there'll be a pent-up demand, but the whole point of a proper health service is that it gets progressively cheaper. When people are given the proper treatment they've been denied through poverty—not to mention given better working conditions, better houses, and a higher standard of living from decent wages—the need for medicines and doctors will simply diminish. We'll all live healthier and longer. Eh, Sir Graham?' He grinned. 'As a medical man, mustn't you agree?'

'But if we all live longer we'll simply suffer more intractable ailments and need even more doctors.'

'Sir Graham! You're belittling your profession. What about the inevitable great advances in curative medicine?'

'And the inevitable increases in expensive drugs? Penicillin's a dreadful price as it is.' Graham felt uneasy entering in an argument with a professional debater, but to his relief the waiter interrupted by serving the main course. 'What on earth's this?' he exclaimed in surprise.

'Whale steak,' the M.P. told him proudly. 'We're importing tons of it to eke out the meat ration. I assure you it's absolutely delicious.'

Then the young man began talking equally energetically about India, a subject which bored Graham even more than cricket.

It was clear that Haileybury was enjoying the occasion immensely. He rose to make a short if wholly unmemorable speech, and as they prepared to break up Graham noticed with amusement he was noticeably flushed with official port.

'Graham, old fellow, if you're going my way perhaps we can stroll together?' Haileybury suggested with an unknown heartiness.

'I'm not going anywhere in particular. Shall we take a turn round St James's Park? We've plenty to talk about.'

As they walked round the lake, the chilly spring air restored Haileybury to his usual oppressive sobriety. They talked animatedly for half an hour about the first steps for bringing the new unit into being, until Graham broke off unexpectedly, 'You know, Eric, this new task you've saddled me with has saved my life. Literally, I mean. I've never thought of suicide —and I know a surprising number of one's acquaintances have at least once, quite seriously. But I wouldn't have been too sure of myself, not at this stage of my life, without some fresh interest.'

'You're being fanciful again,' Haileybury told him with a thin smile.

'I suppose you're entitled to think so. You know me better than almost anybody. But I mean it. Without something big to tackle, some worthwhile achievement to make, I'd get depressed. Dreadfully depressed. It seems to get worse with age. And when a patient's depressed, you know well enough, they've a different personality, there's no knowing what they might do. It's as dangerous as walking along the edge of a cliff.'

Haileybury nodded slowly as they walked. 'What makes you imagine I haven't suffered myself?'

Graham looked at him sharply. He had imagined Haileybury's personality breasting the tides of life with the unexciting stability of a coal-barge on the Thames. It struck him that although Haileybury had grown to understand a good deal of his own inner workings, he knew absolutely nothing of Haileybury's.

'I hope the intolerable amount of work you are about to undertake will put such unpleasant notions from your mind,' Haileybury added.

436

'I'm safe as long as I'm occupied every minute of the day. I hate living alone.' Graham hesitated, but decided to go on. Haileybury, of all people, had become his only confessor. 'I'd hoped to cure that particular deficiency, but I'm afraid it's not to be.'

'You're thinking of taking a companion?'

'I notice you avoid the word "wife", and I can't blame you for that either.' Graham sounded a shade weary. 'You know I lived with a girl during the war? She was my ward sister from the annex. We've met up again. I want to marry her. I can't live without her. That's a stupid expression, much overused, but as I explained a moment ago it might have been quite literally true. But she doesn't want to take the same risk with me twice, and I can hardly object to her point of view.'

'Who might this lady be? Would I have met her?'

'I should imagine so. She's the children's ward sister at the Kenworth.'

Haileybury stopped dead. 'Sister Mills? But what an amazing coincidence!'

'It isn't at all. John Bickley got her the job after I kicked her out in 1944.'

'I see,' said Haileybury. He put his fingers together and blew on them.

'I do wish you wouldn't do that,' Graham burst out. 'It's irritated me for years.'

Haileybury hastily thrust his hands in his pockets. 'I'm sorry there's a difficulty between you,' he sympathized.

'She can't understand that I don't *want* to go back to my old ways—because of the war, or old age,' Graham ended gloomily, 'or perhaps just disgust with myself in general.'

'I suppose to some extent the seven ages of man are all strangers to each other,' Haileybury observed.

'Just look at those ducks,' said Graham, pointing across the lake. 'They must run up a tremendous oxygen debt, keeping their beaks under water as long as that.'

He didn't care to reveal more of himself to Haileybury. He had said too much as it was. He had written Clare a long and thoughtful letter, uncloyed with passion. There had been no reply. It seemed best to forget about her, as deliberately as he had once forgotten about Edith. As the two surgeons resumed their walk, Graham began with growing disquiet to hope that Haileybury would forget about her too. Haileybury had been his enemy once, and in this shifting and faithless world who knew when he might be again?

27

BUT HAILEYBURY did not forget about Clare at all.

He had heard some rumour during the war of Graham living
'in sin' at Smithers Botham, but had vaguely imagined his
consort some painted and skittish female of the type portrayed
on his rare visits to the cinema by Dorothy Lamour (Haileybury suffered a guilty affection for the comedies starring Bing
Crosby and Bob Hope). That she was the quiet and efficient
Sister Mills, whom he had encountered almost weekly for a
year, seemed inconceivable. But Haileybury decided he had
never been able to comprehend the powerful mysteries of sexual
attraction, no more than he could grasp those of the atomic
physics you were beginning to read so much about in the newspapers. He had never felt drawn to one woman rather than
another in his life. He felt annoyed that John Bickley had kept
Sister Mills' relationship from him—but he supposed it wasn't
a matter you wanted revealed in such a gossip-ridden place as a
hospital. He anxiously tried to recall if he had made any
particularly uncharitable remarks about Graham in her
presence.

Haileybury thought about it all the week-end. He kept
shaking his head and chuckling faintly to himself, much
alarming his sister. It certainly took him back. The only other
of Graham's women he had met was that girl Edith, secretary
on his plastic surgery unit in 1918. He had taken a distinctly
dim view of *that* connection, Haileybury remembered. But that

was long ago; now they were growing into old dogs and learning not to bark and bite so much. He began to wonder if he might say something on Graham's behalf to Sister Mills. An outrageous idea, of course. But Haileybury was a fair man and felt the lady was perhaps being unjust. As for the injustice he had himself done Graham in 1942, he felt it more keenly than Graham now did himself.

Sister Mills might make the man a good wife, Haileybury speculated. Graham had sobered down, there was no doubt about that. For him to have thrown away his profitable private practice would before the war have been as inconceivable as his entering a monastery. But no, Haileybury finally decided, he had no right to intervene. It was a personal matter for the pair of them. Besides, he was still not entirely certain how much in these strange postwar years he had come to like or even to tolerate Graham.

On the Monday, Haileybury was visiting the Kenworth Hospital to see his patients. He had two cases of cleft palate recovering in the children's ward, which he usually visited ceremonially escorted by his house-surgeon. But this young man, whose services he shared with the throat department, was occupied in the theatre with the emergency of a postoperative bleeding tonsil. Haileybury found himself alone with Sister Mills in a small room off the ward known as the nursery, which contained a slide, a rocking horse, and various toys, all of which some half-dozen small children were enjoying with an amazing amount of noise.

'I believe you know Graham Trevose?' Haileybury asked her suddenly, above the din.

'Yes, that's quite correct,' Clare told him calmly. 'I was one of his ward sisters during the war.'

'How very strange.' Haileybury looked uneasy. 'I have enjoyed his acquaintance for years, you know.'

'Yes, he used to talk a lot about you. Particularly when there was that fuss in 1942.'

Clare noticed Haileybury had the grace to turn pink.

'I think we have made all that up between us, Sister.'

440

'I hope so, Mr Haileybury. He was very upset at the time. Almost out of his mind.'

Haileybury made no reply. He had long ago ceased caring what Graham said to him, but the cloaked rebuke from Sister Mills was surprisingly wounding. A shocking illogical thought crept upon him—perhaps it was he who had behaved so badly over the years of their acquaintance rather than Graham?

'I hope I have undone any damage by arranging to some extent his appointment to our fine new accident hospital. You must have seen the place mentioned in the papers, surely?'

'I don't think anything could compensate him for those few terrible weeks. He had built up the annex at Smithers Botham, and it was to be taken away from him.' She paused, and added, 'It was like a mother losing a child.'

Haileybury didn't know what to say. So he put his finger-tips together and blew on them.

'I saw Graham just before the week-end,' he admitted. 'Naturally, with the new project we shall be thrown on each other's company a good deal.' He hesitated and added, 'I understand he wishes to marry you, Sister?'

He could not remember uttering anything making him feel more uncomfortable in his life.

'That is correct, Mr Haileybury.'

Clare leant down to pick up a crying child who had tripped over a pile of wooden bricks.

'Forgive me—this is really nothing to do with me—but I gather you are not agreeable?'

'That too, is correct, Mr Haileybury. I am not agreeable.'

Haileybury hesitated again. He decided that having got this far he would charge bravely on. In 1942 he may not have been motivated by spite, as Graham suggested, but he had found the delicate negotiations leading to the man's dismissal from the annex not wholly unpleasurable. Yes, he must make amends, it was his duty. The new job was not enough. After all, Graham could have earned that easily on his own merits. It was only a matter of his stooping to take it.

'I'm sorry to hear that,' he said, quite sternly. 'I hope you

441

appreciate the extent of his emotional disturbance? I have known him for years—since before you were born—and *I* can appreciate it very keenly myself. Quite frankly, he talked to me of suicide. Oh, I know it's a common enough threat in such circumstances. From a boy of twenty, perhaps. But not from a mature man. And a man of the world, like Graham.' He saw she looked alarmed, and went on, 'Perhaps I can see your point of view. He would never conceal from society that he was lavish in his affections. But he's a better man. It was a process which probably started during the war, when he had no alternative but to follow his natural instinct and devote himself to others. I fancy his life in the world of fashion merely expressed his taste for self-indulgence, pursued with the energy which he devotes to everything.'

There was a pause, filled with the screaming of children.

'Perhaps so,' was all Clare said.

Haileybury shrugged his shoulders. He felt no need to say more. He had done the duty. He made a peculiar jerky bow and sidled away. He sincerely hoped the girl would take up with Graham again and marry him. After *that* conversation, it would be outrageously embarrassing always meeting her in the hospital.

Clare went to her small office and sat at her desk. It was all dreadfully confusing. Of course, she still loved Graham. Of course, she would happily marry him. Had she been five years younger she wouldn't have hesitated. But the lesson of Cosy Cot was not one she was anxious to learn over again—unless that funny old stick Haileybury was right, and Graham had really shed his old habits. When they had lived together she had seen mostly Graham's best side, and that was certainly something worth taking a risk for. On the other hand, with Graham you could never tell how he **was** going to behave about anything, even the way he liked his shirts ironed.

There was a knock. A cheerful curly-headed young man in a white coat, the thoracic surgeon's houseman, put his head inside. 'All right if we have a look at that patent ductus, Sister?'

'Yes, of course, Mr Cooper.' Clare got up. The surgeons

442

were daringly starting to operate in the area of the heart itself, and had tied off an abnormal blood-vessel in a little girl suffering this congenital defect. She gathered up the notes. 'The patient's doing very well, I'm glad to say.'

'That's splendid. Then we'll have another one for you to nurse next month.'

'I'm afraid I shan't be here by then, Mr Cooper. I'm leaving to get married.' Clare stood looking at him, still wondering why she had said it.

Graham found a wedding in middle life a surprisingly agreeable experience. Though after all, he told himself, unlike most bridegrooms he wasn't marrying an almost total stranger.

Graham's first marriage had been one of the social landmarks of 1920. Maria had worn a train twelve feet long, there had been a shoal of expensively outfitted bridesmaids, all of whose names and faces he had long ago forgotten, and the first Lord Cazalay had driven her up in a brand-new Rolls Royce. The young John Bickley had been his best man, and the second Lord Cazalay, now calculating his chances in a remand cell, had become embarrassingly drunk. The reception had been in some official building, though Graham had gathered the bride's father would have preferred Buckingham Palace could he have arranged it. As Graham had expected, nobody had taken much notice of himself. He had later come to appreciate this was true of even the humblest marriages, which he supposed were largely occasions for the parents to entertain their friends and show off without risk of later backbiting.

His own wedding was the first Graham had attended since the miserable afternoon at the marriage of Peter Thomas— who Graham was delighted to find from the newspapers seemed to be making a fortune with some sort of cross-country air service. There were to be only four onlookers at the registry office. Clare's mother and father appeared from Bristol, to Graham's relief too flattered by their daughter's unexpectedly turning herself into Lady Trevose to utter anything but the platitudes of the occasion. He asked John Bickley to repeat his rôle of best man. Denise had to be invited as well, of course, but to Graham's intense joy was too ill on the day to go out.

Afterwards, Graham stood them all lunch in a hotel, where they had champagne and *snoek piquante*. There was a wedding-cake, with an iced covering made, in the way of the times, from detachable white cardboard. There were no speeches, though Graham's new father-in-law had by then so fallen under the influence of his charm and his title that he had to be restrained from making one. They caught the train for a week-end's honeymoon at Bognor Regis. Everything was punctiliously correct. The rushed two weeks since Clare had accepted him were too occupied with her work in hospital and her visits to Bristol to give them more than a moment or two together over lunch in Claridge's. Graham mounted to their seaside bedroom reflecting with amusement that he was facing his bride like the most moral of newly wedded husbands—if one overlooked a year or two during the war. He got into bed making jokes about consummations and such other horribly dignified words festooning the sexual relationship. This time he put out the light, feeling he wanted to be as respectable about everything as possible. Then suddenly he broke into tears.

Clare held him tight in the darkness. 'Darling, what is it?' Weeping was something she had never known in him before. 'What is it? What's upsetting you?'

'I don't know, I don't know,' Graham told her. 'For once I just can't express myself any other way, that's all.'

Her hand under the bedclothes stroked his penis, that organ of superb anatomical ingenuity.

'I thought I'd lost you for good, Clare—I really did. I could have taken it a few years ago, but not now. Not any longer.'

She said nothing for a minute, then confessed, 'We have a fairy godfather. Someone who came and changed my mind.'

'Oh? And who might that be?'

'Mr Haileybury,' she told him cheerfully.

Graham sat bolt upright. 'Haileybury? My God! That pie-faced fossil Haileybury?'

'He told me you could be relied upon to be a good boy in

444

future,' she added teasingly. 'And of course, nobody could possibly doubt the good word of Mr Haileybury.'

'Good God!' muttered Graham.

But the news was too much. For almost the first time in his life when in bed with a woman, Graham was put off his stroke.

28

AT THE BEGINNING OF JUNE in the hot and thundery summer of 1947, it was starting to sink into the British public that of all the 'shortages' bedevilling the country, which ran from electricity-generating stations to milk chocolate, a lack of United States dollars was the most serious, intractable, and baffling. After all, General Marshall was proposing to give dollars away by the shipload to European countries who had spent the war defeating one another—even to Germany, or the bits that the Russians had left of it. And we were the victors. We had fought the war from the first shot, we had won it (admittedly with a little American assistance), we had paid our whack of it. It was most frustrating. Why, the Government were even contemplating an unbelievable economy—of denying the twenty million weekly cinemagoers their accustomed Hollywood films.

Graham then had a letter from Edith, demurely congratulating him on his marriage. He supposed she had learnt of it from some regular bundle of English newspapers dispatched to soften her exile. But most of the half-dozen pages in her large round hand concerned her son Alec. She was dreadfully worried about him. He had written early in the year explaining he was in hospital with some mild psychological disturbance. She just couldn't understand it. Alec had been a highly strung child, of course, and was still inclined to be excitable, but he was perfectly normal, and very clever, really. There was certainly no madness on *their* side of the family (Graham felt slightly irritated at the barb, but supposed it unintentional). Edith hadn't heard from Alec since. She has no idea if he were still under treatment, or where he was. She hesitated troubling Graham, who must be terribly busy, but she was becoming desperate. It seemed such an awful pity that all Alec's splendid education should go to waste.

Graham tossed the letter on to the desk in his Marylebone flat. Edith was always a great admirer of education, he reflected. Even as a girl she placed it among the noblest of human qualities, when it was only another pair of hands, to be used for good or evil, but mostly for feeding yourself.

But he supposed he had better do something about Alec.

He knew the young man had been discharged from Smithers Botham, taking some new drug which Dr Dency assured Graham would have a tranquillizing effect, rather than a soporific one like the barbiturates. Graham telephoned the psychiatrist's consulting room, to learn that Dr Dency had left for a six-months' lectureship in the Union of South Africa, where he was doubtless enjoying steaks and as many eggs as he cared to eat for his breakfast. He telephoned Smithers Botham, but could get no sense from anybody. The next afternoon he was himself delivering a lecture at Addenbrook's Hospital at Cambridge, and had arranged to dine in hall afterwards with his son. Perhaps Desmond might be able to help, Graham wondered. He had more reason for keeping track of Alec than anyone.

'How did the lecture go?' asked Desmond, welcoming his father amiably enough with a glass of sherry in his rooms.

'I don't really know. It was my standard one. I've delivered it so often it comes out automatically. It's a useful opportunity for me to think about other matters.'

Desmond gave a faint smile. Now that he's started wearing his hair long, thought Graham, he really does look tremendously like Maria.

'How's Clare?' Desmond asked.

'She's splendid! You didn't particularly want to attend the wedding, I suppose?'

'I'd have come if you'd asked me.'

'Then perhaps I saved you some embarrassment by omitting to. By the way, you don't happen to know where Alec's got to, I suppose? His mother's worried stiff about him.'

447

Desmond looked surprised. 'I was going to ask you the same thing. I heard some sort of rumour that he was doing anaesthetic locums round London.'

'Then perhaps John Bickley might have a clue,' Graham suggested hopefully.

'I'm not going to let him get away with it, you know,' said Desmond more severely. 'The money's mine, and he's showing absolutely no inclination to pay it back whatever. It's just as if he'd put his hand in my pocket and stolen it.'

'My dear Desmond!' Graham leant back in his armchair. 'One of the things you should now be learning in life is the right moment to cut your losses. With either bad debts, bad women, or bad operating techniques. Enjoy your mistakes, but don't lose sleep over them.'

'*I* didn't want to pay for his bloody upbringing! It was you who took it on.'

'I agree, but anyway the unpleasant experience will do you good.' Graham sipped the sherry, which was really rather good. It was stupid to worry about grabbing money all the time, he told himself. One of the more depressing of the herd instincts. A wonder he had fallen for the idea for so long. Since marrying Clare he was becoming quite righteous.

'If I'm going to start making self-improving donations to charity I certainly wouldn't begin with Alec,' Desmond declared crossly.

'You've got paranoia about him, haven't you? That's a waste of time, too. Old Haileybury and I were daggers drawn for years, and it didn't get us very far. Only recently I've realized that everyone was killing themselves laughing behind our backs. I'd forget Alec, if I were you.' As Desmond continued looking disagreeable, Graham added, 'All right, all right, once I've got my affairs straight I'll make up the sum to you. Does that make you feel better? Count your blessings. You're set for a brilliant academic career, while Alec will never come to anything.'

Desmond seemed to consider this proposition for some moments, then announced, 'You know I've decid d to prepare a new edition of grandfather's book? There's a tremendous amount of work involved, but I think it will be worth while.'

'That's excellent news.' Graham felt deeply gratified. ' "Trevose on the synovial membranes". I remember the old boy writing it, donkey's years ago, when I'd escaped with my life from that sanatorium. He'd be pleased to think the family were keeping it going. There's a weight of medical tradition on your shoulders, you know, Desmond. It gets heavier every generation, like our debts.'

'Perhaps that's why I decided on the task,' said Desmond solemnly. 'It's something for posterity. It doesn't seem I shall father another generation of Trevoses. Our branch of the family will die out.'

'Oh, I don't know,' Graham told him cheerfully. 'You've forgotten about Clare and myself.'

'Good God,' murmured Desmond, looking thoroughly alarmed.

Graham decided to take Desmond's guess about Alec's whereabouts as fact, and wrote Edith a consoling letter saying her son was making his way in the newly flourishing specialty of anaesthetics. He supposed he could have made more energetic enquiries, but he was tremendously busy with plans and committees for the new hospital. For the third time in his life he was starting a new unit from scratch—first at Blackfriars in the twenties, backed by Val Arlott, secondly at Smithers Botham, discouraged by everybody, and now in the abandoned American building with the full resources of the Welfare State at his elbow. It was the most exciting, if the most exhausting, of all. He could hardly be expected to play Alec's nursemaid at the same time. Anyway, the man was in his middle twenties, a qualified doctor, and should be able to look after himself. Edith wrote again rather pathetically. Graham finished her long letter with a deep sigh. The woman really was rather a nuisance. She'd never missed a chance to make use of him. Never since he'd deflowered her in a seaside summerhouse during the warmer months of 1918.

Graham let young Alec drop from his mind. Then one afternoon in November he was hurrying along Shaftesbury Avenue from a lunch appointment in Soho, and saw the name ALEC TREVOSE facing him from a placard outside a theatre. Graham stopped, frowning. He felt for his newly prescribed glasses, the announcement not being in particularly large type. The name was among three others claiming authorship of a revue, which Graham vaguely remembered as wringing amiable notices from the critics (he had turned his back on the theatre of late). Lower down, there was Alec Trevose again, in even smaller letters, among the cast. Well, it was not an uncommon name, Graham reflected, and sounded well enough for any player to sport. There was no immediate way of telling if the actor-dramatist might be his own nephew. The simplest course seemed to buy a couple of tickets for the show, which he obtained for the following evening, with the greatest difficulty.

A glance at Clare's programme as they took their seats told Graham it was Alec right enough. The sketch he had written and in which he was about to display himself was entitled simply *At The Doctor's*. The pair of them sat through the foregoing scenes, which struck Graham as exactly like every other revue he had seen, with mounting impatience and foreboding. Then Alec finally appeared. He acted a patient, subjected to an ingenious variety of indignities and discomforts by a dozen white-coated doctors. The audience bellowed. Once recovering from the shock of his nephew's entrance, Graham had to admit it was well put together and surprisingly funny, perhaps because every line that Alec had written and every situation he had depicted occurred often enough in a real hospital. He turned his head, to see Clare dabbing away tears of laughter with her handkerchief. He wondered what Edith would have thought.

After the final curtain Graham said without enthusiasm, 'We'd better go round and have a word with him, I suppose?'

'Yes, I'd love to,' agreed Clare eagerly. 'I've never been behind the scenes before.'

Graham gave his name to the stage-door keeper, who directed them down a flight of stone stairs leading to a narrow, green-painted, ill-lit passage, smelling strongly of disinfectant.

The dressing-rooms that Graham had visited during his theatrical phase had been spacious flower-filled apartments, but Alec's seemed hardly bigger than a railway compartment, with a wooden stand in the middle for the mirrors fringed with electric bulbs, at which three other young men were busy wiping away their make-up.

'Why, it's Uncle Graham!' Alec leapt up, a scrap of filthy towelling in his hand. 'But what a lovely surprise! And Auntie Clare. I say, I should have congratulated you or something, shouldn't I? I'm dreadfully sorry. Life's been an absolute rush, I've had hardly a moment to think of my nearest and dearest.'

'Perhaps it is we who should congratulate you?' remarked Graham rather drily, shaking hands.

'Did you enjoy the show?' asked Alec, with a pressing eagerness he shared with even the greatest actors.

'I'd hoped we clapped loudly enough to make that an unnecessary question.'

Alec lit a cigarette. 'I expect it shattered you a bit? Seeing me from out front?'

'It's admittedly an unexpected talent brought to light.'

'It all started in Smithers Botham. Dency thought it would help if I tried some form of self-expression. He knows someone in the management here, and sent the sketch along. At first I was only supposed to help out with the technical details— you know, wearing your stethoscope the right way round, putting on gloves the regulation way, that sort of thing. After I'd been fooling about at rehearsals one of the cast went sick. So they gave me a chance. Success story.'

One of the other young men, none of whom Alec had introduced, picked up his jacket and with a call of 'Good-night, darlings,' left them. Graham noticed with amusement Clare looked shocked. He himself had come to learn the endearing expression was merely the equivalent of the Communists' 'Comrade' in an ever-shifting and commendably classless society.

'A success story so far,' Graham agreed, nodding.

'Now, Uncle, you're being damping. But I've half another

451

show written, I'm getting work on broadcasting—I've even got an agent. Oh, I know it isn't a solid job like medicine, but you can't imagine how much better I've been feeling since I tried my hand at it. And this poisonous underground atmosphere has absolutely cured my asthma. The pollens can't get at you.'

A girl, who seemed to Graham to be wearing only her underclothes, put her head round the dressing-room door, said, 'Oh, sorry,' and disappeared again.

'I was a misfit in medicine,' Alec continued cheerfully, wiping off the remains of his grease-paint. 'God knows why I started it in the first place. Mother, I suppose. Weight of family tradition. Or perhaps you think I've let the side down?' he asked, genuinely concerned.

'Not entirely. I was something of a misfit myself.'

'Well, I'm not the first doctor to make an exhibition of myself in public. The great Charles Wyndham was qualified. He ended up a grand actor-manager, with a knighthood and a theatre called after him.'

'I don't think Wyndham ever played in revue,' Graham observed. With the vague feeling that Alec was probably starving in some attic, he added an invitation to supper. But his nephew declined graciously, explaining he was already engaged to sup with some important director who thought highly of his work. Graham imagined the girl in the underclothes his more likely companion, but was glad enough to accept the refusal.

'You really ought to send some sort of word to your mother,' he finally admonished him. 'She's written saying how disturbed she is about you.'

'Dear mother!' Alec started putting on his shirt. 'She always did fuss so. Yes, I really must send her a line.'

'Or perhaps you'd prefer me to write?' Graham saw Alec in his present mood as a doubtful correspondent.

Alec turned with a bright smile. 'Just do that little thing for me, will you, Uncle?'

In the taxi going home, Graham said, 'God knows what will come of Alec's wild ideas. It *is* a bit of a let-down for the family, however broadminded you try to seem about it. A hell of a lot of people took enormous trouble teaching him medicine. Now he throws it all away to become a professional buffoon.'

'Haven't you said often enough, darling, you can't suppress a true artist? Even if he can only chalk sunsets on the pavements? You never let them suppress you.'

'Perhaps so,' he admitted. 'Perhaps Alec and I are the same thing, really.'

He took her hand and stared gloomily out of the cab window. It would all be intolerably difficult to describe to Edith. But his thoughts as usual turned back to the new hospital, and he said, 'Remind me I've got to go to the Board of Trade tomorrow afternoon. Something about importing American equipment. I'm seeing the new Minister—fellow called Harold Wilson. One of Attlee's bright boys.'

Clare said, 'Tomorrow I'm going to listen to the wedding on the radio.'

'Wedding? What wedding?'

'Oh, Graham! Princess Elizabeth's wedding, of course.'

'I'm sorry, it was out of my mind for the moment.' After another long silence he said, 'It's odd to think that one day we shall have a Queen on the throne again. Though I shan't be alive to see it. I just remember when the last Queen died. At least, I imagine I do. I have a mental picture of my mother telling me the news in father's old study in Hampstead. I could only have been seven years old at the time. It was just before my mother died herself of T.B., and I remember that well enough. "Queen Elizabeth" has a fine ring about it, hasn't it?' He began to sound more cheerful as the problem of Alec settled into its true insignificance. 'The country's having a pretty thin time of it at the moment, but perhaps a new Elizabethan age will dawn upon us. Oh, we'll end up top dogs again, sooner or later, like we were before the war.'

That so many fellow-countrymen imagined the same as Graham Trevose at the time was the great mid-twentieth-century British tragedy. Or perhaps comedy. They are only two ways of looking at the same thing.

453

29

WHEN THEIR TRIDENT landed at Heathrow there was a reporter and a photographer waiting. Graham had lost nothing of his attraction for the Press.

'How kind of you to come along,' he smiled. He had also lost nothing of his touch with newspapermen.

'Good evening, Sir Graham. I hope you had a good trip?'

'Splendid, thank you, splendid. Aeroplanes make everything so convenient these days. I still haven't quite got used to them. All that messing about one used to do with trains and boats was quite exhausting. Yes, Rome was wonderful. In September I think the light is just right. In summer the sun's too strong, and the shadows are the most intriguing part of any building—or of any human face.'

'I gather you made a quite sensational speech to the Plastic Surgery Congress, Sir Graham?'

He chuckled. 'Hardly sensational. My days for making sensations are past. But I put over a few of my old ideas, which still hold good. The basic principles have been rather swamped by the enormous advances in surgical technique and technology. But to my mind, it's as important to grasp them as firmly in 1968 as it was in 1948, when I took over the Directorship of the National Accident hospital. In fact, these basic principles haven't changed since 1940, when I was proud of being in a position to put them to good use.' He always referred to 1940 in front of the Press.

'I hope you've managed to get some holiday in Italy at the same time, Lady Trevose?' the reporter asked Clare.

'Yes, we had an absolutely wonderful fortnight in Positano.'

'Despite the continuing currency restrictions?' grinned the reporter.

'We are extremely modest abroad,' Graham told the man, quite sharply.

It was nine o'clock before they emerged from the Customs into the bright and confusing concourse. 'It's strange how this place always looks entirely different depending on whether you're going or coming,' Graham observed. 'It's the difference between hope and anticlimax, I suppose. A common enough sequence, in my own experience.'

'You've nothing to complain about this trip, darling.'

'Perhaps a little. They didn't take my speech seriously at the Congress, you know. Not entirely.'

'But they were absolutely charming,' Clare protested. 'Particularly the Russians.'

'Yes, but they think I'm old hat. Perhaps they're right. I'm a realist. Anyway, I livened them up. We'll see how the Americans take to me in Baltimore next spring.'

Graham looked round hopefully for the chauffeur booked to drive them into London. He felt that at his age the shunning of airport buses was a luxury worth indulging in. He was spry, and as thin as ever. He let his wispy hair grow overlong, and strands of it poked under his hat. He wore glasses all the time, large and round, making his eyes look more owlish than ever. He had grown rather untidy in his clothes, presenting an amiably donnish look to the world. Clare thought fondly he resembled an elderly elf.

The car had hardly reached the M4 before Graham fell asleep. Clare picked up the tartan rug provided by the hire firm and carefully laid it over him. This was less to prevent any malevolent chill taking advantage of his unguardedness—her nursing training enabled her to take a strictly scientific view of Graham's management—but an indulgence on her part, an expression of the steadfast tenderness she had shown towards

455

him in their twenty-one years of marriage. She settled back in her corner, looking at the street lights, trying to correlate them with the necklaces she had admired from the air. She had grown fatter, but kept her pale good looks, and, with assistance, her fair hair. Graham tended to drop off to sleep rather often these days, she reflected. Perhaps he shouldn't gad about the world so much. But seventy-three, though a respectable age, was hardly over the threshold of senility. If she remembered, Churchill was rather older when he became Prime Minister through the persuasion of the ballot-box rather than the approaching muzzles of the German guns.

They had a small flat in Chelsea, and an unimposing house in the country on the way to Oxford, past the National Accident Hospital. Graham had worked there almost a dozen years, until his retirement in 1959. They had been the happiest of his life, happier even than at the annex. It was mainly because nothing had happened to him. He sometimes wondered if it were the security of a settled job, or the fires of his personality dimming to a comfortable glow, or simply Clare keeping a firm hand on him. He had busied himself with his work, developed a relish for committees, lectured enthusiastically, and drew veneration from the world as effortlessly as a well-established oak draws moisture from the soil. He enjoyed the respect, though it amused him. It was not so much the poacher turning gamekeeper, as the swashbuckling pirate becoming Admiral of the Fleet. Perhaps he possessed the same luck as his seafaring Cornish ancestors, he wondered, who had never turned from a chance of smuggling and generally ended clothed with gold lace and dignity.

There was a pile of letters inside the door.

'I can't face that lot at this hour of the night,' Graham said, as Clare started gathering them. 'I'll have a go at them in the morning. Anything from Dick?'

Their nineteen-year-old son was on holiday in Spain, with, Graham suspected, the girl he had met at the university. Well, it would be a bit of fun, he wished he'd had the chance to do the same at Dick's age, but then trips to Spain were only for the

456

rich and venturesome. And the sunshine would do the girl good, he thought. She had struck him as a dismally anaemic young woman.

'There's a letter he seems to have sent from Malaga.'

'Read it to me, darling, will you?' Graham sat in the armchair. 'I'm rather tired, and his handwriting's dreadful.'

'And there's something from Blackfriars.' She tore open a large envelope. 'They've made it at last,' she exclaimed. 'They're actually going to open the new Arlott Wing by Christmas. Of course, they want you to perform the ceremony.'

Graham laughed. The rebuilding of Blackfriars beside the Thames had long ago become a harmless joke. When the war had ended, the staff imagined they would quit Smithers Botham in a year or two, but the volume of hospital work so increased with the National Health Service, and the volume of hospital building so diminished with the national bankruptcy, the country was several times on the brink of another war before they finally parted company. 'I think we've beaten St Thomas's to it, haven't we?' he asked. 'Or is it more or less a dead heat?' He opened and closed his hands. 'Perhaps they might ask me to perform an inaugural operation on some unlucky fellow? It's an amusing thought. I wouldn't mind having a knife in my hands again. After all, John Bickley's still giving anaesthetics for private cases all over London. Though perhaps he only does it to get away from Denise.'

John had worked for Graham again. Graham's private practice had in fact continued almost as busily as ever, through an interesting fraction written into the Health Service known as 'nine-elevenths'. The consultants were paid for the nine-elevenths of their time spent in the Service, the other two-elevenths being free to extract money from those members of the public feeling disinclined to accept its benefits. And two-elevenths of a consultant's time, with evenings, early mornings, and week-ends, was a handsome period for profits. Without this concession, the consultants would have dug in their toes and there would have been no Health Service at all. But Nye Bevan was an even more penetrating realist than Graham.

457

Clare read their son's letter, which said a lot about the sunshine, wine, beaches, and bullfights, but nothing about girls. The omission confirmed Graham's suspicion. He got up to pour himself a drink, and said, 'I suppose he'll get married pretty soon?'

'I don't know. He's no one in mind.'

'But they all seem to get married these days as soon as they're legally entitled to. Perhaps they look upon it in the same light as learning to drive a car. Once the obstacle to any enjoyment's removed, you indulge yourself automatically.'

'He'll wait until he's qualified, surely?'

'In my day, even in Desmond's day, that seemed to be the rule. But of course we lived on our parents or our wits. Now they live on everyone else's parents. Doubtless it's all a good idea.'

'He'll wait till he finds the right girl. He's terribly sensible.'

Graham smiled. 'I had to wait a very long time till I found the right girl. Even then I didn't realize it, did I?' She said nothing. He seldom brought up their times at Cosy Cot. She felt he liked to imagine the episode had never happened, that he had met her for the first time when he had entered, extremely dramatically, her children's ward one wet March morning in 1947. It was a forbidden topic, just like Maria's divorce.

Graham sipped his whisky. 'Do you know, Clare, I'm beginning to think that life resembles something I haven't experienced for donkey's years—it's like Saturday night in an old-fashioned public house.' As she looked puzzled, he gave a grin and said, 'It gets better towards closing-time.'

When they went to bed he lay reading for half-an-hour. He snapped the book shut and said, ' "Birth, and copulation, and death. That's all the facts when you come to brass tacks:" Strange how those lines of Eliot's keep coming back to me. I must have read them years ago, when I first started at the annex. But it's right, isn't it? Everything else is the trimmings. It's the most useful thing you can learn from medicine. How to sort the two out. What's the time?'

'Half-past midnight.'

458

Graham turned over. 'For God's sake remind me in the morning I'm due to see a fellow at the Royal College of Surgeons. He wants to touch me for some charity, I imagine.'

He turned out the light. At twenty to four he woke, switched on the light, gasped at the pain exploding from his throat into his left arm, and died.

30

CLARE HAD RATHER HOPED for something at the Abbey, but whoever invisibly decides such delicate questions demurred. Official memories are long and not subject to the mellowing of human ones. A knighthood for Graham Trevose had been acceptable, in times when a man's merit mattered more than the man himself. But a memorial service at the Abbey . . . the doctor, though distinguished, was far from impeccable. Someone in some small quiet office remembered there was really a bad scandal—he had lived openly with a mistress during the war.

In the end, the final pageant was held in St Pancras Church, a frequent choice for such affairs in memory of medical men, possibly because of its nearness to the red-brick ramparts of the British Medical Association in Bloomsbury. It was a befittingly miserable day in late September, with cold wet winds from the north blowing down the railway lines to the termini which dominate that depressing area of London. Haileybury stumped along, a thick overcoat over his blue suit, wondering if it were going to trigger off his bronchitis again. It was becoming increasingly burdensome to run the laps of the years. It occurred to him to list mentally his own infirmities. Apart from the chest, there was presbyopia, ptosis, arthritis of the left hip, a bilateral hallux valgus, a small inguinal hernia he ought to have something done about, and of course the piles. But a man was as old as his arteries, as the physicians kept saying when everything else was falling to bits. He supposed if his number didn't come up in the cancer lottery a good surgeon and antibiotics would keep him going a while. At least that morning he was alive, while Trevose was dead. To Haileybury's mind, death restored the formality of surnames.

'Excuse me, Sir Eric—'

Haileybury paused on the pavement outside the church, staring blankly at a young man in a raincoat.

'I'm from the *Daily Press*,' said the young man.

Graham deceased had the news value of Graham alive. The London evening placards had announced FAMOUS SURGEON DEAD, and middle-aged men in crowded trains heard the echo of Churchill's funeral drums. Sir Graham Trevose was part of the legend. And if young pilots in Spitfires and Hurricanes had shot out of the sky only half the enemy aeroplanes they thought they did, the legend could shine when required as brightly as ever. It seemed about the only thing the country had got out of the war.

'Do you think,' the young man continued, 'that Sir Graham deserved his distinction as "The Wizard" of plastic surgery?'

'I don't know. How could I know?' Haileybury started edging away. 'Wasn't the term invented by you people in Fleet Street?'

'I understand you had certain differences with Sir Graham?'

'I was never aware of any,' Haileybury muttered.

'Do you think it morally wrong, using surgery to construct new noses and such things for people who can afford it?'

Haileybury sniffed. 'I have never given the matter any thought.'

'Perhaps, Sir Eric, you have a comment on Sir Graham's great work in the war—'

But Haileybury had escaped into the sanctuary of a holy place, like a medieval criminal.

The church was crowded and warm and smelt of damp overcoats, reminding Haileybury of the out-patients' clinic. He was shown to a pew at the front. He decided his arthritis put even a perfunctory kneel on the hassock out of the question. At least the service would be short and businesslike. Services for

461

dead doctors generally were. Medical men live in far too close intimacy with death to regard its arrival as other than an unexpected stroke of treachery. And at his age, Haileybury reflected, such functions become occasions less of pain than foreboding. He adjusted his glasses and reached for the folded sheet of printed paper set before him. Experience told him they would have *O God, Our Help In Ages Past.* He found he was right. He felt pleased with his little guess, it brightened his morning considerably.

He folded his arms and stared along the pews. The widow, of course. Rum sort of business, really all over and done with now. Her son. The first son, now an academic, he believed. He'd forgotten what line. These days they made professors in all sorts of peculiar little subjects. Woman doubtless his wife. Been trouble there in the past, too, he seemed to remember. Trust the Trevose family to make fools of themselves when a female came into it. Other man the nephew, Alec. Always seeing him on the television. Looked damned prosperous. Needed a haircut. The other people around him were elderly men of washed-out military appearance, and of course the surgical big wigs. The biggest wig was giving the address. Wouldn't say anything about Trevose, really, of course. At least, Haileybury reflected, he sincerely hoped not.

Odd chap, Trevose. Neurotic, of course, but he supposed all medical men were to some degree. You must be, to pick such a strange occupation. As slippery as a snake, unreliable, abominably self-centred. Fond of fame, money, and women. The first two failings didn't matter much, but the last did. Women were human beings. Trevose always seemed to forget that little fact. Of course, it all changed in the last twenty years of his life. I always rather liked Trevose, Haileybury decided, even when I didn't care to admit it to myself. He livened things up. Didn't take life too solemnly. I rather wish I'd had the courage to be more like him myself.

Haileybury looked behind him. Full of Trevose's patients. It suddenly struck him these men had hardly aged. Over twenty-five years ago they had been dragged from blazing

462

aeroplanes, shattered tanks, and ships' scalding engine rooms; now the skin collected in bits from all over their bodies had frozen on their faces in unwrinkled youth. He supposed it was some compensation for having your features ravaged by a shell-splinter at twenty, if you were immune from the ravages of time at forty-five. He searched for some more delicate examples of Trevose's reconstructive art. But all the worldly and often charming men and women who had besought Trevose at considerable discomfort and expense to make them new faces seemed disinclined to show them in public.

A fitting epitaph, Haileybury thought, dragging himself to his feet as they began.

ABOUT THE AUTHOR

Richard Gordon, the pseudonym of Gordon Ostlere, received his M.D. degree from Cambridge University. *The Facemaker* is a result of rarely combined medical and literary careers.